'The fifth and final book in a gripping series of crime novels . . . the last outing does a credit to our 17th-century hero. I will miss Damian Seeker' *The Times*

'The end of a tantalising mystery that pits the wits of Captain Damian Seeker against a set of enemies both ruthless and violent' *What's On North*

'MacLean guides her characters through the twists of an intriguing plot with great aplomb' *The Sunday Times*

'Excellent at conveying the insecurities and unsettling memories that bedevil Cromwell's dying Protectorate, the author brings a fresh perspective and gold-plated research to a period which has been unfairly eclipsed by the popularity of the Tudors' *Daily Mail*

'MacLean has the first-rate historical novelist's gift for bringing to life any period she writes about' *Sunday Express*

'A writer of immense talent who seems to be getting better with each book' *Historical Novel Society*

'The plot is full of twists and turns, edge-of-the-seat excitement and intrigue . . . this series is addictive' *Crime Warp*

'MacLean effortlessly achieves the delicate balance of immersing readers in a time and place rife with deception and precarious loyalties' *Crime Review*

T0026190

Shona (S.G.) MacLean has a PhD in history from Aberdeen University, specializing in sixteenth- and seventeenth-century Scottish history. She has written four highly acclaimed historical thrillers set in Scotland, *The Redemption of Alexander Seaton* (shortlisted for the CWA Historical Dagger), *A Game of Sorrows*, *Crucible of Secrets* and *The Devil's Recruit*, and a series of historical thrillers set in Oliver Cromwell's London. The first and third books in the series, *The Seeker* and *Destroying Angel*, have won the CWA Historical Dagger and the second and fourth, *The Black Friar* and *The Bear Pit*, were longlisted for the same award. S.G. MacLean is married with four children and lives in Conon Bridge, Scotland. Follow her on Instagram @iwritemybike2 and Twitter @SGMacleanauthor.

Also by S.G. MacLean

The House of Lamentations

S. G. MACLEAN

Quercus

First published in Great Britain in 2020 by Quercus
This paperback edition published in 2021 by

Quercus Editions Ltd
Carmelite House
50 Victoria Embankment
London EC4Y 0DZ

An Hachette UK company

A CIP catalogue record for this book is available
from the British Library

PB ISBN 978 1 78747 366 9
EB ISBN 978 1 78747 364 5

10 9 8 7 6 5 4 3 2 1

Typeset by CC Book Production
Printed and bound in Great Britain by Clays Ltd, Elcograf S.p.A.

MIX
Paper from
responsible sources
FSC® C104740
www.fsc.org

Papers used by Quercus are from well-managed forests and other responsible sources.

To Lachlan

PROLOGUE

London

July 1658

Hate upon hate. Fear upon fear. Where was God in this? On men's lips, but nowhere else. Lawrence Ingolby and Elias Ellingworth forced themselves to watch as men whom they had never encountered but whose politics happened to be different from their own, were untied from the sledges on which they'd been dragged through the streets from their prison. The thin shifts which were the only clothing the prisoners wore, were stained from their captivity and from the missiles thrown at them by the populace as they'd passed. Lawrence and Elias looked on as these men, Royalists of no loud repute in the world until now, taken in taverns and coffee houses while musing on half-formed plots against Cromwell, were pushed towards the scaffold on which they would die.

The two men were brought forward, the executioner begging forgiveness of each and of God before he did his work. With differing success, each victim sought to hide his terror. Lawrence remembered hearing that the late King, before his execution, had worn two shirts, lest the cold of January should cause him to tremble and the people think it fear. It wasn't January now though, but the blistering heat of summer, and the stench of London was high enough. Their valedictory speeches, whether repentant or defiant, Lawrence didn't hear, so full were his ears of the growing rumblings and mumblings of the people around him.

The executioner knew his business well: he knew to tie his rope short, enough to hang a man, to choke the breath almost out of him, but not to snap his neck. This expertise was clear from the first victim's performance. Just as the legs were tiring in their thrashing, the one-time Royalist colonel was cut down. A foolish hope appeared in the eyes of his companion, already on the scaffold and awaiting his own turn. Elias saw it too. 'Dear God, Lawrence – does he think it's a reprieve? Can it be that he doesn't know what's coming next?'

If the second condemned man had truly not known, he was a short time in finding out. The executioner was at work again, tearing off the first victim's shift, exposing his emaciated body and his privy parts for all to see. Lawrence looked away and heard Elias wince as the half-hanged man was castrated, his manhood then burned before his eyes. A boy near Lawrence fainted; a hearty drayman a few feet from him vomited, but the butchery went on. The hangman, much bloodied now, took a heated poker and seared a line down the dying man's abdomen, along which he next plunged his knife. To the sound of bestial agonies from his victim, the executioner played his weapon in the man's very bowels and drew them out before his eyes to throw them, also, in the flames. Only when he held aloft the vanquished Royalist's heart was it clear that the ravaged carcass's agonies were at last over.

'I cannot watch another,' said Lawrence, as the second man, shaking uncontrollably and now almost beyond the capability of standing, was dragged beneath his own noose that the ritual might be repeated.

'Aye, but you must,' said Elias as the crowd around them, at last disgusted and murmuring that this was surely not God's plan, began to thin. 'We both must. How else shall we bear witness? How else shall we say in truth that we know what England now is?'

When at last it was over, the gaping, bloodied heads of the traitors set on poles and their severed limbs thrown in a basket like so much offal, Lawrence turned away from the spectacle he had forced himself to watch. He had seen less butchery at Smithfield, and better done. The beheadings of June had been bad enough, but those, at least, had been swift. These latest though, would the stench of the barbarity ever clear?

Elias waited longer, looking on the scene as if to carve every detail into his mind. Lawrence walked as far as Seething Lane and then waited for him. Crowds filed past, returning from what they had thought might be an entertainment but now understood to have been a descent into something else.

London was subdued, disgusted. Royalists scarcely heard of, caught in some conspiracy against Cromwell that had never seen the light of day, were condemned to brutal ends by a court the Protector had had invented for that express purpose. The deaths were to serve as a lesson to any who might have been tempted to similar thoughts of treason. The look on the faces of those who passed him, the muted expressions of dismay, suggested to Lawrence it might have been a lesson too far.

He and Elias walked on in silence a good while until at last Elias turned in at the Rainbow. 'I have hardly the stomach for the law, Lawrence,' he said as he led Elias into the tavern rather than continuing to Clifford's Inn.

'I think the law must be engaged elsewhere today, in any case,' said Lawrence, following him into the tavern.

The Rainbow was busy, many others perhaps wanting to shake off what they had just seen rather than carry it back with them to the business of their everyday lives. Lawrence sought a place where they might not be overheard. He knew from the look on Elias's face what the tenor of their conversation would be.

Once they were seated and served, Lawrence said, 'How long do you think this can go on?'

'What, the persecution of the Royalists? Their purging from London? The suspending of Parliament in the name of the rights of the people?'

'All of it, I suppose,' said Lawrence.

Elias shook his head. 'I don't see an end. Even those who were his closest friends, his greatest supports, are cast out or worse, for that they dare question him or advise the reining in of his power, while we must call Cromwell's children "Highness" and watch as he marries them into titles and lands and Royalists of the highest ranks who so lately supped with Charles Stuart.'

Lawrence looked around him. 'Hush, Elias, or you'll be up on that scaffold next.'

Elias took a long draught of his ale before speaking again. 'No, Lawrence. I'm done with it.'

Lawrence chanced a smile. 'You, Elias, done with sedition? Never.'

'With sedition? Who knows? I hope so. I hope to be somewhere where sedition is not a thing that is necessary.'

Lawrence put down his own tankard and looked closely at his lawyer friend. 'What are you talking about?'

'England, Lawrence. I'm done with England.'

Lawrence contemplated the words a few moments, but they still didn't make any sense to him. 'You mean, you've no hopes it'll get better?'

'Well, yes, I suppose that means the same thing in the end, doesn't it? I had hopes for Cromwell, for the Commonwealth, so, so long ago. But where is our freedom now, where our humanity?' He laughed. 'Where our parliament even? Protector or King, what does it matter to you and I, Lawrence? Those men we just saw butchered, in a different time, would you not have sat a while with them, smoked a pipe, learned something of their families, their hopes, their cares and then moved on without caring to know of their politics? My England never was, Lawrence, and I am done with this one.'

There was silence between them as the sounds of the tavern travelled all around them. And then at last, in low and very measured tones, Lawrence said, 'What are you telling me, Elias?'

Elias looked him directly in the eye. 'I am bound for Boston, Lawrence.'

Lawrence screwed up his face. 'Lancashire?' But even as he said it, he knew he was wrong. 'Tell me you're not talking about Massachusetts.'

Elias gave one, slow nod.

Lawrence sat back and attempted a laugh. 'No, Elias, you can't. I mean Grace . . .'

'Grace is less than a month from her time, and she no more than I wants our child to grow up in the world we have made here. Whispers, lies, fear, always looking over our shoulders for who might be listening and not liking the gist of what we say. Hypocrisy everywhere.'

'But what of her uncle, what of Samuel?'

'He's coming with us. Samuel can make his home any-where, with anyone, so long as Grace is there.'

Lawrence felt like a child watching his favourite dog be sold away. The dog beside him, Damian Seeker's dog, stirred and placed a heavy paw on his foot, as if guessing his thoughts.

'But what about Kent's?' tried Lawrence, his voice trailing off hopelessly. A man who could speak with such certainty about taking his wife and yet-to-be-born child, along with her lamed and elderly uncle across the world to begin again, would hardly be put off by concern for the fate of a coffee house.

'Samuel is giving it to Gabriel. The boy's seventeen or eighteen now, as far as he can tell, and as able as any merchant in the city. He'll buy and sell them all by Candlemas.'

'You've decided this, haven't you? You've got it planned already.'

Elias let out a long breath. 'It was when Cromwell dissolved the Commons, in February. After two weeks of sitting. *Two weeks*, Lawrence. I'd had enough. And nothing that's happened since then has made me anything but more certain. It's taken this long to put arrangements in place – somewhere that I might practise, a suitable house, possibly the acquisition of a printing press . . .'

Lawrence felt the indignation growing in him. Not even as a child, with his slattern of a mother, had he felt hurt like this. 'And you didn't even tell me . . .'

Elias lowered his voice and leaned further across the table towards Lawrence. 'I couldn't. It's Maria, you see . . .'

'Maria?' And then Lawrence did see. 'Oh, don't tell me,' he said, an incredulous half-smile on his face. 'You haven't told her, have you? You haven't told your sister.'

Elias flushed and looked about him. 'We cannot talk about it here.'

It was several hours later, in his own chamber on the upper floor of the Black Fox on Broad Street, that Lawrence finally took up his pen. The tavern was shut up for the night, the doors locked and his landlady, Dorcas, and the girls all sleeping. Nevertheless, the sounds of the argument he'd witnessed earlier in the evening in the garret of Dove Court were ringing so loud in his ears that he wondered they did not carry all the way to Flanders.

Maria had been towering in her anger. 'Massachusetts? I will not come!'

Elias had been equally vocal. 'You will, Maria, for you cannot stay in London on your own!'

That was when she had gripped the edge of the small table in the attic apartment that they had shared but was now, since his marriage to Grace and to the scandal of the neighbourhood, occupied by Maria alone. She had leaned forward and eyed her brother with such contempt that Lawrence had been afraid to breathe.

'I have no intention of staying in London.' She enunciated every word as if releasing a predator into the room.

'Then what?' Elias was perplexed, though only for a moment. 'Oh no! Absolutely not. I forbid it!'

This was when Maria actually laughed in his face. 'Forbid it, brother? Oh, no. I don't think so. I don't think so at all.'

So now, in his chamber in the Black Fox, with the rest of the house and most of London sleeping, Lawrence took up his pen. In response to the pleas of Elias Ellingworth, who by rights should not have known it was possible for Lawrence or anyone else to write a letter to such a person, he began an urgent missive to Damian Seeker.

ONE

Bruges

The parlour of De Vlissinghe was beginning to empty, most of the inn's patrons having at last decided to return to their own homes. Those who remained were either travellers passing the night on their way elsewhere or those with no real homes to go to. De Vlissinghe and the other inns and taverns of Bruges had seen more than their fair share of those in late days. In the far corner, their demeanour discouraging others from occupying the tables and benches close by, four Englishmen, Cavaliers of sorts, looked at a news-sheet, a week old. Not long brought from an English ship come in at Ostend, the booklet had lain on the table between them all evening. Usually, they would have fallen upon it, eager for news of home, but tonight it was as if it was a thing infected.

'It's true then,' said one, at last, an Irishman. He might once have cut a figure of some style, when his russet velvet coat had not been patched and faded, the ostrich feather in his hat not grey with failure, the heels of his fine Spanish boots not ground away to nothing. Somewhere in the faces of his companions too were the traces of better days, the memory of a long-gone lustre.

Seated opposite him, Sir Thomas Faithly finally picked up the news-sheet and began to read aloud the names he found there. The sleeves of his blue velvet suit were worn and dull, lace cuffs that might once have been white now a hopeless grey.

'Stop, I beg you,' said a third Cavalier, thin-faced and hollow-eyed. 'I cannot listen to another word of it.'

'Aye, but we must, Ellis,' said Sir Thomas. 'They suffered and we must know it and acknowledge it.'

'Acknowledge it?' asked the Irishman, his voice rising in disgust. 'We must avenge it. They were hanged, drawn and quartered, made a spectacle for the masses, all at the behest of Cromwell's new High Commission of Justice. They were our friends, and they were betrayed and butchered for their service to the King.'

The fourth Cavalier, Sir Edward Daunt, was a fleshy, slow-looking fellow, called 'Dunt' by his companions, in an affectionate bow to his universally acknowledged dim-wittedness. Having until this point appeared to be in contemplation of nothing more than the stein in front of him, Daunt now looked up. 'But how? How can it be that their plans were discovered? The Sealed Knot . . .'

'The Sealed Knot is finished, Dunt,' said the Irishman. 'Thurloe has unravelled it and it is done, and the Great Trust broken.'

'But how? How could he discover plans first laid here, amongst the King's own friends?'

His companions made no response, other than to look at their friend as a fond mother might regard a simpleton child.

It was perhaps an hour later that they finally left the inn, taking the reek of their tobacco smoke into the warm night air, to mingle with all the other aromas rising over the scarcely moving waters of the canal. Their boots sounded loud on the cobbles, and their voices had a dismal echo in the near-empty streets. Bruges had become a place of echoes and absences. It was hardly three weeks since they, fighting alongside Spain in the name of Charles Stuart, had been defeated at the Battle of the Dunes by an unholy alliance of Cromwell's forces and the French. The fugitive King himself had removed his rag-tag court for the summer from Bruges to Hoogstraten, while the rest of his supporters were dispersed throughout Europe, genteel beggars living on long-exhausted credit.

It was not a great distance from the cosy parlour of the inn on Blekersstraat to their lodging at the Bouchoute House on the corner of the Markt. The house was also now a place of empty spaces, dust and echoes. It had been different when the King had first come with his threadbare court to Bruges, and taken up residence there, and even after he had shifted to a grander house elsewhere in town, his proximity had lent a veneer of something finer to the everyday drudge of his adherents' lives. But it had only been a veneer and had grown thinner by the day. There had been little enthusiasm amongst the Cavaliers of the Bouchoute House to remove for a summer's sport further north, with the rest of those same tired faces that had hung about the King in his exile for years now, and so they had stayed in Bruges, for want of anything better.

The men had hardly crossed the Strobrug when the hindmost of their number, who had been fussing with his cuffs, called out that he had left his gauntlets in the tavern and must return for them. Laughing at talk of the dangers of the town at night, he refused all offers of company, and promised his companions he would join them soon in a last bottle of brandy from their cellar.

The others carried on and the straggler turned back across the bridge. He was within sight of the hostelry when a figure stepped out of the shadows from an alleyway to his left. The Cavalier stopped but he did not look round. He knew who it was. He had seen the carpenter sitting obscured from the sight of the rest of his companions, in a far corner of the parlour in the shadow of a high-backed oak dresser. As they had been leaving, he had risked a glance that way and the carpenter had lifted his head enough to afford him the merest of nods. That was why he had come back – because he had been summoned.

He followed the carpenter back into the darkness of the alley. 'What is it?' he asked, though he suspected he knew.

'They're sending someone to find you.'

'What? They know I've been passing secrets to Thurloe?'

'If they did you'd be dead already. But your Royalist

friends in England know someone in your circle's been reporting to us. They just don't know who yet, so they're sending someone to find out.'

'When?'

The carpenter had started to turn away. 'She's probably already here.'

The Cavalier felt suddenly sick. He walked unsteadily to the edge of the canal, steadied himself on a post by the end of the bridge, and vomited up his dinner. By the time he'd recovered himself, the carpenter was gone, having left on that same post the gauntlets he'd picked up earlier from the Cavaliers' table.

A short while later, in the loft that had been his home for a year and a half now, the carpenter looked again at the inventory that had come to him that day, accompanying a box of tools from a ship not long landed at Ostend. At the bottom was a note in a familiar hand.

Delivery on its way to you, but goods faulty. A chisel of English manufacture, ordered for the repair of a faulty window catch at the Lion House.

The code was a simple one, and well-suited for a recipient masquerading as a carpenter. Thurloe's message clear enough. 'Faulty goods' were Royalists; 'A chisel of English manufacture' was an Englishwoman; 'repair of a faulty window catch' meant putting a stop to the leakage of intelligence; and 'the Lion House' referred to the Lion of Flanders, the sign by which the Bouchoute House, in which the last of the Cavaliers were ensconced, was known. Royalists in England had finally understood that their plans for uprising had been revealed to Cromwell's intelligence services by means of a source embedded in the King's own circle in Bruges, and they had sent someone – a she-intelligencer – to find out who that source was.

Damian Seeker carefully put the note to the flame of his candle, and just as carefully made safe the glowing ashes. He had warned their source, their double agent, and what remained was for Seeker to find this Englishwoman before she uncovered the identity of the man she had come to find, and, possibly, his own. A swift death in a dark alley was the best any Royalist caught in such treachery to his own cause could hope for, and there had been such deaths in cities throughout Europe. No more than was deserved. Seeker didn't like double agents, didn't trust them. Men and women who could be turned through bribery or blackmail, who'd sell out their friends to save their own skin, should be prepared to take the consequences. But Thurloe valued their services, and so, for now, must he. He'd kept an extra close eye on this one. It hadn't been difficult. The Cavaliers who'd settled in Bruges over the last months could generally be found in one or the other of their preferred taverns; if not, between those and a brothel. It was in such places in this small, half-forgotten Flemish city that plot after plot against the Protector had been hatched before being sent out onto the wind and across the Channel to land amongst people it should not. But those plotters were being betrayed now, and they knew it. The difficulty was in remaining incognito amongst those who had once known him. The growing of his beard, the new scars from the struggle with the bear, different forms of clothing and headgear, a practised change to the way he walked and carried himself. Every morning on waking he took a moment to remind himself, to step into the persona that must now be his. Most of all, though, there was vigilance, that he should not be seen. What the Cavaliers would do should they find one of Secretary Thurloe's own handlers also in their midst was not something Seeker was going to dwell upon.

It was late now, and dark. He would begin his search for the Royalist she-intelligencer at first light, but for tonight, there was something else that required his attention. He set his candle carefully in its niche and drew from his leather apron the second letter he'd received that day.

This second letter had come into his hands hours after Thurloe's missive warning of the woman spy. A shore-porter on the Langerei had handed it to him as he'd passed on his way to his vigil at the Vlissinghe. 'You're popular today, John Carpenter,' the man had said.

Seeker had looked at the direction on the front of the letter, and the hand in which it was written. 'John Carpenter, Englishman, Sint-Gillis in the city of Bruges.'

'From my mother,' he'd said, slipping it into the pocket

he'd stitched into the lining of his buff jerkin. 'When did it come in?'

'Late barge from the coast. Horse-feed and ironmongery.'

Seeker had nodded and gone on his way without saying anything else.

Now, back in his stable loft in Sint-Gillis, he turned the letter over in his hands, almost afraid to open it. To anyone other than the man for whom it was intended, this missive would read as a dull account of family life from an elderly woman in a Kent village to her dutiful and far-travelled son. To Damian Seeker and to Lawrence Ingolby, however, the only two people who knew the cypher in which the letter was written, it would be something else entirely.

Seeker received a coded letter every two months from Lawrence Ingolby. Lawrence kept him abreast of many things – the rumours from the Inns of Court and Chancery that never reached Whitehall; the rumours from the lips of Sam Pepys or Andrew Marvell of goings-on at White-hall that never reached the ears of John Thurloe; news from the North Riding, home once to both Ingolby and Seeker; news from Kent's coffee house and of the people beneath its roof; and, most of all, news of the Black Fox, of Dorcas, and of Manon. Seeker had made it plain, through Lawrence, that Dorcas should not live her life as if bound to him, but as the free woman she was. Nothing in Law-rence's responses suggested that Dorcas had as yet taken him up on this suggestion. And Manon; Lawrence told Seeker of Manon. Even through the cypher, Seeker could see the young man's struggle for formality, his eagerness to give nothing away, to keep all feeling hidden. Seeker should have told Lawrence that he had decided, before he ever left London all those months ago, that he would let him marry his daughter. Not yet though. Enough for now that the infuriating, clever, stupidly courageous young Yorkshireman was there, watching over her.

This letter hadn't come by the usual channels, and it had come at the wrong time – he'd had one from Lawrence only three weeks since. Checking the seal and the folding pattern for any signs of tampering, Seeker opened the single sheet carefully and began to read. The contents showed every sign of having been written in haste and ill-humour, the hand was sloppier than Lawrence's usual precise script. For all that, this letter was indubitably from Lawrence. Seeker read it through and closed his eyes, letting out a deep breath, then read it through again.

You'll excuse what follows, but this is no time for me, you, Elias or Maria herself to keep up the pretence that no one but you and she knows of your past connections, though it appears that unbeknownst to the rest of us, they're not in the past at all. Regardless – you should know that Elias has finally given up on hope of anything better from Cromwell and is set on taking ship, with all his family, to Massachusetts. Not only has his sister declared she will not go, she has announced her intention of making instead for Flanders. Mistress Ellingworth, it appears, is remarkably well-informed of the details of your

whereabouts and the means by which you pass yourself off in
your chosen place. I know for a certainty that I've told her no
more than that you are safe and will be back, one day. How
she has discovered the rest I'd warrant you'll know better
than I. Only one thing more will I say: this is trouble of your
doing, and Elias Ellingworth asks in no uncertain terms that
you put it right.

    Your friend, L. I.

Seeker put down the letter and lay back on the soft clean straw of the floor. Through the open shutter in the gable he could see over the nearby rooftops to a black sky studded with stars. 'Oh, Maria,' he said aloud, shaking his head and smiling. 'Only my Maria.'

Just one time had he seen her, one time since that terrible night a year and a half ago on Bankside, when a trio of Royalist conspirators had left them deep underground in a disused bear pit, as if for dead. They hadn't been dead, but they had been taken away to their separate places to have their injuries tended to and the world informed that he was dead. Only Lawrence, Dorcas and Seeker's daughter Manon were to have been told the truth of his survival and posting to foreign shores. Maria absolutely was not to know it. But Lawrence had told her, only that he lived and would one day return, because how could he not?

Once. Last summer, when Seeker had been recalled, incognito, to England, to bring in person to John Thurloe the intelligence he had gathered for the commencement of the Flanders campaign. Not risking London, they had met instead in a small town near the Essex coast. Some madness, some exhilaration to be back on English soil, had made Seeker send a message to Dove Court: a piece of winter jasmine he had plucked one day in front of her in a garden in Lambeth, bound in a thin ribbon of silk she had once made play of tying around his finger. They were wrapped in a piece of paper with only the name of the town on it. Seeker should have gone back across the Channel on the next tide after Thurloe's return to London, but he hadn't. He'd waited, and on the second day she had come. Two days and a night they had had together, in an empty fisherman's cottage in that little Essex town. What she had told Elias he never asked. After that there had been no more doubt, no more pretence between them. 'I will come back,' he had told her as they had lain together in that one-roomed cottage. 'When my work in Flanders is finished, I will come back, and I swear I will make you my wife, even should the Lord Protector himself forbid it.'

A year had passed, and Thurloe's promises that he would be brought back from Bruges and settled elsewhere – Ireland, or Scotland perhaps – had drifted away on the polder mists. But the news from England grew worse on every tide – the House of Lords revived, the Commons suspended, the Protector's daughters married amongst the scions of lords and earls, generals Seeker liked and revered dismissed, for that they did not want a monarch in all but name. The worse the news was, the more likely he was to hear it first not from Thurloe, but from Lawrence, or by means of newsletters. Seeker was resolved that, come what may, John Carpenter would be gone from Bruges by autumn. Now, lying on his back, looking up at the black sky and its diamonds, he made a promise. 'This is the last thing, Maria. I will find out this she-intelligencer, then it will be done.' He would get this business over and done with long before Elias Ellingworth ever shifted to get himself and Grace and Samuel, never mind Maria, on a ship bound for Boston. He looked a third time at Lawrence's letter. 'But first of all I'll have to get Lawrence Ingolby to make you stay put.' He tried not to think of the complexities that might await him should his former wife, Felicity, also have made her way to Massachusetts, as had been her plan.

At last he snuffed out his candle and finally fell asleep to the distant rumbling of carriage wheels along the Langerei.

TWO

The Engels Klooster

Sister Janet almost jumped out of her skin when the bell by the night door of the Engels Klooster began to clang, only a few feet from her ear. It happened every time it was her turn to watch; she drifted into sleep only to be rudely awakened at the most inopportune of times. The warmth of the fire and the comfort of the cushion that she smuggled under her habit every night made it almost impossible to keep her eyes open. She had heard the young novices giggling about it once, but at sixty-seven years of age, and thirty of them spent here at the Engels Klooster, Sister Janet feared neither novice, Mother Superior, nor the Pope himself, should he appear in Bruges and choose to take issue with her cushion.

Muttering loudly about inconvenience and lack of consideration, Sister Janet straightened her veil and shuffled towards the door. Lifting her lamp, she drew back the small wooden panel that was level with her eye and peered out.

'Well? Who is it that disturbs the peace of an honest Christian woman tonight?'

The response was in Flemish, and the voice instantly

recognisable. Jakob van Hjul, the carter. 'Well, Jakob,' she demanded, also in Flemish, 'and who have you brought to me tonight?'

'I think it is surely your sister, for never have I come across a more disagreeable woman, unless all Englishwomen of your years be the same.'

She tried to peer out beyond him but could make out nothing. 'I never had a sister save those called to God in this house, you rogue. Have you come from the coast tonight?'

'Aye, and a troublesome journey I've had of it.'

Sister Janet slid back the bolt and opened the door. 'When did you ever claim anything else? You are paid well enough for your trouble. Now step aside and let the lady come in.'

As the carter went to see to his cargo, Sister Janet saw that not one but two women were perched up on the driver's bench. She took a step out onto Speelmansstraat, and then another, then held up her lamp, very close now to where the women sat. The younger of the two, clearly a maid-servant, was readying herself to get down in order to help her mistress alight, as the carter was showing no sign of doing so. Like most people, Sister Janet paid little attention to maidservants, and craned her neck a little to see past her to the mistress. What she saw almost made her drop her lamp. The woman looked back at her and favoured her with that well-remembered crooked smile.

'Well I'll be damned,' said Sister Janet at last.

'Yes, Janet,' returned the woman. 'I've no doubt you will.'

★

It was a good half hour and a great deal of grumbling from the carter later that Lady Hildred Beaumont was finally settled beside the fire in the little guest parlour of the Engels Klooster, Sister Janet's cushion at her back. The stable boy who looked after Mother Superior's horse had been roused and commandeered into assisting the carter in unloading Lady Hildred's possessions from his cart. The lady herself had watched as every item was lifted down and had charged her maid with accompanying it to the empty cell Sister Janet had proffered as storage. The last item, evidently a framed painting of some sort, was padded and bound in several linen sheets, and that the maid herself was charged with carrying.

Sister Janet had looked from the maidservant with her burden to Lady Hildred. 'Guy?'

Lady Hildred nodded. 'Though I am sure he was never so tumbled in sixty years on horseback as he has been on the back of that donkey-cart.'

By the time the maid had finished preparing the beds in a guest room for herself and Lady Hildred, Sister Janet had readied a spiced caudle to warm the two women.

'You have grown fat,' said Lady Hildred, watching the nun bustle about the small room.

'And you old,' said Janet.

Lady Hildred laughed. 'I've missed you, Janet. No one in fifty years has dared to speak to me the way you do.'

'Well, I have not missed you,' said Sister Janet. 'Why are you here, Hildred?'

'Ever to the point. Good. You know that Guy is dead?'

'Yes, I do. fourteen years ago, at Marston Moor. And sorry I was to hear it.'

Lady Hildred nodded. 'He died as he lived, without compromise. He died for his King.'

'Well, he certainly didn't compromise when he married you. He could hardly claim he hadn't been warned.'

Hildred snorted. 'He was pleased enough with his bargain.'

'More pleased than the Parliamentary troops that descended on Beaumont House after he'd gone, I hear. Did you truly take a crossbow to them yourself, from the battlements?'

'Only when I ran out of shot for the guns. I'd promised Guy before he left that I'd be in my grave before they took Beaumont House.'

Sister Janet narrowed her eyes. 'And yet you are not in your grave, Hildred, but you are not at Beaumont either.'

For the first time since they had left England under cover of darkness from a tiny Norfolk beach, Lady Hildred's maid saw her mistress's shoulders sag.

'Why are you here, Hildred?' the nun repeated.

'Because England is finished. Cromwell would have himself made king, and those of our people left at home who have the courage to try to stop him are betrayed and butchered. I'll have no more of it until the King is returned to his throne. I've sold everything I could not carry and come to wait upon His Majesty.'

Her maid, astonished already at the tone of the conversation between the two women, knew this was true, for she herself had watched as Beaumont House and its policies had been cleared of every moveable object – whether stick of furniture, piece of plate, carpet, drape, painting, horse or dog – and the proceeds converted into coin, to be carried to the Spanish Netherlands and laid at the feet of Charles II. Lady Hildred had left the place a shell, and if she could have dismantled the house itself, and sold it too, stone by stone, she would have done. But she hadn't been able to sell Beaumont House, because Beaumont House wasn't hers to sell.

'But your son . . .' began Sister Janet.

'I have no son.'

Janet's hand went to her heart. 'Forgive me, Hildred. I had not heard he was dead.'

Lady Hildred's face set like stone. 'He died to me sixteen years ago, when he defied his father and abandoned the King's cause to take up arms with the rebels. He has not been welcome across my door since.'

An hour later, as she lay down on a pallet at the foot of the bed in which her mistress slept, Lady Hildred's maid thought over the exchange she herself had had with the nun when Sister Janet had shown her out to the well in the yard, where she might draw water for the morning.

For the sake of conversation with the prickly old woman she had ventured, 'Lady Hildred had not told me that she was coming here to an old friend.'

'She wasn't.'

'She didn't know she would find you here?'

'Oh, I've no doubt she did, for I have been nowhere else these last thirty years, and Hildred makes it her business to know what she needs to, but she was never my friend, nor I hers.'

So astonished had she been by this declaration that the maid had been unable to think of anything further to say. This seemed to be as the other woman wished, but after the bucket was filled and they were making their careful way back inside, the nun suddenly grabbed her right hand to examine it. 'Soft hands,' she said, looking the maid right in the eye. 'Just as I thought.'

A bright moon in a cloudless sky meant that the cell allotted to Lady Hildred was never truly dark, all the whole night through. Despite her exhaustion from travelling, the maid lay awake a long time, gazing at the night blue whiteness of the walls. The crucifix above the bed troubled her, but Lady Hildred's only comment had been that she supposed it might please her son well enough to see her in a nunnery. The maid had murmured an appropriate response, which was all that was required. For a woman who for sixteen years had been declaring him dead to her, Lady Hildred spent a great deal of time talking about her son. The maid glanced over to the small side table on which Lady Hildred had laid out her travelling jewels and the red leather box, engraved with the Beaumont crest, that accompanied her everywhere she went. Inside was a large silver locket. Nan had only seen into the locket once, a brief glimpse. On one side, as she might have expected, was a miniature portrait, not well executed, of Sir Guy, who had died at Marston Moor. On the other side was a much finer portrait of his son, who had not. George Beaumont, though legal heir to his father's estate, as ratified by Parliament, had respected his mother's wishes and never returned home after the battle which had killed his father – the battle in which he'd fought on the other side. He'd made his home with the army, and left her to see out her days in the house to which she was no longer entitled. It was widely believed that only George Beaumont's high standing with the Protector had kept his ardently vocal Royalist mother out of gaol. Lady Hildred claimed to have kept his portrait only because it had been her husband's last gift to her, but her maid suspected otherwise. She wondered what that handsome young boy of nineteen, who would now be a battle-weary soldier of thirty-six, might look like now, and whether his mother would ever set eyes on him again. As if she had uttered her thoughts aloud, her mistress's voice came clear to her across the stillness of the small room. 'Go to sleep, Nan. There is much to be done in the morning.'

THREE

Bartlett Jones

The bells of the English Convent – Engels Klooster – rang as Seeker made his way to the Kruispoort. Everywhere, across this city, cowled or veiled figures, arms encased in wide, overflowing sleeves, shuffled, heads down, to prayer. Benedictines, Carthusians, Dominicans, Capuchins, Carmelites and others he hardly knew names for – there was no end to the religious in Bruges. Sometimes Seeker fancied he could hardly sleep at night for their murmuring. And then, of course, there were the Jesuits, that priestly cohort sent out by Rome to penetrate the society and infiltrate the governments of nations that had got out from under her dominion.

A line of Benedictine nuns flowed past Seeker – their eyes firmly averted from his, their faces so encased in white linen wimples and shrouded by their black veils that their own fathers would not have known them. His first thought had been that the she-intelligencer sent by the Royalists in England to track down Thurloe's double agent would be a person of rank and wealth. His years in Cromwell's service had taught him that Royalists were drawn to espionage for the love of the cause. For those on the other side, however, it was different. Thurloe had a knack for finding persons too poor, or compromised, or disappointed to turn him down. But now Seeker realised that the woman he had been warned about might be anyone. She might be concealed beneath layers of cloth and whispered prayers, one amongst ten, twenty, a hundred women, all dressed the same, going anonymous and unnoticed in a town full of women who looked almost exactly as she did.

He had been here too long. Something in the air of the place had begun to seep into him. The flatness of the polder, the plaintive calls of the geese overhead, the dark canals, the constant ringing of bells, and the lavish palaces and churches that told of a glory that was past – all spoke to him of a powerlessness to change, of the futility of trying to act upon the world. It was a city fading into itself, like a painting fading on its canvas. Anyone who stayed here too long would risk fading away with it.

Bruges was not London. London was constantly growing, changing, moving, building layer upon layer on top of its old self, layers he knew how to peel back, to push aside, to find what he knew was hidden beneath. Here, he was always watching for what was in plain sight – Royalists turning up where they weren't supposed to be, English travellers making arrangements to go somewhere it did not suit the Protectorate that they should go, talking to people they should not be talking to, and the endless flow of the hopeful or desperate to the court of Charles Stuart. He listened in inns and taverns, befriended ostlers and stable lads and boatmen, the English carpenter who'd come as a journeyman to Bruges. The city was a scene for him to observe, a tableau on which he could cast his eye, ready to spy any movement, any change of shade. Seeker flexed his shoulders and strode past the file of Benedictine women who had just overtaken him. A man who could trace traitors and murderers on the ever-shifting streets of London could surely find one Englishwoman in Bruges.

He'd start at the Kruispoort and make his way from the north-east of the city down its western side, gateway by gateway, getting into conversation with the gatekeepers, making casual enquiries about any work that might be needing done, complaining about the Spaniards, not needing to ask about visitors newly arrived from England because the gatemen always told him about them anyway. In the last few weeks, since the victory of France and the Protectorate at the Dunes, far fewer English travellers had ventured from the coast to Bruges. The Protectorate navy had virtually cut off Ostend, and the French handed Dunkirk to Oliver's commanders. Only the desperate would now find a way through their lines and across the polder.

It was at the Donkey Gate – Ezelpoort – that he struck lucky. 'Poor Jakob had one of yours last night. A real old tartar. There'll be work for you there in a few days, you may rely upon it. Rich old Englishwoman come to settle in Bruges. The sort that nothing pleases. She'll be bound to be looking for a carpenter to change whatever she finds here.'

Seeker laughed and thanked the gateman, of whom he'd made a friend. 'Where would I be without bad-tempered old women who don't like foreigners, Theo? I'll have a sniff about in a day or two – who should I ask for?'

Theo called to his companion to bring him the ledger. 'Beaumont,' he said, carefully enunciating each syllable. 'Lady Hildred Beaumont. On her way to the Engels Klooster.'

Beaumont. The name rang a bell in Seeker's head somewhere, and he was in the course of tracking it down when his attention was taken by Theo breaking into English. He and the gatekeeper always conversed in Flemish, but Theo could pass himself off in several languages when his duties so demanded. Seeker moved further around the curve of the western gate tower and listened as the gateman, in his heavily accented English, questioned a newcomer.

'Your purpose in the town?'

'To find my sister.'

'You will stay with your sister?'

'Yes.'

'How long do you intend to stay in Bruges?'

There was some hesitation in the voice before the young man made his response. 'Ten days.'

'Name?'

'Bartlett Jones.'

'Your sister?'

'Ruth. Ruth Jones.'

'And where does Ruth Jones reside?'

Again there was some hesitation before the young man, picking unfamiliar words as if from the air said, 'Engels Klooster.'

'Ah, of course,' said Theo, handing Bartlett Jones a pass to be in the city for ten days. 'The English Convent.'

The young man, travel-worn and weary-looking, slipped his pass inside a dusty but serviceable buff coat. 'How do I get there?' he asked.

Theo looked beyond him to where Seeker had just stepped out of the shadow of the gatehouse. 'Perhaps my friend there will show you.'

Bartlett Jones shifted his gaze to Seeker. 'And who are you?' he asked.

Seeker turned away to walk again down the Ezelstraat. 'They call me John Carpenter.'

Like a barn door, thought Bartlett as he picked up his pack and began to follow the Englishman. Bartlett, who was two or three inches shy of six foot, would have fancied his chances with most folk in a fight. Not this one though: Bartlett's stocky strength would avail him nothing against this fellow, should things turn awkward. He'd needed his wits about him to get this far – and more than half the money he'd brought with him when he'd left home, too. Now that he was finally in Bruges he'd have to be even more careful. Carpenter. Maybe that was this man's real name, maybe it wasn't. There were probably a good few Englishmen had crossed the sea to France or the Low Countries and taken themselves a new name when they'd landed. Bartlett had no interest in them. He was only here for Ruth. He wondered though, what name Ruth might be going by now.

As if reading his thoughts, the man in front of him threw over his shoulder, 'So, your sister's in Bruges.'

'I said so, didn't I?'

'Nun, is she?'

'That's my business,' said Bartlett.

The man shrugged. 'Fair enough.' The rest of their journey continued in silence. The further into the town they got, the fewer were the gardens and spaces between buildings, the higher and grander the walls. There were spires almost everywhere. They followed a canal in one direction for a while before crossing an old stone bridge and soon finding themselves following another. Halfway along the second canal, the big man in front of him stopped outside the door of an inn and turned to look him up and down. 'When did you last eat?'

Bartlett swallowed and tried to remember. 'Last night,' he lied.

'Right, then,' said the man. 'You'll be needing some breakfast. The good sisters up at the Engels Klooster'll still be at their morning mutterings just now at any rate. Come on.'

Carpenter stooped as he went through the door, and Bartlett had little option but to follow him. The place was cooler inside than out, where the heat was already building, despite the early hour. Bartlett summoned the grace to mumble his thanks when a large jug of beer was put down in front of him and didn't argue when it was followed a few minutes later by bread and a dish of herrings. He looked uncertainly at the fish.

'You'll get used to it,' Carpenter said, downing one whole.

The late-morning murmur of voices around them was mostly in the guttural-sounding Flemish Bartlett was becoming accustomed too, but some he recognised as Spanish, and one or two were English. He glanced in the direction of the English voices, but they were paying no attention to him.

Suddenly, the carpenter, who he'd noticed observing him from time to time said, 'You'll not be able to stay with her.'

'What?'

'Your sister. If she is a nun at the English convent. You'll not be able to stay with her, not there.'

'I don't plan on staying,' said Bartlett, looking the man very clearly in the eye.

'You don't know if she's there at all, do you?'

Bartlett swallowed down the last of his ale and stood up. 'My business is none of yours,' he said. He threw down some coins he could not spare on the table. 'I'll find my own way from here.'

He made to walk away but the carpenter placed a heavy hand on his wrist so that couldn't move it even if he'd wanted to. The man was looking very closely at him.

'If you find yourself in trouble – you or your sister –

ask for me, the English carpenter. You'll find me over by Sint-Gilliskerk.'

When the hand lifted, Bartlett swept his own away. 'I don't need your help, Mr Carpenter, and neither does she.'

Bartlett could feel his cheeks flaming by the time he was back out on the canal-side. He looked all about him for some sign of where the English convent might be, but it was hopeless. On their journey in from the city gates, they'd passed countless churches, and he didn't know what any of them were. He was still deciding which way to set off when a man, somewhat unkempt and looking as if he had slept in his clothes, swaggered towards him and addressed him in English.

'You've the look of one that's lost, friend,' he said, the words in English but the voice thick and Irish.

Bartlett wondered whether a man might walk two yards in this city without being accosted by some wanderer from the British Isles. He had hoped they would all be gone from Bruges by now. This latest one at least looked friendly, and Bartlett knew he'd never find his way to the convent without help.

'I'm looking for the Engels Klooster.'

The man made a play of being alarmed. 'Nuns, is it?' Then he laughed and threw an arm across Bartlett's shoulders, enveloping him in smells of stale wine and tobacco smoke. 'Well, aren't you in luck then, for I'm just going that way myself.'

★

Seeker watched through the window of the inn as the Irishman propelled Bartlett Jones up the Spiegelrei. This was not a good start to Seeker's day. His interest was in the woman who had arrived in Bruges last night and made straight for the Engels Klooster, but seeing this young newcomer with a rogue like Glenroe did nothing to assuage Seeker's suspicions that Bartlett Jones's visit to the same place was not quite for the reasons he would have people believe. Seeker downed the rest of his own ale, swallowed another herring, and pocketed what was left of the bread. Bartlett Jones was a person of interest to him now, whether the young man liked it or not.

By the time Seeker was back out on the canal-side, Jones and Glenroe had already crossed over the bridge into Sint-Anna and were heading up Carmersstraat towards the Engels Klooster. The Irishman still had his arm around the other's shoulder, and even at this distance, Seeker could see that he was hardly drawing breath. It would be one story after another: Glenroe was a good old boy, asked for nothing more than a drink and a song and a fight with his friends now and again. A good old boy who would cut your throat as soon as look at you. As for Jones, his hair black as coal and sticking out in all directions in straight, unruly spikes with not a curl in it, broad shoulders, sturdy legs and a face that looked ready to take offence wherever there was a chance it might be given – he'd blend in to Bruges as easily as Seeker might into a lacemaker's window. If Bartlett Jones had been hoping to go through Bruges unnoticed, he'd picked for himself the wrong companion.

Seeker took a slightly different route to the pair he was following, to take up position opposite the corner of the Engels Klooster. Glenroe and the young Englishman had almost reached the convent's main doorway when a Jesuit priest carrying the host and attended by a gaggle of altar boys crossed their path. It was the Spaniard, Father Felipe, whom Seeker knew to be suspected of having made clandestine visits to England. Whilst the Irishman stopped and genuflected, Jones merely stood scowling at the inconvenience he had been put to, not a trace of reverence showing on his face.

'Not a Papist, then,' said Seeker to himself. 'So what's your sister doing in an English convent in Bruges, Bartlett Jones?'

Once the priestly party had passed, Jones was about to cross to the door of the convent when his companion put a hand on his arm, and with a disappointed gesture indicated that he himself would need to be on his way. To his credit, in Seeker's mind, Jones looked happy to see the back of the Irishman. Glenroe dispensed with, the young man approached the solid doorway set into the convent wall and rapped three times, hard, with the brass knocker. After a moment or two a small panel, a little lower than Bartlett's eye-level, slid open. Bartlett leaned in towards it and spoke. He could hardly have had time to give much more than his sister's name before Seeker saw his shoulders sag and heard the door panel slide firmly shut again. That confirmed what Seeker had already suspected. Bartlett Jones had spoken not of visiting his sister, but of *finding* her. This young, angry man who had come to Bruges looking for an Englishwoman called Ruth Jones really had no idea where that woman was.

After staring at the closed panel of the door to the Engels Klooster for a good minute, Jones, shoulders slumped, began to trudge back down the street in the direction of the bridge and the heart of the town. At the top of the same street, waiting outside the Schuttersgilde of Sint-Sebastiaan, Glenroe had been paying close attention to his new young friend's progress. Once he was out of sight, Glenroe finally knocked at the Schuttersgilde door and was let in. That at least was a relief to Seeker. He could leave Bartlett Jones to his own devices for a while, safe in the knowledge that Glenroe would be passing his idle hours at the butts, rather than leading the new and naive young arrival into all manner of vice. He waited another few minutes, to make certain that Glenroe did not reappear, then crossed the street to the Engel's Klooster.

Seeker went not to the main door of the convent, but to a small entrance off Speelmansstraat, through which tradesmen were granted entrance. He knocked at the gate and it was soon opened by a novice, who was quickly moved aside by an elderly nun, over twenty years his senior, a foot and a half shorter than him, and almost as wide as she was long.

'Sister Janet,' he said.

'John Carpenter,' she replied, in Yorkshire tones broader

than his own, though she had not been home in fifty years. 'I swear you've the nose of a bloodhound, though it looks better on a dog.'

He laughed. 'You've no care for a man's heart, Sister.'

The woman snorted. 'Your heart's as hard as your head, John Carpenter, and that head could fell a tree on its own. I know what you're here for though. Never saw a man sniff out a full purse as quick as you. You'll be wondering if Lady Beaumont's looking for work done, I suppose? You might wait till she's got her hat off.'

'A man could take offence, Sister. What would I know about this Lady Beaumont or anyone else you have stopping here? I only called to see whether a young man I gave directions to earlier had managed to find his way here. He was looking for his sister.'

The sparkle in Janet's eyes hardened to sharp pins. 'Well, he didn't find her,' she said briskly. 'No Ruth Jones here, nor any girls of her age that haven't been here a good long time already.'

'And she's definitely not one of them, then? This lad's sister?' With most people, Seeker would have had to be more circumspect in his questions, but Sister Janet loved few things better than a little innocent gossip and speculation.

'No, she isn't. The only younger woman we've had arrive of late was last night – Lady Beaumont's maid, but she's thirty years old if she's a day. And her name's not Ruth Jones.'

Sister Janet's tone made clear that the carpenter's time was up.

'Well, I'm glad he at least found his way here, Sister,' said Seeker. 'And you'll remember, won't you, to mention me to Lady Beaumont?'

The nun laughed as she closed the door on him. 'John Carpenter, you're the Devil's own Yorkshireman.'

Sister Janet's smile lasted just as long as it took for the catch on the door to click shut. Her back once turned to the door, her mouth had become a thin line. One such enquiry would have been enough to concern her; two called for action. She was considering how she should proceed when Hildred Beaumont's familiar voice sounded sharp through an opened upper casement.

'Nan! Close that window – the breeze disarranges my papers.'

Janet glanced up to where Hildred's maid was standing at the window, looking out over the wall onto the street below. Her brow was slightly furrowed, as if something she'd seen confused her, but then she shook her head as if to dislodge the confusion before closing the window.

FOUR

The House of Lamentations

The loft above the stables of the inn in Sint-Gillis had been Seeker's home since his arrival in the town. The place was cold in winter and too warm during the summer months, but it suited him well enough. At the other side of the courtyard from the stables was the carpenter's workshop in which he had found occasional employment. The proximity of the horses, the sounds, smell and warmth rising up from their stalls offered a familiar comfort. The inn itself was well placed, not far from the Langerei, where travellers entering Bruges by barge from the north would first alight. Just as the proximity to the quays allowed Seeker to become familiar with the stevedores and their knowledge of what was coming into and going out of the city, his place above the stables gave many opportunities to pick up information from ostlers and drivers. Often, Seeker had merely to listen to learn where travellers had come from, where they were going to, sometimes what they had talked of on their journey or who they intended to meet with now they had arrived in Bruges. Travellers by coach rarely came into the stables, riders on horseback more often, but neither riders nor coach passengers paid anything but the most cursory attention to the carpenter stooped over his workbench across the yard.

The space he had claimed as his own was at the far gable end of the loft from the stepladder leading down to the stalls. Shutters in the gable opened over a little canal that ran along behind the inn, allowing loading and unloading of hay and wood direct from the barges. In the summer months, and sometimes in winter, Seeker slept with the shutters open. Even in sleep, he was alert to noises that were not of the everyday. He was not the hunter in Bruges, but a man more like to be hunted, should his identity be discovered by those on whom he reported. He would wake in the morning to the shifting and soft whinnying of the horses in their stalls as they waited for the stable lad to bring them their breakfast, and remind himself that only vigilance would see him through to the next morning.

In the simple wooden chest that also served him as table and desk, Seeker kept copies of the news-sheets that found their way to Bruges from London. In them he read things that might have been true, things that might have been lies and things that Thurloe never told him. At such a distance now from Whitehall and Milton's censor office, he took time to consider what amongst them might be truth, and what lies. And of late, with every new month, if not week, things that had not seemed possible before became more likely, and sometimes certain. In the beginning, Seeker had never questioned why Thurloe chose to withhold certain information from him; he had never questioned Thurloe's view that it was not relevant to Seeker that Cromwell had considered long and hard before reluctantly refusing the Crown, or that Cromwell's daughters and Fairfax's daughter were marrying themselves to aristocrats and Royalists almost as quickly as the banns could be read. Neither did Thurloe think it Seeker's concern that minor players in the royalist intrigues were hunted down, given show trials and publicly executed, whilst senior figures were increasingly tolerated and intrigued with by the Protectorate authorities. Thurloe didn't tell him of such things because he did not regard such things as being Seeker's concern.

Seeker opened the chest, lifted out a paper, and lit the lamp he kept hanging from the crossbeam of the roof. The news-sheet he held out beneath it was the one abandoned the night before by the Cavaliers in the inn on Blek-ersstraat. It was one that rarely found its way to Bruges, for the Royalists had little interest in the ramblings of a former Leveller. *And yet they should have*, thought Seeker, they should have, for in *The London Lark* Elias Ellingworth called Cromwell's government more thoroughly to account than any of the papers supporting the Stuarts ever could. If Seeker had still been in London, he would have been shutting the thing down. He would have broken Elias's presses and gone to Dove Court to arrest the lawyer and face the wrath of Elias's sister. But if Lawrence Ingolby was to be believed, Elias's presses would soon fall silent, and the wrath of Maria Ellingworth directed not at himself, but at her brother.

Each night before he slept the last thing in his mind's eye was her face, as they'd lain together for untold hours in that underground cavern on Bankside, him holding her, she scarcely knowing he was there. Over them had been the half-ton carcass of a bear shot dead at the last, desperate moment, by Rupert of the Rhine. Had it not been for the warmth of the near-immovable beast, they might both have died of the cold. As it was, Maria, badly injured by her fall from the gallery above, had been almost lifeless when the soldiers under Colonel Pride had at last found them. For himself, a twisted ankle, a broken arm and a row of gashes from the first tear of the bear's claws down the side of his face had been all the harm that had come to him. He'd been covered in blood though, not only from his own wound, but from the shot animal, and the soldiers who had first come upon him had thought him dead. It had been Colonel Pride, bending down to feel the pulse at his neck, who had declared that he was, whilst taking a moment to bend closer and caution him, in a whisper, to silence. Pride had himself carried Seeker up from the pit, assisted by Seeker's own sergeant, John Proctor. By the time they emerged from underground, a crowd had gathered to see what the commotion at such a time of night could be. When he was satisfied that enough of them had witnessed Seeker being carried as if lifeless from that pit, Pride had covered Seeker's face and pronounced him dead.

Colonel Pride. Illiterate. A brewer by trade. Pride understood men, how their minds worked. When he had explained his idea to Thurloe, the Chief Secretary had been charmed by the simplicity of it. A plot, hatched in Bruges, to murder Cromwell, had been brought by Seeker to its bloody and ineffectual end in a Bankside yard. Soon the main conspirators and everyone else would believe Seeker dead. But Seeker was not dead, and when he was recovered, he would go to Bruges, and there observe the Royalists at their centre. No plot against the Protector must ever again come so close to success as had that lately put into action by Rupert of the Rhine.

And so it had gone. Seeker, quickly recovered save for a slight limp that he soon put to good use in adopting for himself a new walk, had been got away to Bruges, found employment and given a roof over his head where Cromwell's enemies, believing him dead, would never think of looking. Thurloe's plant amongst Charles Stuart's courtiers at the Bouchoute House had soon learned he must pass his coded messages to Damian Seeker and that it would be more than his miserable life was worth to think of giving Seeker away. And now both their lives were endangered by the arrival in the city of an unknown Englishwoman.

Hildred Beaumont had been a name to him up until now, a story that had almost become a legend. The kind of legend soldiers joke about, when they've got far enough away from it, and that ordinary people don't really believe. Seeker hadn't believed it himself when first he'd heard it

– this woman, well beyond middle age, standing on the battlements of her house, shooting a musket alongside the old men and young boys left on her estate, and finally wielding a crossbow and bolt when the shot ran out. But he'd heard it from so many who said they had been there and seen it with their own eyes, that he'd come to believe it to be true. The news that the real flesh-and-blood woman had appeared in Bruges had turned the legend of Hildred Beaumont into something that Seeker couldn't ignore.

There had been an unfamiliar look in Sister Janet's eye when the subject of Hildred Beaumont had come up, a shadow of something colder behind the usual irascible good humour, and Seeker couldn't tell whether it was himself or the woman in question Sister Janet was displeased with. She could hardly have known Hildred Beaumont – he had had it from the old nun herself, and from others, that Janet had fled England fifty years ago, when her father's crypto-Catholicism had come to light. There had been rumours of the hiding of Jesuit priests. Those had not been the days to be a Catholic in England. The smoke of Guy Fawkes's attempt on Parliament had still been in King James's nostrils, and there had been little sympathy for more Catholic Yorkshiremen. Janet's father had died a traitor's death, and she herself had only escaped overseas with the help of good friends. Old troubles from other days. Seeker would go back up to the Engels Klooster tomorrow, to see what he could learn.

★

It couldn't have lasted for ever. Ruth Jones had known that, and yet she had begun to feel safe in the House of Lamentations. Ruth opened the shutter a few inches and looked out over the Spaanse Loskaai – the Spanish Quay – and the canal. Darkness was encroaching on the town. Soon, the night-light men would go through their parishes, lighting lamps over bridges and along canal sides. Ruth wasn't afraid of the night: it was the daylight she feared. It was in daylight that she had run from her tormentor – broad daylight – and he had watched her run and laughed and said it hardly mattered, for he would find her before nightfall.

But night had fallen many times now, and still he hadn't found her. She welcomed the advent of the night-light men more than any other. She didn't know when last she had been out in daylight. She had gone from one sanctuary, that was not a sanctuary, to another, that was. The women of the House of Lamentations had taken one look at her damaged face and understood that Ruth could not earn her keep as they did, by night, when the House came to life. It was an irony indeed that his marking of her had served to protect her from being subjected to other men. And so by day, as the other women of the house slept, Ruth swept, and washed and scrubbed, cleaned out fires and set new ones, peeled vegetables, dressed meat and gutted fish. When night came Ruth would go to her own little room, out of sight behind a wall of old herring barrels stacked one upon the other, in the cellars of the House of Lamentations. She would take the pole she kept for the purpose and prod tentatively at the pile of warm blankets piled on her straw mattress, for fear of rats. And then, reassured, Ruth would take from beneath her mattress the pot of salve of prunella and briony root she had been given, and rub it into the sores on her flesh, as she had been shown. Finally, before snuffing out her candle, she would take the concoction of wine with melancholy thistle that had been urged upon her to stave off the melancholy and fear that had become her constant companions. Then Ruth would pull her blankets up around her and go to sleep to the sound of the bells of the Augustinians as the business of the House of Lamentations began.

Sometimes, Ruth would wake with a start, fancying she had heard the turning of the heavy iron ring on the door at the far end of the cellar. The women of the house had assured her she had nothing to fear by it – and indeed she knew she did not. On the other side there was only a tunnel, old beyond memory, running from behind the cellar wall beneath the canal into the cellars of the Augustinians' priory on the other side. None but themselves and those who wished them well knew of the tunnel. An old tale told of a doomed love between an Augustinian monk and a Carmelite sister of the House of Lamentations when it had known more respectable days. The monk, driven mad by his obsession, had murdered the nun. But that was just a tale – Ruth should not fear ghosts. Flesh and blood and the smell of one man's sweat and warm breath were what

Ruth feared. Whenever she woke, thinking she heard the ring on the tunnel door begin to turn, Ruth would take the knife from beneath her mattress and watch until her ghosts retreated into the darkness.

Tonight though, as she closed the shutters to the tolling of the Augustinians' bells and the carillon from across the city, Ruth Jones already had her knife in one hand, and a crumpled piece of paper in the other. She had read the note on the paper so often since its arrival two hours ago that its contents were burned into her brain. A man had come to Bruges, and gone to the Engels Klooster, asking about her. The man had claimed to be her brother. Ruth would not be lying down to sleep tonight.

FIVE

The Bouchoute House

As the carillon from the Belfort across the market square ricocheted around his skull, Sir Thomas Faithly cursed himself for not having pulled close the shutters of the window when finally he had tumbled into his bed in the early hours of the morning. After the despondency of two nights ago, when they had read of the butchering of their friends on Cromwell's scaffold, they had gathered last night at Sint-Walburgakerk, to listen to the mass Glenroe had insisted on having said for the souls of the dead men. Faithly had little time for the mass, still less for the Jesuit Felipe, in whose thrall Glenroe appeared to be, but he had been able to offer no alternative means to mark the passing of their comrades. They should have left it at that, but then Dunt and Ellis had insisted on further honouring their friends, and they had all but drunk Bruges dry. Glenroe had not even made it into his bed, but was still prostrate on the floor, his head turned to the pewter bowl some thoughtful soul amongst the servants of the Bouchoute House had placed there. Sir Thomas wondered for a moment whether he should check that the Irishman was not dead, but a first attempt to lift his own head from his pillow produced only agonies.

A groan from the floor reassured him. 'Dear God, Faithly! The sun, for mercy's sake put out the sun.'

Thomas made another effort, this time rolling over on to his side and gradually sliding down to the floor. This had been the last time – they all knew it. Glenroe, in fact, had been adamant: one more carouse and then revenge! *And Then Revenge.* By the end of the night, which was in truth the early hours of morning, that had become their motto and they four, who had hardly known each other a few weeks earlier, were a band of sworn brothers.

At last Thomas hauled himself to his feet and, shielding his eyes from the searing sunlight, he lurched towards the window. When he undid the catch and threw open the window to take hold of the shutter, all the warmth and sounds of the Markt below came flooding into the room, as if they had been waiting there on purpose. The world had been up and about and going about its business a good while, whilst Thomas and his companions had been sleeping off the previous night's adventures. Thomas breathed deep. Across the wide-open square, the breezes from the polder brought a hint of salt air. The sea. Always a channel of escape for him before, but now, with the Protectorate's navy controlling the Channel, it hemmed him in. His choice, such as there was a choice, was to remain here or to go further into Europe. No choice at all.

Thomas closed his eyes and opened them again, gradually

acclimatising them to the light. Each day, he searched the square for familiar figures, figures that might be looking for him, for Thomas knew he was a hunted man. This morning, he saw at first nothing to alarm him, but then something across and over to his left caught his eye. Two women were emerging from the end of Vlamingstraat. There was nothing unusual in seeing a wealthy woman and her servant coming into the Markt, but there was something different about these two. They weren't Flemish − that much was evident from their clothing − nor Spanish either. These were Englishwomen, and after watching them a moment longer, Thomas realised that they were headed his way.

'Up, Glenroe, quick! There are women coming.'

'Women?' groaned Glenroe. 'Speak no more of women. I am done with women. The House of Lamentations has finished me.'

'Not whores, you fool! English women. A lady, if I'm not mistaken, and her maidservant, and they are coming this way.' The stream of English Royalists finding its way to their door had become a trickle of late weeks, but those still determined to make their way from England to join the King in Flanders knew to come here first, to the Bouchoute House in Bruges, to make their arrival known.

Glenroe sat up at last, but then veered over and made use of the pewter bowl. Thomas, tucking his shirt into his breeches, thrust the water ewer at him, but he shook his head. 'I can't, Faithly. I'm not fit for ladies or their maid-servants. Rouse one of the others to go down with you.'

Thomas couldn't even remember if the other pair from their quartet had come home with them at all, but a cursory glance into the tumult of the neighbouring bedchamber – boots tossed into corners, hats hanging where they could only have been flung, and the aromas of the morning after with which he was all too familiar – reassured him. Marchmont Ellis was beyond rousing, but Daunt at least was awake, if deathly looking.

Thomas lifted a pair of breeches from the floor and dropped them on to Daunt's bed. 'I need you to come down with me, Dunt. There appears to be an English gentlewoman headed this way. Whatever her business, I cannot see her alone.' It had become an unspoken rule amongst those who clustered around the King that any visitors to the Bouchoute House should be received by at least two people. The Stuart court had always been a cauldron of rivalries and cabals, but the betrayal of their comrades in England had set them all looking over their shoulders at one another, wondering about every conversation they had, every letter they wrote. As Daunt heaved himself reluctantly to his feet, Thomas realised that this bold new brotherhood of theirs might be built on sands just as shifting as all the others.

Even in these benighted times, Lady Hildred was not used to being kept waiting. It was a quarter hour at least since she had given her name and demanded an interview with whoever was most senior amongst His Majesty's courtiers remaining here. The footman had given her a very peculiar look, before ushering her maid to the kitchens, where Nan was to enquire of the housekeeper where the most reliable servants were to be got, where the best tradesmen, and other matters that were the business of servants. Lady Hildred herself would take charge of the selection of a suitable lodging, but first she must see to the business she had come here for. She considered her surroundings as she waited. The ceilings were of an appropriate height, and if nothing else the windows allowed for a good deal of light and permitted a more than adequate view of comings and goings in the heart of the town. It was, in all, a townhouse, in a marketplace, in a fading Flemish town. She might well have been in Norwich or some such place, and whilst the house might serve for a merchant of an unremarkable town, she could hardly believe it had ever been deemed a fit residence for the King of England.

At last a low rumble of male voices echoed across the tiled entrance hall and soon was followed by the entrance into the reception room of two characters she would think twice about entrusting with the sweeping of a barn, never mind what she had been considering. The arrival of the men was accompanied by a reek of stale tobacco smoke, sour wine and unwashed linen, and Lady Hildred made no effort to mask her distaste.

The one in the faded blue velvet suit spoke first. 'Lady Hildred, I must apologise that there was no one here to receive you. My companions and I were—'

'Drunk,' she interrupted. 'It is as well His Majesty is not

in residence, the disgraceful standards that you keep!' The second man, who had not yet made any effort to speak, looked determinedly at the floor in a passing imitation of a schoolboy who had not done his lesson. He had married a grey velvet coat and half-done-up brown doublet with green hose that looked a good deal too small for him. It appeared to Lady Hildred that he swayed on his feet rather than stood, fixing his eye to a point on the floor as if it might be the only thing keeping him upright. Both men made an effort at a bow, but green hose winced noticeably as he shakily straightened himself.

'You will do me the honour of introducing yourselves, sirs.'

'Of course,' said the one in the blue suit, who looked to have a better grip on himself than his companion. 'My name is Sir Thomas Faithly, and this is Sir Edward Daunt.'

Lady Hildred was unmoved by this information, other than to inform them that she knew of the Faithlys of the North Riding, but the provenance of the Daunts was a mystery to her. After indicating that they might sit, she lost no time in coming to the point. 'I am informed His Majesty has gone to Antwerp for the summer.'

Thomas Faithly nodded. 'Hoogstraten, your ladyship. To the north. The wildfowl are particularly good there, and it was thought, given the naval situation in the Channel—'

'That His Majesty should be got further away from the coast,' she finished for him.

Faithly began to nod again but appeared to realise that

it was not required of him to say anything else, simply to listen.

'I have come here expressly to wait upon His Majesty and to deliver to him funds for his own use. On learning he is removed from the town for the summer, I had thought to engage some gentlemen of his court to take those funds to him on my behalf.'

Daunt, in the green hose, made a perceptible effort at sitting straighter. 'Your ladyship, it would be an honour . . .'

'I've no doubt it would be, but after the disgraceful spectacle of your appearance, half-dressed and unable to stand, and your companion there scarcely in better order, I have no intention of trusting my money to your care. I did not attain my current number of years by being an imbecile.'

'N-no, your ladyship,' stammered Daunt.

Thomas Faithly broke in. 'Of course. But we cannot be certain when His Majesty will return, and if it were to become widely known that you were keeping a large sum of money here . . .'

Lady Hildred bridled and leaned a little forward in her seat. 'I will not be keeping a large sum of money here. Whilst I had intended taking up residence in Bruges and engaging some reliable gentlemen to take the funds to the King, I see now that I will have to take them to Hoog-straten myself.'

This seemed to startle both men into a greater degree of sobriety. 'Yourself!' exclaimed the fat one, Daunt. 'Madam, the roads are not safe. There are disbanded mercenaries and

Spanish soldiers everywhere, to say nothing of Cromwell's spies. We could not in all honour permit you to go.'

Hildred moved quickly to disabuse the man, cutting him short. 'I have been fourteen years a widow and asked no man his permission for many years before that. I will take the money to Hoogstraten myself, and two of your number, sufficiently sobered and appropriately dressed, will escort me. We set out from the Engels Klooster shortly after dawn tomorrow. See that you are not late. Now,' she picked up a pair of long kidskin gauntlets she had laid down on a side table, 'I'll thank you to have my maid sent for. It is time for us to leave.'

The maid was sent for as Lady Hildred made ready to depart. She had warned Nan of the reputation of the circle around the King. She was glad to see that despite Daunt's scarcely concealed interest, Nan kept her head down when she emerged from below. The creature could be excused the brief glance she had given Faithly, for even Hildred would acknowledge that he was an attractive man.

'They are a disgrace,' she said after they had been shown out of the Bouchoute House and begun to make their way back across the Markt.

'Utterly,' agreed Nan.

'But they will have to do.'

'Do, your Ladyship?'

'We are going to have to go to the King at Hoogstraten ourselves. I have informed them that we require two from amongst their number to escort us.'

The look on Nan's face was not one that Hildred had ever expected to see on one of her servants. It was the look of a person who has an opinion.

Hildred stopped. 'This is of some inconvenience to you? You can scarcely have been in any doubt that engaging yourself in my service would bring many discomforts. Loyalty to His Majesty in these times of ours exacts a great price. I am honoured to pay it, and I expect my servants to be so also. Besides, the journey to Hoogstraten will hardly be more perilous than what we have already endured to get here, and poor specimens though they are, those two are at least English gentlemen, and trusted by the King. We will go to Hoogstraten, and they will escort us there.'

Nan lowered her eyes. 'Of course, your ladyship.'

Lady Hildred looked back once more at the Bouchoute House. As she did so, she noticed that a man whose face she couldn't properly see was watching them from a window in the uppermost storey of the house. Realising he had been seen, the man hastily pulled close the window shutter. Lady Hildred was not a nervous woman, and only appropriately suspicious, but there had been something malignant in the look she had felt from the unseen man. She quickened her pace and was glad to see her maid do likewise.

Seeker had risen early in his stable loft, but some work in the carpenter's yard that required his attention had prevented him from going over into Sint-Anna and the Engels Klooster as early as he had planned to, and he learned from the Mother Superior's stable lad that he was too late to catch sight of Lady Hildred Beaumont. The boy was happy to inform him that after a day's resting yesterday the rude old English lady had been up and out this morning, before breakfast in the refectory was even cleared, and that whatever her business was, her arrival had put Sister Janet into a mood like thunder. The boy was also able to tell him that Lady Hildred had been on her way to the Bouchoute House – he himself had given her maid directions.

And the maid was English too? Seeker had asked. Certainly. But the boy didn't think Sister Janet much liked her either.

Why was that?

In a hushed tone, as if the wrath of the redoubtable old nun might be about to descend on him, the boy confided that he had had it from one of the novices that Sister Janet had made a search of the maid's belongings as soon as she and Lady Hildred had safely disappeared down the Carmersstraat. 'Christiana said she was pretty sure Sister Janet would have done it the day before, when the maid had gone down into town by herself, but she'd not been able to get in because Lady Hildred was in there resting.'

'Oh? And did she find anything this morning?'

The boy had shrugged. 'Christiana doesn't know. She just said Sister Janet came out looking very pleased with herself, then hurried away to her cell to write a note.'

'A note?' It was too much to hope that the boy might know its contents, but Seeker was a veteran of many years of extracting information from people who hardly knew they were giving it, and he was certain the stable boy had a little more to give. 'Something for Lady Hildred's maid, I suppose.'

The boy shook his head and looked about him to check that they were not overheard. 'Not for Lady Hildred's maid. She had me call Jakob van Hjul. I heard her tell him to take it to the House of Lamentations. Jakob grumbled that he'd had to take one there for her yesterday, too.'

Back in the centre of town, Seeker had taken up position at the top of Vlamingstraat from where he had a good view of the Bouchoute House. The Markt was busy, as ever, but the House seemed to have shrunk in on itself somewhat. There was a good deal less coming and going now than there had been over the previous few months, when Charles Stuart had been in residence in Bruges, and whatever lustre his tattered name might have brought with it was now gone. An aura of gloom seemed to pervade the air around the place. Repeated failure and bloody retribution had at last put an end to the plots emanating from that house. Sealed Knot, Action Party, Great Trust: it didn't matter what the Royalist conspirators called themselves any more. They were finished.

And yet. The arrival from England of a legendary royalist matron at the very time Thurloe had warned him of a woman coming to Bruges to hunt down their source suggested that there were some in Charles Stuart's service who had not yet accepted they were finished. That Hildred

Beaumont, whose contempt for the Protector was infamous, had gone directly to the Bouchoute House within two days of arriving in Bruges suggested the place still needed watching.

Seeker ran his eye over the front of the house. Presumably Faithly was downstairs now, dealing with Lady Hildred. This at least gave Seeker some pleasure. If even half of what he had heard of the woman were true, it would be an uncomfortable encounter.

That night eighteen months ago in the underground cavern, the bear pit, Seeker had sworn he would find Thomas Faithly and he would kill him for the danger in which he'd placed Maria. Faithly had claimed to love Maria, he'd tried to persuade her to leave London, to leave England with him. Even now, in his nightmares, Seeker saw Thomas Faithly looking on as the Frenchwoman Clémence Barguil held a knife to Maria's throat; Thomas Faithly's uselessness as Clémence pushed Maria from a ledge fifteen feet above the pit in which Seeker was trapped; Thomas Faithly's inertia as the Frenchwoman released a half-starved bear into that cavern. And Seeker had meant the threat, every word. But over the weeks of recuperation and the months of absence that had followed, he had realised it had not been Maria's connection to Thomas Faithly, but to himself, that had endangered her life. The most searing memory from that night was of Maria's response when Faithly had asked her to go away with him, and she had refused because, she said, she was in love with Damian Seeker. She had said that at the edge of a pit, with a knife at her throat, and he had gone away and left her again. But Seeker was determined this would be the last task he would complete for Thurloe, and then he would disappear, become someone else as he had before, start a new life as he had before. With Maria.

Even so, the first time he'd spied Thomas Faithly here, in Bruges, he'd been so overwhelmed with rage that he'd almost done it, almost taken the chisel from his carpenter's bag and driven it into the passing Cavalier's neck. It had been a dog, a daft big beast he'd never seen in his life before, that had stopped him, bounding out from behind a cart to jump up and lick him just as he was drawing the chisel from his bag. For a ridiculous moment he'd thought it was his own dog that he'd had to leave behind in London. It was as if Maria had sent the thing. And then the dog and the moment were both gone, and with them the killing rage. It chilled Seeker sometimes, to know how closely Thomas Faithly had been to death and not known a thing about it. Even so, from the shadows, in his altered persona, Seeker had observed that Faithly often looked over his shoulder, as if fearing a sinister presence somewhere, just out of sight.

Across the Markt, the door to the Bouchoute House opened, and a woman who could only be Lady Hildred Beaumont appeared. Even at this distance, her entire demeanour exuded displeasure. Seeker smiled. 'I'll bet you've given Sir Thomas a hard time,' he murmured to himself. Lady Hildred was richly dressed in a style that hadn't been seen much in England since Henrietta Maria was in her pomp in Greenwich – no demure Puritan bib and tucker for her. A sudden breeze from the polder caused her skirts to balloon and her cloak to fly up almost in the face of her maid who was partially obscured by her mistress as she followed her out into the marketplace. Lady Hildred was tall and bore herself with a lifetime's experience of telling others what to do. The maid was more drawn in on herself, as though bowed by the burden of a life spent doing the bidding of others. Her ladyship was clearly admonishing the younger woman about something when she suddenly looked up towards a window on the second topmost floor of the house. Seeker followed her line of sight, just in time to see a figure hastily pull the shutter closed. Lady Hildred saw it too and he could see she was troubled by it.

Seeker was considering which route he might best take to follow the women unseen when a young man, not looking where he was going, ran into him.

'Hoi!' said Seeker. 'What's the hurry?'

The man didn't stop, but side-swerved Seeker to continue on his way. 'I need to get to the Burg. Body in the canal. Augustinians' Bridge.'

Seeker felt an unaccountable chill at the young man's words. He glanced back over towards where the women had been, but they'd moved out of his sightline now. There'd be time enough later to track them down again. He turned instead in the direction of the Augustinians' Bridge.

Still some distance away, he could see a small crowd gathered on the quay, just across from the House of Lamentations. Men on a barge working long-handled hooks beneath the bridge were hauling something out of the water. Seeker slowed his pace. By the time he had reached the back of the small crowd of curious onlookers, the dock hands had swung the object up out of the water and it was being lowered on to the Spaanse Loskaai.

All around him, when the inevitable low groan of surprise that always greeted these things had subsided, voices, mainly Flemish, began to chatter. Who was it? No one knew. A foreigner. Spanish? No. Too pale. A soldier? Peasant, more like. Fallen drunk into the canal? A fight perhaps.

'Got thrown out of there, like as not,' said one grey head, indicating the House of Lamentations nearby.

'No.' Another shook his head. 'Not finely dressed enough for there.'

'Stealing perhaps?'

'Likely. Stealing, or a woman. Usually is.'

The crowd began to drift away, even before the town's officers arrived from the Burg. They'd seen it all before, and they had other things to be getting on with. It had been a diversion, but one that would be forgotten by most of them before dinnertime. Soon, only the porters, and one or two aged burghers for whom this was an entertainment at least worthy of a morning's interest, remained.

Seeker drew closer to the corpse on the ground, on the pretext of saving the porters the trouble of getting off their barge to unhook it. As he did so, his heart sank. Seeker knew, before he even turned the body over, what he was

looking at. The black hair not sticking out in all directions now, but plastered to the pallid cheeks, the stocky,
belligerent form of Bartlett Jones. But Bartlett Jones wasn't
belligerent now – Seeker could see that he had been scarcely
more than a boy. The anger, the hostility, the bravado: it
had all been to mask the fear of a boy far from home and
with no one to trust.

Feeling his years, Seeker sat back a moment on his
haunches, his stomach hollow. 'Why didn't you trust me,
Bartlett?' he murmured. The boy's face was curiously
unmarked. Carefully, Seeker moved the head slightly, and
was not altogether surprised to see a deep and expert gash
across Bartlett's throat. An assassin's cut, sudden and from
behind. 'Why did you really come here?'

The process of straightening the boy's limbs, removing
tendrils of plants and other canal debris from the body
allowed Seeker to make a search of Bartlett Jones's clothing.
In an inside pocket of the leather jerkin was a sodden Bible
and the remains of what looked to have been a pass. Hooked
onto the breeches was Bartlett's money pouch, which felt
no lighter than it had looked the previous afternoon. Seeker
removed both and secreted them in the front pocket of his
carpenter's apron. He was just examining Bartlett's hands,
which showed little sign of having put up a fight, when a
now familiar respectful murmuring behind him alerted him
to the fact that a priest had arrived. He wanted to say, 'He's
not a papist.' He wanted to hurl the priest's beads and the
man after them into the canal. Instead, he stepped back to

let the priest, and the town's officer with him, take charge of the earthly remains of the scared young Englishman who'd come to Bruges and died there.

The officer asked the usual questions of the onlookers – who had found him? Bert, the bargeman. When had he been found? A little after ten. His body had been caught by a pier of the bridge. Had anyone heard an altercation the previous night? No. Did anyone know him? Had anyone seen him about the town before? No. No. 'And you,' said the officer, to Seeker, who had remained silent throughout the questioning. 'Do you know him?'

'No,' said Seeker, at last beginning to walk away. 'I don't.'

Through the small window that looked out from the back stair of the House of Lamentations to the Spaanse Loskaai and over the canal, Ruth Jones watched the big Englishman walk away from the huddle around her brother's body and thought she might collapse.

SIX

The Road to Damme

Sister Janet attempted to stifle a yawn but then gave up. It was natural enough, surely, that a woman of her years should show signs of tiredness now and again. The life of a bride of Christ, even in the congenial surroundings of this town, was not an easy one, and the unlooked-for arrival of Hildred Beaumont had caused her no little inconvenience. Nobody would question the yawn.

Yesterday had been a long day, and fraught with difficulties. Hildred had always had remarkable stamina – Janet should have remembered that. Barely a day's rest had been sufficient for her to recover from the rigours of her journey from England and the late-night arrival in Bruges. Even then, she had already been up and about by the time Janet had emerged from seeing her confessor, Father Felipe. Hildred had even had the gall to question her on the priest afterwards.

'That man is a Jesuit?' Hildred had enquired with a degree of impertinence.

'Father Felipe is our confessor. You should remember,

Hildred, that you are no longer in England. A father of the Society of Jesus may move freely here without fear of persecution. It is *you* who are the heretic here.'

Hildred had only been temporarily put in her place by the rebuke and looked as if she would say more, but the arrival of two sisters in dispute over laundry duties called Janet's attention elsewhere.

Then, when Hildred had gone to make herself known to those shiftless fellows at the Bouchoute House, Sister Janet had taken the opportunity to search through Hildred's personal effects and those of her maid. There, amongst them, was a locket which opened to reveal a miniature of Guy as a young man. The years had fallen away from Janet, and she'd stood a good long time gazing at that portrait. When a concerned novice had asked a little later about her red-rimmed eyes, Janet had blamed the poor standard of dusting in the chapel and ordered the girl to see to it. The locket also held the image of another young man, facing Guy. Janet didn't know him and supposed he must be their son. She had taken note of the case in which Hildred kept the locket, and left it there, for the time being. It was amongst Hildred's maid's belongings, however, that Janet had made the most interesting discovery. It was a copy of a book which she had heard of from English visitors from time to time, *The Compleat Angler*, by one Izaak Walton. That a lady's maid should possess such an item was an object of only mild curiosity to Janet, and she would have paid it little more attention, had it not been that in returning it to its place a thin sheet of paper had fallen out from between its leaves. Janet could make very little of the marks and assortment of words and names on the paper, and that she found very interesting indeed. So interesting did Janet find this that she made a short visit to her own cell to copy down what was written on the sheet before returning it to where she'd found it.

Janet had then devoted a considerable length of time to compiling a list of likely properties which Hildred might consider renting in the town. There should be little difficulty in finding something suitable. Since the King's departure for Hoogstraten with most of what remained of his court, properties that had once been rented by the English were now empty. The Spanish, too, were going or gone, in the hope of reaching Brussels before the advancing French did. The town was returning to the jaded obscurity that Janet so much preferred to its many other incarnations. There would be plenty of vacant lodgings and available houses soon in Bruges, and the further away from Sister Janet's little world of the Engels Klooster the better.

Janet had been thus pleasantly occupied when a novice had tentatively knocked at the door of her small parlour.

'Forgive me, Sister,' said the novice, never raising her eyes from the floor, 'but there is a . . .' she paused, '*person* asking for you.'

'"Person"?' she had queried.

The novice's cheeks had started to deepen in colour. 'It's the English carpenter, Sister. He will talk only to you.'

This explained the novice's blushes. Janet might have guessed. She could not have said when, exactly, she had become aware of a slight change in the air within the walls of the convent whenever John Carpenter was at work somewhere there – a stall in the choir needing repair, a cupboard door requiring replacement, a rotted window-frame to be removed and a new one put in – somehow, over the past months, it had been John Carpenter they had turned to. And when he came to do the work, Sister Janet would always find two or three novices and nuns – some whose youth was almost as distant a memory as her own – who had apparently found it necessary to carry out their own duties somewhere from where they might catch a glimpse of him, or even hear the sounds of him at work. He was hardly a young man, goodness knows – well over forty, if Sister Janet was any judge. But he was tall, and strong, spoke little, and had gentle eyes – a deep brown, framed by dark lashes. Almost black brows matched the remaining black in his hair, whilst the rest was a steel grey. Janet had long ago relinquished any interest in dark lashes: what she knew of John Carpenter's eyes was that they took in everything they lighted upon. She had enquired and found that he had come to Bruges alone, and was unmarried. She knew his voice to be Yorkshire, but a man's voice might be set before he was twenty. His history, or some of it, could be read in the scars on his face and his hands. She had commented on them once, and he had given a low laugh and said the other fellow had come off worse. Janet had seen plenty of scarred men in her time – fifty years in the Low Countries had taught her enough to know Carpenter's wounds had been garnered over a long period. 'More than one fellow, I'd wager,' she'd said, and left it at that. One day Sister Janet would take the time to find out what lay behind his watchful eyes and easy humour, but not today. What Sister Janet would require of John Carpenter on this occasion would be to know why he had come to the Engels Klooster three times within the last two days.

'You'd best send him along then,' said Sister Janet. 'And if you happen to see Sister Marjory lurking in his vicinity, you can tell her that I recall the vows she made even if she doesn't.'

The novice lowered her head even further, but not so far that Janet couldn't see her wide-eyed shock. 'Yes, Sister,' the girl mumbled before hurriedly leaving the room.

A few minutes later, John Carpenter stood in the doorway. Sister Janet made a shooing gesture to the novice who had brought him.

'Well, then. Don't just loom there like a drawbridge about to crash down.'

He nodded, and came in, closing the door carefully behind him.

'So?' she asked, feigning lack of real interest. 'You wished to see me. Best get on then, for I'm a busy woman.'

'That's not in dispute, Sister.'

'Oh?' Something in his tone had suggested that something else was. It was not what she expected from a tradesman.

'The man Bartlett Jones that came here looking for his sister.'

'You're disturbing me for this again? I'll tell you again what I told him. She isn't here. Never was. Now what's it to you?'

'I don't know, Sister. Not yet, anyway. But not half an hour after he left here, you sent a note to someone in the House of Lamentations.'

Sister Janet put down her quill pen and stood up, investing her five feet and two inches of height with all the menace she could summon. 'You are *spying* on me, John Carpenter?'

'Not spying, Sister. Just something I happened to hear of.'

'When you were sniffing around in the stables, I'll warrant.'

He didn't deny it. 'Repairs to be made to a gate on one of the stalls. Took some time.'

She sat back down and considered him. 'Who are you?'

He looked around the small, spartan parlour, his gaze coming to rest on the portrait of St Livinius behind her. 'Just an Englishman,' he said, 'trying to make his way. Trying to look out for others who might have lost theirs.'

'Like?' she said.

'Like Bartlett Jones.'

'I haven't seen Bartlett Jones since I sent him away.'

'But I have.'

Sister Janet felt a strange sense of dread begin to take hold. 'Where?' she demanded, a little too quickly.

He looked at her very closely, as Guy's older brother

had looked at her, that day all those years ago when the news had come that her father had been taken. He spoke slowly, and very clearly. 'An hour ago, at the Augustinians' Bridge, within spitting distance of the House of Lamentations, being fished out of the canal.'

'Dead?'

'As my great-grandfather.'

Janet was conscious of her hand gripping her pen as if it was the only thing keeping her upright. She forced herself to loosen her fingers around it. She wanted to close her eyes, shut out the reality of the man standing in front of her, saying these things. But she didn't. She kept herself sitting straight up and she kept her eyes open, looking at him.

'Who *are* you?' she said again, finally.

John Carpenter looked at her a good long while before replying: 'No, the question is, Sister Janet, who are *you*?'

But that had been yesterday, and the long day had been followed by a long night. It was almost morning now, though, with that grey, pre-dawn light that she so liked – the air was cool and the sun yet to burn the low mist from the canals. She might have been home in England, but she knew she would never see England again.

Out in the courtyard Hildred was already up and break-fasted, and anxious to be on the road. The maidservant looked exhausted, and Janet knew why. It was seldom that the right circumstances presented themselves to Janet as fortuitously as they did now, and she had expected to encounter a great deal more difficulty in putting her plan in place, but after what she had observed only two hours ago, in the darkness of the city, she felt a good deal more confident of success. On the pretext of needing help with a hamper of provisions she had prepared for the journey to Hoogstraten, Sister Janet told Lady Hildred's maidservant to come with her to the kitchens. Halfway there, she stopped and looked out the length of the cloister walk. No one was watching them. Quickly, she lifted a key from the chain at her belt and turned it in the lock of the door they had stopped next to. 'In here.'

The maid was startled but had the sense not to say anything. Without protest, but with a look that said she was very much on her guard, she did as she was bid. Sister Janet quickly pulled the door to behind them and turned the key once more in the lock. She had many years ago selected this room – a store for old habits, reeking of damp and dead moth – as somewhere suited to her private purposes, and had consequently made sure that all keys to it but hers had gone missing. Only a little light came through the storeroom's small, round window, but that was quite enough. She turned now to look at her companion. Hildred's maid was an attractive woman if no longer young – somewhere over thirty: dark hair, good cheekbones, fine skin. A woman like this must surely have been married once. Janet wondered what could have happened to the husband, that his wife should find herself here.

'Nan they call you, isn't it?'

'Or Nancy, according to preference.'

'Not your preference, I'd wager. You're no Nancy, nor Nan either. But that's your business.'

The woman opposite her didn't even blink.

'What do you want, Sister?'

Janet felt herself smile. She always did prefer people to be direct. The novices were too terrified to open their mouths to her, and Mother Superior had long since learned to know her place, so people were seldom direct with Janet.

'I want you to take something to Hoogstraten with you.'

'Then surely it's her ladyship you should be asking—'

Janet interrupted her. 'Hildred's head is full of her own concerns, and she has no interest in anyone else's. Besides, I trust her ladyship about as much as I'd trust a Toledo cutpurse.'

'And you have better cause to trust me?'

Janet smiled. This young woman had some mettle, which no doubt stood her in good stead for dealing with Hildred. 'Much better cause.'

The woman looked even more puzzled, and Sister Janet might have strung her along a good while longer, but time was pressing.

'I saw you, you see, my dear. I saw you earlier this morning – two hours ago. I saw where you were and I saw what you did.'

Even in the poor light of the storeroom, Janet could see the other woman's face pale. She had her.

'Now, I won't be telling anyone about you clambering

out of a ground-floor window of the Bouchoute House in the middle of the night, or that you appeared to be secreting some item – the size of, shall we say, a book? – in amongst the folds of your habit once you had done so. No, there's no need whatsoever for me to mention that to anyone. If you do me a small favour in return.'

The woman had quickly regained her composure, and her gaze didn't waver. 'What favour?'

Sister Janet turned away and a little breathlessly pushed aside a laundry hamper near the wall, indicating what was behind. 'I want you to take this person to Hoogstraten.'

The surprise on the woman's face was as she had expected. 'I . . . But how?'

'The clothing chest.'

The maid went through several objections – all of which Sister Janet had anticipated and taken steps to eliminate – before eventually admitting defeat.

'And when we get there?'

'When you get there – having of course checked at regular intervals on the journey that all inside is as it should be – you will remove Lady Hildred's clothing and deliver the chest with its contents to the Begijnhof there and that will be the end of your involvement in the matter. I daresay my memory of what I witnessed out in the town in the early hours of this morning will desert me, when I receive confirmation that you have completed your commission.'

Janet knew there was nothing the other woman could do but agree. She unlocked the door and sent the maid down to Lady Hildred's cell as quickly and quietly as possible, to wait by the open chest.

It was less than half an hour later, and now truly dawn, when Thomas Faithly appeared in the courtyard of the Engels Klooster, ready to act as escort to Hildred and her valuable baggage. Janet liked Sir Thomas and did not envy his escort duty. She raised an eyebrow in enquiry when she saw he had arrived alone.

'I have no doubts as to your capabilities, Sir Thomas, but surely if it should become known that Lady Hildred is carrying half the Beaumont fortune to the King at Hoogstraten, a larger escort would be advisable.'

Sir Thomas nodded. 'You're right, as ever, Sister, but have no fear. Sir Evan is waiting for us at the Speye Poort with all the requisite travel passes. We will escort Lady Hildred as far as Damme, where she will join a larger, and well-protected party also making its way to His Majesty. You need have no apprehension for your friend. Lady Hildred will be safe in our care.'

Janet contented herself with a smile and murmured as she turned away from him, 'It was His Majesty's money I was concerned about.'

Jakob van Hjul and the stable hand grumbled heartily about the weight of Lady Hildred's baggage, particularly her clothing chest, and earned themselves many rebukes as they did so. Both Hildred and her maid were dressed against every eventuality of weather, although it had been a parching summer and the heat of the sun would be searing before they were many miles up the road. Hildred wore a heavily embroidered brocade cloak, pinned at her shoulder with a pearl and ruby clasp Janet had last seen on Guy's mother, over fifty years ago. The maid had shrouded herself in a much simpler garment, a short cape of grey wool, the hood of which was up and covering most of her face. She was fearful, no doubt, that the early morning moisture would make tangle-weed of her hair. Or perhaps it was Janet she feared, for she never lifted her eyes as she followed her mistress into their carriage. It was good that she was afraid, reflected Janet. Frightened people were more inclined to do as they were told.

Farewells were brief, with Hildred declaring she would be returning to the convent to collect the rest of her goods and chattels and establish herself in Bruges before the end of the month. Sister Janet was happy to see the small party at last ride away from the Engels Klooster. She was so happy, in fact, that she went out onto the street to follow its progress to the top of the street, and from there, to the accompaniment of the creaking of the windmills on the ramparts, she watched them draw up at the Speye Poort, and finally pass over the bridge and out of the city. Sister Janet smiled to herself, lifted her crucifix to her lips and kissed it, then turned to go home.

Thomas Faithly rode a little ahead of the carriage, with Evan Glenroe behind. Lady Hildred had treated Glenroe to some forthright views on the Irish and he, making an ostentatious bow and sweep of the hat to her, had delivered to her in Gaelic a stream of invective on the English, smiling all the while. Thomas was fairly certain Lady Hildred could not speak Irish, but just as certain that she had understood very clearly the tenor of what he had said. She had settled for giving them both a sour look and chastising her maid about the distribution of the carriage blankets. Every so often, Thomas would hear the old woman make some disparaging remark about the polder – 'Flat as Norfolk, or the Fens' – to which her maid would make some muted response. Thomas himself had taken a long time to get used to the flatlands and the ubiquitous water, to the nothingness of the horizon, the stark landscape broken by windmills, smallholdings, the odd, regimented line of trees. He longed for the high moorland and crashing streams, the crags and the dales of the North Riding. Glenroe sometimes spoke of Ireland as if it was a woman he had loved and abandoned. England was not a woman to Thomas, but a companion, ready for adventure but ever sturdy and dependable. It was the rock he had been cleaved from and to which he wanted to return.

Two things drove them on now: the desire to avenge their friends, and the need to be home. Charles Stuart came third, a more distant third with every month that passed. He was the companion of their sufferings, but in Thomas Faithly's heart at least, he was little more now.

They hadn't been on the road very long – the spires of

Bruges were still clearly in sight should they turn their heads – when something odd about a windmill a little ahead, on the other bank of the canal, caught Thomas's eye. It took him a moment to realise what was wrong. It was not just that the sails were not moving as they should, but one was missing altogether. Only a few yards ahead, the torn sail was lying on the road, blocking their path.

'What in the name . . .' said Glenroe, trotting up to join Sir Thomas to inspect the obstacle. It was one of those moments when everything came together with a slow, stark, clarity, a realisation that came upon Thomas too late. This was an ambush. Thomas saw Glenroe open his mouth exactly as a loud bang and a flash emanated from a narrow window slit in the mill. Twenty yards back, beyond the rearing and panicked whinnying of the horses, came a horrified shriek and scream from the carriage. Thomas wheeled round in time to see the maid throw up her hands and spin around as Lady Hildred appeared to slump in her seat. Another shot came, the coachman struggled to control his beasts, and Glenroe's horse was taken out from under him.

The Irishman tumbled to the ground as his horse fell. It was fortunate that his feet had already been loose in the stirrups or he would have had slim chance of getting them free and throwing himself to the side before the animal crashed to the ground. The fall dazed him so that when he managed to haul himself to his feet he immediately keeled over again. Through the dust of road and gunshot, once he had his own horse under control, Thomas could see a commotion of blankets and cloaks and women's skirts in the carriage.

There was no time to lose – the attack had come from the far bank of the canal and their assailant was already at an advantage. 'You stay with the women,' Sir Thomas shouted to Glenroe, who was still attempting to stagger to his feet. 'I'm going after them.'

Glenroe nodded groggily as he extracted his pistol and checked for powder, and Thomas set off in pursuit. The canal itself was not a possibility – silted in parts, still too deep in others, he couldn't risk the horse in it. The nearest crossing appeared to be a wooden footbridge, a good distance further up, but he had no choice. He dug in his spurs and urged the horse eastwards, further from Bruges and closer to Damme, expecting every moment to hear further gunshot, feel the hot agony of being hit, or his horse go from under him. But there was nothing, no further shot. He turned as often as he could to see what was happening behind him, but there was no approach of horsemen to the stricken carriage, which Glenroe, pistol ready, had almost reached. At one point, Thomas thought he saw a disturbance in the water, a dark shape move below the surface of the canal, but the darting of a horseman from behind the windmill forced his attention elsewhere. Thomas lifted his pistol and shot. He was certain he'd caught the horseman on the arm, but the man continued to career southwards, beyond a line of spindly trees. By the time Thomas reached the bridge, his quarry was completely gone from his sight.

He had little chance of catching him now, but at least he had driven him off. Giving up his prey as lost, for now, Thomas wheeled back towards the carriage and its occupants.

Glenroe, still unsteady and with his pistol extended, was scanning the landscape and cursing mightily by the time Thomas got back.

'Are you badly hurt?' Thomas asked the Irishman.

Glenroe dismissed the idea. 'Bumped, nothing more, but my horse is done for.'

'Poor devil,' said Thomas, looking down at the animal whose eyes had now glazed over and whose blood was slowly crawling from the wound in its neck. 'And the women?'

'Her ladyship was hit – in the arm, I think. The maid is attending to it – there has been much ripping of linen and some astonishing language from the old woman. I wouldn't get too close, if I were you. The maid says the sooner we get her to Damme and a physician, the better.'

Thomas risked a glance into the carriage where the maid was on her knees with the clothes chest open, ransacking it for linen to serve as bandages. The old woman's colour was not good.

'Are you badly hurt, your ladyship?'

'Hardly a scratch,' Lady Hildred replied testily, 'and more petticoats than enough torn and ruined over it. They have not got my money chest?'

'No.'

'God be praised. Then we must make haste.'

'We can be back in Bruges within—'

She roused herself to protest. 'Bruges? We go on to Damme. And when I have had a surgeon look to whatever this fool girl has done to my arm, we will continue to Hoogstraten, and the King. And you can tell that Irish bog-dweller to keep his head out of this carriage, too.' The effort of her outburst was almost too much for her, and her maid laid a calming hand on her arm. 'You must not upset yourself, your ladyship.'

'Is she fit to travel?' asked Sir Thomas, his voice lowered.

The maid nodded. 'Yes,' she said quietly, never taking her eyes from her work.

Behind him, Glenroe had managed to climb up beside the driver, who had taken some time to calm his horses. 'The old woman's insisting on Damme then?'

Thomas nodded. 'I'd rather go back to Bruges, but we're closer to Damme now. The sooner we get her into the care of a physician the better. As soon as we have her settled we'll get back to Bruges to consult with Ellis and Daunt. We can decide what to do from there.'

'We can start by finding whoever it is wants to kill me,' said Glenroe.

'You?' said Thomas.

'What else? The shot that got the old woman was clearly meant for me – why else would he have tried with the second? And they never went near the money either, so it wasn't that they were after. The old woman's a tartar, granted, but why should anyone go to such lengths to try to kill her?'

But Thomas knew what skill it must have taken to fire a musket from a narrow aperture in a windmill at a moving carriage and still manage to hit one of the occupants. He was certain it had been the old woman, and not himself or Glenroe, who had been the target, for if they had been, they would surely be dead by now. 'I don't know, Evan,' he said. 'I truly do not know.'

It was with some relief all round that they finally arrived at the house of De Grote Sterre in Damme. Although the Spanish military governor had already set out for Brussels, the house still rang with the calls of officers and civil servants preparing to follow him. An embassy from the Duke of York to his brother the King, also bound for Hoogstraten, was already assembled in front of the Stadhuis, in expectation of the arrival of Lady Hildred and her precious baggage. The lady had grown a good deal weaker over the course of their short journey from the site of the attack, and by the time the coachman drew up at the front steps of the house, her maid was having trouble keeping her from falling into a faint. Nevertheless, Lady Hildred made it clear that her money was not to be transported to the King until such time as she was sufficiently recovered to accompany it.

'That day will never be,' murmured Glenroe, and Thomas could not help but agree. A boy was immediately sent to fetch a physician, and a sturdy young English soldier stepped forward to lift Lady Hildred from the carriage, her maid hurrying afterwards, uttering words of exhortation and consolation. Thomas accompanied the man carrying Lady Hildred into the house, and despite his urging of Glenroe to rest, the Irishman also came in, so that he might assure himself of her condition. The old woman was laid on a settle in a grand room on the first floor, where her maid hastily asked that the large empty fireplace might be set and lit.

'Come on, Glenroe,' said Thomas, as a servant began to go around the room, closing shutters against the late morning sun, 'we can do nothing further here.' They went out to the backyard of the Grote Sterre to supervise the unloading of the women's belongings – other than the money chest, which they had agreed to take back, for safekeeping, to Bruges, until they should have word from the king about what should be done with it. The large clothing chest that had been loaded at the Engels Klooster had clearly been ransacked by Lady Hildred's maid in her search for suitable linen to be torn into bandages, and many ruined and bloodstained garments still lay about the carriage floor. Thomas took a moment to throw them back into the chest – something for the laundresses and seamstresses of Damme to exercise their talents upon. As he did so, he was momentarily struck by how empty the chest still appeared to be, given the trouble the men had had loading it in Bruges.

As he finished packing in the scattered and stained clothing, Thomas noticed the chest had been damaged – at first he thought some shot must have hit an end panel, but then he realised both ends were similarly marked, and not by chance: six holes, that he might stick a finger through, at each end, and another dozen, which he had at first thought to be studs, at the back. They looked to be recent, and he dared say the owner of the chest knew nothing of them. But he reminded himself that Hildred Beaumont had greater concerns just now than the defacing of her property, and he had not the leisure to muse on such matters. Thomas slammed the lid shut and called to the two men nearest to him to carry it into the house. Meanwhile, Glenroe had bargained the borrowing of a new mount, and they were soon on the road back to Bruges, and their comrades.

'I fear for old Dunt, though,' said Glenroe, as they discussed how they should proceed.

'Why?' asked Thomas.

'He is losing his sight or his senses or something.'

'What do you mean?'

'That maidservant.'

'The woman attendant on Lady Hildred?'

'Yes, her. Dunt waxed long and lyrical over her beauty after she'd been in the house yesterday morning with the old lady. Said she was just the woman to set him on the right path. He raved of her looks – eyes like almonds, skin as rich and pure as cream – all the usual nonsense.'

Thomas considered. 'She has a fine enough figure.'

Glenroe scowled. 'What? You too?'

'Well, I saw little of her at the Bouchoute House and even less this morning, such pandemonium were we all in.

Her hood billowed out a time or two, and I saw nothing to disconcert me, for all that I looked.'

'Well I did,' said Glenroe, 'and "skin as pure as cream" is about the last way I would choose to describe her face. She has a scar, as livid as a burn, from above her right eye, across her nose, to below her left ear, and another that must have split her lip. It is as if someone had once taken a belt to her with the end of removing her face.'

Thomas stared at him. 'Glenroe – your fall, the bump on your head . . .'

Glenroe was exasperated. 'I'm telling you, man. I saw it not twenty minutes since, as clear as I'm seeing you. That girl's face is ruined.'

Thomas tried to make sense of what Glenroe was saying. 'There was only one maid with Lady Hildred, was there not?'

'Of course,' said Glenroe, 'and it was that one. I saw her with my own eyes get out of the carriage at Damme after her mistress was carried out, and not another soul left inside.'

Thomas spoke slowly. 'Glenroe, I saw her only briefly, and hardly bothered to look, but the woman I saw follow Hildred Beaumont into that carriage at the Engels Klooster in Bruges this morning had no scar across her face, and the carriage they got into had not another soul in it.'

Back in Damme, in a shuttered room in De Grote Sterre, while a physician and a surgeon tried and failed to save the life of Hildred Beaumont, Ruth Jones put a finger to her own scarred lips as if exhorting herself to secrecy. It was a blessed thing, the secrecy of women. From Sister Janet in the Engels Klooster who had first given her sanctuary, to Madame Hélène in the House of Lamentations who had ordered that any man coming within the walls of the brothel, as her brother's murderer had done only last night, and asking for Ruth Jones should be told that no such person had ever been there. And now, the last act of a dying English noblewoman was to keep Ruth's secret. Ruth had woken in the early hours of this morning a scullery maid in a brothel. Yesterday's dawn had shown her the body of her brother, hauled from the canal to lie on the quayside just a few feet from her window, and now, with the blessed dusk of today still many hours off, she was maidservant to a woman who would soon be dead. But it would be all right. She was out of Bruges, and she was safe.

SEVEN

Sanctuaries

Seeker felt the women's eyes on him as he reached up to fix the shutter back in its place. The light did the older of the two no favours, but the shutters couldn't be fixed properly when they were closed. The house itself was not made for brightness, but for darkness, where the glow of candles might rest for a moment on a length of silk, a velvet cushion, a heavy drape, and then move on, leaving hints of shadows and secret places. What must have looked luxurious, enticing by night, looked shabby and worn, dusty past its time by day. They called it a clean house, the House of Lamentations. As soon as a girl showed any sign of the pox she was out – cast off to try her luck in Amsterdam or Rotterdam or one of those other places where foreigners and sailors, too drunk to look properly or to care, might pay them.

He'd spotted the shutter weeks ago, old and green, the paint flaking, and so swollen with damp it didn't close properly. He made it his business to note such things, as he went around Bruges. The habit served him well. If there was a house of particular interest, a house that he might want in to, to take a closer look at, he could present himself, the jobbing carpenter, offering to fix something he had noticed needed fixing. It didn't matter that what he'd noticed was on the outside – they'd always have other things, behind their otherwise closed doors, that needed fixing too. And so it was with the House of Lamentations.

He'd avoided entering this place until now. Like so many places in Bruges this last year and several before it, the brothel was a hive of exiled Royalists, some of whom had cause to remember having crossed paths before with Damian Seeker. Instead, he'd made acquaintance of the servants of such places – they could always be met with somewhere in the town's marketplaces, taverns or churches. Each parish within the ramparts and the ring of canals was its own community, with its secrets and hatreds and certainty of its right to know each other's business. It rarely took as long as a morning or afternoon to find someone who knew what Seeker needed to know. Taverns were the best for garrulous servants, the marketplace for observing clandestine encounters masquerading as something else, the church to watch without being noticed, and to observe others try to do the same.

But now the death of Bartlett Jones demanded more of Seeker. The fact of the young man's body, pulled from the canal beneath the Augustinians' Bridge, a few yards from the House of Lamentations, would force him through doors he would otherwise never have crossed. Perhaps if

Seeker had not discovered that Sister Janet had sent a note to someone within the walls of that house scarcely an hour after Bartlett had presented himself at the Engels Klooster, he would have let it and its inhabitants be. But Sister Janet had sent such a note, and Seeker knew of it, so now he must find out who that note had been intended for, and what that person had to do with the death of the angry young Englishman whose trust he had been unable to gain.

Had this been London, he would have been told to leave it alone, but here in Bruges, there was no Thurloe to tell him the drowning of naive young men in foreign towns was no concern of the state's. Here, there was no Andrew Marvell to send to places that he himself couldn't go, to listen to things that people might not say in front of him. There was no Lawrence Ingolby, even, to send on the murkier business, to the darker edges, where Seeker's authority wouldn't allow him to go. Seeker didn't need to be in the same room as them to know what they would all have said — they would have told him to leave Bartlett Jones on the quayside in Bruges and forget about him. So here he was now, in a private parlour of the House of Lamentations, overlooking the Spaanse Loskaai and the Augustinians' Bridge, fixing a faulty shutter.

'Bit of trouble out there yesterday morning,' he observed, as he carefully planed the edge of the shutter.

'You mean the foreigner washed up on the quay? That had nothing to do with us,' said the older woman, who seemed to have the running of the place. 'We sleep late in the House of Lamentations. The excitement was over and the body gone before we were awake.'

'Ah, so not one of yours, then.'

'One of ours?' The woman arched her eyebrows at the affront. She had forgotten to remove a black, heart-shaped spot from above her lip from the night before. Her pink fur-trimmed velvet jacket hung open, revealing emerald silk stays. Her slippers were of emerald satin, and Seeker could see that she wore no stockings. She took no trouble to conceal her profession and had no shame in it either.

'Customers,' he said, still appearing to concentrate on the wood. He could, nevertheless, see the anxious look that crossed the younger woman's face.

'We do not have "customers", we have patrons. And no, I am assured by our laundry maid, who was the only one to witness that morning's business, that he was *not* one of our patrons. When you are finished here, there is some work to be attended to in the cellars. Beatte here will show you the way.'

And so, the desired effect achieved, Seeker was left alone with the young whore. And she was young. Too young to be in a place like this. Safer here than on the streets, though, or following some army or other.

'Your mistress there takes a pride in this place,' he began, casually.

The girl nodded. 'Madame Hélène answers to no one.'

'Especially not a foreign carpenter who doesn't mind his place, eh?'

'She answers to no one,' the girl repeated. 'Carpenter or King.'

'Even the Scottish King?' That was what they'd taken to calling him, since the Scots had crowned young Charles Stuart seven years ago at Scone, after the English had dealt with his father at the edge of an executioner's axe. Young Charles had soon learned the Presbyterian price of his crown and hadn't much liked it. Happier in exile, probably.

The girl said nothing.

'One of his courtiers, was he?'

'Who?' asked Beatte.

'The drowned fellow,' said Seeker, nodding out towards the quay on which Bartlett's drowned corpse had been laid the previous morning.

The girl frowned and shook her head. 'Not him. He was just . . .' She stopped. She'd already said too much.

'What?' pressed Seeker.

The girl shrugged, her face hardening a little with the lie she was preparing. 'Nobody. Some poor fellow who ended up in the canal. As Madame Hélène said, he was no patron of ours. If you're finished there, we should go down to the cellars. Madame Hélène doesn't like tradesmen hanging about in the house.'

As they crossed the black and white tiled entrance hall, hung on all sides with looking glasses framed in gilt, Seeker glanced upwards, past brass and crystal chandeliers to where a winding staircase gave access to the upper floors of this former convent – panelled walls and doors hiding private parlours and bedchambers where half the secrets of the city were laid bare. A fug of stale perfume, sweat and tobacco smoke that had not quite cleared from the night before mingled with the smell of baking bread rising from the kitchens. Housemaids with buckets, scrubbing brushes and mops, or bundles of linen, scurried about, never lifting their heads to look at him. The presence of a man was not quite the novelty in the House of Lamentations that it was in the Engels Klooster.

'Down here,' said Beatte, opening a door in the far corner of the hallway. Behind it was a stairway leading down to the kitchens, and then the cellar.

The kitchens, like the hallway and stairs above, were a hive of domestic industry – fish being gutted, poultry plucked, and an abundance of fruit and vegetables that would have astonished an English housewife being prepared for the coming evening. Seeker stood aside to let pass a boy carrying an enormous cheese.

'Not down here, but in the cellar, some of the shelving down there is decayed,' Beatte said, as she carefully picked her way down a darker, narrower set of stairs, holding high her lamp. 'Rotted with the damp.'

It was colder down in the cellar, a long dark place whose wooden ceiling and cross beams gave off the damp smell of an old church. It had the echo of a church too, though overlaid by sounds from the kitchens above. Seeker wondered aloud at the depth into the ground of this cellar.

Beatte shivered. 'We're beneath the level of the canal now.'

He nodded towards the row upon row of barrels of different sizes that stretched down the room. 'You'll not go thirsty here.'

'Canary wine, sweet Madeira, olive oil from Andalucia, the finest Rioja. It's not all bad, having the Spaniards for our master.'

'You're Flemish then?'

The girl nodded. 'We had a farm near Ghent. One spring the Schelde flooded and we lost everything. I was sent to the city for work, but my mistress thought the master took too great an interest in me, so I ended up here.'

'I'm sorry.'

'Don't be,' she said. 'I prefer it here. Madame Hélène protects us. Everyone knows what the men are here for – there is no pretence. It's more honest.'

'Aye,' conceded Seeker. What was the good in telling her she should deserve better – she would never get it. 'I suppose it is. So are all the girls Flemish then?'

Beatte shook her head. 'Some French, Dutch, Spanish.'

'But no English?' he asked, examining the joist on a shelf supporting barrels of olive oil.

An unmistakable look of fear crossed Beatte's eyes. 'No. No English girls here. No.' She wiped imaginary dust from her hands on her apron. 'Anyhow, Madame Hélène will be wanting me. All the shelving here needs to be looked at.'

Seeker straightened up, folding his measuring rule. 'And in there?' he said, indicating a door set into the wall at the other end of the cellar, near to the bottom of the stairs.

'There?' She glanced quickly across. 'A cupboard. That's all. It doesn't need looking at. Only this shelving. Please do not be long.'

As she left, Seeker saw her look over, just once, to an oddly stacked collection of barrels, just beneath a small window set high up in the outer wall, before reminding him once more not to be long.

Seeker quickly took the measurements of the shelving to be repaired, then went over to the barrels. As he drew nearer, it was evident to him that they weren't actually set against the wall, but about two feet out from it. Behind was a straw pallet, a pile of abandoned blankets, a stove with dead ashes and the remains of a meal. Seeker tasted a small piece of a hunk of bread left on the round wooden platter. It had started to harden, but wasn't stale. It couldn't have been left there more than a few hours ago. The ale left in a beaker beside it was unclouded by dust, and free of floating insects. A small barrel had been set beneath the window. Seeker moved it aside and hauled himself up by the window bars to edge open the shutters. As he expected, he was looking out upon the Augustinians' Bridge and the Spaanse Loskaai on which the previous morning he had seen Bartlett Jones's body laid out.

Jumping down, he went quickly over to the door of what Beatte had claimed was a cupboard. It was locked. In England, he would simply have kicked it in, or had his men batter it down, but now he lived the life of an agent, not a handler or army officer. Now he had to work clandestinely, cover his own tracks. At his tool belt, never having drawn remark, was a set of keys, designed before he'd left London by a blacksmith out past Limehouse. Seeker had yet to come across the lock to which one or other of these keys didn't hold the solution. He set to work at the lock with them and it was only a moment before the door was open.

Seeker bent down to pick up the lamp Beatte had left with him and held it up to reveal what was beyond the door. At first, what he saw didn't make sense to him. It certainly wasn't a cupboard. Instead, it was a structure of curved stone walls, as if he was stepping beneath an endless arch. He was in a vault, whose far end he could not see. He held out the lamp with one hand and reached the other into the darkness beyond to test the depth. Nothing. He took a step, and then another and then another, trying again each time, lifting the lamp each time. Nothing. There was no back wall, this was no cupboard, room or recess – he was in a tunnel. He reached out his arms and soon touched walls on either side. It was not quite as broad as the span of his arms. He summoned in his mind an image of the house, the street outside, the bridge, tried to position himself and where he was now in all of that and realised this tunnel could only be in one location – underneath the canal.

He was but a few feet in when he heard the sound of the handle at the top of the cellar stairs turn. He was back out of the tunnel and relocking the door within moments. By the time the hem of Beatte's skirts appeared at the turning in the steps, he himself was at the bottom of them.

'Finished?' she asked, as he pulled close the buckle on his carpenter's bag.

'Finished.' He told her his price, and she said she'd inform her mistress and let him know whether he was to have the work.

'If your mistress has any doubts, tell her to ask Sister Janet, she'll vouch for me, I'm sure.'

'At the Engels Klooster?'

'That's right,' he said. 'Sister Janet at the Engels Klooster.'

He didn't ask her, for he was certain she wouldn't tell him, how it was that a fifteen-year-old Flemish brothel worker could know a seventy-year-old English nun who rarely ventured out of her convent. Instead, he told her where his workshop was to be found. Beatte opened the door of the House of Lamentations for him, and he stepped once again into the heat of the bright day.

It was only when she was locking the door behind him that Beatte realised, too late, that she probably shouldn't have let the English carpenter know she knew who Sister Janet was. Madame Hélène had warned them all that no word of the connection between the House of Lamentations and the Engels Klooster should ever escape their lips. Any who transgressed would merit a visit from Father Felipe, and there were few things Beatte dreaded more than the sight of the Jesuit priest.

At the Engels Klooster, after the departure of Lady Hildred for Hoogstraten, life had returned to its peaceful pattern of performance of the daily offices, work, and quiet companionship. Nevertheless, Sister Janet had pleaded a surfeit of flatulence, blaming Sister Marjory's overuse of parsley in almost every dish presented to the sisters from the convent kitchens. Mother Superior had hastily granted her permission to observe the hours and to take her meals that day alone, in her cell. In the course of the day, as her community dutifully measured out their time from lauds to compline, Janet had gone over another day, in another place, over fifty years ago.

They had lived in the same household, Beaumont House, she and Hildred, learning the duties and expectations of an English lady of good family. At Oxford, Janet's brother had been the bosom companion of Guy Beaumont, younger son of the house. Janet's own mother being many years dead, it had swiftly been agreed that Janet should receive her education from Guy's mother. Hildred, a distant cousin to the family, had already been there. Guy loved nothing better than to hunt and then to dance and sing, and very soon, Janet had come to love nothing better than Guy. Every sight of him had delighted her heart. Guy's older brother, Edmund, was a fish of a distinctly different flavour, already in the service of Lord Cecil, and known to the King. Whilst Janet had been enchanted by Guy's gaiety, Hildred's only interest had been that as his older brother Edmund rose at court, she should rise with him.

And so it had gone until that day, that terrible day. Early in the morning, a rider had arrived, near dead, after riding for days on end from Janet's own home in Yorkshire. Her father had been taken, arrested, on the charge of harbouring in his household a Jesuit priest. Janet must lose no time in fleeing to Yarmouth, where a passage to the Netherlands awaited her. It came back to her now as if the years in between had never been. She remembered the fluster, Lady Beaumont's anxiety at the taint that might attach to her own house and distress for what might await the young woman she had grown so fond of. She remembered Guy's indignation at the idea she should be sent away at all, his determination that he would go with her as escort. She remembered his brother Edmund's absolute forbidding of such a move. And most of all, what she remembered was the look on Hildred's face as she, Janet, had left Beaumont House for the last time. The gardener had been her only escort, leading her on a ragged pony that no one would miss, with all the earthly goods that remained to her in a bundle at her side. The look on Hildred's face had been one of quiet triumph, and Janet had seen something of that same look on it just the other morning, when she had found Hildred lurking outside the room in which she had met with Father Felipe.

It must have been five or six years after her flight from England, but still a good while before the Engels Klooster had ever come into being, that another refugee of their faith, fleeing England for the sanctuary of the continent, had stopped for a night at her convent near Antwerp. It was then that Janet had heard the truth of it. It had been

Edmund Beaumont, Guy's brother, a guest oftentimes in her father's house, who had spied upon and betrayed her family to Robert Cecil; Edmund Beaumont who had consigned her father to a traitor's hideous death and her to this lonely exile, all for his own advancement. The worst of it then was that Janet had been unable to do anything with her new knowledge, aside from nurse her private anger and despair; Edmund Beaumont had died of a quatrain fever, not six months after his treachery had forced her flight from England. And on Edmund's death, Guy had become the Beaumont heir. Janet wished she could have been more surprised to learn that he had been married off to Hildred before the twelvemonth was out. 'You knew, didn't you, Hildred?' she said to herself, as she looked at the shadow of the crucifix spread across the bare white wall of her cell in Bruges over fifty years later. 'You knew what was going to happen to my father and to me. I could see it in your face the day I was sent away. You knew because Edmund had already told you, and you never said a word.'

EIGHT

News from Damme

In all of his researches into any Englishwoman who might have appeared of late in Bruges, the only name which Seeker had so far come upon was that of Lady Hildred Beaumont. He had sent word to Thurloe's agent at Hoogstraten that Lady Hildred was on her way there, under escort, and had also sent a message to Chief Secretary Thurloe in London, to inform him of her movements and intended destination. He had reported that although Lady Hildred had visited the Bouchoute House, there had been nothing to suggest that she had identified their double agent whilst there. Lady Hildred was gone from Bruges and his work in that respect was done, for now. He had included in his missive to Thurloe a request that he might return to England. Separately, he had told Lawrence Ingolby that he must communicate to Maria, in no uncertain terms, that under no circumstances was she to come to Bruges, but to wait, in London, for his return. For now, until he received Thurloe's response, he could concentrate on the matter of Bartlett Jones.

After going back and working at the carpenters' yard in Sint-Gillis, Seeker returned in the afternoon to the vicinity of the House of Lamentations and the Augustinians' Bridge. He had pondered Jones's most likely route from the quiet environs of the Engels Klooster, just within the outer canal and ramparts of Bruges, to the busy Spanish quay at the trading heart of the city. It offered as close to a straight line as was to be had here and would ask not much more than a quarter-hour's walk from a sturdy young man. But Bartlett Jones might have taken a hundred turns on such a journey, gone anywhere in the city, before finally finding himself out of turns and options, and thrown helpless into the canal, there to drown. What Seeker really needed to discover was where Bartlett Jones had gone and what he had done between the last time he'd seen him alive and yesterday morning, when he'd come upon him dead.

The English who came to Bruges tended to congregate, unless they were in the orbit of the King himself, around Seeker's own parish of Sint-Gillis or in Sint-Jakobs, to the north-west of the Markt. None of Seeker's enquiries there bore any fruit so he returned to the centre and worked his way along the quays and all the taverns, yards and workshops encompassed by the inner canals and bridges. Everywhere, it was the same story. No one had noticed an awkward young Englishman, looking for his sister. But then, at the bottom of the Spiegelrei, Seeker looked across to the opposite quay and saw that the drinkers outside the tavern there would have a clear view down the canal almost to the Carmersbrug, which Bartlett would most likely have crossed on his way back into town from the Engels Klooster. He went over and put his question.

'Sister! Hah,' scoffed an old soak, seated on a bench outside. 'Looking for a *woman*, more like.'

'You saw him?' asked Seeker.

'Aye. Trouble, he was. You could tell by his face.'

Another man laughed. 'Just because he wouldn't buy you a drink, Dirk.'

'No harm in being friendly, is there? Especially when you're a stranger new in town.'

The others grumbled their assent, and then a young apprentice from a nearby brewery spoke up. 'He had a name though, for the girl he was looking for. Something from the Bible – Rebecca? Rachel?'

'Ruth?' offered Seeker.

'That was it,' said the boy. 'Ruth.'

'Pah! You weren't even here,' said the soak.

'But I was, as they were leaving,' protested the apprentice.

'They?' said Seeker.

'The two Englishmen.'

'It's a lad on his own I'm looking for,' said Seeker, about to turn away.

'No, but there were two. There was the young one, looking for his sister, and the other who was taking him to her.'

Seeker now gave his full attention to the apprentice. 'Taking him where?'

The boy shrugged. 'I don't know. I couldn't understand what they were saying, but I heard the girl's name a few times. The older man had his arm around the young one's shoulder as they left. He was nodding, reassuring. I remember thinking it was good the young one had met someone who knew his sister, when they were so far from home. I wouldn't like to think of my sister in a town full of strangers, and none to help me find her.'

'*Your* sister? They'd throw her out of the whorehouse – she's as ugly as you!' called out another drunk. The boy went crimson with anger.

'Ignore him,' said Seeker. 'Tell me about this older man. Do you know where he was taking him?'

'The whorehouse,' insisted the second drunk, leaning across to get Seeker's attention. 'That's where he was taking him – where else? Probably robbed him when they got there.'

The old fellow seemed, momentarily, to have sobered up. Seeker knew the look in his eye – a drunk's moment of lucidity before the descent into incoherence. 'You saw them go there?'

The sage nodded. 'Headed that way. House of Lamentations.' Then he returned to his beer, the lucidity gone and the matter closed.

The apprentice boy was still on the verge of tears of rage, and Seeker steered him further away from the other drinkers. 'Tell me about the older of the two, the one who knew where the sister was. What did he look like?'

The boy wiped a sleeve across his nose and made an attempt to reclaim his dignity. 'I don't know. Like an English soldier, maybe.'

'An officer?'

The boy shrugged.

'How old? Old as me?'

The boy scrutinised him a moment, then shook his head. 'Younger. Shorter. Lighter hair. Longer too.'

'What kind of face?'

The boy shrugged. 'I didn't really see it. I hardly saw him, only when they were leaving.'

'Beard?'

The boy wrinkled his mouth as if in thought, but Seeker could see that he didn't truly remember. 'I think so.'

'All right. Have you seen him around before – with those who hung around the Scottish King, perhaps?'

The boy looked down at his apron then over at his older, drunken companions. At first he appeared bewildered at the question but then his face broke into an unexpected smile. 'What would I know of the Scottish King, or any other? Their doings are nothing to me, and mine none to them. Men are masters or they are servants, that's all I know. This man you're asking about, the older one, he's a master, and that's all I can tell you of him, and I'd warrant, should you find him and ask him, he could tell you nothing at all of me.'

Seeker gave the boy a coin and told him to keep an eye out for the Englishman, and to get word to him should he ever see him again. The boy nodded and, deciding against the ribaldry of the older men, left to go home. The other drinkers had nothing to add to what the boy had told him, but the parlourmaid remembered a little more. 'He wore a grey wool suit, good quality. Not fancy, but better condition than most of the Englishmen hereabout. Linen collar and cuffs. No lace, but clean.'

'Slashed sleeves?' he asked.

She thought for a moment. 'No.'

'Hat?'

She nodded. Black. A brown band. No feather.

Had she ever noticed him before?

No. Nor the young man looking for his sister either and she knew nothing of any Ruth Jones.

It was little enough to go on, but it was more than nothing. The description didn't sound much like any of the inhabitants of the Bouchoute House, but he would check that when he got a safe opportunity. Two of the courtiers from the Bouchoute House were absent today, on escort duty with Lady Hildred Beaumont. Ellis and Daunt had not gone with her to Damme. Seeker would have to be certain that they were all out of the house before he could search through their belongings for evidence of the good grey woollen suit. But there were dribs and drabs of other English officers still in the city too, and Seeker knew where they could generally be found: the Schuttersgilde Sint-Sebastiaan. The meeting place of the Archers' Guild, almost within the shadows of the ramparts, was within a longbow's shot of the Engels Klooster. It had been a much-favoured haunt of Charles Stuart. Seeker had often wished he could have climbed up the steps of its hexagonal tower, a needlepoint in the sky of the north of the city, from the windows of whose eight-sided turret the whole city and all the countryside around must be visible, but the officers of the Schuttersgilde guarded their privileges with pride and were in no hurry to open their doors to an English carpenter. He had, therefore, found it necessary to establish another means of getting information on the English patrons of the Schuttersgilde. So, now, instead of crossing over the canal into Sint-Anna, he went to his favourite hostelry in his own parish.

The small tavern by the Duinenbrug was full of craftsmen like himself – carpenters, masons, potters, plumbers. Their homes huddled happily in the quiet backstreets around Sint-Gilliskerk, back from the busy quays and the trading centre of the town. Seeker should have felt at home here. Thurloe himself had said it: 'Your old life, Seeker – what better cover could there be? You will slip into it like a favourite old coat.'

An old coat that had been made for someone else. His had never been the life of a town craftsman. His had been an itinerant life, working with the seasons across woodland and moor, doing jobs in manor houses and small villages that local craftsmen couldn't master. And when he had shed the coat of that old life, the new one offered him by England's brutal war with itself had made him someone else. Thundering across a battlefield in the midst of a cavalry charge, fighting hand to hand through dirt and mud, marching through the corridors of Whitehall, across Horse Guards, breaking down doors in the city to haul reprobates from their hiding place: Seeker had built such barriers around himself that almost none could touch him. For good or ill, that was who he had become. What use to say to John Thurloe, though, that he did not want that old coat that he had cast off so many years before? What choice had there been? None. But Lawrence Ingolby's news about Elias Ellingworth's plans to shift to Massachusetts and to take his sister with him meant that the time for throwing off that old coat Thurloe had thrust on his shoulders had almost come.

For now, he would play the role the tradesmen of Sint-Gillis had come to know him in. Amongst those whom he regularly encountered here were those engaged upon the work of the banqueting hall in the Schuttersgilde Sint-Sebastiaan. Charles Stuart was said to have promised money for it, but Seeker could not think that Charles Stuart had any money to give. The work went on, nonetheless, and the workmen were here tonight, shedding the cares of the working day before going home to their wives and families. They had begun a familiar round of song just before Seeker entered, and they carried on with it as he crossed the room to take up a stool at the far corner from them. This wasn't London, and John Carpenter was not Damian Seeker. As the first song came to an end and the next was taken up, an old fellow who generally listened more than he spoke left his group to seat himself on a bench a little along from Seeker. He took out a deck of cards.

'A hand of something, John Carpenter?' he asked.

'Lansquenet?' suggested Seeker.

They often played cards in here of an evening, John Carpenter and Berndt, and most nights their game of cards was simply a game of cards, but sometimes it was not. Seeker took the pack from Berndt and began to lay out the cards for Lansquenet, the old mercenaries' favourite. Berndt, appearing to pay close attention to his cards as they were turned, waited.

'The Schuttersgilde . . .' began Seeker.

'Yes,' murmured Berndt, laying his stake beside his first card.

'Anyone new there of late?'

Berndt frowned and shook his head. 'Not since before the Dunes.'

'You're sure? A few years younger than me, bit shorter, longer hair, maybe a beard. Dressed in a good grey wool suit?'

Berndt gave a good-natured laugh as Seeker's card was matched. 'They're all younger than you, John Carpenter, all got longer hair, all a bit smaller. Not many good grey wool suits, but you can give or take the beard.'

'*Any* grey woollen suits?'

Berndt thought a minute longer. 'No. Still hanging on to their fine silken rags and shreds of velvet, most of them, leastways when they're up at the Schuttersgilde.'

Seeker grunted his acknowledgement. Berndt knew nothing of anyone fitting the description of Bartlett Jones either. 'This young fella wasn't travelling with that old woman, was he?'

'What old woman?' said Seeker, pausing in his gathering up of the stake he had just won.

'The English one, that left the Engels Klooster today.'

'No,' said Seeker cautiously. He himself had watched from the deck of a barge only a few yards away as Hildred Beaumont's party with its escort had passed through the Speye Poort that morning. 'He wasn't of that party.'

'As well for him, then,' said Berndt, suddenly smiling and laying down a winning card.

'Why?'

'Because sometime this afternoon,' the old stonemason said, 'a good while after I'd had my dinner, two of your Englishmen came tearing along back the way they'd left by this morning. They almost fell from their horses such was their haste to dismount. One of them was wounded.'

'Who?' said Seeker.

'The one who is always drunk or fighting. Dark red hair.'

Glenroe, thought Seeker. It was hardly worth explaining to the Flemish stonemason that Glenroe was no more English than was the Infanta in the Escorial.

'And the other?'

'The one with the long fair hair, that arrived here with Prince Rupert last year.'

'Thomas Faithly,' said Seeker.

'Aye,' nodded Berndt. 'Him.'

'Not wounded?'

'Not that I could see,' said Berndt.

'Those were the two men that left Bruges this morning, escorting the old Englishwoman bound for Hoogstraten.'

Berndt took a draught of his ale and wiped his lips. 'I know. And she'll never see it.'

Seeker paused in the act of laying down the queen of spades. 'Why's that then?'

'Ambush, they said. Somewhere on the road before Damme. The red-headed one had his horse shot from under him and the old woman was killed.'

Seeker thought again about the party that had left Bruges by the Speye Poort. 'And the other one?'

'Who — Sir Thomas?'

'No,' said Seeker. 'The other woman — the maid.'

'Maid?' Berndt seemed not to have considered the question. 'No one said anything about her. The money's all right though, that this old woman was carrying to Hoogstraten. Redhead and the other one took it back from Damme, after they'd left the lady at the Grote Sterre. Everyone seemed more concerned about that than they were about the old woman. God rest her soul,' Berndt added, in pious afterthought.

Almost two hours later a heron, illuminated by the moonlight and reflected on the still surface of the Minnewater, dived suddenly into the lake to emerge a moment later with the fish it had been watching. 'Skilfully done,' murmured Seeker, who'd been watching from the shadow of a small boathouse. The surface was still again by the time the man he'd been waiting for at last appeared, emerging out of the darkness at the far side of the Wijngaardplein and coming towards him.

Seeker stepped out of the shadows. 'I've been waiting an hour,' he said.

The other man looked about him, as if checking he was not followed. 'What? You think it was easy to get out of the Bouchoute House tonight?'

'Why should tonight be different from any other?'

The man stared at him. 'You have surely heard what happened on the road to Damme today? Why else have you called me here?'

Seeker loomed a little closer to him. 'Oh, I've heard, all right, but not from you.'

A sudden look of fear crossed the man's face.

'I – I . . .'

'You what?'

'I was struggling to . . .' he paused, 'fully understand what had happened.'

'Oh? The way I heard it, there was an ambush, an old woman and a horse were shot, the culprit never went near the money but rode off and didn't get caught. Did I miss anything?'

'No . . . but . . . you must understand, Seeker, everyone is watching everyone else now. It is no easy matter to leave the Bouchoute House without some explanation. And to get out without one of the others in attendance is almost impossible.'

How was it that Thurloe had considered continuing to retain this man to be a worthwhile exercise?

'So they were after the old woman?'

The man held up his hands. 'I don't know.'

Seeker was coming close to losing his patience. 'Well, they never went after the money, did they? And they attacked the horse as a distraction, to buy them time. They hit Lady Hildred in a moving carriage from the other side of the canal because they meant to hit her.' Sometimes Seeker wondered how Charles Stuart's forces had managed to put up any kind of fight at all during the last wars. 'Were you behind it?'

'What? Me? Seeker, why would I—'

'Because I told you I'd had word there was a royalist spy, a woman, being sent to Bruges to find the source of the leak in intelligence from Charles's circle in the Bouchoute House – to find *you*, in other words – and Lady Hildred showed up in Bruges that very night. It wasn't long before she found her way to the Bouchoute House, and then this morning, she set out for Damme under the escort she'd got from there. Now she's dead. So I'll ask you again, and don't even consider wasting my time by lying to me: are you behind it? Did you hire someone to kill her?'

'No, Seeker, I did not! But if I did, what of it? If she was the spy, surely to kill her would have been to protect—'

'And if she wasn't?'

The man stopped. 'What?'

'If she wasn't the spy? You think Mr Thurloe would give you the authority to murder an old woman simply because you thought she *might* be a Royalist agent?'

The man sank down on a bench at the side of the boathouse. 'Might? Who else could it have been, Seeker?'

'You tell me.'

The man shook his head, his frustration scarcely kept in check. 'I don't *know*! All I know is that if it is found out that I have betrayed the King—'

'That you have informed on traitors to the Lord Protector,' corrected Seeker.

'Aye, that,' the man almost spat. 'When that is discovered, they will not wait for darkness or a lonely alley to slit my throat in. They will do it in broad daylight, before all who care to watch, in the Markt.'

'I think that would be the best you might hope for, should your services to Mr Thurloe become widely known. Given the justice meted out to those you have informed upon.'

'What?' The man looked at Seeker in disbelief. 'It was you who brought me to this, and yet you judge me?'

'You brought yourself to it, and I have no respect for any man who'd betray his friends to save his own skin. Or kill a woman on the off-chance that she was a spy.'

'I did not kill her. But if not her, who, Seeker? Where is this spy?'

'Where's the maid?'

'The maid?' The man screwed up his face. 'What's she got to do with it?'

'That remains to be seen. Now where is she?'

The man threw up his hands, dismissive. 'Damme. She stayed there to see to the old woman's comfort in her final hours, to see to the making decent of the body, and . . .'

Even by moonlight, Seeker could see horror dawn on the man's face. 'Oh, God.'

'Go on,' said Seeker, a very bad feeling beginning to take hold of him.

'The maid. I don't know how it can be, but . . .'

'What?'

'She wasn't the same one. Not the one that had come to the Bouchoute House with Lady Hildred or left the Engels Klooster with her this morning.' Seeker listened with a growing sense of certainty as Thurloe's double agent went on to explain about beautiful faces and harsh scars, about confusion at the site of the ambush, in the carriage itself, the tumble of skirts, the dishevelled clothing chest. About one maidservant leaving Bruges at the side of Lady Hildred Beaumont, and another arriving with her at Damme, solicitously bandaging her wounds and mopping her brow.

Seeker shook his head. 'I've come across a good few fools in my day, but I've never heard the like of this. Not ever.'

'I – I don't understand,' the man said helplessly.

'Then let me explain to you,' said Seeker. 'She's been under your very nose, this spy that's been sent to hunt you down. In the Engels Klooster, and the Bouchoute House, and in a carriage bound for Damme at the side of Lady Hildred Beaumont. She knows, from the ambush, that we're on to her, and she's given you the slip.'

'But . . . how? I don't understand. The maid?' He screwed up his eyes and held his head in his hands before looking up. 'But where is she now, Seeker?'

'That's just what I was wondering.'

Sister Janet turned over in her cot. Really, after so many years, surely she should be permitted a more comfortable bed? But tonight, her dreams had been sweet. When she had closed her eyes, the rhythm of the wheels of Hildred's carriage, carrying her far away, had played her to her slumbers. But now, a window shutter was rattling, and Janet had been certain the night was still as a millpond. She turned again and covered her head with her pillow – new-stuffed with goosedown, with which the flocks that lighted on the polder, thank God, kept them well-provided. And still the shutter rattled. God blast the thing! She would have to have John Carpenter see to it.

Pulling her shawl over her shoulders, she heaved herself up and swung her old feet to the floor. The flagstones grew colder every year, she would swear it. She stepped gingerly over to the window and undid the catch before reaching for that of the shutters. Just as she touched them, they rattled again, suddenly and with great force, nearly bringing her heart out of her mouth.

'In the name of God who's there?' she cried, finally forcing open the shutter, before jumping back with a start.

Before her, hair bedraggled and trailing canal weed, clothing muddied and soaked through and a desperate look in her eye, was the woman she had watched leave the Engels Klooster that very morning, seated in a carriage alongside Hildred Beaumont.

'You!' she exclaimed.

'Yes, Sister,' said Lady Anne Winter. 'Now would you be good enough to let me in?'

NINE

Mons Pietatis

Faithly, Ellis and Daunt had all been there at the appointed time. Only Glenroe was late.

'Damn his eyes, I have missed my dinner for this!'

'You'll get your dinner, Dunt. That belly of yours would keep you going a week.'

Edward Daunt muttered another oath and took himself off through an archway to the side on the pretext of inspecting the Flemish family portrait at the end of that corridor: a self-satisfied merchant two hundred years dead, and his emaciated wife, no doubt glad of the fact. Edward knew nothing of art, or much else, save how to sit a horse, how to run a man through with his sword, and how to do justice to a well-laden table. For these attributes, he had been called 'Dunt' since his schooldays. Edward knew there was affection in it for the most part, but still, he had given much, and lost much, in support of the King, and even a sturdy man of Kent tired, eventually, of being taken for everyone's fool.

Almost a quarter hour after the bells of the neighbouring Onze-Lieve-Vrouwekerk had stopped ringing, Evan Glenroe wandered into the pawnbroker's salesroom from the main courtyard of the Gruuthuse, bestowing his presence upon his fellow Cavaliers like a man without a care in the world. Daunt abandoned his pretended examination of the well-fed fifteenth-century burgher and strode back up the hall to where Faithly and Ellis had been examining a pair of spurs and a saddle for sale.

'Spanish leather,' Ellis was saying. 'That would sit on your horse like a glove.'

'A glove I could not afford for a horse I can barely feed,' said Faithly, turning away in disappointment from the tack stall. Even at the knock-down prices of this *mons pietatis*, this vast pawn emporium that was the former Palace of the Lords of Gruuthuse, once home to one of Bruges' richest merchant families, Sir Thomas knew his pockets would come up short.

'Ach, we should have stolen the old witch's money ourselves, Thomas,' said Evan Glenroe who had now come up beside them and was also admiring the Spanish leatherwork.

'Lady Hildred's money is intended for the King!' protested Daunt.

'Well, much good may it do him, when his best cavalrymen can hardly afford a decent saddle.'

'Keep your voices down,' pleaded Ellis. 'Would you have the whole town know our business?'

'The whole town knows it anyway,' said Glenroe. 'I heard of little else on my way down here from the Schuttersgilde.'

'And what are people saying?' asked Ellis, turning away

from the saddlery stall and walking towards a less exposed alcove in which old books had been stacked.

'What are they not saying?' asked Glenroe in response. 'The old woman was shot in error, and it was me the assassin was after . . .'

'The idea is not without merit . . .' observed Daunt, to a friendly dig in the ribs from Glenroe.

'Or, they were after Sir Thomas – an affair of the heart – or it was one of Cromwell's men, sneaked over to Bruges practically in her baggage and after her money, or, that Lady Hildred was a man in disguise and—'

'Enough,' said Faithly. 'Was there no information of use?'

Glenroe became serious. 'One thing.'

'Then tell us, for God's sake!' said Daunt, who was no admirer of the preamble.

'Not here,' said Faithly, looking around the hall which was filling up with bargain hunters. 'Come on.'

They were soon all seated in a pleasant alcove in the Gruuthuse garden overlooked by a fountain and a range of ancient mossy busts with none but the passing swans to overhear them.

'Well then,' said Ellis, looking around. 'We are alone.'

As Glenroe was gearing himself to speak, Daunt plucked at a cherry from an overhanging branch. 'I still fail to see why we could not have discussed this in our own lodging, without this fuss.'

Ellis gave an exasperated sigh. 'Because secrets have been spilling through the walls of the Bouchoute House . . .'

'Aye, weeks and months ago,' protested Daunt, 'when the King was still in residence in the town and plans for the Usurper's overthrow were still being made. But now His Majesty is elsewhere and we are somewhat out of strategy.'

'Well we'd better get a new one,' said Glenroe, 'because what I heard today was that our friends in England – those of the Great Trust who are still at liberty, that is – have sent over a woman to discover who the traitor to His Majesty is, that is passing on information to Thurloe. Now, it strikes me that that woman might well have been Lady Hildred.'

Daunt was perplexed. 'But why would they not have told us, or the lady herself done so?'

Ellis let out a heavy breath. 'Because they think it's one of us, Dunt.'

Daunt's hand went to the hilt of his sword. 'I'll slay the first man to say so!'

'Stop!' said Faithly. 'We cannot be at odds with ourselves, but we must accept that we will all fall under suspicion.'

Daunt grumbled but left his sword where it was.

'How are we to proceed, though?' asked Ellis.

'Well, there are three things,' said Sir Thomas. 'First: Lady Hildred – was she indeed in Bruges to discover the identity of the traitor? Second: who is that traitor? Third: did he or she kill the old woman?'

'That's two too many questions for Dunt there,' laughed Glenroe.

'Too many for me also,' said Ellis. 'But you say he or *she*, Faithly?'

'Think about it,' said Sir Thomas. 'The Bouchoute House is full of women, even now that the King has gone. Do you know one housemaid or scullery maid from another? Can you tell the bootboy from the stable lad, for that matter? And then there is the brothel – how many men have not lost their wits a while in the House of Lamentations? Who knows what has been said there that shouldn't have been. And then think, who *knew* the details of when Lady Hildred was to be on the road to Damme?'

It was Ellis who got to it first. 'The Engels Klooster. They knew of her plans up at the Engels Klooster.'

'What? One of the nuns?' said Daunt in disbelief.

'Or a stable lad or . . .'

'No, wait,' said Glenroe, leaning forward with the beginnings of a gleam in his eye. 'The very day her ladyship arrived and took up residence there, I met with a young fellow, said he was just over from England, and looking for his sister. Wanted to know the way to the Engels Klooster.'

'Did you show him?' asked Faithly.

'Aye, I did. And told him to watch out for that old tartar, Sister Janet, too.'

'I hope you also warned him against that Jesuit, the Spaniard, that's always gliding about the corridors up there too. Shifty-looking as a Seville cutpurse. Don't know why he can't stick to his own billet in the Sint-Walburgakerk.' Daunt shivered, but then his brow furrowed as a memory stirred itself. 'Yes, though, the young fellow. I remember. I met him on the way down from my afternoon's practice at the Schuttersgilde. Sister Janet had turned him away with a flea in his ear. Ruth something, his sister's name was.'

'I haven't heard of an English girl called Ruth at the Engels Klooster,' said Ellis.

'No, nor I,' said Daunt. 'But I'm certain there's one in the House of Lamentations. One of the kitchen maids. Can't say that I've ever seen her, but I've overheard Madame Hélène a time or two addressing a servant in English and calling her Ruth.'

'And did you tell him this?'

Daunt coloured and coughed. 'Well, no. I mean, I could hardly tell the fellow his sister was in a brothel now, could I? I merely gave him directions back into town and wished him well.'

'You didn't show him the way?' asked Ellis.

'No, I did not,' bridled Daunt. 'I had not had my dinner, and I can't be showing every waif and stray that lands from England the delights of Bruges.'

'Perhaps this Ruth is the woman who has been sent to find out the traitor in His Majesty's court,' said Thomas Faithly, 'and this "brother" no brother at all, but one of Cromwell's henchmen sent after her. She will be in need of our protection.'

Glenroe agreed. 'A nice little visit to the House of Lamentations tonight to make our enquiries should be just the thing, don't you think? And if we can discover from her who the traitor to our friends is . . . well, how much quicker our revenge than we could have hoped.'

'Perhaps so,' said Daunt, who was not quite as slow as they often decried him to be, 'but if the she-intelligencer is indeed this Ruth, why is it Lady Hildred who is dead?'

Seeker had watched Faithly, Ellis and Daunt go through the main gate into the courtyard of the Gruuthuse in the late afternoon and seen Glenroe follow them in a short while later. He'd waited a moment then crossed the street to go in after them, in time to see Glenroe disappear through the door of the *mons pietatis*. What they were up to in there, he didn't know, for they had little enough money to spend, even at those reduced prices. They might be equipping themselves for some new endeavour, or just simply idling away more of their pointless days. They should have been gone from Bruges by now, the whole lot of them, either to the forces gathering around the Duke of York at Nieuwpoort or somewhere deeper into the continent where they could forget their hopeless cause and be forgotten by it. It would be too risky to follow them into the narrow confines of the pawnbroker's hall, but the fact that they were all in there gave him an opportunity, however brief.

Seeker was soon letting himself in by the back gate to the yard of the Bouchoute House. The elderly cook, bent over her leeks in the kitchen garden, made a great deal of her shock at seeing him standing there all of a sudden.

'John Carpenter! You English will finish me off, always creeping about!'

'Not before you've got that lot in the stockpot, I hope,' he said.

'Well, there'll be none of it for you.'

'Still got a houseful then?'

'Down to the last four, and them nearly down to their last penny. We thought we might have a bit of luck when a rich Englishwoman turned up at the door a few days ago, but she took herself off to the Engels Klooster instead.'

'An old woman, was it?'

'Older than me, and on the move with all her worldly goods, they say. England must be a terrible place under this Cromwell, that so many of you leave it.'

Seeker let that pass. 'I was hoping she might have been younger – with all respect to yourself,' he added hastily.

She straightened up as far as she could and fixed him with a look of interest. 'You looking for a wife then, John Carpenter? My Minne's last husband has been dead near a year, and she's as good a breeder as you'll get this side of the Maas.'

Seeker laughed. 'I've seen your Minne, and her brood. They'd be too much for an old bachelor like me. No, it was the sister of a friend I was wondering about.'

'Pah, man like you doesn't have friends. You'd better come in and tell me what you're really wanting. And you can sort out my kitchen steps while you're at it.'

Seeker followed her up the path and into the huge kitchen of the Bouchoute House. Despite the heat of the day, steam was rising to the high ceiling from a fish kettle over the fire, and the smell of loaves fresh taken from the oven filled the air. Game hung from a pulley suspended from the rafters and a scullery maid was busied in sorting through a mound of soft fruits. A lazy cat observed Seeker warily from the corner of the hearth. Seeker gave it a wide berth – it was his considered view that most cats were, inherently, royalist.

The cook watched Seeker with amusement. 'Man your size, scared of cats?'

'Wary,' he said, giving the beast a last, distrustful glance. He looked over to where a set of steps was propped against a bare portion of wall. 'These them?' he asked.

The cook nodded. 'Either they're squint, or I am.'

Seeker suppressed a grin as the scullery maid, cheeks bursting with mirth, let out a snort.

As Seeker examined the steps and got out his plane, the older woman set a bunch of leeks in front of the girl and herself settled to plucking a duck that was lying on the table. 'So,' she said, 'you're looking for a young woman.'

Now the scullery maid's eyes widened and she bent lower over her berries.

'Just wondering,' said Seeker. 'A young fellow I met the other day, not long arrived in town. Looking for his sister – young woman by the name of Ruth Jones. More like to be a servant than a lady though. She hasn't been here at all, I suppose?'

The cook considered. 'No young Englishwoman in this house since before the Dunes. And the ones that were here before – well, they called themselves ladies . . .'

Seeker knew enough of the nature of Charles Stuart's pastimes in Bruges not to need further details. 'But the old woman – Lady Hildred. She didn't have a maidservant with her at all?'

The cook nodded. 'Oh, she had a maidservant all right. Not Ruth though – what was her name now?'

'Nan,' offered the girl.

'That's right, Nan. But she wasn't that young – thirty at least. Older than my Minne,' and here a meaningful lean in towards Seeker, 'and a good deal skinnier. Not much of a breeder I'd say.'

'Not much of a servant, either,' mumbled the girl.

Seeker turned his attention towards her. 'Why do you say that?'

'Well, I was supposed to be telling her which were the best markets to buy at, what prices were fair and who would cheat her mistress, but she had no interest in that sort of thing. Wanted to know about nothing but the gentlemen that were here with the King, what hours they kept, what their pastimes were, where they went, who they saw. And her hands – not used to hard work and skin as white as my cap, hardly done a day's work in her life, I should say, and not much intention to. All shiny hair and dark eyes and asking about the bedchambers! After a fine husband if you ask me. The old lady would have lived to regret taking that one over from England as her lady's maid.' She lowered her voice and started with some vigour on one of the leeks. 'If she hadn't been dead, that is.'

'Mmm,' said Seeker. 'She'd have been nosing about the house too, I'll bet.'

The girl nodded. 'I caught her looking up the back stairs – told her she'd no good reason to be up there. Then off out the back she went, wandering around the garden, poking about here and there, looking up at the bedroom windows. When I asked what she was up to, she said she was admiring the shutters!'

'You're right then, Dora,' said the cook, 'for I never heard of a servant yet that had time for wandering about and admiring shutters.' She turned to Seeker. 'We had enough of that sort of thing when the King and all his court were still in Bruges – these pretty women with their white skin and their dark eyes are nothing but trouble.'

Seeker couldn't help but smile. 'Oh, I know that well enough. But it doesn't sound like this one was my friend's sister. I don't suppose they called here, my friend and his companion?' He gave the cook and the scullery maid a description of Bartlett Jones, and what he'd been told of the Englishman in the grey woollen suit who'd been seen leading Bartlett off in the direction of the House of Lamentations, but neither meant anything to the women.

As Seeker was finishing off aligning the wooden shafts of the steps, the scullery maid suddenly said, 'The library.'

'What?' said the cook.

'They've broken the catch on one of the cabinets for housing the books. Not that they said anything about it, but it swings open now when there's a breeze, and bangs, and Femke is sure the glass will shatter if the catch is not fixed.'

A few minutes later, Seeker found himself on the second floor of the Bouchoute House, in the library. No one but the servants being in the house, the scullery maid had taken him up by the main stairway. The panelled walls showed light patches where paintings had been taken down to be shifted to some new home or to be sold. A huge, moth-eaten tapestry depicting a hunt in the age of Charles the Bold dominated the landing. Seeker stopped in front of it and thought of being out of the town, on horseback, a hound at his heels. The scullery maid gave an impatient cough and he continued after her, into the library.

The place had a musty, unused air, as if it had hardly been entered since Charles Stuart had last left it. The chair by the empty fireplace might still have borne his imprint, the volume left on the table might have lain there, untouched, since set down weeks ago by the pretended King. The room was lined with glass-fronted cabinets, most of them empty, but some showing the spines of ancient, dusty books. The cabinet with the broken catch was different, not only in that its door did, indeed, swing open, but that the books were not ancient, calf-bound tomes inlaid with gilt, the half of them in Latin and beloved only of gentlemen and scholars, but modern works, known as well to the common man as to his masters, and they were in English. Seeker cast his eye along the shelf. Nothing in it surprised him – not even to see dog-eared copies of *Mercurius Fumigosus* with its foul and lascivious lampoons of honest working women next to the *Book of Common Prayer* that had started the revolution in Scotland over twenty years ago. There too was Edwards' *Gangraena* with its attacks on the sectaries who gave Cromwell as much trouble as they gave the Stuarts, alongside Culpeper's *English Physitian*, which Seeker had seen even his old friend Samuel Kent pore over more than once. Seeker picked it up and leafed through its pages, for old times' sake. His eye was caught by a favourite passage of Samuel's where Culpeper claimed papists had bad breath from 'maintaining so many Bawdy Houses by authority of His Holiness'. His mind went to the House of Lamentations, the brothel that had once been a nunnery, and the notes sent there by Sister Janet. The scullery maid, who'd been moving around the room plumping cushions and exclaiming on the dust, caught sight of him. 'Please will you put that book back exactly where you got it? There's been a to-do already, with one of the books gone missing. One of the gentlemen's been hunting high and low, and even been down to the kitchens to ask if one of us has taken it. As if I could even read Flemish, never mind English.'

'Oh, English book, was it?'

'So he says. About fishing, or some such thing.'

'Fishing? Would it be *The Compleat Angler* maybe?'

The girl frowned. 'Say it again.'

He did, repeating the English words slowly, watching her concentrate.

She nodded. 'That sounds about right. Hmph. As if any

of us below stairs have time to go fishing! At any rate, that's the cabinet with the broken catch. I'll leave you to it. You can find your own way down, but mind you put back that book.'

Seeker returned *The English Physitian* to its place and looked more closely at the shelf. There was a gap between the last book on the row – an older book, *Urania*, that Seeker had seen elsewhere and knew to be filled with the kind of rubbish Andrew Marvell would write, and the end of the shelf. A channel through the dust where a book had been pulled out was clearly marked. It was just the right size of gap for the particular edition of Izaak Walton's *Compleat Angler* that had been provided to Thurloe's double agent in the Bouchoute House from which to take the coded words for his encrypted messages. The fuss made in the house about the disappearance of the book suggested it had either been lost, or stolen. The fact that the catch to the cabinet from which it had gone missing had clearly been forced suggested it was the latter. Someone knew what Thurloe's code book in Bruges was, and it appeared that that someone had already found their way into the Bouchoute House. The question was, whether they'd been there all along, or whether the theft was the work of the she-intelligencer he'd been warned of. Checking that the scullery maid had indeed disappeared back downstairs, Seeker went out into the hall. Several doors gave off the central corridor around the stairhead. He tried the two closest to him – bedchambers, although one was devoid of any bed and filled instead with the discarded belongings of those Seeker suspected had left the Bouchoute House some time ago, expecting to come back and never had done. Each door he opened revealed a bedchamber or a linen press until he reached the door set at the far corner of the landing. It was smaller than the others, and its trimmings plain. It was the servants' stairway. He slipped through the door and carried on up to the next floor, where he found the two bedchambers that must have been occupied by the house's four remaining Cavaliers. In each, he searched without success for the missing book. Mindful of the tale of the Englishman in the grey woollen suit who'd been seen leading Bartlett Jones towards the House of Lamentations, Seeker also checked what clothing he came across. What he found amongst the chests and draped over chairs or hanging from hooks was a motley selection of shabby items that had been meant for and seen better days. Nowhere, though, was there any sign of a good grey woollen suit. Neither was there such a thing in evidence in any of the other rooms he'd searched.

Seeker was leaving what appeared to be the chamber occupied by Ellis and Daunt when he heard the sound of the main door on the ground floor opening, and the voices of the four Cavaliers as they came in. He heard Glenroe lament the lack of a bootboy and declare that his feet would be the death of him if he did not get his boots pulled off this very minute. He heard Daunt calling down to the kitchens, asking about his dinner, and then he heard the voices of the other two, Marchmont Ellis and Thomas Faithly, talking in low tones as they came up the stairs. Whatever else was to be learned from the Bouchoute House would have to be learned another time. He reached the small door to the servant's stairway just as Ellis and Faithly reached the landing of the main stairs below. The doorknob turned, then stuck. Seeker cursed under his breath and turned it again. This time he felt the click of the mechanism and the door opened at last in front of him. He cast one last glance backwards just as the top of Ellis's hat emerged beneath the banister, then slipped quickly through the door to the servant's stairway, closing it softly behind him.

'What was that?' he heard Ellis say.

'A servant, that's all,' said Faithly, and then Seeker was too far down towards the kitchens to hear anything more.

It was growing dark by the time he left by the back gate of the Bouchoute House, having promised to return later in the week with a new lock to fit to the book cabinet door. The heat of the day had been searing, and a late evening breeze had got up that would have been refreshing had it not been for the stench coming up from the canals. Usually, such things did not trouble him – all the years living in London had accustomed him to malodorous air, but tonight it was as if the breeze had got up expressly that the memory of Bartlett Jones's corpse lying on the Spaanse Loskaai would follow him everywhere he went.

But the tragedy of the previous morning and the odours of the stagnant water were not all that followed Seeker as he walked the streets from the Markt back to his stable loft in Sint-Gillis. It was not unusual for people to be out on a pleasant summer evening, crossing the squares, sitting at canal-side taverns, taking a turn out through the quiet back lanes leading towards the city ramparts or the Minnewater. Sounds of laughter and song from the taverns, of arguments between drunkards on the quays, of religious singing their devotions in the town's many churches or of lovers laughing as they scurried up lanes or whispered in courtyards accompanied him on his journey through the town. But there were other sounds too, and Seeker had first become aware of them as he'd turned down the Kortewinkel. The street curved down to meet the canal just by the House of Lamentations. To his right as he approached the Augustinians' Bridge, the high walls were punctuated by candle and lamplight glowing through the brothel's windows, but to his left was only a sharp drop and the inky waters of the canal itself. He could not have said whether he heard the noise or felt it: an echo of his own footsteps so light they might have been muffled, a sensation of a presence that was entirely focused on his own. He turned his head slightly, and a dark figure moved into the greater darkness of a coach house, just where the buildings between street and canal tapered to nothing. Seeker didn't alter his pace but continued over the bridge into the quieter backstreets of Sint-Gillis. The sensation of being followed down the narrow streets didn't leave him and neither did the soft echo to his own footsteps. He cut through the precincts of the church itself, the darkness deepening, and when he came out at the other end, in sight of his lodgings, he knew he was still being followed.

Once back in the stables, he spoke softly to the horses in their stalls as he did every night, but instead of continuing up the stepladder to his loft, he stepped behind the door, and waited. He didn't have to wait long. The footsteps coming through the yard were clearly audible now, and then Seeker could hear the man breathing. He felt the other's presence in the doorway little more than two feet away from him, and then a dark shape started to move past him. Seeker, who had unsheathed his dagger before crossing the Augustinians' Bridge, waited until the man had his foot on the second rung of the ladder then stepped quietly behind him and touched the point of his blade to the side of the man's neck. With the other hand, he removed the sword hanging at his mysterious visitor's left-hand side. 'Now, friend,' he said. 'If I were you, I'd turn around very, very slowly.'

Without attempting anything foolish, the man did as he was bid. Seeker couldn't make out much in the darkness – a tall, slim-built man of about thirty, short hair under a plain green hat, brown buff coat, dark doublet, hose and boots. 'Damian Seeker,' the man said. A statement, not a question.

Seeker advanced the tip of his knife a little closer to his visitor's neck. The signal was swiftly understood.

'My name is George Beaumont,' he said. 'I'm a soldier in the service of the Lord Protector. My mother was lately murdered on the road to Damme. I need your help.'

TEN

George Beaumont

Having directed Beaumont up to his stable loft, still at the point of his dagger, Seeker indicated a pile of sacking his visitor might sit himself down on whilst he himself lit a lamp. As the glow of light spread out across the loft, Seeker saw that the man claiming to be Hildred Beaumont's son was dust-covered and looked weary near to exhaustion. That he had a look of Lady Hildred was beyond question. Beneath the hat, which he had asked permission to remove, was pale red hair, close-cropped at the sides and with a stubborn wave at the front, recalling the traces of auburn that even in her last days could be discerned in his mother. His cheekbones, beneath the pale skin, were a softened version of hers, his eyes, when the light caught them, a paler green. Everything about him was like a diluted version of Hildred Beaumont. An observer who knew nothing of him might have said her arrogance had been replaced in him by diffidence, hesitance, but Seeker knew better: George Beaumont had a reputation as uncompromising as any soldier in Cromwell's army. The voice too, in the few words he had spoken, recalled the Beaumonts' native Leicestershire. Seeker was satisfied that this man was who he said he was, and that being so, he had taken a considerable risk in coming to Bruges.

Seeker sat down to begin removing his own boots. 'Well, Major Beaumont, you'd better start talking.'

It took the best part of an hour. George Beaumont had been part of the New Model Army's expeditionary force which had allied with the French against Spain and the Duke of York's Royalists at the Battle of the Dunes. One hundred Protectorate army losses to a thousand on the Spanish and Royalist side. Ten days later, Beaumont had been one of the first English officers to walk into Dunkirk following the town's surrender. It had been at Dunkirk, early yesterday, that news had reached him of the attack on his mother on the road to Damme, and of her subsequent death.

'How did you come to hear so quickly?' asked Seeker.

'The French had an agent embedded with the Spaniards at Damme. He had just been recalled and was in no hurry to stay amongst them. When he arrived at Dunkirk, he passed the information to the army council as something of note but, he imagined, little consequence. I had to hear him through twice before I understood that the woman he was talking about was my own mother.'

'You didn't know Lady Hildred had come to the Netherlands?'

Beaumont's mouth narrowed and he looked away. 'My

mother and I had been estranged a long time, Captain Seeker.'

'And you'd no one keeping an eye on your interests in England?'

Beaumont shrugged. 'I wasn't interested in the house or the running of the estate after my father's death – I was too taken up with the business of our great struggle to worry myself over one modest family estate. My mother might well have wished to disown me, but I had no desire to render her homeless. I drew what I needed from Beaumont Manor and trusted my father's factor to continue to manage it. Which I must say, he has done.'

'Up to the point when your mother sold everything that wasn't hammered down.'

Beaumont gave a humourless laugh. 'She sold a good deal that was as well, by all accounts.' He paused and ran a hand through his short hair. 'The establishment of our authority in Dunkirk and Mardyke has demanded my every waking hour. Information that should have reached me from England hadn't done. A letter from a well-affected neighbour, written over a month ago, had lain unopened amongst the posts.'

'Aye, that sounds like enough.' There was little there that Seeker couldn't have guessed. 'But what do you want with me?'

Beaumont straightened himself and all the diffidence was gone. 'You're Thurloe's best tracker-dog, or at least you were. I thought you were dead until a returning agent told me differently, yesterday.' Beaumont named the man – a protectorate agent in Bruges up until the previous year. A few weeks' acquaintance had persuaded Seeker that he was utterly useless as a source of intelligence, or for the planting of false information.

Beaumont made to reassure him. 'He only told me after I'd made it clear I was coming to Bruges regardless of the danger. He hardly needed to warn me what would happen if I was found out by the Royalists here, after what happened to our agents in Madrid and elsewhere.'

He didn't need to elaborate. There were men in the Protector's service whose blood had long dried across the cobbles of Europe.

Beaumont continued. '"Filleted in the street", I think was his best prediction about what would happen to me should I be discovered. When he saw I wasn't to be dissuaded, he told me to ask for the English carpenter and find my way to you.'

Seeker cursed. The agent would have to be shut up or half of Flanders would know who he was, and where. 'Well,' he said, 'so much for how you come to be here. What about *why*?'

'There's no great mystery to it, Captain: I need to find out who killed her. For all that we were estranged, she was my mother. And even were I a man devoid of all feeling, which I am not, no man could let such a thing pass. I intend to make him pay, whoever he is.'

Seeker could tell there was something else. He waited, and Beaumont continued.

'And once I've done that, I intend to get my money back. Letting my mother live off it for her last few years was one thing but handing it all over to Charles Stuart to use as he pleases is another thing entirely.'

This sat better with the man across from Seeker than the idea that he had breached Royalist lines in order to avenge his estranged mother. 'Fair enough, but you should know that whoever killed your mother made no attempt to get at the money during the ambush of her escort.'

Beaumont got the point. 'You mean it was her rather than her money they were after?'

'Probably.'

'Probably?'

Seeker unfurled his bedroll on the straw and sat down on it. 'I'll help you, Major Beaumont, but with due respect to your rank, there are aspects of my business – Mr Thurloe's business – that you've no call to know. You'll be told what you need to be told, and nothing else.'

Beaumont nodded slowly. 'All right.'

'Good. Well, the first thing I would do is take a good look at the escort charged with getting her to Damme.' He told George Beaumont about his mother's visit to the Bouchoute House and the men resident there. Seeker ran through the names. Beaumont knew something of Faithly and Glenroe, but had never met either of them, and the names of Ellis and Daunt were entirely new to him. 'They're a mismatched crew, thrown together by their own ill fortune and no idea what to do next. You'll need an alias if you're going to infiltrate them. You might not have heard of them, but you can be all but certain they'll have heard of you.' It didn't take long to flesh out a background for Beaumont as a cavalryman in the Royalist armies, serving in different parts of the country, under different commanders to the men of the Bouchoute House.

'And then?' asked Beaumont.

Seeker considered. 'You came to the continent. Followed Montrose.'

'Well, that's true enough,' said Beaumont, his face grim. 'I followed Montrose all the way to the scaffold in Edinburgh. Seven years up there under Monck I had, with the wind nearly chilling the flesh from my bones, before I went south to join the expedition that brought me here.'

Beaumont's tale was likely enough. His name, moreover, wasn't one that had ever come to Seeker's attention as one of suspect loyalty to the Protector. Nevertheless, Seeker wasn't ready to trust him with everything he knew of the inhabitants of the Bouchoute House. There were things, though, that Beaumont would need to be clear on. What Seeker had heard of George Beaumont, aside from that he was remorseless in battle, was that he was a firm and uncompromising Puritan. 'You should know, Major, that their moral code is not as yours or even mine. They breathe in the Papist incense here like it's fresh air, and don't think twice about bending the knee before their altars. When Charles Stuart was here he worshipped at the English convent, Engels Klooster. There's a Jesuit priest always slithering around up there that I wouldn't trust as far as I could throw him. The Cavaliers left in the town haven't two pennies to rub together, but are seldom sober two nights in a row, and they wouldn't know an honest woman if they fell over one. The Bouchoute House is a cesspit, Major Beaumont. You'll have to mask your distaste when you fall in with them, or your cover'll be blown by dinnertime and you'll be dead by nightfall.'

George Beaumont's genuine disgust was written on his face. 'I daresay I can school myself to stomach it until I have found what I've come for.'

'See that you do nothing to give yourself away,' said Seeker. 'I've no desire to be the one explaining to Secretary Thurloe what your guts were doing smeared all over the streets of Bruges. And one more thing . . .'

'More than my guts smeared on the streets?' enquired Beaumont.

'You'll need a safe house. You'll need somewhere to bolt to, should things go wrong. And you can't come here again.'

Beaumont looked around Seeker's stable loft, not quite managing to mask a degree of dismissiveness as he did so. 'I've already taken lodgings in town – a one-room house in some backstreet, over by the Smedenpoort.'

'Good.'

Seeker stretched out his arms. He'd told George Beaumont as much about the Bouchoute House as he intended to. He didn't waste much time wondering whether to alert Thurloe's double agent in the house as to the identity of

George Beaumont, or George Barton, as he would present himself as, because he didn't fully trust their agent. And he wouldn't be telling George Beaumont about that source either, because he most certainly wasn't ready to trust George Beaumont yet. The only person who needed to know the truth about either of them was himself.

Beaumont had got up to leave and was standing by the hatch at the top of the stepladder when he turned back to Seeker. 'My mother wasn't in Bruges very long, I understand, before she left for Hoogstraten. I take it these men – Faithly, Daunt, Ellis and Glenroe – were the only people she knew in the city?'

Seeker shook his head. 'No, they weren't. She put up at the Engels Klooster while she was here. But you be very careful if you go anywhere near there. There's something going on in that convent – I don't know what yet – that may or may not have something to do with your mother. I'm certain there's an old English nun at the back of it, but she wasn't born yesterday, and I'd warrant she'd give you a tougher grilling than any of that lot in the Bouchoute House if you turned up there asking questions. You just concentrate on Faithly and Glenroe and their cronies, and I'll deal with the Engels Klooster and whatever's going on up there.'

Anne Winter examined her reflection in the dark glass of her cell window. She would have been interested to see in a looking glass, to know what picture she now presented to the world, but she had not been entirely surprised to find that such an item was not permitted to the sisters of the Engels Klooster. Sister Janet had tutted as she'd helped her fix on her wimple. 'One of those faces.'

'Which faces?' asked Anne, trying to hide her amusement at the other woman's irritation.

'*Noticeable*. The kind of face that ends up a chatelaine or a mother superior. Not the sort of face to blend in amongst thirty others. Sister Agnes, now. Exemplary face.'

'Sister Agnes, I don't think I . . .'

'No, and why would you? Here ten years before I could even remember her name. Face like a lump of fresh-kneaded dough. Exemplary.'

Sister Janet had taken some persuading, that night, when Anne Winter had staggered, exhausted and soaked through, to her window. It had been a gamble, but Lady Anne's choices had been limited, and none of them attractive.

She'd been certain, almost as soon as she'd registered the crack of the assassin's musket, that the shots from the wind-mill on the road to Damme had been intended not for Lady Hildred but for her. The terrible confusion when the older woman was hit had made Anne forget for a moment about the anonymous young woman secreted in the clothing chest at the back of their carriage. Her first concern had been to improvise bandages to staunch the old woman's bleeding, but even as she'd turned the key in the lock of the chest, air holes drilled discreetly into each side of the lid, the fact of the young woman being there had come back to her, and the plan had begun to form in her mind.

The girl had been terrified as she'd scrambled from the chest and Anne spoke quickly as she ransacked the linen for suitable dressings. 'Switch places with me.'

'But I—'

'Whoever you are, you clearly need to get away from Bruges, and I need to get back there.'

She'd then bent down to whisper in Lady Hildred's ear as she had applied a pad to try to staunch the blood. 'Lady Hildred, I am on His Majesty's secret business. Will you take this girl with you and pass her off to the people in Damme as me?' The old woman had nodded, a little spark in her eye, despite her weakness, to be at the heart of an intrigue.

Anne had turned back to the frightened stowaway. 'I don't know who you're fleeing from, but what better way to hide than to disappear altogether, to become someone else?'

The girl's decision had been made on the instant, and soon they were exchanging their outer clothing as quickly as it might be achieved, fingers fumbling and cloth tearing, as Lady Hildred rallied to field the intrusive enquiries for her welfare from Glenroe and the coachman.

'One more thing,' said Anne, as she hastily thrust her arms into the girl's worn green jacket before preparing to leave the carriage to disappear into the still, dark waters of the canal. 'Is Sister Janet to be trusted?'

The girl had nodded and spoken the only other words Anne would hear from her. 'More than anyone I know.'

And so, over a period of several hours, Anne had found

her way back to Bruges. She had remained in the dank canal waters, shielded from view by a small tethered boat, a hundred yards or so down from where the ambush had occurred, until Lady Hildred's party had set off again. Not trusting to the open road, she had followed the banks of the canal back towards the city, sheltering in thickets of wood or gardeners' huts whenever she felt the need, before finally accepting a lift from the kindly wife of a carter, whom by a mixture of Flemish and French, and a series of signs, she was able to make understand she did not wish to be seen entering the city. Only once they were safely through the Speye Poort had she emerged from the cover of blankets and pressed a few stuivers into the woman's hand, before disappearing into the quiet backstreets of Sint-Anna. Near a corner within sight of the Engels Klooster was a house fallen into disrepair that Anne had noticed two days previously. She had hidden herself in a derelict outbuilding of the abandoned property until well after nightfall and then, when she had been as sure as she could be that she would not be seen, she had made her way back into the grounds of the convent, and to Sister Janet's window.

There had been a moment, as they'd looked at each other, she and the old nun, through that opened window, when Lady Anne's entire scheme had hung in the balance. Sister Janet might have called out to the other sisters, to Mother Superior, or the stable hands or for the watch, but Sister Janet hadn't done.

The old woman had let her in, warmed water for her

to wash with and found her a change of clothing before setting some bread and cheese in front of her. Only once she had forced her to swallow down some vile decoction fetched from the convent's apothecary did she allow Anne to speak.

'Well,' she said, gathering up for laundry the faded green jacket and brown woollen dress that she had last seen that morning being worn by Ruth Jones, 'I daresay you've a story to tell me.'

So, over the course of the next hour, Anne had told her. She told her about the ambush, the injury to Lady Hildred, the swap with the stowaway Sister Janet had only that morning blackmailed her into taking out of Bruges, and her own escape and journey back to the city.

Janet had been delighted with Anne's quick thinking over the swap. 'Well done, well done! I would not have thought of that myself. And Ruth was unharmed?'

'Ruth? Yes . . . but the scars . . .'

Janet ran on though. 'And Glenroe, the Irishman? He is not badly injured?'

Anne had been somewhat surprised that Sister Janet enquired after the condition of Evan Glenroe before that of Hildred Beaumont and then she had understood, before Janet told her, that it meant news had already reached the convent that Hildred was dead. She had forced herself not to think of it, that she had left the old woman whose companion she had been on their long and perilous journey from England, to die attended only by strangers. It was as if her thoughts registered in her face, for Janet leaned close and made her look at her. 'Hildred knew the risks she was taking. It was her time. We will all have our time, one day. Today was hers and there was nothing you could do about it.'

To Anne's repeated enquiry as to the full identity of the young woman who had taken her place as Lady Hildred's maid, she was told to mind her own business. To her enquiry as to why the girl was running, Sister Janet had looked surprised. 'Why do you think? There's a man looking for her that she doesn't want to be found by. You did a good thing, in helping her get away.'

'Thank you,' said Anne.

Sister Janet's mouth pursed slightly – the giving of the compliment had clearly pained her. And then her eyes narrowed, as if she were preparing to thread a particularly awkward needle and Anne knew the questioning was about to turn upon herself.

She was right. 'But now for you,' said Sister Janet, 'I would be very interested to know what *you* are doing back here. And don't for the merest minute consider lying to me – a woman who turns up at a near-stranger's window in the middle of the night with canal weed in her hair and wearing someone else's clothes has already run out of options.'

'Where would you like me to begin?' asked Anne.

'Your real name,' said Sister Janet.

'I am Lady Anne Winter. My family held Baxton Hall near Oxford. My father and brother served the late King and died for it. For my own protection, I was married to an officer in Parliament's army who is over four years dead. Since his death, I have worked for the restoration of His Majesty to his father's throne, in whatever manner has been required of me.'

'And what is required of you now is that you be in Bruges?'

Anne nodded. 'Even here, in this convent, you must have heard of the atrocities meted out to those in England who have been working to remove the usurper Cromwell and bring back to England her rightful king.'

Sister Janet's response was delivered in a monotone that chilled Anne to her heart. 'Fifty years ago, my father was hanged from a gibbet, his body cut down before he was dead, his entrails drawn and his corpse quartered, all at the behest of Charles Stuart's grandfather. But do continue, Lady Anne.'

Anne looked over to the door. It was locked, and the key was on Janet's chain. The window had now also been locked.

Sister Janet smiled. 'Even wet and exhausted and no doubt brewing a fever, you could overwhelm a woman of near seventy if you wanted to. You are quite safe, Lady Anne, but it is very late, and I *was* asleep before your arrival. If you could get to the point of why I saw you climbing from a window at the back of the Bouchoute House in the early hours of yesterday morning, I would be most obliged. Oh, and I know about the cypher key, too. I took the trouble of copying it the other day, whilst you and Hildred were out and about in town. I imagine you thought it safer to leave it here than carry it about town on your person, but really, I would advise you to greater caution in future.'

Unthinkingly, Anne's hand went to the leather satchel she had kept close to her all day.

'Oh, yes, I put it back amongst your belongings, my dear. I may be incorrigibly curious, but I am not a thief.'

Now that she had a better idea of what she was dealing with, Anne felt less constrained by politeness. 'An old woman who listens at keyholes or inspects her neighbour's linen basket might be incorrigibly curious. A supposed nun who searches her guests' belongings and transcribes documents she finds amongst them is something else.'

'Oh? And what might that something else be?' asked the nun.

Lady Anne spoke very clearly. 'A spy.'

Sister Janet tilted her head. 'I'd be interested to know who you think I might be a spy for.'

Anne said nothing and the old nun continued. 'I do, however, like to know who *is* — a spy, that is — especially if she is sleeping under my roof pretending to be a lady's maid. I don't think I have met a she-intelligencer before, Lady Anne. How very interesting.'

Anne decided there was nothing to be gained by denying it.

'And would you care to tell me who it is that you are spying on?'

'I would,' said Anne, 'but I don't know yet.'

At Sister Janet's impatient sigh, she continued, 'The executions in London are the direct result of the betrayal to Cromwell's intelligence agents of the plans of the Sealed Knot and the Great Trust. That betrayal has its source here in Bruges, amongst the inhabitants of the Bouchoute House.'

'I see. And what did you find on your midnight expedition to that house?'

'Little of interest,' said Anne. She was not going to tell Sister Janet any more than she absolutely had to. But then the nun reminded her that it was she who held all the best cards.

'Other than the book, I suppose.'

'The b—'

'Izaak Walton, *The Compleat Angler*, I think, was it not? Of course, I'm not sure why you should have gone to the trouble of stealing it, when you already had a copy of your own amongst your belongings when you came to Bruges. And then to leave both here in Bruges when you left for Hoogstraten.'

In response to Anne's look of amazement, Janet flicked her hand. 'It was nothing. I had another look through the items you left here in storage. Imagine my surprise to find you now had two copies of the same book – one I assume to be the one you arrived here with, the other I expect is the book I saw you tuck away in your clothing after you climbed out of the Bouchoute House window the other night. Are you very keen on fishing?'

Anne remained silent.

'Or perhaps,' continued Sister Janet, 'you are less talented in the use of cyphers than those who sent you here hoped?'

Lady Anne could almost hear her own heart thumping in her breast as Sister Janet unlocked a small cabinet by her bed and produced the copy of the Izaak Walton book that she had indeed stolen, only two nights ago, from the library of the Bouchoute House, and with it a copy of the one she had arrived in Bruges with. From a small drawer in the same cabinet Sister Janet produced a sheet of paper almost completely filled with columns of paired symbols. Anne recognised it straight away as a copy of the cypher entrusted to her in London by her friend Elizabeth Carey whose husband, John Mordaunt, had so recently escaped the fate of the other conspirators of the Great Trust. Without the book, Anne would have no means of entrapping the traitor in the heart of the Bouchoute House, and no means of proving to the rest that she had done so. 'You must give that back to me, Sister Janet,' she said.

It was as if she hadn't spoken. 'It's an ideal text, of course, as the basis for secret communications. What better than something as innocuous as a book on fishing, which might be owned and enjoyed by anyone, be they ever so humble, so long as they be literate? What more suitable for the repetition of code words which might otherwise attract attention? Each person of significance given the name of a fish – though I do not entirely think the Halibut would be happy with her code name, do you?'

In spite of the uncertainty of her situation, Anne laughed. The exiled Queen Mother, Henrietta-Maria, would doubtless not have been flattered by the accolade.

'And as for His Majesty,' continued Sister Janet, affecting shock, 'to be designated the Sargus, or, now, how does Walton put it?' She made a show of leafing through until she found the correct page. 'Ah, here it is:

> "The adult'rous Sargus . . .
> As if the honey of sea-love delight,
> Could not suffice his ranging appetite,
> Goes courting she-goats on the grassy shore,
> Horning their husbands that had horns before."

'Dear me! Think if Sister Blanche or Sister Cecily had come across this book. There would have been mass swoonings in the refectory and hysteria before compline.' She was clearly enjoying herself as she returned the book to Anne. 'I really must counsel you to be more careful where you keep it in future.'

Anne nodded her mute thanks and slipped the book into her satchel.

'So,' the nun continued, 'I take it the volume you stole is what the spy on whose trail you have been set is using as the text for his communications?'

'So we believe,' conceded Anne.

'And the cypher?'

'A rare slip on the part of Thurloe's people. It was left

within sight of one of His Majesty's agents employed at Whitehall.'

'Thus enabling you to decipher any further communications you might be able to intercept from the same source.'

'Yes.'

'But why go to such lengths and take such risks as to steal the book? Given you already had your own copy. Surely you don't think the loss of the book will make the man you are looking for throw up his hands in despair and stop sending information to his Cromwellian masters? He will simply purchase another copy.'

At last Anne felt she was on surer ground. 'And that is precisely why I stole that one from the Bouchoute House.'

Sister Janet's face wrinkled. 'I don't understand.'

'It's simple. If his own copy has been stolen, he will have to get another one. The day after we arrived, I went around every bookseller in Bruges, asking them to let me know whether anyone came looking for that particular edition of Walton's book. I told them I would pay double the price of the book if they would only let me know who they had sold it to.'

'Indeed?'

Anne was pleased to see she had at last surprised the old nun.

'And how should they communicate this information to you?'

'I asked that they should send it to me here, addressed to Mlle Nanette, Maidservant to Lady Hildred Beaumont.

Lady Hildred's decision to go on to Hoogstraten was an unexpected inconvenience.'

'Which you are now rid of,' said Sister Janet with a shrewd look in her eye.

'I take no pleasure in how it came about.'

'No, but your activities may well have aroused suspicion about the true purpose of Hildred's trip. We shall have to think carefully about how you proceed from here.'

'We?' said Anne in some surprise.

'We,' said Sister Janet.

And so now, just a night after that bedraggled request for help from Sister Janet following her escape via the canal, Anne found herself attired as a nun of the Engels Klooster.

'Liberating, isn't it?' commented Sister Janet, observing Anne's smile as she looked down at her new incarnation.

'Yes,' she said, 'it is.'

Lady Anne had worn many disguises over the last year and a half. It had taken her some time, after the death of Damian Seeker, to realise that no one was watching her any more, and then she had redoubled her efforts in the Stuart cause. Disguised as a washerwoman, an elderly spinster, a seamstress and a preacher's wife, she had travelled between London and the coast, the coast and the north, the north and Wales, carrying information between those who actively sought the overthrow of Oliver Cromwell's government and the restoration of the King. She had learned every manner of folding a letter so that it might not be opened and resealed without that fact being evident; she had learned the use of dyes, so that a piece of paper might show nothing but a laundry list, until held against a light in a certain way or wetted with the proper solutions. She had learned codes, carried cypher keys, hidden symbols and notes about her person. She had flattered bores and flirted with drunks, played the damsel in distress and the woman without shame, all to entice information out of those who might otherwise have kept their lips sealed. Twice before, she had travelled to the continent. More than twice, she had come close to discovery, but immediately after she felt herself encased in the habit Sister Janet had found for her, she did indeed find it liberating – truly liberating. Who, she realised, would question, or look twice at, a nun in a town like Bruges? Lady Anne Winter could not recall the last time she had felt so safe.

She wondered what Lady Hildred would have made of her current incarnation and then she remembered what, in the tumult of the last few days, she had forgotten about. Smoothing down her surplice she turned to Sister Janet.

'There was something,' she said, 'that Lady Hildred said when she was here, in the convent. I had been going to ask her what she meant, but we were interrupted and then it was gone from my mind.'

'And you have remembered it now?' enquired Janet.

'Yes.' Anne thought back to the exact words. They were simple, and yet they might have meant much. 'It was when we lay down to sleep the night before setting out on our journey to Damme. She said, "I am sure I know that fellow."

I asked her what she meant, but she only said, 'That fellow we saw today. I have seen him before, in England. And he knew me too – I am certain of it. I will have it by morning.'

'And did she?' asked Sister Janet, busy packing away threads and pins back into her workbox.

'I forgot to ask her,' said Anne. 'I was so taken up with my night visit to the Bouchoute House, I forgot to ask her.'

ELEVEN

New Friends, Old Enemies

Thomas Faithly looked out over the Markt. Bruges was a nice enough town, as towns went, but he craved the openness and hidden places of his own country. Here, in this town house, at the very centre of a city itself encircled by ramparts and water, and pressed on all sides by the flat polder, Thomas thought he might suffocate. It had been a stiflingly hot summer, and the heat of the day became more oppressive by night; Thomas didn't know when he had last truly slept. Sometimes he thought he would either suffocate or go mad. He had gone mad, almost, at the Battle of the Dunes. When the Spanish had fled in the face of their English and French foes and the Duke of York had rallied his forces to a last charge, Thomas had insisted on being at the front, hoping his final moments would come at the end of a fellow Englishman's pike. Somehow, as comrades fell around him, he had survived. Glenroe it had been, who, almost as mad as himself, had pulled him away when all was done, and disconsolate, they had dragged themselves back here, to Bruges.

They didn't know, Glenroe, Ellis and Daunt, what Thomas had done when last he had been in England. All they knew was that he had left the King's court in Cologne over three years ago to slip back to Yorkshire in the hope of stirring up an English rising. The hoped-for rising had never come to be, and Thomas had reappeared in Bruges eighteen months ago with Prince Rupert, their venture failed and Oliver Cromwell still ruling England with an iron fist. That was what they thought they knew, Ellis, Daunt and Glenroe, but they were wrong. Thomas had returned to England because he was sick of life away from it. '*Heimweh*' – homesickness – Prince Rupert had called it, who had never had a home. As the price of his return to England, Thomas had agreed to spy for Cromwell's regime and he had reported directly to Damian Seeker. The arrangement had brought them all near to disaster, and only his desperate flight from England with Rupert had allowed him to escape it. Damian Seeker was dead, because of him. Many thousands had already died in the wars and their aftermath, and Thomas shouldn't have cared that Seeker had joined them. But when all was said and done, there was a part of him that had liked his fellow Yorkshireman. There had been something of an England he had understood in Damian Seeker, and there was little of it here.

Should any of this become known to his companions in the Bouchoute House, Sir Thomas would be able to count his breaths thereafter in minutes rather than hours. There would be no mercy for the man discovered to have acted the double agent, and he would deserve none. Moreover, Thomas knew that should the truth of his own past activities come to his friends' ears, he would swiftly be pronounced to be the spy whose treachery had lately consigned their comrades at home to their barbaric deaths. But Thomas knew he had not been that traitor, that he would never again be a traitor to the King's cause. As the bells of Bruges, the interminable bells, rang out from every part of the city, he wondered which of the three men with whom he had sworn brotherhood and revenge was the viper in their midst.

As he was about to turn away from the window, Thomas saw a man approaching the front door of the house. Something in the way the man walked held his attention – he was looking neither left nor right, but clearly set on the front door of the house. Something in the manner of his walk, the sash he wore, his boots, had the look of an Englishman and a Cavalry officer.

By the time Thomas got downstairs, the newcomer had been let in by the housemaid, behind whom lurked the old Flemish cook, who regarded the visitor with a degree of disdain very familiar to Thomas. The man was tall and slim-built, but wiry, and for all his gentleman's dress had the look of a battle-hardened soldier. Beneath a weather-beaten face the skin was pale. The hair and lashes were like washed-out straw. The light green eyes were disconcertingly unblinking. A killer, then, but Thomas didn't know when last he had met a man who was not.

Before addressing the newcomer he turned to the house-maid and said, in Flemish, 'A visitor, Femke?'

It was the cook who answered. 'Another English beggar.'

'He doesn't have the look of a beggar,' said Thomas.

'None of you do,' muttered the cook, 'but you all turn up under this roof, expecting to be fed just because His Majesty slept under it.'

'I think you have no cause to complain of your wages, Vrouwe Mytens.'

'No, but of the butcher's bill and the dairymaid's and the candlemaker's – of those I have grounds for complaint. Complaints about those you may have with my compliments.'

Thomas was glad the newcomer did not appear to be fully able to grasp the details of their impoverished existence in the Bouchoute House. He now turned to him and changed to speaking in English.

'I bid you welcome, sir, but am curious to know your business here.'

The man gave the very slightest of nods, not quite an inclination of the head and certainly not a bow. 'My name is George Barton. I was in Newburgh's regiment at the Dunes. The coast is crawling with Cromwell's men and the French. I came to Bruges in the hopes of joining with other officers in the service of the King.'

Sir Thomas relaxed a little. It was a familiar enough story. Another English Royalist abroad, with nowhere to go. Thomas took a few steps closer to George Barton and gestured for him to move further into the light. Closer up, it struck Thomas that there was something familiar about the officer. 'Have we met before?'

The man shook his head. 'I don't think so. The women' – here he indicated the housemaid and cook, still observing the exchange they could not understand – 'would not tell me the names of the officers domiciled here.'

Thomas introduced himself and named the others. Barton shook his head. 'They are but names to me. I cannot say I know them, although we will have shared a battlefield. I was in a dungeon in Edinburgh for three years after the defeat of Glencairn's rising. Until I joined Newburgh's regiment, I had not been on the continent in nearly ten years, since I left it with the Marquis of Montrose.'

'Days of hope and better men. Much blood spilled since then.' As he said it, Sir Thomas saw Barton glance involuntarily to a not-quite-healed gash on his right hand. The man looked almost ready to fall over, as if he had hardly slept or eaten in days. Thomas felt suddenly sickened by himself and the suspicions every new face aroused in him. He turned to the housemaid, reverting to Flemish. 'Femke, get this man some food before he drops.' Then he settled the Englishman in the dining hall and went to fetch the others.

He found them upstairs, in various states of indolence. Glenroe was in the library, and Thomas called the others there. Ellis opened a window, to let in some air, and the sudden draught caused a door in the bookcase to bang. Daunt tried to close it and then complained that the 'damned catch' was broken. 'Even the house is coming apart around us,' he said. No one asked him what else he referred to.

Thomas told them about the new arrival. Glenroe was sceptical. 'He could be anyone, Thomas, and we can't take in every Englishman that turns up in Bruges. We've hardly enough to keep body and soul together ourselves.'

'He'd have to pay his own way,' said Thomas. 'I think he's just looking for some companions and some shelter until such time as we are called upon to fight again.'

'Still,' said Ellis, 'we must be cautious. The servants claim the house was broken into but three nights ago.'

'Nothing was taken,' interjected Daunt.

'Can we be certain?' continued Ellis. 'It can hardly be coincidence that the very next day Lady Hildred Beaumont was shot, dead, in the course of a journey planned in a room downstairs.'

'But the fellow wasn't even here then,' protested Daunt. 'Might as well say it was one of us!'

The stony silence that followed this remark was broken by Daunt awkwardly clearing his throat. 'Well, it may be a coincidence, but I cannot for the life of me see what the connection is.'

'The money,' said Ellis.

The others nodded, even Daunt eventually seeing it. 'They were after the lady's money chest, and they thought she was keeping it here.'

'Which we weren't,' said Thomas.

'No, but we are now,' said Ellis. 'If anything should

happen to that chest now, who do you think will fall under suspicion?'

'I'll tell you right now, and for nothing,' said Glenroe, 'the Irishman, that's who. The rest of you need never worry, for they'll never look at any of you so long as there's an Irishman to blame.'

'Is it any wonder?' said Daunt. 'I am convinced those stockings you are wearing . . .'

'The thing is,' said Ellis, 'we cannot just invite a stranger into the house. The fellow could be anybody. The ambush in which the old woman was shot . . .'

'It's not him,' said Thomas. 'I saw the marksman ride away, remember? Different shape. Different man.'

'Of course,' said Glenroe, idly flicking a coin up in the air and catching it, 'it could always be the one our friends in the Great Trust sent over here in order to discover which one of us is the traitor. How would it look if we were to send him away then?'

No one had any response to this. Glenroe caught the coin a final time then tossed it to Daunt. 'For the rent of your stockings, Dunt. Now what say you all we don't let this fellow sleep under this roof, but we befriend him all the same, just to keep an eye on him until we know for certain who he is?

As they drifted out of the library to head down to the dining hall to inspect their new companion, Glenroe leaned closer to Sir Thomas. 'Have you really no worries, Thomas, that this new friend of yours has been sent to Bruges to spy upon us?'

'I have nothing to fear from that, Evan. Do you?'

'Me, Thomas?' murmured Glenroe. 'Oh, no. Nothing at all.' And he followed Daunt down the stairs, whistling a tune he usually reserved for the night before battle.

It was a good deal later that afternoon, in a modest tavern near George Beaumont's own lodging, far from the haunts of the Cavaliers, that Seeker met the officer for the second time.

'I was expecting you earlier,' said Seeker.

A look of irritation flitted across Beaumont's face. The senior officer of the two, he'd clearly never been spoken to this way by a subordinate. Seeker decided it would save a deal of wasted time to make clear to the major that here, in Flanders, on Thurloe's business, it was he, Seeker, who was the senior officer, and Beaumont the subordinate. The explanation didn't take long and at the end of it Beaumont turned up his palms in conciliation.

'Of course, Captain. I will study to adapt to my new circumstances.'

'Good,' said Seeker. 'So – what kept you?'

'In a word? Glenroe.'

'Go on.'

Beaumont sniffed and arranged himself more comfortably on his stool. 'For all his bonhomie, I don't think he trusts me – or rather "George Barton" – one bit. I've met enough Irishmen of his sort to know that. You know the kind of thing – a laugh, a wink, a twinkle in the eye and a slap on the back, and all the time they're watching you – sharp as a razor and twice as deadly.'

Seeker nodded. George Beaumont's assessment corresponded almost exactly with his own. 'And the rest of them?'

'His companions at the Bouchoute House? An ill-assorted quartet, if ever I saw one. The fat Kentish one, Daunt, isn't quite as stupid as his fellows would have him believe. I've seen it before – there's a kind of safety in feigned stupidity. People don't ask you to do so much, when they think you stupid. And sometimes they underestimate you so far that they make the mistake of trusting you.'

Seeker doubted many people made the mistake of underestimating George Beaumont for that reason.

'Still,' continued Beaumont, 'I don't doubt Daunt can be relied upon, from time to time, to be remarkably stupid.'

Seeker laughed. 'And the other two?'

Beaumont furrowed his brow. 'Ellis. Ellis is a different proposition. He has the look of a lawyer, or a clerk, or a scribbler of news-sheets. A clergyman even. One of those thin, sour-looking people who takes care over what he says, and looks you over as if calculating how much he might get for selling you.'

'And Thomas Faithly?'

Beaumont looked surprised that he should ask. 'I'd assumed Faithly reported to you. I mean, wasn't he on Thurloe's payroll around the time of the attempts on Cromwell last year? Wasn't it him that gave away the plotters?'

'No,' said Seeker, struggling not to grind his teeth. 'It wasn't. And he doesn't report to me. I've taken very great care that he shouldn't even know I'm here, and we'll be keeping it that way. Thomas Faithly is a desperate man, and there's no telling what a desperate man will do.'

'Kill an old woman for her money, perhaps?'

Seeker had already asked himself the same question. 'Perhaps. There was a time I'd have said not, but now, I don't know. He might come in handy for us, at some point, all the same. His companions don't know about his past service to us, and I don't think he'd want them finding out.'

'So you'll just leave him there, dangling like a worm on a hook, until you're ready.'

'If you like,' said Seeker, musing on the image a moment before returning to the point. 'So, you've got the measure of our Cavalier friends then. And you tell me Evan Glenroe already has his eye on you.'

George nodded. 'He "invited" me to join him this afternoon, that he might show me the town. Show me to the town, more like, and everyone else.'

'Oh?'

'He asked me first if I'd ever shot a bow . . .'

'Which no doubt you have.'

George smiled, self-deprecating almost. 'From as soon as I was old enough to lift one. Before that even. My father would take me out to the butts at Beaumont Manor, and I grew up listening to my grandmother's tales of the tournament they had had there, when old Queen Bess had visited Beaumont, how Her Majesty had won, of course. My grandmother was fond of lamenting that the kingdom would go to the dogs, if young men did not practise at their bow. There were the hunts, too, of course: my mother always said we had the finest park in Leicestershire. She wasn't wrong. I spent most of my youth ranging over it; hunting an animal, bringing down a doe with my bow.' He smiled. 'No meat tastes better than that you kill yourself, does it, Seeker?' As he spoke, he brought the toe of his boot down on a beetle Seeker had noticed scuttling around. There was a slight crunch as Beaumont, smiling, ground the life out of the creature.

Seeker averted his face. But he remembered the excitement and the fear of poaching for game with his father and brothers across the moors and through the woods of Yorkshire, the ever-present fear of being caught by the gamekeepers, hauled to the landowner's justice.

'I daresay you and I had a different experience of the chase, Beaumont. But I hope you didn't tell Glenroe all that – remember you're supposed to be from a hard-pressed family of little account.'

'Don't worry,' said George. 'I told him I'd maybe shot the odd coney, or pigeon perhaps. Said my father's was not a great estate and the park not well kept.'

'And Glenroe was happy enough with that?'

'Oh, he was still very keen that we should test my prowess. Specifically, that I should accompany him to the shooting range up at the Schuttersgilde Sint-Sebastiaan where we could 'get some air and test our mettle'. He said there'd been some strange happenings of late at the Bouchoute House and when I asked if he intended to shoot intruders with a crossbow he commented that a crossbow would deal with unwanted visitors as well as a pistol shot.'

'You think this might have been a warning to yourself?'

Beaumont shrugged. 'Why warn me? No, I think he just wanted an excuse to keep me close for a few hours, find out what he could about me, see if my face registered with anyone else. On our journey up to the Schuttersgilde, Glenroe grilled me about every battle I'd been in, every commander I'd served under. Each time, I reversed the truth, put myself in the camp of the opponent I'd fought on any particular day, told what I knew of the opposing commander.'

'Good,' said Seeker. 'Anything else?'

'Oh yes.' Beaumont swallowed down the last of his beer and wiped his mouth. 'He seemed particularly keen that I should steer clear of the Engels Klooster.'

'Did he say why?'

'He tried to make a joke of it, made play of having a terror of nuns, that sort of thing. But he wasn't joking about it. He was warning me off, I'm certain of it.'

'What exactly did he say?' said Seeker.

Beaumont took a moment, seemed to hesitate as he tried to recall the Irishman's exact words, and then said, '"The last Englishman I took up here went looking for his sister there. Next I heard of him he was fished up like a flounder on the Spaanse Loskaai, dead as old Queen Bess."' Beaumont sat back and looked directly at Seeker. 'Now what's that all about, Captain? What do you know of this? Are Englishmen in Bruges being murdered by the nuns of the Engels Klooster?'

Seeker took a moment before answering. 'I don't know, Beaumont. But there's something going on up there, and if Glenroe's trying to warn you off, I'd say that means he's up to his neck in it. He didn't stop there himself when you were with him?'

'No, went right on past it, to the Schuttersgilde at the top of the street, but he did make a point of speaking to a couple of nuns we encountered back out in the town later in the day.'

'Oh, did he now?' said Seeker. 'Well, we'll get to that later. Tell me first what happened at the Schuttersgilde. I've never been in the place.'

'I didn't get to go up the watchtower, more's the pity. I'd say you could shoot at anything from there, see into practically anywhere from there to Sint-Gillis to the south and all around the polder to the north. Probably see right into the grounds of the Engels Klooster too.'

'Like I say, I've never been in it,' said Seeker. 'They don't let the likes of me in. Charles Stuart and his younger brother idled away a good part of their time in Bruges there. I think he liked the deference. The pretence that he was King of something.'

'I expect it's like that for him in most places around these parts.'

'Do you?' Seeker was unable to keep a hint of derision out of his voice. 'I can easily see you haven't been on the continent long. A pauper's a pauper, and if Charles Stuart is anything in the Spanish dominions, or anywhere else for that matter, it's a pauper. Anyway, what happened once you were in there?'

'Oh, Glenroe took some time over the selection of our weapons. He took a longbow and handed me a crossbow. It was an exquisitely crafted weapon. The tiller was inlaid with beautiful ivory plaques sporting the crests of the city and of the Schuttersgilde itself. The balance was perfect, as if it had been made expressly for my arm.'

'If you could get to the point . . .'

Beaumont smiled and shook his head a little, as if storing the memory away. 'Well, once we were set with our weapons, Glenroe took me outside. The heat of the day had started to abate slightly, and there seemed to be a good few prosperous-looking burghers and a collection of straggling Spanish and English officers out on the lawns or at the ranges. Glenroe had a word for everyone we passed, and a word about them after they were out of earshot. A litany of every vice and failing you might expect to find in the moral quagmire the Stuarts and their kind inhabit. I did my best to laugh, as at a farce, although in truth my stomach churned, but I believe he was testing me.'

'Who was there?' asked Seeker.

Beaumont named a few Royalists whose history was well-enough known to Seeker. 'He was putting you on show, testing whether anyone recognised you.'

Beaumont nodded slowly. 'I only had one close shave. A Scottish officer of Newburgh's regiment – the one I'd told Glenroe I fought in at the Dunes. Fortunately, the fellow was more concerned with getting money he said Glenroe owed than with looking too closely at me. All he had to say to me was that I shouldn't trust the Irishman an inch.'

'And do you think that Irishman had come to trust you by the end of your afternoon together?'

Beaumont took a moment before replying. 'I'm not convinced of it. But at least his parading of me amongst the other exiles up there will make it easier for me to go back to the Schuttersgilde myself, should that become expedient.'

Seeker looked at the officer sitting opposite him. He had no doubts – had heard it given as fact – that George Beaumont was fearless and tireless, ruthless even, on the battlefield, but he was not certain he wanted him becoming too deeply involved in the role of agent. 'Best, I think,' he said at last, 'that while you're in Bruges, you let me decide what's expedient. Speaking of which, you'd better tell me now about those nuns.'

'Well, after we left the Schuttersgilde, Glenroe appeared to have little in mind than to have me trail around Bruges in his wake, giving the impression that he had a retainer, and to keep me away from the others in the Bouchoute House. Whenever we met one of his acquaintances, he'd don his genial, roguish persona then drop it like an old cloak whenever the acquaintance was out of sight. I've seen it before – men who've been fighting so long they can scarcely remember the life they started out fighting for. I think he's questioning what he's doing here, what the struggle is about. I think he's losing his grip on things. Particularly after our encounter with the nuns, he was uncommunicative and morose, and I was able to get very little of use out of him.'

'The nuns,' repeated Seeker. 'Tell me what happened with the nuns.'

'We were coming up Spanjaardstraat when Glenroe spotted them outside the Poortersloge; a short, fat sort of a woman, with a younger companion. Sister Janet he called the older one. He seemed particularly wary of her.'

'Aye, well, he's not wrong to be wary of that one.'

'Why?'

'I don't know for certain, but she's up to something she doesn't want anyone to know about. I've had my eye on her a while.'

George nodded. 'There was something in the way they talked with one another, sparred with one another, that was false, as if they were really talking about something else. I don't know if it's to do with the girl perhaps, whose brother went to the convent looking for her.'

Seeker was surprised. 'I should think any tension between Glenroe and Sister Janet would be more likely to do with your mother being shot whilst under his protection, on the way from Sister Janet's convent to Damme, don't you?

Anyway,' he continued, 'what do you know about that – the fellow going to the convent looking for his sister? Where did you hear about it?'

Beaumont looked slightly taken aback, as if unused to having to explain himself. 'It was just what Glenroe said today. The brother's name was Bartlett Jones.'

'Aye, well, I hope he gave Sister Janet pause for thought.'

'You hold her responsible for the boy's death?'

'I think she had her part to play in it, whether she meant to or not. Like I said, Glenroe's right to be wary of her.'

'You don't trust her?'

'About as much as I'd trust a starving dog with a mutton chop. Two people, your mother and Bartlett Jones – both English, mind – went to that convent for help of some sort in the last week, and they were dead within twenty-four hours of each other. I don't know much about the boy, but the old termagant had no love for your mother, for all they hadn't seen each other in fifty years. You'll need to go carefully though – I wouldn't put it past her to notice your likeness. She didn't appear to recognise you?'

'A glance, that's all. I'm not sure about the other one though.'

Seeker hadn't considered the other nun might be of relevance. 'What about her?'

'I caught her looking at me once or twice, for all she made a show of keeping her eyes lowered. I'm pretty sure she was paying close attention to what was being said between Glenroe and Janet too.'

'Describe her,' said Seeker. He listened a while, and didn't much like what he heard. 'I'm in and out of that place a lot, and I haven't come across one that fits that description. Your mother had a maid about that age and height with her though, who disappeared during the ambush.'

Beaumont was interested. 'You think it's her?'

'I think there's a good chance it might be.'

TWELVE

Encounter

Anne Winter couldn't help but marvel at the effect: her nun's habit, the wimple and veil, were like a shroud masking her from curious eyes. The townspeople she'd passed on the streets saw *what* she was and didn't waste any time wondering *who* she was. 'Nobody ever asks you,' Sister Janet had told her, 'who you have been. They make up their own stories for what brought you here.'

And yet, the events of the afternoon had reminded Anne that even in a nun's habit she was not entirely invisible. They had set out from the convent together on Sister Janet's 'errands' about town. As they meandered through the streets to the Markt, Janet pronounced on the various churches and religious houses they passed along the way. The churches were categorised as too large, too small, too ostentatious or too plain. All were decreed to be too cold. Neither was there a religious foundation, other than her own, that met with Sister Janet's approval. This one was too lax, that too strict, the brothers of that order were drunks while those of another were frequenters of brothels. As Anne absorbed the information with mounting amazement, it was clear to her that the old woman was thoroughly enjoying herself.

As they passed the Poortersloge Anne saw two men coming towards them from Sint-Jansplein. The taller, slimmer man with the pale complexion reminded her of someone, but she couldn't place him. She tried to think if she had seen him around the Bouchoute House, for he was evidently connected there. He caught her looking at him and she turned away too late, inwardly chastising herself for being so careless. It was his companion she should be paying most attention to, for it was the Irishman who, along with Thomas Faithly, had formed Lady Hildred's escort from Bruges to Damme. She had taken great care that neither he nor Sir Thomas saw her face properly, but still she felt a tingling of apprehension at the sight of him. She bent her head down, quickened her pace slightly, and hoped Sister Janet would be willing just to pass on by. Her hope was in vain.

'Well, you Irish rogue,' said the old nun, 'much good as an escort you were. I'd have been better to take Hildred Beaumont to Damme myself, on the back of my old donkey, than entrust her safety to you.'

'Ah, but there's wickedness outside the walls of your convent that you could hardly begin to imagine, Sister.'

'Oh, could I not?' she said. 'And what are you doing about apprehending the culprit in this heinous business?'

'Ellis and Dunt have begun to search property between here and Damme, in the hope of coming across someone who gave the fellow shelter or sustenance or saw him ride by.'

'A terrifying duo to confront any malefactor, I am sure,' said Sister Janet. 'Surely Thomas Faithly would be the better choice for that – he did see the assassin, after all, did he not?'

'Not exactly, Sister. Not enough that he'd recognise the fellow again. He did get a decent look at the horse though. He's going round every livery and stable in Bruges to try to find it.'

'Well, that's something, I suppose,' said Sister Janet.

'That's Thomas's view at any rate. Find the horse and you'll find the man.'

'Well, it's not the most stupid idea I've ever heard,' said Sister Janet. 'So much for Sir Thomas, Marchmont Ellis and the idiot Daunt. What about you, Glenroe?'

'Me, Sister?' Glenroe feigned surprise. 'I am the thinker amongst us. Now, I know that Ellis is given out to be a great scholar, and he would obviously be a boon to any counting house, or the ornament of some dusty high table in a college no one has ever heard of, but he lacks the necessary cunning for this type of business.'

'Well, we can rest assured that you do, I'd warrant.'

'Oh, yes, Sister, you may absolutely rest assured on that front.'

Lady Anne was not sure if she was observing some performance, a good-natured sparring between adversaries of old, or an elaborate game of strategy between two practised foes bent on outwitting each other. Whichever was the case, the man accompanying the Irish Cavalier was observing the exchange just as closely as she was.

Sister Janet, evidently content with the progress into the hunt for Lady Hildred's assassin, as relayed to her by Glenroe, now whipped her head round and fixed her gaze on the Irishman's companion. 'And who might this be?'

'Ah,' said Sir Evan, 'now that is the question. I would not like to speculate as to who he might be, but he claims to be George Barton, gentleman. He has fetched up in Bruges, I daresay, because we all do eventually.'

The man called George Barton appeared to take the Irishman's barbed comments in good spirit.

Sister Janet wrinkled her face. 'Barton? Never heard of them. New gentry, no doubt.'

Glenroe leaned in to whisper very audibly in the new Englishman's ear, 'Sister Janet here is of an age when a lineage of less than five hundred years consigns a man to the yeomanry, at best. Fortunately,' he said, 'that cannot be applied to the True Irish.'

'Perhaps not, but there is much that can. I would warn you, young man,' the old nun said, giving her attention once more to George Barton, 'this fellow will cheat you at cards, drink you senseless, and inveigle you into the company of wicked women.'

Glenroe laughed. 'Ah, you need have no fears there, Sister, I've already warned him away from your convent.'

Anne was not sure she believed her ears. The old woman's

cheeks went a dangerous shade of crimson. 'Evan Glenroe, you go too far!'

Glenroe's face now became more serious. 'A little humour, Sister, that's all. But these are dangerous days in Bruges. What with the business of Lady Hildred, and then that young chap looking for his sister, Bartlett Jones, he said his name was, that I showed up to your convent turning up dead the very next day. You couldn't be careful enough who you let within your gates, or who you talk to.'

Anne had the impression that Glenroe was giving Sister Janet more than just friendly advice to be careful about newcomers to the city. This impression only grew stronger as Glenroe, who had removed his hat on greeting them, now put it back on. 'I'll bid you good day, Sisters. But remember: take especial care to lock *all* your doors and be wary of strangers.' The man Barton gave the women an awkward smile as he also tipped his hat to them before following Glenroe away up the street.

Sister Janet watched with pursed lips until the men rounded the corner. 'That fellow is always so impertinent, he puts me quite out of kilter. I feel I need to sit and rest a moment.'

Anne cast about her for somewhere they might go inside. She suggested they ask admittance for a few minutes to the Poortersloge. She quickly realised she would have been wiser to bring to life the bear whose statue guarded the corner of the building as it faced down the canals.

'Poortersloge? A front for wealthy merchants to drink

and play at cards and utter profanities all the live-long day whilst they make their plots to plunder the poor. I'll not set foot in it. But come, we are no great distance from Sint-Walburgakerk. A moment's prayer and quiet contemplation will be all the restorative I need.'

Anne was certain there were half a dozen places they might have stopped and rested a moment before they finally reached the Walburgakerk. Protesting that she was perfectly all right, Janet nevertheless permitted herself to lean on Anne's arm as they went up the steps, before shaking it off at the top and bustling purposefully inside.

Following quickly after her, Anne remembered just in time to cross herself with holy water and then to genuflect before the altar before joining Sister Janet who was already on her knees in prayer. It was only the second Romish church Anne had set foot in, and she could not help but look about her in wonder. Whereas the chapel of the Engels Klooster was almost oppressive to her in its closeness and ornament, this was a revelation of space and pure light. At first all she was aware of was that the heat and harsh brightness of the sun were here moderated by swathes of white marble into something cool and clear, giving blessed relief from the heat and dust of the street, but then into her throat crept the first trickle of incense and into her head the murmuring of black-robed priests. Lady Anne caught her breath. She had met Jesuit priests before, in English Catholic houses loyal to the King, but those men had always been moving around the country incognito, constantly in danger of their lives. It was a shock to see them walk openly here. Anne could not quite master a sensation of fear at finding herself in such near proximity to men she had spent her life being taught to see as cunning of intellect and sinister of purpose.

Sister Janet was on her knees and in prayer before Anne had completed her genuflection. When Janet's lips had finished moving, and the beads she had been passing through her fingers lay still in her hands, Anne helped her to a sitting position on the wooden seat behind her.

'Ah, these old bones,' said Janet, letting out a long breath.

'Are you recovered a little, Sister?'

An irate face whipped round. 'There is nothing whatsoever wrong with me.'

'The Irishman was very insolent . . .' began Anne.

'Ho! You will be on your knees a long time if you take to prayer every time you come across an insolent Irishman,' said Janet. 'I am just getting a little tired. I've been fighting a long time.'

'Fighting for what, Sister?'

It looked to Anne as if Janet would say more, but suddenly a shadow fell across the floor in front of them. Anne looked up. Emerging from behind a close-by marble column was Father Felipe, Sister Janet's confessor and the Jesuit whom she and Hildred had encountered on that first morning after their arrival at the Engels Klooster.

'Sister Janet,' he said, whilst looking at Anne, who lowered her head further over the beads. 'I see you have a new companion.'

The young Jesuit wasn't a particularly tall man, but his soft brown eyes and the gentle contours of his face would have made him very appealing to look at were it not for the predatory expression that came over that face when he spoke. It was an expression that told Anne he had no difficulty in seeing past her nun's habit in the way other men might not.

'She is not long arrived from England, Father, and I have taken her under my wing. Bruges can be a dangerous city for young women unfamiliar with its ways. I shall be keeping a particularly close eye on her welfare.'

'Of course,' said Father Felipe, taking a half step back and looking less pleased with Sister Janet's response than he pretended to be. 'And you have brought her here to see its most beautiful church?'

'It was the first sanctuary that came to my mind, for a moment's repose and reflection, after an encounter with the Irishman, Evan Glenroe.'

'Oh?' Real interest flashed in Felipe's eye. 'I hope the reprobate did not upset you unduly, Sister.'

'His attempts to impress his new companion, some fellow also lately arrived from England – Barton, as I recall – veer to the somewhat vulgar. No doubt he will be leading the fellow astray, at the House of Lamentations and other such wicked places.'

'Indeed? Then we must pray that his new companion finds a better path.' Father Felipe inclined his head to Janet, cast another unsettling look at Anne, and turned away, trailing aromas of sandalwood and lemon behind him. A moment later, Sister Janet was once more genuflecting before the altar, and making her way back out of the church. It felt to Anne that they had taken an unduly long diversion to spend such a short time 'resting', and as they made their way back out into the sunlight of the street, Anne could not help feeling that what she had just witnessed was the delivery of a message of some kind. What she was not so certain of was whether the message was *about* Evan Glenroe or from him.

By the time they were making their way back along Sint-Annarei, Anne felt emboldened to ask Sister Janet about something else that had been preying on her mind. 'The girl you had me smuggle to Damme, and with whom I changed places – was she the sister of the young drowned man that Evan Glenroe spoke of?'

Janet stopped, heaved a great sigh and at last said, 'Yes, she is.'

'Then why did you send her brother—'

Janet interrupted her. 'I could not be certain it was her brother.'

'But could you not have asked her? Where would have been the harm?'

'Ruth Jones was not present at the Engels Klooster when the man claiming to be her brother came asking for her. I sent her a message after I had sent him away.'

'Where to? Where was she?'

'Somewhere safe.'

'From what?'

'The man she was running from.'

'This Bartlett Jones?'

Sister Janet shook her head. 'No. She wouldn't tell me the name of the man she so feared. All I know is that he is an Englishman, and that she has been fleeing him for some time. She came to Bruges because she had heard she might find sanctuary here. But of course, Bruges is full of Englishmen and I had to keep her presence at the Engels Klooster and – *elsewhere* – a secret. She is too terrified to trust anyone completely, even me. She fears there is no one he cannot win to his side, and nowhere he cannot reach. I could only press her so far. And as for this poor boy – Bartlett Jones – it seems he was indeed her brother, God rest his soul, come to Bruges to bring her home safe. He will never do that now. I would never have turned him away if I'd known it was truly him, and what was going to happen to him.' She swallowed, then looked up at Anne, vulnerable, old, and almost defeated. Almost. 'Ruth saw him the next morning, on the Spaanse Loskaai, dead. Her own brother.'

Anne thought of the girl with the badly scarred face with whom she'd frantically exchanged clothes in Lady Hildred's carriage, tried to imagine the horrors she had seen and was running from. 'And that's how you knew about his death before Evan Glenroe told you?'

But Sister Janet shook her head. 'I already knew he was dead. John Carpenter told me that morning. He'd met Bartlett Jones when the young fellow had just arrived in Bruges, and the next day he saw him lying dead on the dock.'

'Who is John Carpenter?' asked Anne.

Janet's face lightened at last and she laughed. 'So much has happened since your arrival in Bruges, I had almost forgotten how little time you have really been here. He is an English carpenter, who seems to come from nowhere and yet be everywhere you least expect him. I think little happens in Bruges that he does not make it his business to know about.'

'An English carpenter?' said Anne, the hairs on her neck suddenly prickling. Back into her mind had come an image from her first full day at the Engels Klooster, and the glimpse of a man she had seen Sister Janet speak with at the convent garden door.

'Yes, well, if Yorkshire is to be counted as England. Certainly, there are arguments against but . . .' Sister Janet suddenly stopped and reached a hand over to take hold of one of Anne's. 'My dear, is something the matter? You've gone very pale.'

'I . . . no . . . it is not possible.'

'Anne? What is wrong? We have walked too long in the heat this morning.'

Anne shook her head, screwing shut her eyes as if blanking out what they might show. 'It's nothing,' she said at last. 'Foolishness, nothing more.'

But even now, hours after they'd arrived back safe within the convent's walls, Anne couldn't quite shake off a deep sense of foreboding. Nor could she quite rid her senses of the trailing aromas of sandalwood and lemon that clung to the priest, Father Felipe.

THIRTEEN

Oude Steen

The stonework of the archway Seeker was leaning against was pleasantly warm in the early evening sun. George Beaumont had been somewhat vague when telling him where he had taken his lodgings in 't Zand, in the sleepy south-west of the city, so Seeker had made a point of following him that first night. Beaumont's lodging was in fact a trim little cottage on Kreupelnstraat, very close to the Blindekenskapel. Seeker was impressed – it was a well-chosen spot, with absolutely nothing in the vicinity likely to incite the interest of the Cavaliers. Beaumont would be able to come and go from here relatively unobserved.

Seeker had not been there long before he saw George Beaumont appear at the end of the street. He stepped out of the shadow of his archway and saw that his sudden appearance had given his fellow Englishman a jolt.

'I . . .' Beaumont took a moment to recover himself. 'I hadn't expected to find you here.'

'Well, as long as you can be found wherever I might expect to find you, you needn't worry yourself about being able to find me. Come on.' Seeker had already started up the way George had come.

George Beaumont hesitated, then followed after him.

As they passed Sint-Salvatorskerk, Seeker said, 'You been back at the Bouchoute House since we spoke earlier?'

Beaumont still seemed unsettled by Seeker's appearance. 'No, I've . . . just been wandering around town, trying to familiarise myself with it. Where are we going, by the way?'

'Oude Steen,' said Seeker.

Something like alarm passed over George Beaumont's face. 'The prison? Is this some sort of trap, Seeker?'

Seeker screwed up his face. 'A trap? What on earth for? This is about your mother. If it was one of that crew in the Bouchoute House that shot her, they won't have risked doing it themselves – they'll have paid someone to do it for them. They'd not have had much trouble around Bruges finding someone desperate for money who can handle a musket. Whoever that was has more than likely gone back to the hole he crawled out of. We start tracking him down by asking the low-life in the prison. We find him, and with a bit of persuasion – be it fiscal or physical – he'll tell us who it was that paid him to silence Lady Hildred.'

'Silence her?' George gave an awkward laugh. 'I'm not denying that my mother could be a harpy, Seeker, but even I wouldn't have shot her to shut her up.'

'Even if you were a traitor who thought she'd come to Bruges to discover you?'

They were now making their way up the Oude Burg. George stopped. 'What are you talking about, Seeker?'

Seeker had considered very carefully how much to tell Beaumont of his own particular interest in the Cavaliers. 'Secretary Thurloe has a spy, in the Bouchoute House. He's provided us with some very useful information over the last year or so. He sends his reports, in cypher, to England, through me. The Royalists have uncovered that much, but they don't know who he is, or who I am, so they've sent someone – a she-intelligencer – over here to find out. I received this information and reported it to my source a few hours before your mother's arrival in Bruges. Two days later, she was dead.'

George Beaumont appeared to hear the words Seeker was speaking but didn't seem entirely able to make himself understand them. 'My mother? A she-intelligencer?' He laughed. 'I have heard of such women, though I can scarcely credit a woman could truly be capable of espionage. It's hardly what one looks for from them, is it? And even should such women actually exist, I cannot believe even the deluded fools of the Sealed Knot or the Great Trust or whatever name they now manifest themselves under would think Hildred Beaumont up to any enterprise requiring even a modicum of subtlety.'

'Oh, you wouldn't believe what some women are capable of, but no, on this occasion, you're right: I don't think Lady Hildred was the person sent to ferret out our spy.'

Seeker had started to walk again, but George Beaumont

remained where he was. Seeker turned to him, impatient. 'They don't let people into the Oude Steen at all hours, you know.'

But Beaumont was shaking his head, his lip slightly twisted. 'You know.'

'I know what?'

'Who Thurloe's agent is. Which of them in the Bouchoute House is the traitor to the rest. Of course you must know who your own spy is. What farce are you having me play?'

Seeker walked back towards Beaumont and stopped very close to him. 'I'll remind you again, *Major*, that I am the senior officer in our current situation,' he said, his voice very quiet. 'I'm not telling you who my source is because firstly, you have turned up in Bruges without me having had any warning of it and without Mr Thurloe's knowledge – I have not the authority to give you this agent's name. Moreover, I'm not telling you because it isn't certain that it was him who shot your mother.'

Beaumont looked as if he was struggling to keep his temper. 'Oh, come, Seeker, of course it is. Who else might it be?'

'Any number of people. The man denies it, quite strenuously.'

Beaumont looked incredulous. 'Well, he would, wouldn't he?'

Seeker shook his head. 'Not to me. If you think about it, he has no reason in the world to deny to me that he has removed a Royalist agent sent here to uncover our activities. More like to take the credit for getting rid of our common problem.'

Seeker could see that George Beaumont followed the logic of what he said. 'What's more, I've learned over the past few years that more than one person may have a motive for killing a particular person. I think you and I have a much better chance of getting at the truth if you can start with the fact of your mother being shot rather than him being someone in whose interest it was to shoot her.'

George gave a crooked smile. 'I had not heard you were a philosopher, Captain. Clearly you favour the empirical over the teleological approach.'

Seeker gave a dismissive grunt. Republican or Royalist, sometimes the gentry just couldn't help themselves. 'Call it what you like, Beaumont,' he said, 'but we'll do this my way or you'll depart Bruges now. You're fresh eyes, and after a year and a half of keeping track of these vipers, fresh eyes are exactly what I need.'

The self-satisfied look on George Beaumont's face was gone and was replaced by a flash of temper. 'Fresh eyes? The Cavaliers don't trust me, you don't trust me. I go not with fresh eyes but half-blind.'

Seeker had already started walking again. 'Half-blind is better than nothing at all, which is what you came into Bruges with. That's your choice, take it or leave it.'

Beaumont had no other choice and he knew it. He started to walk after Seeker. 'And how are we to comport ourselves in this prison?'

'Well, I'm visiting a friend down on his luck. It's not the first time I've been there to see him, and I've bailed him out before. No one will think it strange . . .'

'And what role do I play in this?'

'The one you're already playing. A comrade of the officers at the Bouchoute House, making investigations into the shooting on the road to Damme. You're not long arrived in the city. I was doing some work at the house and am simply showing you the way. You need to remember: people aren't wary of me here. Here, I'm just the English carpenter.'

They turned on to Wollestraat and the prison soon came into sight. They gained admittance from the doorkeeper and began to descend the steps to the dungeon. Once at the bottom, Seeker exchanged a few words in Flemish with the warder and they were each given a candle in return for dropping the requisite number of coins into the warder's palm. There could be no telling for the inmates incarcerated at this level whether it was day or night. Such things could lead to madness.

As the clanking sound of the gate shutting behind them reverberated around the walls, Seeker was acutely aware of the smell. It was as bad as a barrack room in high summer. Proximity to the canal meant that the air that did find its way through from the high barred windows of the ground floor of the Steen brought with it fetid humours, rank odours, and flies. At least it was cooler below ground. Cold, in fact, and the rasping coughs and shivers of many of the inmates did not bode well for those forced to have any more than a fleeting acquaintance with the Oude Steen. Interspersed with the coughs were mumbles and sudden shouts, offensive catcalls and pleas for help.

'Dear God, it is surely Bedlam,' said George.

'I doubt even the souls of Bedlam have undergone what has been undergone here,' remarked Seeker, lifting his candle to illuminate for a moment an iron spike, remnant of some hideous torture inflicted on those unfortunate enough to find themselves here in years past.

George stared at the thing a moment, apparently fascinated, but Seeker had seen it all before. Ignoring the insults and outstretched hands of a dozen malcontents, he made for a small cell at the far end of the passageway. 'How's your Flemish?' he asked Beaumont as he laid a hand on the bolt of the door.

'Functional. I've let the Cavaliers believe I don't understand any of it. Certainly, I can barely speak the language but I can more or less follow a conversation between two or three people.'

'All right. You'll have to listen hard then.'

The door creaked open towards them and Seeker went first into the small, windowless room. A stream of curses greeted their arrival.

'Mind your manners, Dirk, I've brought a friend for you. He's brought a few schellings for you to invest as you wish, if he's a mind.'

The lump of sacking and old blankets in the corner stirred itself and rose to a sitting position. Dirk was short and rotund, and probably around Seeker's age. He was relatively well dressed and certainly no beggar.

'Dirk here has a problem with the piquet,' Seeker explained to Beaumont, 'and more often than not is unable to honour his obligations, isn't that so, Dirk?'

'Just another hand, another turn of the cards, and I would have won back all I owed, but you know Beertelmaans – he's a vulture. I think he has his eye on my wife.'

'Well, if you're helpful to my friend here, I suspect he'll be inclined to pay the warder something for your comfort.'

Seeker turned again to George. 'Dirk here pays attention to the world around him. He generally knows what's going on – a useful man to know.'

The small fat man sat up and checked the points on his breeches. 'So what's your friend's interest then?' he asked.

'Tell him,' Seeker said.

George's Flemish proved unequal to the task, so Seeker took over. 'He's employed on the business of the English gentlemen, resident in the house lately occupied by the Scottish King.'

Dirk nodded. 'I know them. I am certain the Irishman has his dice loaded.'

Seeker said nothing to this. 'They were lately escorts to a party on the way to Damme which fell under ambush.'

Dirk nodded.

'What my friend would like to know,' said Seeker, 'is whether anyone's been throwing money about who doesn't usually have any, anyone who's handy with a musket.'

Dirk laughed. 'This is the Netherlands, John Carpenter, half the musketeers in Europe have tramped through this town, and they're all looking for money. But, yes, there is someone. A fellow who was in here the other day, taken in for drunkenness and fighting. Bleeding and bandaged when he came in, worse when he left, mind.'

'Why worse?' asked Seeker. 'Fighting in here too?'

'Not exactly. He was just bragging so much Big Johann had to give him a thump or two to shut him up.'

'Bragging of what?' said Seeker.

'Oh, that he was a person of standing now. That history would speak of him. That some English gentlemen had paid him a king's ransom to shoot the Queen of England.' To this promising information, Dirk had nothing to add. He couldn't have said whether the braggart's injury might have come from a pistol shot or not. They left his cell, repeating their promise to pay the warder something for his comfort.

On their way back through the dungeon, the catcalling and outstretched palms resumed. There was scarcely an insult in Flemish or French that didn't fly through the air on waves of laughter and invective behind them.

Back up in the ward room, a couple of extra coins to the warder extracted at least the Christian name of the prisoner who'd bragged of killing the 'Queen of England' – Piet. And then they were back outside. As they reached the end of the Wollestraat, Seeker said, 'You'll find your own way back from here; I've got things to do.'

Beaumont gave Seeker a curt bow and headed off back

in the direction of 't Zand, and his own lodging. By dint of a couple of turns through darkened passageways and the use of some shortcuts, Seeker soon had Hildred Beaumont's son in view again. There was something about the man's increasingly uneasy manner, something in the kind of questions he asked, that made Seeker even more than usually distrustful of him. His distrust was soon rewarded by his sighting of Beaumont on a street that would take him not to 't Zand, but to the Markt.

Keeping out of Beaumont's sight, Seeker followed, and was not greatly surprised to see Beaumont approach the entrance to the Bouchoute House. What did surprise him though, was that the very flustered-looking maid who answered the door would not let the Englishman in. As Beaumont remonstrated with the girl, Seeker drew as close to the building as he could without being seen. Thomas Faithly was soon brought to the door, and Seeker strained to hear what he said.

'Sorry . . . circumstances have changed . . . Glenroe insists . . . no admittance . . . I cannot . . . No, not tonight.'

As Faithly shut the door on George Beaumont, Seeker stepped further back into the shadows of the neighbouring house and watched as Beaumont, fists clenched, eventually walked away from the Cavaliers' lair and across the Markt. Again Seeker followed him. He realised with growing unease that Beaumont was walking in the direction of the House of Lamentations. Seeker felt a surprising wave of disappointment that this officer, so reputedly firm a Puritan, should show himself as morally compromised as the Royalists he had fallen among. But Beaumont did not enter the House of Lamentations, nor even approach the brothel's door. Instead, he stood a moment looking up at its windows before turning away and tracing his own footsteps back to 't Zand, where Seeker finally saw him enter his own cottage on Kreupelnstraat and soon afterwards extinguish his light.

FOURTEEN

The Book-Buyer of Sint-Donatian's

Anne supposed the garden of the Engels Klooster was as close an approximation as might be found to the poets' view of earthly perfection. She was on her knees, weeding amongst the peas, and occasionally popping a sweet, fat pod into her mouth. To her right, a honeysuckle clambered over a brick wall, driving Sister Ignatia's bees almost to distraction. A breeze reaching the garden from the west carried to her the scent of the lavender grown for the convent's apothecary. This wasn't like an English garden, like the gardens she'd known as a child and a young woman, with their knots of hedges and mannered walks, promenades for the discussion of policy, arbours for the whispering of sweet nothings or the hatching of intrigues. This was a place of industry and utility, where everything, however lovely its effect, had a purpose beyond the facilitating of leisure or the pleasing of the eye. And yet, there was something, amongst the buzzing of the bees, the flitting of the butterflies and the contented chatter of the nuns as they bent to their work amongst the vegetables and flowerbeds, that kept Anne on the alert. It was a tableau to delight the senses, and it masked something else. Andrew Marvell would have seen it for sure, would have found that something, laid it bare with his pen. But Marvell was not here, he was in London and, despite Lady Anne's best efforts, he was still on the wrong side.

Thoughts of Marvell brought to Lady Anne's mind memories of past failed endeavours on the King's behalf, of friends lost. Anne rallied herself and concentrated harder on the harvesting of the peas. She was nearing the end of a second row when she became aware of a hush descending amongst the novices and a stiffening in the posture of Sister Euphemia, who had charge of the gardens. On glancing up she saw the Jesuit, Father Felipe, emerging from the cloister walk in the company of Sister Janet. They took the path towards the orchard and as they passed the novices lowered their heads. The Spanish priest accorded them a perfunctory nod. Father Felipe, after all, was the son of a count, and his mother a cousin to a cousin of the King of Spain. A bishop's mitre and possibly a cardinal's hat lay somewhere in his future; it was hardly to be expected that such a one would take novices under his notice.

The workings of religious orders and the relationships between them were still largely a mystery to Anne, and yet, that the priest should be so often at the Engels Klooster struck her as strange. Stranger still was the fact that most of the Spaniard's interactions seemed to be not with Mother Superior, but with Sister Janet. She knew, from what Janet herself had told her and what she had gleaned from others in the convent, that the English nun's exile so many years ago, in the reign of King James, had been occasioned by her father's imprisonment and execution for the harbouring of Jesuits. Anne had at first wondered whether there might be some family connection between Janet and the priest, but then the nun must have left England many years before Felipe had been born, and Anne could not see that she could have any connections with the harbouring of Jesuits in England now. Besides, the doings of a Spanish Jesuit were not the reason she had come to Bruges: all her focus must be on the uncovering and removal of Thurloe's double agent.

As they walked along the path to the convent orchard, the priest occasionally inclined his head slightly, as if to catch something said to him by the English nun. On one such occasion, Sister Janet broke off from her narrative and turned her head to look directly at Anne. Father Felipe followed suit and looked at her too, and it seemed to Anne that something in what he saw displeased him.

She was still pondering what Sister Janet might have said about her to the priest when one of the novices brought to her a note that had been delivered to the convent gate.

The note was in Flemish, but its contents easily understood.

Two gentlemen have come to me asking about the book you were recently enquiring about. If you are of a mind to fulfil our arrangement under the terms already proposed, you should come this afternoon to me at my shop by the entrance of Sint-Donatian's. I have asked the gentlemen in question to return at 4 o'clock. Balthasar van der Velde, Bookseller.

At last, her tour of the booksellers of Bruges on that first day in the city, when Lady Hildred had been recovering from their journey from England, had borne fruit. Anne only managed to stop herself from cursing out loud at the dilatoriness of the convent gatekeeper. The bells of the Engels Klooster had sounded three o'clock some time ago. She abandoned her trug of pea pods, hastily undid the strings of her apron and ran to wash her hands at the garden pump. Sister Euphemia was all astonishment but couldn't get her words out in time to ask Anne what she thought she was doing. Quickly, Anne went to her cell and took her money bag from the small case that Sister Janet had permitted her to keep there.

Anne Winter had spent almost all of her time since she had heard of the death of Damian Seeker moving as quickly as possible, on horseback or on foot, from one part of England to another, whilst trying her best to attract no attention. In that sense, Bruges was no different to her than anywhere else. She arrived at the Burg just as the great bells of Sint-Donatian's tolled four. Quickly, she threaded her way through the crowd of booths and booksellers clustered around the steps of the cathedral and positioned herself to the side of a stall selling devotional tracts and gruesome German woodcuts. The bookseller, engaged in attending to an elderly Flemish matron, smiled broadly on noticing her and lifted a hand to wave. With tightly pursed lips and a firm shake of her head she tried to communicate to him that he shouldn't draw attention to her. How could she have been so careless as to forget to impress on the bookseller that her identity should be kept secret from the man looking for a copy of Walton's *Compleat Angler*?

She didn't have long to berate herself for soon she saw two of the men from the Bouchoute House – the Englishman Ellis and the Irishman Glenroe – approach the bookseller. Minutes later they were stepping back out on to the square, each with a package under his arm.

Once they were safely lost in the crowds of the square, Anne hurried over to the booth. 'Well,' she demanded of the slightly startled man, 'which of them was it?'

The man blustered for a moment, protesting that one Englishman was much like another to him. Anne realised that to distinguish an Englishman from an Irishman would be utterly beyond him. 'The red head or the thin one?' she said at last.

'Oh.' He smiled, on surer ground now. 'The thin one.'

'You did not tell him where you had got the book?'

The smile disappeared. 'Only that it was from a sister at the Engels Klooster.'

Anne felt a chill go through her. She paid the bookseller what had been agreed between them for keeping her informed and began to make her way back to the Engels Klooster, feeling somewhat shaken and nauseous. After crossing the bridge at Molenmeers she stopped and forced herself to consider what she had just learned. The man whose treachery had led to the deaths or imprisonment of so many of her friends in England was Marchmont Ellis, and the unthinking bookseller of Sint-Donatian's had just told him where he might find her.

As Anne had been crossing back over the Molenbrug, she had been too taken up in her thoughts to notice the carpenter crossing over from the other direction, but he had noticed her.

It was her walk. It had bothered Damian Seeker the day he'd had a brief glimpse of her crossing the Markt in the company of Lady Hildred Beaumont, and it bothered him now. It had bothered him then because he hadn't been certain why it had caught his attention, but now he knew, and it hit him like an iron bar to the chest. Anne Winter. Lady Anne Winter, dressed first as a maid, and then gone missing, and now back in Bruges and dressed as a nun. Seeker stopped in his tracks, astonished. It was all he could do not to lay hold of her there and then and ask her what she thought she was up to.

But he didn't need to ask. Seeker knew precisely what Anne Winter was doing in Bruges, and he could not believe he hadn't guessed it before. Who else would they have sent? Was there a more brazen Royalist in the whole of England? What was Thurloe thinking of, to have taken his eye off her just because he, Seeker, had gone to Bruges?

Seeker was so out of countenance he almost walked into a group of three old women on their way to mass at Sint-Annas. The old women apologised and got quickly out of his way. The near collision had brought him back to his senses. He had been halfway to deciding to go and pound on the door of the Engels Klooster and demand to know what was going on. But then his game would have been up before Sister Janet even had her wimple straight, and once it was discovered who he was, the odds were not good that Damian Seeker would depart this city's gates alive.

Anne Winter, Hildred Beaumont, the Engels Klooster, Ruth Jones, Bartlett Jones. It was to the first three that he should be giving his attention, yet his thoughts constantly returned to the young Englishman who'd survived little more than an afternoon in Bruges. That Anne Winter had been Lady Hildred's 'maid' he had no doubts. But Seeker knew better than most how many aliases an agent might go by. Whether Anne Winter was also the 'Ruth Jones' that Bartlett Jones had gone to the Engels Klooster in search of was another question.

Seeker had spent much of the afternoon walking the parts of the town where he knew the remnants of the English soldiery to be billeted but found no one who answered the description of the man in the fine grey woollen suit. It would have suited his purposes, quite wondrously, if the man he sought turned out not to have been a man at all. Certainly, Seeker didn't regard Anne Winter as a woman. To him, she was neither male nor female; she was simply a person capable of great deviousness and someone who was constantly to be watched. Even so, while she might successfully have passed herself off first as a lady's maid and then as a nun, he doubted very much that she would be able to disguise herself as a man.

In London, Seeker would simply have marched to Anne Winter's house and arrested her. Never, since he had come to Bruges, had he so much regretted the power that he could not wield. He took great care, usually, not to come within sight of those whose paths he might have crossed in England. That Anne Winter had not recognised him was a chance that he could not rely on occurring again. Sister Janet's new suspicion of him was already making visits to the Engels Klooster more dangerous. The information with which Mother Superior's stable boy could provide him was useful, but limited. Seeker had almost reached the carpenter's yard in Sint-Gillis and was just considering whether he might need to send to the agent at Dunkirk or Hoogstraten for help to further infiltrate and investigate the Engels Klooster, when he saw the solution to his problem crossing the street ahead of him.

George Beaumont had a haunted, anxious look to him, much as he had had before when he had turned away from the House of Lamentations. Now he was plainly headed towards the inn above whose stables Seeker lodged. Seeker called over to him. Beaumont looked up quickly but seemed to take a moment to realise who was addressing him. He straightened his shoulders and summoned the expression he more habitually wore, but Seeker wondered if what he had just seen was a man more affected than he would wish to admit by the death of an uncaring mother.

'Are you looking for me?'

Beaumont nodded. 'Something has—'

Seeker stopped him. 'Not here.' A short while later they were stooping beneath the doorway of De Garre. It was a place generally patronised by local craftsmen, and they were unlikely to be observed or overheard by English soldiers. Seeker selected a bench on the ground floor, from where he could keep an eye on the doorway from the narrow alleyway and any new arrivals. He waited until the tavern maid had filled their tankards and left.

'Well?' said Seeker.

'I'm finished at the Bouchoute House.'

'What have you done?'

'Nothing, but when I called there yesterday they wouldn't let me in.'

Seeker refrained from telling him he already knew that. 'Why not?' he said.

'Glenroe's decision. Thomas Faithly was very apologetic. They're expecting a new arrival there and they're all on edge. No recent or new acquaintances allowed.'

'Who are they expecting?'

Beaumont shook his head. 'I contrived an encounter with the scullery maid at the Vismarkt this morning. She wasn't very forthcoming. The cook muttered something about Mr Longfellow or something like it. Whoever it is, they don't want any strangers around, especially not English strangers. It's been made plain to me that I am not to show my face there again.'

'Have they ever spoken of this "Longfellow" before?'

'No. Not in my hearing.'

'And do you plan to leave Bruges now?'

Beaumont shook his head. 'Not until I've got what I came for.'

'All right. Well, I still haven't tracked down this "Piet" who brags of having shot your mother, but I will. What of the money she took with her out of England – are you any closer to discovering what they have done with it?'

'I'm certain it's somewhere in the house. Every time any of the four of them come back from somewhere, the first thing they do is go scuttling up the stairs to check upon something. They've never left me alone in the house long enough that I can do the same.'

'All right. Leave that to me,' said Seeker. 'I have another job for you.'

Beaumont's face became stony. 'I'm not one of your agents, Seeker.'

'This is to do with finding your mother's killer. If you have some other reason for being in Bruges that you've neglected to apprise me of, you'd best tell me now. You've deliberately come into hostile territory and have sought me out. Every encounter, every conversation I have with you risks exposing us both. Now, you can walk out of here and go your own way, you see to your business and I to mine, and we need never acknowledge each other in the street nor anywhere else again. Or you can help me, and I you.'

Beaumont said nothing but took a draught of his beer, as if deliberately to calm himself. He nodded his acquiescence.

'Good,' said Seeker. 'Now, the point of you being in the Bouchoute House was to get close to the Cavaliers. It's not something I can do myself – there is too great a likelihood that Thomas Faithly would recognise me. As to the house itself, though, I can get access to it as long as they're not in it. I'll get myself in there and find out where they have stashed your mother's money. I'll get it out of there if I can.'

'And what do you wish me to do?'

'The English convent. The older of the two nuns that you met with Glenroe in the street . . .'

'Yes?'

'She has her eye on me too. And as to what it is has Glenroe's back up, I don't know, but she's sheltering the woman the Royalists have sent over to sniff out Mr Thurloe's spy, and I'd wager she's doing it knowingly.' As Seeker told George Beaumont about Anne Winter and her being incognito at the English Convent, he could see Beaumont's interest growing.

'The one accompanying this Sister Janet when she and Glenroe had their exchange in the street – she was my mother's maid?'

'That's what she was passing herself off as when she first came to Bruges at any rate.'

George shook his head as if in admiration. 'Well, that I would never have guessed. I remember thinking it was a pity she was a nun.'

'What?' said Seeker, not liking the way this remark was tending.

'Well,' said George, smiling in an almost devil-may-care way that Seeker would not have thought him capable of, 'she's too fine-looking a woman to be wasting away in a nunnery, do you not think?'

'No,' said Seeker, 'I do not! She is a spider, a viper, a vixen more cunning than any you have ever run to ground. Don't forget it, not for a moment. She has but one aim in sight, one purpose: the restoration of Charles Stuart to the throne of England. Nothing else. Do I make myself clear?'

'Very much so,' said George, his face becoming more serious. 'Not a woman to keep her place.'

Tell me a woman of worth who does, Seeker wanted to say. Never in his life had he encountered a woman who meant anything to him who would have done something simply because he told her to. But it wasn't George Beaumont's business to know his life. 'No,' he said instead, 'she is not.'

George Beaumont contemplated his beer for a moment. 'And do you think she is in some way connected with the death of the young Englishman who went to the convent, searching for his sister?'

'That I don't know. It's one of the reasons I need you to find a way into that convent, but not the main one. I need you to find out how much Anne Winter knows about Marchmont Ellis.'

'About Ellis?' queried Beaumont. But then his face cleared. 'Marchmont Ellis is your source in the Bouchoute House.'

'That's right.'

'Why have you chosen to tell me of this now?'

'Because he's gone rogue. This "Mr Longfellow" that's coming to the Bouchoute House – I should have heard it from Ellis, not you. That means he's planning some way out, probably involving your mother's money. He hasn't kept up his side of our bargain, and that releases me from mine. He has no right, any more, to my protection. But I need to know what he's up to, and I need to know how much Anne Winter has discovered about him, and me. Sister Janet is already becoming suspicious of my visits and my questions, and Anne Winter knows me far too well. I can't show my face around the Engels Klooster as long as she's there.'

'But I can,' said Beaumont, understanding.

Seeker nodded. 'Let them get used to seeing you. See what you can learn, and I'll attend to the business of your mother's money.'

Agreeing when they would next meet, they parted company, Seeker to his lodgings in Sint-Gillis, Beaumont to his over at 't Zand.

Back in his stable loft, Seeker was troubled. Whatever Sister Janet was concealing at the Engels Klooster would come to light in the end, and he had a feeling that what-

ever it was might prove to be just as bad news for his
enemies in Bruges as it would be for him. What troubled
him more though was the imminent visitation to the
Bouchoute House that had put its inhabitants so much
on the alert. Mr Longfellow. Seeker had guessed as much
even before Beaumont had mentioned the name he'd got
out of the scullery maid. Intelligence sent to Whitehall,
and arrived some days ago back out in Flanders, had
spoken of a 'Mr Longfellow' as a Royalist of the highest
standing. It was suspected that Mr Longfellow was one of
three people: the indefatigable Irish intriguer the Duke of
Ormonde, Prince Rupert of the Rhine, or perhaps even
James, Duke of York. The Bouchoute House was getting
ready for the arrival of someone of the utmost importance
to Charles Stuart's cause, coming back to Bruges to fetch
for themselves the money brought there by Lady Hildred
Beaumont. It was not so much, in itself, the imminent
return to the city of such a person that bothered Seeker,
as the fact that Marchmont Ellis had very signally failed
to inform him of it.

Even so, Seeker might have closed his eyes and slept,
in the knowledge that the best manner of his proceeding
would be clearer to him when he woke, had it not been
for the letter in his possession that had been passed to him
tonight by his landlady on his return from De Garre. It
was in Lawrence Ingolby's hand.

With a degree of foreboding, Seeker broke the seal and
opened it.

August, 1658, Clifford's Inn

I waste no time with niceties, that I might catch the next posts.

You should know that Maria has at last been dissuaded from attempting to make her way to you in Bruges, not, you will understand, from any common sense that has been spoken to her by myself or Elias – the woman is beyond the reach of such argument, and how you think you will manage her is beyond me. Between us we had laid before her, in no uncertain terms, and with a degree of embellishment on Elias's part, the dangers to anyone attempting to journey in Flanders whilst Cromwell's forces still fight it out with the Spaniards and the Duke of York, to say nothing of the added complexities of the French.

Seeker had smiled at that. Lawrence was far down the road to becoming a lawyer if he could speak of the carnage involving Turenne's troops as 'complexities'. He'd read on.

It was Dorcas, of all people, who brought her to a better understanding of the likely consequences of the course she was set upon. She it was who made Maria see what might befall her should she be taken by some foreign force in her attempts to get to Bruges, and then she laid before her quite plainly the fate of women decreed to be camp followers. She asked if Maria would have you have that on your conscience. As if your welfare was of the chief importance! And, fearing that might not be enough, Dorcas added in for good measure that Maria's arrival in Bruges might alert 'nefarious individuals' to the fact that you were firstly, not dead, and secondly, in that city.

As to Elias, since the birth of his child – a girl named Hope, and healthy, thank God – he is more set than ever on Massachusetts. He has secured passage for himself, Grace and the baby, Samuel and Maria (whether she wishes it or not) on George Tavener's ship, The Blade, *on its last sailing of the year for Boston. He can stomach no longer the England that he sees – the shutting down of Parliament, the disregarding of Justice and proper Law, the patent greed and power-mongering of those who claim to speak in the name of the people. He's off to make a new world. Good luck to him, but I'm staying put, for whatever's coming.*

And there is something coming. Marvell has told me. Cromwell's shut himself up in Hampton Court – Thurloe's put it about that it's for grief of his daughter, but Marvell tells me the grief has just about finished him and now he's truly ill. The Committee of State hovers around him and urges him to name a successor. A successor! God knows what will happen if he dies but have no fears for Manon and Dorcas – I'm going nowhere.

Seeker read over the letter twice. Only the last sentence gave him any hope. For all Lawrence Ingolby looked like a reed that might be blown over by the wind, that was deceptive. An early childhood with a feckless mother had taught him to handle himself like a street rat. But also, Lawrence was clever and Lawrence was loyal. There was no one he would sooner trust with the safety of his daughter. Even so, should Cromwell die now, the struggle for control between army and Parliament would make of England a new bloodbath. Seeker needed to get home. And he needed to get home soon. It was already late August, and he knew George Tavener's last ship of the year would leave on its voyage across the Atlantic before the end of the month. He crushed the letter in his hands. He needed this business of Bruges to be finished with and he needed to get home.

FIFTEEN

Hiding Places

Thomas Faithly had breakfasted early and left the Bouchoute House before any of his companions were awake. He had never slept well in the heat and was glad at last to be out in the light rather than tossing and turning through the darkness of the night. The impending arrival of the expected visitor to the Bouchoute House was also preying on his mind. At least out of doors the breeze could be felt, and the sun was just starting to creep up over the horizon. He wanted time to think and space to do it in. He headed outwards from the Markt towards the walls and water that ringed the city.

A good bit before its outer edges, Bruges became a garden city, and the bustle of town life gave way to the sounds of countryside. The rhythm of myriad mill blades as they creaked in the wind above the canal relaxed him and helped the clarity of his thinking as he walked. Rumours had reached Bruges that Cromwell was ill. And then what? Perhaps God was finally taking issue with things in England, perhaps the tide was indeed about to turn. He had no doubt that that would be Mr Longfellow's message when he came. Perhaps Thomas would at last be able to go home.

He'd been following the outer ring of walls and windmills of the city for some time and was almost at the Smedenpoort in the south-west when, to his surprise, he saw George Barton emerge from a street off to his left. He lifted an arm and called out, 'Barton.'

Barton appeared not to have heard him and so Thomas called again. This time, after the briefest of hesitations, his fellow Englishman did seem to realise that it was he who was being hailed and looked his way, smiling and lifting his arm in response a moment later.

'What brings you to this part of town at so early an hour?'

'I might ask you the same question,' George answered.

Thomas told him briefly of his restlessness, and his desire to be away from the hubbub of town.

'Then we are afflicted by the same ailment,' George said.

They walked on together in companionable silence for a few minutes and then Thomas said, 'Do you miss home, Barton?'

George stopped for a moment, as if to consider. 'Not unduly,' he said at last. 'My father is long dead, and I never really got on with my mother.'

'You have no wife or sweetheart waiting for your return?'

'No,' said George, and walked on, as if he had nothing more to say on the matter. But then he stopped again. 'I did love a girl once, a long, long time ago. Before the war, even, if you can imagine that. Her father had the living of the church in our local village. My father had the patronage of the church and so my mother regarded the vicar and his family as little more than menials. When she learned of my affection for Elizabeth, she made sure her father would never allow my suit. He even refused me permission to see her. But even that was not enough for my mother. I came back from Cambridge the following summer to find a new vicar in the pulpit and Elizabeth and her father gone.'

Thomas, who knew from his own family how manipulative some could be in matters of the heart that didn't suit them, murmured some words of sympathy.

'Thank you, my friend,' said George, 'but I got over it long ago. No doubt I'll find myself a suitable wife. If such a thing exists, when the present struggle is over.'

'Possibly even here in Bruges?' suggested Thomas.

'I doubt such a woman is to be found in Bruges,' replied George.

Something in his tone was shaded by that rigidity, that hint of Puritanism, that Thomas had seen in George Barton before. And, perhaps, in fact, he was right, given the only women other than their own servants, with whom they had contact in Bruges were inhabitants either of the convent or the brothel. And George, he recalled, had politely declined any invitations they had made that he might accompany them to the House of Lamentations.

After they had breakfasted at a tavern by the Minnewater they continued their walk around the outer walls until they had passed the Kruispoort and found themselves at the top of Carmersstraat. 'This is where I must leave you, Barton,' Thomas said. 'Unless you will join me for a while at the Schuttersgilde? Ellis, Daunt and Glenroe are to meet me there, but I don't expect them for an hour yet.'

Thomas felt awkward at the manner of his invitation, but the truth was that Glenroe had taken against George and refused to trust him in their company. George Barton saved him further embarrassment by declining his invitation. 'I hoped to gain admittance to the Engels Klooster there,' he said, pointing down the street. 'I believe His Majesty was in the habit of worshipping there when he was in town, and I hoped I might similarly make my devotions.'

'Mind out for Sister Janet, then. Her tongue is as sharp as a butcher's cleaver. But I am sorry you will not come in with me. Glenroe says you have the keenest eye with a bow that he has seen in a long time.'

Barton laughed. 'If you should have learned one thing in this city, Faithly, surely it would be never to believe a word that Irishman says.' Still laughing, he continued down the street in the direction of the Engels Klooster, as Thomas turned to knock at the door of the Schuttersgilde.

Seeker had watched Ellis, Daunt and Glenroe leave their house together and cross the Markt a good while after Thomas Faithly had done the same thing, although Faithly had gone off in a different direction. Marchmont Ellis had a haunted, slightly distracted look to him, and trailed some-what behind the others. Seeker had been of a mind to summon him last night, and ask why he had not informed him of the imminent visit to Bruges of a senior Royalist, but to have called him out so late would have risked exposure that might have been too damaging in its scope. As the three passed, Seeker moved slightly out of the doorway of the baker's shop where he had positioned himself. He made sure Ellis saw him as they passed, and the man seemed then to shrink in upon himself before hurrying on. Seeker had seen it before, an agent taking fright; much worse in a double agent, a man who had been turned and persuaded to betray his first cause. Such men – and women – risked the vengeance of both sides, should they be found out. He wondered how long it was before Marchmont Ellis broke completely and attempted to run.

Whatever the Cavaliers were about so early, it was the ideal opportunity for Seeker to make another visit to the Bouchoute House. He lost no time in presenting himself at the kitchen door of the house and being admitted. His carpenter's bag and a reminder that he was here to fix the broken lock on the cabinet in the library were all that were required to get past what passed for security in this shambolic household.

The library was much as he had left it – apart from one thing. On his previous visit there had been a gap where Walton's *Compleat Angler* had sat, but the book now appeared to have been returned to its place. Seeker picked up the volume and flicked through it. It was the same edition of the book he had handed to Ellis for use as a cypher, and in fact the same copy. He wondered to what extent this fool had exposed himself in order to retrieve it.

The fixing of a new lock on the bookcase was so simple a job that Seeker had it done in minutes. That job done, he quickly returned his tools to his bag. He then proceeded through the bedchambers on the upper floor, searching. In the chamber which Ellis shared with Daunt he found a bag ready-packed with items of clothing, pistol and powder, and papers. Clearly, a sudden journey was anticipated. Seeker sighed and removed the papers. He had plenty of other things to do, but he was going to have to prise this fellow from his companions today and explain to him exactly what was going to happen, and what wasn't. Closing the door to the bedchamber softly behind him, he moved on. It wasn't a packed bag he was looking for, but a hidden safe.

Seeker passed with speed from one upper chamber to another. He'd long since checked the lower floors of the house for such an item and found them wanting. It was on the top floor, in a tiny room beneath the rafters, that he finally found it: a false fireplace with no real chimney. There was a strange pattern to the bricks in the back, and it was the fourth he tested that gave way to reveal a knob to be turned. At the third attempt, Seeker turned it sufficiently far in the right direction to hear the expected click. At that, the entire back of the small, false hearth swung towards him to reveal a cavity in which had been placed the locked wooden chest brought from England by Hildred

Beaumont and carried back from Damme by those who had more concern for the money inside it than for the life of the old woman who had been so determined to take it to the King.

Seeker pulled the chest from its cavity and made a swift assessment of the locks. The chisel he carried in his bag would have dealt with them in short order, but he would buy himself more time if the chest appeared undisturbed, and so he employed once more his set of special keys. Soon, he was lifting open the lid of the chest to reveal as much money as he had ever seen in one place, and a small bag containing more jewels than any one woman should have access to. From his carpenter's bag he removed the stones he had placed there that morning, along with a soft hessian sack. Making as little noise as possible, Seeker moved most of the coins into his bag, then loosening the laces on his jerkin he began to slip as many jewels as he could down into the pockets created by the false lining. He then placed the stones from the bag in the chest and covered them up with the coins and jewels that he had reserved for that purpose. It was a simple deception, and would not bear close inspection, but it might cause some delay in the discovery of the theft and gain him some extra time, should he need it.

His carpenter's bag buckled, and the laces on his jerkin pulled tight again, Seeker returned the box to its cavity and closed over the false brick door at the back of the hearth. He was about to leave when he heard footsteps coming up the last, narrow flight of steps to this attic floor. Slinging the strap of his bag over his shoulder, Seeker strode to the window and forced it open, clapping his hands as soon as he'd done so. Even as the door handle turned and the door opened towards him, a cacophony of squawking and flapping of feathers broke out just outside as disturbed pigeons vented their protest.

Seeker turned towards the door to see Edward Daunt step through it, followed by the flustered chambermaid.

'Who the Devil are you?' demanded Daunt, drawing his sword and brandishing it in the small room.

Seeker held up his hands in a gesture of peaceful intent. 'Carpenter, sir,' he said.

Without lowering his sword, Daunt looked round at the housemaid. 'Is this true?'

The girl confirmed that it was. 'He was to fix the lock on the library cabinet.' Positioned as he was, his attention all on Seeker, Daunt gave no sign of having noticed the degree of suspicion with which her small black eyes regarded Seeker as she said it.

Seeker nodded. 'The library window was open and a bird flew in, a pigeon. Straight out of the door and up the stairs it went, and the Devil's own job I had getting it cornered and out at this window again.'

Daunt appeared unconvinced, but the maid nodded at every word, and was soon off on her own tirade about her difficulties with birds getting into the house, and the mess they made. She was well into an accusation that Daunt himself was responsible for that, as he left crumbs of food in many inappropriate places, when the Cavalier silenced her with a curt, 'Quiet!'

Gone was the cheery, befuddled Cavalier, and in his place was a man who had spent the last sixteen years measuring the margins between life and death, and who had learned to trust no one unless he was looking at his own reflection in a glass.

No one in the room moved. Daunt's eyes went over to the fireplace. 'Take him down to the kitchens,' he said to the maid. 'And you,' he said to Seeker, 'go nowhere until I come back down.'

Seeker said nothing more but followed the maid out and down the steps to the next floor. Once they had gone through the door that led to the servants' stairs and he had shut it behind them, the girl stopped. Without turning around she said, 'There was no pigeon, John Carpenter. No pigeon muck on the stairs, so no pigeon.'

Seeker considered arguing, but instead said, 'You didn't say that to him.'

The girl shrugged and continued on down the dark stairway. 'I am a servant, that's all. And I like you better than I like him.'

They weren't long back in the kitchen when Daunt appeared from the main hall. He must have had time to do little more than open the secret safe door in the attic wall in order to check that the chest was still there. He looked at Seeker. 'All right, you can leave now. But don't come back here.'

'And what if further repairs are required in the house?' asked the cook with some indignation.

'You find another carpenter,' said Daunt over his shoulder as he turned and left the kitchen.

Seeker sat a minute longer at the bench by the door, finishing off the half tankard of beer the cook had given him, before thanking her and walking out into the yard and then out of the gate, carrying away with him in his carpenter's bag almost all of the Beaumont fortune.

Lady Anne had spent the morning in the chapel. Any who saw her there, on her knees, head bent, would have thought her deep in prayer, but Lady Anne no longer prayed. God, she thought, was too beset by the endless petitions of Cromwell and his Puritans to have the leisure to listen to her. So Anne did not pray, but whilst the nuns intoned their prayers, their words rising and falling in centuries' old rhythms that Anne had never heard until she came to Bruges, she thought. Marchmont Ellis. A traitor to the King and to his comrades. Anne's problem was how to transmit this information to those who needed to know it, and then to those who had sent her here. It was to have been so simple. Lady Hildred had been spoken of amongst the leaders of the Great Trust as one whose loyalty to the King was utterly beyond question. With very little difficulty, and very little questioning on the part of Lady Hildred herself, Anne had been placed in her household and recommended as a fit companion for the Lady's planned flight to the continent.

Anne had been assured that when she had identified the traitor, she might reveal her true purpose in journeying to Flanders to the older woman She would have the ear of Lady Hildred, and Lady Hildred would have the ear of the only person who could be trusted for an absolute certainty: the King himself. As to her contacts in England, and the matter of her further instructions, Lady Anne was to have communicated through Lady Hildred's own posts, their passage across the sea facilitated, in as far as they needed it to be, to get out of the Flemish ports by the King's passes, or through his sister the Princess of Orange's court in the Hague.

Now though, Lady Hildred was gone, and with her Anne's direct access both to the King and the lines of communication back to England that the old woman's many connections had made possible. Now there was just Anne, holding the information she had come for, without knowing who in all of this city or the wider ranks of the dispossessed Royalists abroad she might trust. She had hoped, as she'd made her bedraggled way back to Bruges after the shooting on the road to Damme, that she might seek the help of Sister Janet, but Sister Janet was far too much in commune with the Spanish, whom the Stuart supporters had learned to their cost would put the slightest of their own interests against the greatest of the exiled English King. There was some tension between Sister Janet and Evan Glenroe, and Anne did not feel she could fully trust Sister Janet until she knew for certain what lay at the heart of it. Neither could Anne be certain that Glenroe, nor any of Ellis's other comrades in the Bouchoute House, were complicit with him in his treachery and deceptions. She would have to find some other conduit for the information she now held. To make everything infinitely worse, Marchmont Ellis must now know that the person who had stolen his coded book in the first place was a sister in the Engels Klooster. Anne's one consolation was that the bookseller swore he hadn't told him which one.

Crossing herself in imitation of the nuns around her, Anne finally got off her knees and followed the other women out of the chapel. As they went off to their various duties, Anne hung behind to observe Sister Janet. She had noticed that, every day after morning mass, Janet went straight away to the room in which she had first presented Anne with Ruth Jones and the instruction that she was to help smuggle the young woman out of Bruges. Sometimes, when Sister Janet emerged from this room, her fingers would be stained with ink. Once or twice, Lady Anne had seen tiny blobs of melted red wax that had evidently been spilled onto Sister Janet's robes without the nun having noticed. Always, always, Janet took care to lock the door after she came out of that little room, and always, always, she made a point of checking twice that she had done so. Anne had deduced two things from this. Firstly, that Sister Janet was writing something in that room, and secondly, that she absolutely did not want anyone else in the convent to know what she was writing. Anne had tried to recall exactly what she had seen the one time she had been permitted access to the place, but all she could remember were boxes, old habits, and then her own astonishment as she was presented with the terrified young woman with the badly scarred face whom she was enjoined to smuggle to Damme.

Whatever Sister Janet was up to in that small room, if Anne was left with only the old English nun to trust in, she would have to be certain that she could. And if it turned out that Sister Janet did have access to clandestine channels of communication, all the better. Given Janet's frequent meetings with Father Felipe, there was a risk that those channels of communication were run by the Jesuit order. Though far from desirable, this was a risk Anne would have to take. She glanced at the lock to Sister Janet's special room as she passed on her way to the gardens, where she was again to work for the morning. The lock did not appear to be complex, and her lessons from a York locksmith during her exile in that city had provided her with certain skills. All that was required was the opportunity.

The sun had risen far enough in the sky that much of the convent's garden was already in its glare. The older sisters were assigned work in the shade of the walls and the younger out in the open. Anne herself had been assigned weeding duties along the herb borders, where she would do 'least harm'. Sister Euphemia was night and day alert to anything that might 'do harm' to her gardens, and the more recently a new arrival had come to the convent, the greater the harm of which they were suspected to be capable.

Smiling as she thought of this, Anne bent to her pleasant task. One day she might have her own herb garden, when the King was on his throne and the world had at last been set back on its right footing. A short while later her attention was taken by the unexpected sound of male voices at the far end of the garden.

Anne looked up and saw that two men had begun to dig around the roots of a stubborn old ivy known to all familiar with Sister Euphemia's views as 'the work of the Devil'. Sister Euphemia would have no truck with 'choking, creeping things' and had at last persuaded Mother Superior to sanction the removal of what was, to her, a very old enemy. The man directing operations was Gust, who had charge of the convent stables; the other had his back to her and only when he turned slightly did she realise that it was the man she had seen in the street the other day in attendance upon the Irish Cavalier, Evan Glenroe. Anne didn't know what to make of this. She bent her head again to her work, her mind working furiously at the question of whether she might trust this man.

She worked her way the length of the path, keeping a wary eye on the new Englishman and considering the problem of Marchmont Ellis, and what her next steps in the matter should be. She knew, of course, what would happen in the end – Ellis would die. Ellis deserved to die, he had betrayed countless friends and comrades and consigned them to barbaric ends, so Anne had no qualms as to his ultimate fate. What she was not certain of, and what she had not thought would be required, was that she was capable of doing it herself. The plan had been simple, so it had seemed. She would report her findings to the King and the King would appoint those who would serve justice on the traitor, but just like her means of communication, her access to the King was gone. Even if Sister Janet was to be trusted, how could she expect an old nun to know where an assassin was to be found? Anne realised she would either have to kill Ellis herself, or persuade one of the other inhabitants of the Bouchoute House to do it for her. This brought her thoughts again to the new Englishman, and then, as if her thoughts had summoned him, she became aware of his shadow over the path in front of her. She looked up. Again, as she had the first time she'd seen him, she felt a wave of something, as if she knew him from somewhere else.

'I have startled you, Sister,' he said.

'Not at all,' she replied, wiping her hands on her apron,

The man looked a little awkward. 'I . . . I wanted to apologise.'

'Apologise?' she asked.

'For the behaviour of my – associate – towards you and the older sister the other day.'

Lady Anne was standing now. 'I fear His Majesty's subjects will spend a great deal of time apologising if they take the behaviour of all of their comrades upon themselves. Sir Evan's behaviour came as no surprise to me, and I'd warrant he's not the worst that Sister Janet has encountered.'

'I am sorry for it all the same, but,' he hesitated and looked around, before lowering his voice, 'for all Glenroe can be coarse in his manner, you would do well to pay heed to what he says.'

'What in particular?' said Anne, not quite liking the peremptory tone he had used.

The man looked about him again. 'That a woman coming to the Engels Klooster and associating with Sister Janet would need her wits about her. That women who have come here for help have ended up in the brothel . . .'

'Brothel!' exclaimed Anne, only remembering at the last minute to lower her voice. One of the younger sisters looked up. 'Yes, thank you,' said Anne in a louder voice. 'If you come to the stable block, I will show you the one I wish you to move.'

The man understood immediately and followed Anne across the lawn and out of the gardens to the stable yard.

Checking first that they were not seen, Anne said, 'Who are you?'

'My name is George Barton,' he said. 'I've been fighting for some time in the forces under the Duke of York. I came to Bruges masquerading as an officer looking to add my services to those of His Majesty's subjects in Bruges.'

'Masquerading?' said Anne, feeling an increasing sensation of fear.

George Barton took a half-step closer to her. 'It has become known, amongst the Duke's adherents, that there is a traitor in the circles attendant on the King. Information which can only have emanated from those surrounding him in Bruges has been reaching the ears of Cromwell's intelligencers, and good men are dying because of it.'

Anne felt such a wave of relief go through her that she sank down on a bench by the stable door, took in a long breath and said, 'Thank God!'

George Barton gave a puzzled smile. 'You are not shocked?'

She shook her head. 'I am surprised, I think, but not shocked. This is the best news I have had since I came to this city.' And then she told him of her own identity and, careful to leave out the names of those who had sent her, her own true purpose in Bruges.

'I had begun to suspect as much,' he said.

'What? But how?'

He hesitated. 'I fear you are suspected. Faithly, Ellis, Daunt and Glenroe, they know – I cannot tell how – that a she-intelligencer has been sent to find out the traitor in their midst. They each wish to find out her identity – though of course, with different reasons. For myself I have found little welcome, only mistrust among those who should be comrades, and suspicion of everyone else. I think you must look out in particular for Evan Glenroe.'

Anne shook her head. 'It is not Glenroe, unless of course, he is in league with him.'

'With whom?'

'Marchmont Ellis. He it is who has been passing details of our friends' plans to Thurloe's people. Whether he is working alone or not, I don't yet know, but I mean to find out.'

George Barton's face registered his shock. 'Ellis? I would never have guessed it. Have you communicated this information to our friends at home?'

Anne shook her head and explained to him the difficulties that had been caused her as a result of Lady Hildred's death. 'I cannot tell you of my relief to have encountered you.'

'Nor mine at encountering you,' he said. 'I think you will have saved me a great deal of time and difficulty. The question is how should we proceed from here?'

'Tell me about Evan Glenroe,' she said. 'I am not altogether certain that he is not in some way involved. He was with Ellis when he picked up the book.'

'The book?'

She flicked the question away. 'It doesn't matter for now but tell me again what Evan Glenroe said. Tell me what has made you suspicious of him.'

George Barton appeared to choose his words with care. 'Well,' he began, 'he is clearly determined on discouraging too great a familiarity with this convent and appears deeply suspicious of Sister Janet in particular. So wild are his accusations that I would say Glenroe exaggerates or imagines sinister events that never happened, but I feel I should warn you of them at any rate.'

'You still do not tell me what he says,' said Anne.

'It is what he began upon the other day, out in the street. About the woman who came here on her way to the King and found herself the target of an assassin's musket; about young women who come here for help going missing or finding themselves in brothels. He virtually accuses Sister Janet of procurement.'

'He is wrong,' said Anne. 'I cannot speak for what happened to Lady Hildred. She was Sister Janet's childhood friend, and although there appears to have been little love between them, Janet took her loss hard. She had instruction from Damme to pack up Lady Hildred's belongings for sale to raise funds in His Majesty's cause, but only today she took care to set aside a locket she knew had been dear to the old woman, for it contained an image of Lady Hildred's estranged son.'

George Barton looked on the point of saying something, but Anne was determined that no misunderstanding should remain. 'And as for young girls, I cannot speak of those who were here before, but I can assure you, the young woman Glenroe spoke of whose brother he said had died – she was sent to no brothel but got away safe.'

'Are you certain of this? I mean . . .'

At that moment, Gust the stable hand came in looking for George Barton. He glanced suspiciously at Anne, as if knowing her habit and wimple were but a ruse, then spoke to Barton. 'You will find food laid out in the guest refectory, in return for your labours.' Then he looked at Anne, 'And you best get yourself elsewhere, Sister. Mother Superior doesn't hold with you women fraternising with the outside.'

George Barton looked as if he might argue but then

thought the better of it. 'Of course. But you'll let me know if I can be of further help shifting things for the sisters?'

Gust nodded and George Barton, with one more look to Anne as if he would say something, somewhat reluctantly walked off in the direction of the kitchens. Anne closed her eyes. At last, there was someone she could trust.

SIXTEEN

Sister Janet Watched

Sister Janet watched from an upper window as the man she had seen helping Gust dig out the ivy walked through the kitchen garden on the path to the street door. She would have to have a word with Gust: she did not like this coming and going of people she didn't know. Bad enough with people she did. As she watched him approach the door, the man removed his hat and wiped a sleeve across his forehead. It was indeed a hot day, but something in the gesture, in the way he walked, seemed familiar. It was the man who had been out in the town with Evan Glenroe. There was possibly something else, but Sister Janet didn't have the time to stand here and enquire of herself what that other thing might be. If it was indeed the man who had been trailing around Bruges in Glenroe's wake, he should not have been at the Engels Klooster. Glenroe should have made his warnings to stay away clearer. She had warned Father Felipe that the Irishman might prove too volatile a character to admit to their enterprise, but Felipe had not been inclined to take advice from a woman, and the results of that carelessness were beginning to manifest themselves. Too many strangers were arriving at the convent's gates these days. Strangers, and not such strangers. With every newcomer from home, Sister Janet could feel the walls of her convent, so long her sanctuary, move a little closer in on her. The man Barton passed through the door in the outer wall and Sister Janet turned away from the window, her hand going automatically to the key to her special room and tightening around it.

It was his second time inside the House of Lamentations, and this time Seeker was permitted to go alone down into the cellars to carry out the repairs he had been engaged to make. After he'd made two or three trips down the steps with tools and materials, the servants stopped paying any attention to him. He set up his workbench and sawed a couple of lengths of wood as evidence that he had begun the work he was here to carry out. He went over to the pile of barrels behind which he had found a makeshift bedchamber on his last visit. This time he was confronted only with mouse droppings and disturbed dust. Whoever had used this hideaway was clearly not expected back. He then took one of the lit torches set into the wall to help him in his work and went to the tunnel door he had discovered on his last visit here. From his bag, he took out the key that had worked in the lock last time. Soon, he was turning the iron ring and pulling the door towards himself to reveal the entrance to the tunnel.

Seeker moved quickly. The tunnel went straight ahead, without curving, and without any passageways veering off to the side. As he had judged on his last visit, it appeared to go directly beneath the canal. Moving carefully through it, Seeker's mind went back to the mineshafts and tunnels he had been in in sieges during the war, the fear of imminent collapse, suffocation. He could sense the weight of the water above him and was glad eventually to find himself at the other end.

Here he was confronted by two doors. First he tried that to the left, which by means of a turning stairway and outer passageway led out onto Hoedenmakersstraat. Seeker retraced his steps and tried the other door. It was large and heavy and the ring handle rusted from lack of use, but it eventually turned. He pulled it towards him as softly as he could, the creaks from its hinges echoing around him. When he saw what was on the other side he thought for a moment that he had made a mistake and that he was back in the cellar of the House of Lamentations. The smell was the same – old barrels, spilt wine on the packed earth floor, cheeses hanging. He took a step in and raised his torch slightly and listened. The noises coming from above were of a different order from those in the House of Lamentations: lower, less hurried. A door opened at the top of a stairway at the far end of this cellar. Seeker stepped back, pulling the door almost to but leaving a small gap to look through. A light preceded whoever it was coming down the stairs. More lights were lit. A quiet, contented humming passed through the brightening room, and into Seeker's narrow sightline came an Augustinian monk. Seeker let out a long, slow breath. The tales of an ancient passageway connecting this Priory with the former convent of the House of Lamentations were true, and not just the work of some salacious imagination. Seeker thought again of the tale the girl Beatte had told him of the nun murdered long ago by her obsessive lover-monk. He thought again of the dead body of Bartlett Jones, fished out of the canal beneath which this tunnel passed. He thought of the make-shift bedchamber beyond the door on the other side of this tunnel, the girl who Bartlett Jones had come looking for. Had he found her, or had someone else found him first? From the respective conditions of the doors, Seeker was certain that anyone using this tunnel as access to or exit from the House of Lamentations was coming not from the Augustinian priory but from out on the street.

The monk finished filling his flagon from a barrel halfway down the room and took a quick swig for himself before retrieving his torch from the bracket where he had left it and disappearing back up the stairs, still contentedly humming. Once the cellar was again in darkness and Seeker had heard the clicking shut of the upper door, he pulled his own door the last few inches shut and made his way back along the tunnel to finish his work in the House of Lamentations.

Anne was becoming used to the mass now. The other sisters were too intent upon their own devotions to notice any strangeness in her own behaviour in the chapel. But in truth, she had learned to mimic what they did and any onlooker would have thought her little different to the rest of them. Only in the slight hesitations, the slight uncertainty about when to stand and when to sit or to kneel, when to begin the next chorused response, might anyone have suspected that Anne was not as the other nuns were, and even in those, repeated practice and exposure were making her better.

A quick glance at the choir revealed to her that Sister Janet was not in her usual place. Previously, this would not have worried Anne, but after hearing from her encounter with George Barton the insinuations Evan Glenroe had made about Janet, not knowing her whereabouts made Anne feel ill at ease. The mass seemed to her to drag on interminably today, and so great was her hurry to get out when it was over that she almost forgot to bless herself with holy water on leaving the chapel. The nuns in front of her seemed to be moving even more slowly than usual on their way to the refectory. On passing the small room in which Sister Janet had presented her with Ruth Jones, Anne tried the handle as discreetly as she could. It would hardly shift – the door was locked. Anne moved on, wondering whether Sister Janet would appear for lunch, and if not, how soon she might escape to go in search of her. Before they reached the refectory doors, Anne heard a noise back down the corridor and turned her head enough to see Sister Janet emerge from the locked room, quickly lock it again, check that she had done so, and then go off in the other direction, her outdoors cape tied at her neck. She had a small satchel gripped under her arm and a resolute look on her face. Anne stepped out of her place in the line and told the sister walking beside her that she had left her rosary in the chapel and would be going back for it.

Hovering at the chapel door until all the sisters had filed after Mother Superior into the refectory, Anne swiftly went to her own small cell to put on her own outdoors cape and then left through the garden door. It didn't take her long to spot Sister Janet's lumpy little frame making its way down Carmersstraat. Anne wondered if Sister Janet might be going back to St Walburgakerk, to commune in some way over she knew not what with Father Felipe, but instead of turning left at the bottom of the street, she carried on straight over the Carmersbrug and began to make her way along Gouden-Handrei. She lost sight of Janet briefly, only to catch sight of her again bustling across the Augustinians' Bridge. Anne pulled back and concealed herself behind some greenery overhanging the canal. Once over the bridge, Sister Janet continued along by the side of the Augustinian priory.

Carefully, taking pains to conceal herself amongst groups of people on the street, Anne watched Sister Janet pass along beneath the walls of the priory. And then she disappeared. It was ridiculous. Anne had been watching her the whole time, and Janet had not paused to knock at a door or gate. Not caring now for her visibility or otherwise, Anne hurried over to the other side. There was no door in the Augustinians' wall where Janet had disappeared, but a little further on from where Anne had last seen her was the opening onto a dark, narrow passageway. She was about to step into the passageway when a hand caught her arm lightly from behind.

'Really, Sister, I would not advise you to go down there. It is no place for a respectable young woman. Come, let me escort you back to the Engels Klooster.'

It was Father Felipe.

SEVENTEEN

Jesuitical

Lady Anne Winter had endured many discomforts over the last sixteen years, since the wars between King and Parliament had unleashed themselves upon England, but the walk back up to the convent from the Augustinian priory in the company of Father Felipe was one of the most difficult. That the Spanish priest spoke flawless English made it all the more so, for she could not hide behind difficulties of language to avoid his insinuating questions.

'I fear you have got lost, Sister,' he had opened with, once she had conceded to herself that there was nothing to do but go along with him.

'I think I may have done. I had meant to go to the Markt but must have taken a wrong turn somewhere. I thought I saw Sister Janet turn up this street. I hoped she might help me find my way. I must have been mistaken.'

'Yes, I think you must. Sister Janet, as you know, rarely stirs from the Engels Klooster and the precinct of Sint-Anna. I would advise you to follow her example. There are still a few soldiers in the town, and the English ones, as I am sure *you* know, Sister, are of the most desperate sort.'

'I have not found the soldiers of one nation to be any more dreadful than those of another, Father,' she replied.

'For which we must indeed be thankful,' he said, touching his crucifix to his lips, while never taking his eyes from her. Something in the way he looked at her made the hairs on her arms stand up, and her scalp prickle. Not even on her wedding night to John Winter, whom she had not been able to love, had Anne felt as exposed in the company of a man as she did with this Jesuit priest.

Anne turned as if to cross the Augustinians' Bridge, and so go on to the Markt, but Father Felipe stopped her by raising his voice ever so slightly. 'I don't think it a good idea either, Sister, that you should go alone to the Markt, or indeed wander anywhere in the town. Whatever it is that you require I'm sure can be supplied at the convent.'

'I intended to browse the booksellers' booths,' she answered.

Although he could scarcely have been any older than she was, Father Felipe assumed the concerned expression of a disappointed uncle. 'That, most of all, I would counsel you against. The convent library is more than adequately provided with devotional works approved by Mother Superior and myself.'

Anne did not trust herself to respond, and the rest of their journey up to the Engels Klooster was made in silence, save for the frequent times it behoved Father Felipe to acknowledge a sycophantic greeting or to dispense a blessing. The further from the inner canals and their summer odours they got, the more Anne became aware of the aroma of citrus and sandalwood that habitually surrounded the priest. It contrasted with the heavy garlic and wine of his breath which was offensive even in the open air. An image she could not banish presented itself to her mind of the Spaniard applying the fragrant oils as he dressed in the morning. It was with the greatest relief that she finally passed through the doorway into the convent garden. She thanked Father Felipe as briefly and as politely as she could, and made to go, but for the second time that afternoon he placed a hand on her arm. This time, the touch was not light.

'You are but lately arrived in Bruges, *Sister*, and it is understandable that life in England has not prepared you for the proprieties expected of a religious in His Majesty of Spain's dominions, but you must take care that you do not do anything to jeopardise your place here. As you know, I am confessor to Mother Superior and several of the more senior sisters. I sense that you also would profit from my counsel. I will return tomorrow, to hear your confession.' He leaned a little closer to her and she could feel his warm, wine-soaked breath on her. For a very brief moment, Father Felipe's supercilious mask slipped, and she was confronted by a man barely in control of his lust. 'Tomorrow, *Lady Anne*, you will know the benefit of unburdening yourself to me.'

Anne only just reached the latrines before vomiting. One

of the novices, a slight, fair girl whose father had sent her here for lack of any better idea, appeared behind her, offering her a ladle of water from a jug taken from the well. Anne accepted the water then wiped her mouth on the edge of her cloak. 'Thank you.'

'That's all right,' said the girl, leaving without lifting her head. 'Father Felipe confesses me too.'

Seeker could feel the anger rising in him as the time passed. He had told Ellis to be here by two and no later. It had taken him the best part of the morning to complete the repairs to the cellar shelving in the House of Lamentations, and those hours of thought had done little to make clearer to him what might have befallen Bartlett Jones. He was in no mood to be kept waiting by someone of Ellis's degree of insignificance. Every hour wasted was an hour longer before he could begin his journey back to England. The bells of Sint-Gillis had already struck the quarter hour when Ellis finally appeared in the back courtyard of 't Oud Handbogenhof, the hostelry just a few minutes' walk from Seeker's own lodging.

'You're late,' said Seeker as Ellis took up a bench next to his.

'I was at the Schuttersgilde,' said Ellis. 'It is not an easy thing to get away.'

'It's as easy as putting down your bow and walking away,' said Seeker.

Ellis looked at him with an expression he had not quite

managed to banish in his dealings with Seeker, an expression of some social superiority that he still did not understand counted for nothing in their present relationship.

'There are modes of behaviour, civility . . .'

Seeker put up a hand. 'Spare me,' he said. 'The only mode of behaviour you need concern yourself with is the one that says when I whistle you come running, understood?'

Ellis flushed red but said nothing.

'Right, then. I want you to tell me what's going on at the Bouchoute House.'

'The . . . what? Nothing.'

'Nothing? Don't try telling me you all sit there reading your prayer books waiting for Death to come knocking.'

Ellis was alarmed. 'Death? Why – no. I mean, there is nothing out of the ordinary "going on" at the Bouchoute House. Our efforts to find the killer of Lady Hildred have come to nothing, as you yourself predicted they would. We exist from day to day on whatever we can beg or borrow, wait for news of home, take what exercise we can, allow ourselves what entertainments we can. There is talk of moving on.'

'You'll move nowhere without my say-so,' said Seeker.

'But here we have scarcely enough to keep body and soul together,' protested Ellis.

'I'd weep for you if I'd nothing better to do.' Seeker drained his tankard and leaned forwards. 'But are you certain there's nothing *out of the ordinary* going on? There seems to be a lot of bustle and toing and froing amongst the servants for nothing out of the ordinary.'

Ellis attempted to meet Seeker's eyes. 'I don't know. They're clearing things out, I suppose. Selling unwanted furniture, perhaps. The housekeeper doesn't tell much to tenants behind with their rent.'

'And that's all, is it?'

Ellis nodded, more confident now. 'That's all.'

'Right,' said Seeker, standing up and putting on his hat. 'I'll be off.'

'But, what?' said Ellis. 'What about this woman?'

'What woman?' said Seeker.

'The she-intelligencer, sent to uncover me?'

Seeker shrugged. 'I can't help you.'

'What?' Ellis's face was a picture of disbelief.

Having said all that he intended to, Seeker turned away and left the inn. As he walked down the street, he was absolutely certain now of one thing: Marchmont Ellis was not to be trusted. He had given the double agent the perfect opportunity to tell him of 'Mr Longfellow's' intended clandestine visit to Bruges, and Ellis had not taken it. Seeker had never entirely trusted him, and now he had evidence that he had been right. Ellis had finally crossed the Rubicon: from one who watched for Seeker he had become one who would be very closely watched.

Seeker had work to attend to next for a comfortable English merchant, long settled near the Prinsenhof. On the way there he would have time to give thought to the other troubling revelation of this morning, his sighting of Lady Anne Winter, in her nun's garb, emerging from the

passageway behind the Augustinian priory on the arm of
a Jesuit priest.

Back in the cool of her cell at the Engels Klooster, her
nausea subsided, Anne Winter went over in her head what
she had learned that morning, from George Barton and
from her own investigations. Sister Janet was suspected
in the procurement of vulnerable young women for some
unidentified brothel in the city – this from Evan Glenroe
who seemed particularly concerned to dissuade anyone
from too close a familiarity with the Engels Klooster. The
sudden appearance of Father Felipe at the very spot outside
the Augustinian priory where she had lost sight of Sister
Janet made her suspect that the Jesuit, who was so often
at the Engels Klooster, might well be involved in whatever clandestine activities took so much of the nun's time.
George Barton had hinted that Sister Janet was suspected
of involvement in the death of Lady Hildred Beaumont;
the Cavaliers of the Bouchoute House had been aware that
she – or at least some unidentified she-intelligencer – had
come to Bruges to find out the traitor amongst them. Only
one of those matters – the last one – bore any evident rela-
tion to her reason for being in Bruges, and the fact that
the traitor, Marchmont Ellis, now knew the woman on his
trail was in the Engels Klooster, made it even more essential
that she finish this business quickly. Nevertheless, she felt
herself too closely entwined with those other issues to be
able to ignore them. Lady Anne's decision was made. She

got up from her cot, poured water from the ewer into the bowl on her nightstand and washed her face, then retrieved her set of special keys from the small packet of items she had secreted in her mattress. It was not likely that Sister Janet would be back yet from whatever business she had to transact down at the Augustinian priory. Anne might never have a better opportunity to find out what went on in that secret room.

Checking that all the sisters were safely dispersed to their afternoon tasks, Anne went swiftly along the corridor and got to work with her keys in the lock. It took her hand a moment to recall the techniques it had been taught in York, but soon she felt the mechanism turn.

The room had only one small window, high in the wall and set with a grille. Anne took a little time to get used to the poor light. To her left, two large hampers were stacked, one upon the other. They had been moved from the far corner they had been in before, when Sister Janet had brought her in here and shown her the girl she now knew to have been Ruth Jones.

Quickly, Anne undid the leather straps of the top hamper – blankets, nothing more. With some effort she shifted it off and checked the one beneath. Old habits, wimples, veils and sandals. Anne could not see that there was anything secretive about them.

Further back, in the corner behind the hampers, beneath the window, was an old, high writing desk of the type found in the convent's small library and that Anne imagined might have been used in a scriptorium. The seat of the desk had been made comfortable with a cushion of familiar pattern – a match for that which Sister Janet kept for the night-watches. On a small shelf behind the desk were a selection of quill pens, a pot of blotting sand and blotter and a bundle of small red candles. Anne tried to lift the lid of the desk – as she had suspected, it was locked. After a short while working her keys there was a click, and she raised the lid of the desk. Inside, neatly stacked, was a collection of leather-bound ledgers and alongside them, equally neatly stacked if less uniform, a pile of papers tied with a black silk ribbon.

Anne went first to the ledgers. Starting with the one at the top. On the first page was a list of names, some of them familiar to her already from her short time in Bruges. Cavaliers in the King's service who had resided for a time or passed through the town since his exile had begun. They were all names whose origins were somewhere across the sea, in the British Isles. There, three quarters of the way down, was the name of Marchmont Ellis, and below it that of Edward Daunt. Glenroe's name was not there, and neither was Thomas Faithly's. Each name had a page number written alongside it. Anne turned towards the back of the book, the page with Marchmont Ellis's number, and began to read. The script was a dainty italic such as Anne's own mother had used and was familiar to Anne from laundry lists and duty rosters in Sister Janet's hand. In the poor light, Anne struggled at first to make it out properly, and then she had to look again to be certain of what she was reading. Each paragraph highlighted a debauchery or some injudicious speech – the kind of speech that could leave a man with his throat slit in a dark alleyway. The nature of each debauch was communicated in curt specifics, and Anne was shocked that the old woman should ever have learned such terms as she used. At the end of each paragraph were the words 'account verified' followed by a woman's name: 'Account verified Clara'; 'Account verified Magde'; 'Account verified Pernilla'. What was on the facing page was in some senses much more mundane but, in tandem with what had gone before, utterly chilling. It was the name of the wife, mother or sister of the Cavalier in question, and the whereabouts in England, Scotland, Wales or Ireland, of their family estate. Anne realised what she was looking at was the work of a blackmailer. The misdemeanours of men patronising the brothels of Bruges were being reported by the women who witnessed them to Sister Janet, who recorded them in this book, with a view to threatening their exposure to the men's families at home. But to what end? What was the bargain the old nun offered these men in return for her silence?

Anne's eyes travelled now to the last, broad column for each entry. She read through Sister Janet's extremely precise record of her activities, which in each case terminated with the name and whereabouts of a Jesuit priest. And suddenly Anne knew. She knew what Sister Janet was up to, and she knew how Father Felipe was involved. Sister Janet had obtained the detailed testimony, from the prostitutes of the town, of scandalous behaviour or dangerously ill-considered words from exiled Royalists in Bruges. At home in the British Isles these men were considered, at least by friends and family, to be individuals of probity and honour. Sister Janet had presented the individuals thus caught with what she knew and made a bargain not to divulge the distasteful or dangerous details to their closest friends and family, or the wider world. The bargain was that their family should accept and shelter in their home a Jesuit priest sent to England from the Spanish dominions. These innocent family members were to hide and assist these priests, knowing that in doing so they risked exposing themselves to Cromwell's most brutal justice. What was clear to Anne was that they did go along with it, in the main, these men whose incontinent behaviour abroad had put their families at home in jeopardy, because blackmail had no weapon quite as powerful as shame. Amongst the pages in these ledgers were the names of men whose families had been friends of Anne's for lifetimes. For the second time that day, she felt sick.

Anne closed the books, returned them to the desk, shut and locked it and put the hampers back as they had been before she'd moved them. Taking nothing with her that she had not had when she'd come into the room, she went out of the door and locked it. There was no one in the corridor. For a moment's blessed relief Anne closed her eyes and leaned back against the cool wall. And that was when the screaming started.

EIGHTEEN

A Lover's Tale

Lady Anne stood very still, scarcely daring to breathe. Her heart was pounding. At the first outcry, she thought she had been caught. Knowing the brutal punishments meted out to the Jesuits in England and to those who harboured them, she did not doubt that any stranger here who discovered their secrets would be subjected to appropriate retribution. She looked the length of the corridor, but there was no one to be seen. From somewhere, at some distance away, Sister Janet's voice rang around the convent's walls, telling of breakings-in, treachery and theft. Despite the fact that she was alone, Anne felt as if Sister Janet was, in fact, standing in front of her and pointing at her. Only the arrival of a stream of novices, nuns and lay sisters, who then passed by, oblivious to her presence, shook her from this state. They were hurrying in the direction of Sister Janet's cell. Lady Anne composed herself and followed after them.

By the time Anne turned the corner into Sister Janet's corridor, the onslaught of curiosity that had sent streams of religious from all parts of the convent had been brought to a halt, frozen where it stood, by the wrath of the old Englishwoman. The women, now for the most part clearly wishing themselves elsewhere, flanked the walls, immobilised. Standing within the doorway of her small cell, Sister Janet was a bundle of cold fury, quivering as she spoke.

'Who has been here?'

There was silence.

'I'll ask one more time, and you'll all be on night floor-scrubbing duties in the crypt if I don't have an answer. Who has been in my cell?'

Still no one spoke. Anne surveyed the faces of the nuns trying to dissolve themselves into the walls. The younger women seemed to be in various stages of terror, the older were, in the main, enjoying the situation immensely. None of them, however, appeared to show the slightest likelihood of having violated the inner sanctum that was Sister Janet's cell. Lady Anne made up her mind and stepped forward. 'If we might talk alone, Sister.'

Janet pierced Anne with a shrewd look. 'Sister Anne,' she said slowly, laying emphasis on the last word. 'Of course. The rest of you, be about your duties, for I assure you they are not to stand and gape.'

A moment later, the corridor was empty, save for the convent's oldest sister shuffling away. Anne followed Janet into the cell and waited while the door was closed behind her.

'Well?' demanded Janet. 'What were you doing in my cell?'

'I wasn't in your cell.'

'Then why . . .?'

'I wasn't in your cell. What has been stolen?'

'How do you know anything has been stolen?'

Anne had difficulty in not laughing. 'Sister, you have been shouting it to half of Bruges these last ten minutes.'

Janet stared at her and pursed her mouth, but no suitable riposte came. 'Well,' she said, 'is it to be wondered at? Never, not once in all my sixty-seven years, has the privacy of my cell been so violated, my belongings so . . .'

'But you are not permitted personal belongings . . .'

'Do not think to mock me, Lady Anne. There are some things, over a long life, that are not easily to be dispensed with. One day, for good or ill, you may learn that for yourself.'

Anne could have told her of the many things she had had to dispense with over a shorter life than Janet's, but she held back. She knew enough to know that this woman had lost at least as much as she had. It was a conversation that could have gone on a long time and done nothing but open old and painful wounds.

'I'm sorry, Sister. What has been taken?'

Janet crossed over to her bed and folded back the blankets to reveal a box. The box was of old red leather and lined in blue velvet. It was perhaps the length of Anne's hand, but not quite the width. The clasp on it had been broken and the box was empty.

'Lady Hildred's locket.'

'Yes,' said Janet, her voice flat.

'You said you were setting it aside from the things that were to be sold.'

'Yes,' agreed Sister Janet.

'I supposed you meant to return it to England, for her son.'

To Anne's surprise, Janet was indignant. 'Hildred's son is a traitor to the King and to the cause his own father died in. Hildred would never have allowed anything of value, anything that might otherwise be used to further His Majesty's purposes, to be returned to her son. Better by far to sell them and send the proceeds to His Majesty. That would have been Hildred's wish.'

'Perhaps,' said Anne. 'But if that is the case, why did you separate the locket from the other items that were to be sold? The locket should not still have been here for a thief to find in the first place. What was it really doing in your room, Sister?'

Sister Janet sat down on her bed and ran a hand over her face. A straggle of grey hair came loose from beneath the crown of her wimple. For the first time, Lady Anne saw her look almost defeated. She stepped a little closer and touched her hand to the box. 'I saw Lady Hildred open the box sometimes, you know, and run her finger over the locket. I only saw her open the locket itself once. It was as if she was fearful it was too fragile to be opened or worn.'

Janet shook her head. 'No. It was that she feared what was inside would break her heart. Even Hildred had a heart, you know.'

'The portrait of her husband?' asked Anne.

'On the one side, yes, there was a likeness of Guy, when he was young.' She smiled. 'I remember when the original it was copied from was painted. He would hardly sit still for the artist, so anxious was he to be out on the hunt. To be anywhere but cooped up inside, in fine clothes with his hair freshly trimmed.'

'Was it her son on the other?' asked Anne gently.

'What?' said Janet, as if she had forgotten Anne was there.

'The other side of the locket? Was that of their son?'

'Oh, I suppose so. It was of a young man, dressed in more recent fashion. No doubt it was their son. He had Hildred's colouring, at any rate.'

'And nothing else was taken?'

'There was nothing else to take.' Sister Janet looked around the bare white walls, adorned only with a crucifix above the bed. 'What was in that box was the only thing of any monetary worth in this little cell. I suppose someone will get money for the silver, for the portraits will mean nothing to anyone else, now that Hildred is gone.'

Anne didn't want to ask again for she was fairly sure she knew the answer. She lowered her voice and asked as gently as she could, 'But I still don't understand why it was here, Sister, in your room.'

Janet smiled, vulnerable as Anne imagined she might have been as a young girl, many decades before. 'Oh, it's a very simple tale. I loved Guy, you see. And he me – he told me so. We would have married, and we would have been very, very happy. But then there was the King's fear of Catholics, and Guy's brother's ambition. And Hildred's malice. And so we did not marry. I left England at sixteen and I never saw Guy again. Hildred took everything I thought would be mine. I thought I might at least have his portrait, now that she is gone at last, but someone has taken that from me too.'

There was nothing Anne could say by way of comfort, and she reminded herself that she was not here to put right past wrongs, but to uncover the rotten elements at the heart of the King's cause in Bruges. This business of Hildred Beaumont's locket was but a distraction. Anne had come here to expose the treachery of the double agent, Marchmont Ellis, and in doing so she had uncovered the Jesuitical activities of Sister Janet. She had begun to form a plan for dealing with the first problem, but she had no idea whatsoever what to do about the second. What she did know, though, was that her time at the Engels Klooster had run out. Father Felipe had made it perfectly clear that he would be returning to the convent tomorrow, and that his 'confessing' of her would take the most abhorrent form. Anne could not wait here until tomorrow. Promising Sister Janet she would tell no one of the locket and of its particular significance for the old nun, she left.

She was supposed to return to her duties in the convent garden, but instead she took herself to the library, which also served as a scriptorium for the convent's records and correspondence. 'I have some transcribing work to do for

Sister Janet,' she said in response to Sister Olivia's enquiry as to why she needed pen, paper and ink.

Anne returned to her own cell and shut the door. She moved the room's small table against the door and drew up the stool, to make for herself a functional, if uncomfortable, writing desk. From beneath her mattress, she took out her own copy of *The Compleat Angler*. Then, with some awkwardness, she removed the small silk pouch that hung from her neck from its hiding place beneath her habit. Inside was the cypher key she had been given before leaving England, and that she had been careless enough to let Janet discover. She laid out the key on the tabletop, sat down on the stool, and began to write.

His working day as a carpenter over, Seeker had taken an early supper at 't Oud Handbogenhof and taken himself to the Jeruzalemkapel. He had often met Marchmont Ellis here, when the need arose. He had occasionally done work for the Adornes family, and it wasn't unusual for him to stop in at the end of the working day to have a friendly word with the inhabitants of their almshouses before making his evening devotions in the chapel. The place was well situated for Ellis to wander into on his way back into town from an afternoon at the Schuttersgilde, without attracting adverse notice. But it wasn't Ellis he was meeting here this evening. By his failure to inform Seeker of the mysterious Mr Longfellow's impending clandestine visit to Bruges, Ellis had shown himself to have outlived his usefulness.

Seeker couldn't abandon him completely to the fate that awaited him when his Royalist companions discovered he had betrayed them, but he wasn't going to act to remove Ellis from the scene quite yet.

The Jeruzalemkapel was a testament to death. Bruges was clogged with churches wallowing in death, as if the afterlife was a whole new order to be negotiated, and the skill to do so had to be learned now, by the living. Seeker had often thought it a wonder the Papists didn't wear themselves out, living for two lives at once. The Calvinists had it right: once you were dead, there was nothing you or anyone else could do about it, or where you were going. The Jeruzalemkapel was different somehow from the other churches of Bruges; it didn't mince its words, didn't tinker with possibilities. The Jeruzalemkapel spoke to Seeker of a death that was uncompromising and eternal. The altarpiece was no paeon to weeping saints but a white sandstone Golgotha, and above it not one but three plain, empty crosses for the God who'd suffered with fallen man. Seeker liked the darkness here, the lack of choice on offer. He liked the honesty of it. He reached up a hand to touch the pliers, sculpted into the stone alongside depictions of the instruments that had been used to inflict Christ's suffering. Men did this, mortal men. They tortured Christ and killed him. Ordinary, mortal men. If they could do that to the Son of God, what more might they do to their brothers? *Plenty*, thought Seeker.

Just as he was considering leaving, Seeker heard footsteps behind him. It was George Beaumont.

'I was beginning to think the good sisters of the Engels Klooster had done for you.'

Beaumont gave an appraising smile. 'Oh, I daresay some of them would be capable of it, if they had a mind to. But no, I spent some time at the Schuttersgilde after I left the convent. The more accustomed our fellow Englishmen are to seeing me about, the more likely they are to be less cautious in what they say when I happen to be in earshot.'

'And did they say anything?'

'Plenty, but nothing of any value. The most firmly held opinion is that it was the Spanish that murdered my mother. After the debacle at the Dunes, most of them are ready to blame the Spanish for anything.'

'Forget about the Spaniards. The governor's got enough on his mind trying to work out where in Flanders the French are going to march next, without worrying about an old Englishwoman. I'm going to spend tomorrow looking for the fellow we heard about at the Oude Steen, the one who had so much to say for himself "shooting the Queen of England". He's our route to your mother's killer, I'm certain of it.'

'If you say so,' said Beaumont. 'And what should I do?'

'You keep an eye on the Bouchoute House. Oh, I have your money, by the way.'

Beaumont's eyes widened. 'Already?'

Seeker gave a low laugh. 'They might as well have left it out in the back yard with a sign nailed to the box inviting passers-by to help themselves. I've got it stashed away safe

– you can take it with you when you leave. Anyway, you keep an eye on the inhabitants. Follow them if you can – don't bother about Ellis though. Look out for anything that might give us a hint as to when Mr Longfellow is expected to show up in Bruges, and what he plans to do when he gets here. As to the other thing . . .'

Beaumont had been making to leave. 'Other thing?'

'The woman – Anne Winter. Did you get anywhere near her at the convent?'

'I did,' said Beaumont. 'She struck me as a person of some courage.'

'Oh, she has courage all right. But just remember what I said – she's also the most devious woman I've met in over forty years on this earth. I wouldn't trust Anne Winter as far as I could throw my horse. You be careful, Beaumont. If she's gazing at you with those big dark eyes it's to distract you from something else she doesn't want you to see. I'd rather be a fly caught in a spider's web than the man Anne Winter gets into her clutches.'

Beaumont gave a smile of surprise. 'I had not thought you a man to deliberate much over the enticements of women, Captain.'

'I don't. But Anne Winter's a woman the way your sword's a butter knife. And that's where you'll make your mistake. You'll treat her like you'd treat a woman, and you'll be done for. Don't let down your guard with her for a minute.'

'I'll endeavour to remember that, Captain Seeker. But you

may rest easy. Long experience has inured me to the charms of even the most cunning of the more delicate sex. A failed venture into the matters of the heart when I was scarcely more than a boy cured me of such sensitivities. I haven't come to Bruges to contract new romantic entanglements.'

George Beaumont didn't strike Seeker like the sort of man prone to romantic entanglements – too measured, pragmatic. Too much sense.

'Good,' he said. 'But you watch yourself all the same. What did you learn from her?'

Beaumont raised his eyebrows. 'She has discovered Ellis to be your source in the Bouchoute House but is in difficulty as to how to inform those who sent her. Her connection to my mother was to have been her principle means of communication, and now that is gone. This should at least buy Ellis some time. Will you warn him?'

Seeker shook his head. 'Not yet. I'd like to keep him dangling a while yet. Let's see what the lady does for now, who she speaks to, for you can be sure she'll try to draw someone else into her scheme.' Seeker leaned against one of the flights of stairs leading to the gallery above the altar and took a minute to consider what George Beaumont had told him. 'So, if her lines of communication broke with your mother's death, that means Sister Janet's not involved.'

'No,' said Beaumont.

'Well, she's up to something, that's for certain.'

It almost bothered Seeker that George Beaumont had been so successful in his first interview with Anne Winter.

It was impressive that one not used to such subterfuge had carried the thing off so well. Clearly, his old adversary was greatly out of options when she was willing to trust a stranger as readily as she'd trusted George Beaumont.

'And what else did you discover? What about the girl, Ruth Jones? Did Anne Winter say anything to you of her?'

Beaumont looked uncertain but Seeker pressed on. 'The girl whose brother was murdered after going to the Engels Klooster to look for her,' explained Seeker.

He could see George Beaumont thinking. 'She said something to the effect that she was safe somewhere.'

'Did she say where?'

Beaumont took a minute again and then shook his head. 'No, she didn't. What do you know of this girl?'

'Very little. Anyhow, that'll have to do us for now. I'm off for my bed.'

Beaumont looked surprised. 'A little early, is it not?'

Seeker laughed. 'Nothing much changes really, does it? In England, before the war, I was a carpenter and you a gentleman. Here in Bruges I am again a carpenter and you again a gentleman. It was the war that made us something else.'

'And when we go back to England?'

Seeker looked at him a moment. 'When we go back to England we will know if what we have made there was worth it. But for now, Major Beaumont, I'll leave you to whatever it is a gentleman does in these hours, and I'll bid you goodnight.'

NINETEEN

Escape

Thomas Faithly and Evan Glenroe had just left a tavern on the Spiegelrei when they spotted George Barton walking down the opposite canal bank, oblivious to their presence. Thomas began to lift his hand to hail him when Glenroe pressed it back down.

'Don't do it, Thomas! That fellow gives me the shivers. A colder fish than you'll get in the German sea.'

'Wouldn't you be, Evan, if you found yourself friendless and in a foreign town? Your insistence that he should be denied admittance to the Bouchoute House . . .'

'Just till Mr Longfellow has been and got clear, Thomas. We know very little about this Barton fellow. He could be anyone. One of Thurloe's spies even.'

'I'm glad you are not so untrusting of me, Evan.'

'You, I have seen fight for the king. That fellow, I've only heard claim to do it. Besides, have you ever seen a face that looks a more proper Puritan?'

'You cannot condemn a man for his face, Evan.'

'Can I not? We'll see.' Thomas saw a familiar, dangerous

light appear in the Irishman's eye, and before he could prevent him, Glenroe himself had hallooed over to George Barton.

'Barton!' Glenroe said as the three came together by the Poortersloge. 'What a devil of a day it's been. Would this heat not just about finish you?'

'It is certainly very close,' replied George.

'Close!' exclaimed Glenroe. 'It's like a woman I knew in Toledo. Practically had to peel her off my skin.' He let out a long breath and gave Thomas Faithly a conspiratorial look before returning his attention to George. 'Did you ever know a Spanish woman, Barton?'

'Not in that way,' said George. 'Englishwomen are more to my taste.'

'Well, a peachy blush on a creamy cheek and all that has its place, I'll grant you, but how would you *know*, until you tried?' pressed Glenroe.

'I know,' said George, with a finality as though he hoped to cut short the topic.

Glenroe looked at him a little longer. 'You English. Faithly here's almost as bad. It's a wonder you don't die out. But tonight, George my friend, we'll show you something new. See then what you think to your Englishwoman.'

Barton looked uncomfortable and Thomas himself was curious as to what the Irishman had in mind. 'What do you mean?'

Glenroe looked about as if they might be overheard. 'Tonight, we are going to the House of Lamentations.'

'The brothel?' said George.

'Not a word I would use, Barton. Thomas will tell you, I'm sure, that Madame Hélène is a most accommodating woman, and it wouldn't do to insult her hospitality by using such a term.'

'Do you say it is not a brothel, this House of Lamentations?'

Glenroe looked at him in astonishment. 'Not a brothel? Good God, Barton, it's a house full of whores! What do you think it is but a brothel?' He shook his head and then leaned in closer, holding up his fingers as if offering up a jewel. 'But you treat these women like ladies, and they will treat you like no lady on earth would even begin to. I guarantee you, one night at the House of Lamentations and you'll never look at an Englishwoman again.'

'Thank you, Sir Evan, but I have not the funds.'

'Funds be damned. I'm in a generous mood tonight.'

'Do I not recall you telling Ellis the other day you hadn't a penny to your name?'

Glenroe was dismissive. 'Not for his damn fool schemes I haven't. Ellis thinks he might give up the struggle, light out for Maryland, start again. He'd not get as far as Mardijk, never mind Maryland. And for what? Better die in a cause than live without one. But before I die, my friends, I intend to live a while.'

The walls of the House of Lamentations came into view. Thomas himself had little inclination for its entertainments tonight, but George came to an abrupt halt.' You two go on,' he said to Glenroe and Faithly. 'I've no interest in whores, and when I finally have my English wife, I don't intend to gift her a dose of the French pox.'

Glenroe also stopped. 'Ah, come now, Barton. Just supper and a song, then. Tell him, Thomas — isn't there a girl there has the sweetest voice you ever heard? Like your nurse singing to you when you were a baby. I thought I was back in Sligo listening to my own mother. It'll make you weep.'

Barton was unmoved. 'Some other night, Evan.'

Glenroe looked at him. Night had fallen above the still water of the canals and there was no one but themselves out on the street. 'You're a strange one, Barton, aren't you? I'm beginning to wonder if you might not be of the other persuasion.'

George's voice was stony. 'I have no interest in boys, Glenroe.'

'Boys? Oh, if it was boys, I could get you boys, no problem. No, George, what I'm starting to wonder is whether you might not be a Puritan.'

Thomas tensed, ready for the friction already in the air to break out into open aggression, but George stood his ground with notable calm. 'And can a Puritan not also honour his King, can a Puritan not also fight in his King's cause? Must a man be debauched in order to be loyal?'

'No, George, not at all,' said the Irishman. 'It's just, in these days, in Bruges, while we wait about for better news, it helps pass the time.' Glenroe swept off his battered feathered hat in an elaborate bow and carried on down Spanjaardstraat towards the House of Lamentations, whistling.

'You need not go with one of the women,' said Thomas, 'but will you not at least join us for supper?'

'No,' said Barton, 'I will not.' And without further conversation he turned and walked back up the street, in the direction of town.

As the bats emerging from the gables of Bruges swirled in the night sky, Thomas watched George Barton's form dissolve into the darkness, and began to wonder if Glenroe might be right about their recently arrived acquaintance.

Silence permeated the Engels Klooster in the same way that darkness engulfed it. At first it appeared impenetrable, complete, but then, just as Lady Anne's eyes grew accustomed to the darkness and started to notice things emerge from it, so too did she become aware of sounds that in the daytime she would never have noticed: the slight rattle of a window frame, buffeted by a sudden breeze, the creak somewhere above her of a floorboard, or of a bed in a cell as she passed it, the steady breathing of a sister deep in sleep.

There had been no possibility of sleep for Anne. After compline she had imitated all the other women in going quietly to her cell. There, she had removed only her headdress, and lain down beneath the rough woollen blanket. As the sounds of the sisters making their usual bedtime preparations had abated to be replaced by the occasional creak or snore, Anne had risen again, and moving as quietly as she could, gathered up the sack she had kept under her bed. Ruth Jones's old brown woollen dress and green jacket were in it, laundered and dry, along with a small bag of money and the scrip of paper she had begged from Sister Olivia in the scriptorium. Her own copy of Walton's *Compleat Angler* was there too, and in the cloth pocket she wore around her neck, hidden beneath her habit, were the cypher key she had carried with her from England, and the letter, addressed to Marchmont Ellis, that she had written that afternoon. She glanced down at the sandals she had been given to wear with her habit and wished she had managed to keep her shoes in the flight from the ambush by the Damme canal. There was nothing she could do about it now. Slipping the sandals into the sack with everything else, Anne lifted her candle and crept out into the corridor, closing the door of her cell behind her with as little sound as possible.

After the heat of the day, the flagstone floor was pleasantly cool beneath her bare feet. She had six hours, she calculated, before the sisters started to rouse themselves for lauds. All day, it had felt as if the air had been building for thunder, and Anne prayed the clouds would stay, obscuring the moon, but that the thunder and lightning would leave off long enough for her to get her business done and then be gone from the convent.

As quickly as she could, Anne moved along empty corridors to arrive, without incident, at Janet's secret room. She managed to turn the key as easily this time as she had done the last.

The ledgers were where she had found them before, and where she had left them. The light from her candle was not great, but it was enough for her to see and do what she needed to. She found first of all the list of Jesuit priests who had been sent to England, and the names of those families they had been forced upon. Her plan had been to copy it, but now she realised it would be quicker simply to tear the pages from the book. This she did, wincing at the sound with each rip. Next, starting with the most recent ledgers, in which were kept the accounts by the women of the House of Lamentations of the behaviour and injudicious utterances of their clients, she began to put as many of them as would fit into her sack, going back ten years. That would have to be enough. She would have liked to set light to the rest, but feared they would take too well, and burn down the convent. Instead, she poured as much as was left of her own ink, and what she could find of Sister Janet's, over the remaining ledgers, and left it to do its worst.

Anne put her skeleton key back in the lock, ready to turn it again, when the first rumble of thunder followed, at no great distance, the first flash of lightning. Lady Anne's hand stopped at the lock as a shriek rang out along the corridor. Poor Sister Assumpta, whose small village on the Maas had been blasted out of existence by the endless contentions of foreign armies: the horrors of her childhood had left her fit for little but the folding of laundry. Now Assumpta screamed fit to wake half the convents in Bruges.

Anne froze. From all directions came the sounds of those

going to comfort Sister Assumpta, and of others waking, troubled by the storm. Doors were opening, more light was seeping in under the bottom of the door from the corridor. There was little hope that all the sisters would be safely back in their cells and slumbering before lauds, and none whatsoever that Lady Anne could simply walk out of the Engels Klooster in the dead of night, escaping Father Felipe and taking with her evidence of Sister Janet's blackmailing activities, as she had planned to.

Her candle was out now, and she stood with her hand still on the key and her heart pounding. Anne thought of all the things she had done to get to this place: a tiny, locked dark room in a Romish convent in a foreign country. She thought of the men she had seen only a few weeks ago, executed, torn piece by piece before the mob on Cromwell's orders. She thought of her own friend and servant who had died such a death only three years ago, trading with Damian Seeker to spare her life. What was the worth of that life, of that trade, now? She thought further back, to her father, her brother. She must not shrink in fear from Jesuits who would infiltrate her country whilst Cromwell's spies consigned her friends to torture and judicial murder. Straightening her shoulders and taking a deep breath, Lady Anne turned her key and walked out of Sister Janet's secret room.

There was nobody in the corridor now, all the sisters who cared enough to deal with Assumpta already having passed. Anne was calm. She walked in the opposite direction until she reached the internal iron gate at the foot of the main stairs. Sister Bethany was on duty there tonight, obviously not long aroused from her sleep by the thunderclap or Assumpta's screams.

'Sister Anne?' she said, straightening her headdress that had been knocked askew by her having slept with her head against the wall. 'Is all well with Assumpta?'

'She is almost calmed,' said Anne, 'but begs to see you.'

'Me?'

Anne nodded, astonished, as so often she had been over these last years, by her own ability to manufacture and tell a lie. 'She will not be persuaded that you have come to no harm.'

'Me?' said Sister Bethany again in genuine surprise.

'She is convinced a lightning bolt will have come through the door grille to strike off the inner railings and smite you. Mother Superior begs that you should go to her and reassure her that all is well. I will take your place on watch here.'

'Of course, of course,' said Bethany, hurriedly getting up and starting down the corridor.

'Sister,' Anne called after her.

'Yes, Sister?' said Bethany.

Anne pointed to the huge lock on the iron inner gate. 'We may well be called upon to give shelter to some unfortunate traveller on a night such as this. Had you not better give me the keys?'

'Oh, of course, Sister, of course,' said Bethany, hastily removing the key chain from around her waist before hurrying back down the corridor.

At another time, Anne Winter might have felt sorry at her deception of such a kindly soul, but not now. As soon as Sister Bethany was out of sight, she unlocked the inner gate, then hurried across the flagstones of the vestibule to open the door into the outer courtyard. Only now did she remember that she was still in bare feet. She hastily pulled her sandals from her sack and slipped them on. Taking a quick look out into the street through the eye-level grille in the outer door, she unlocked that door and was about to step into the street when a new and far more terrible scream rose up from within the walls of the Engels Klooster. It was the voice of a young nun, and the scream one not of fear, but of horror. While logic told Anne to flee the sound, concern for the women inside urged her otherwise. She let drop her sack and ran back into the convent.

All was chaos. The troubles of Sister Assumpta were forgotten as the women rushed once more towards Sister Janet's cell, younger sisters forgetting their place and rushing past their elders to reach the source of the crisis. Anne outstripped all but the foremost. The screaming continued, and only after Anne rounded the corner to see an hysterical novice slapped hard across the face by Sister Bethany did it stop. And then she knew she was too late. Sister Euphemia, the gardener, was standing, aghast, in the doorway, a younger nun, her face pressed to the door-jamb, was wracked with sobs, another, slumped to the floor, howled in grief. Anne summoned her courage and went past them, gently moving Euphemia aside. Janet's room was lit by a solitary lamp, held aloft by Sister Ignatia, her face frozen in horror. In the pool of light cast by the lamp, Anne could see Mother Superior slumped on her knees, her arms flung across the figure on the bed and repeating, 'Oh, Janet, oh, Janet.' And there, in blood-soaked sheets, her eyes locked open as if in surprise, lay Janet, the bolt from a crossbow lodged in her unmoving chest.

Anne stumbled out of the room, into the corridor, and fled.

TWENTY

St John's Hospital

Seeker didn't know which was worse, the smell of the Oude Steen first thing in the morning, before the night slop buckets had been emptied out, or later in the day, when the heat had warmed the fetid air trapped below ground and brought new flies to antagonise the guards. He reasoned that last night's storm should have improved things one way or the other and took a chance on early morning.

He turned through the narrow opening on Wollestraat and exchanged a few grumbles with the upper guard before descending the stone steps. The heavy lower door of the Oude Steen was firmly locked, and he rapped hard on it. The disgruntled doorkeeper eventually shot back the iron cover on the eye grille and grunted, 'You again? Why not take a cell here and be done with it?'

'I prefer my landlady's housekeeping, thank you. Now are you going to let me in, or shall I take my money elsewhere?'

The guard snorted and began the process of unlocking the door. 'What you here for this time?'

'There's a fellow ran off that owes me money. Thought Dirk might know where he was.'

'Fair enough.' The guard unlocked another door and jerked a thumb in the direction of the dungeons. 'You'll know your way by now.'

Seeker took a breath and stepped into the cavern of misery that was the Oude Steen. Some of the faces and shapes gurning or shifting as he passed were the same as on his last visit, some different. It was one of those places a man was glad there wasn't much light: dark stains on the walls, like rust that wasn't, bore testimony to centuries of incarceration and interrogation. All the ingenuity of man to torture whatever he wanted out of his fellow man had had its day in the Oude Steen.

Dirk was snoring like a shire horse when Seeker entered his cell. He was the only person in the whole prison to have a space to himself – there were plenty others as well as Seeker who were prepared to pay him for information. He'd once asked a guard why Dirk didn't just buy himself out of the Oude Steen. 'Because living with his wife is worse,' had been the response.

Seeker shook Dirk a couple of times by the shoulder, but making no headway reached for the jug of tepid water on the floor and splashed most of it over the slumbering man's face. He stood back and waited for the expletives to run their course.

Dirk finally shambled to a sitting position, coughing as if nothing but heaving up his lungs would set him up for the day. Seeker took a couple of steps back and waited for the performance to be over.

'Aah, that's better,' said Dirk at last when he had projected sufficient phlegm onto the dirt floor. He then took to scratching. 'So, what is it this time, John Carpenter, that's so important you rouse a man of business at this ungodly hour?'

'I'm sorry to intrude upon Your Excellency's rest,' said Seeker, 'but it was you who sent me a message, if you recall. So if you could accord me a moment out of your busy morning I'd be most grateful.'

'How grateful?' asked Dirk, leaning forward and remarkably wide awake now.

Seeker produced a coin from his pouch. 'That do?'

Dirk went back to a mild scratching. 'Not for what I've got for you.'

'Which is?'

'What you were here asking about the last time. That old Englishwoman killed on the road to Damme. '

'Go on,' said Seeker.

'Might have heard something more,' speculated Dirk, eying Seeker's pouch.

Seeker took out another coin, a little greater in value than the last. 'That's all there is. Take it or leave it. I haven't the time to waste.'

Dirk shot out a grubby hand and took the coin. 'Vagrant in here yesterday – said he was a soldier, might have been . . .'

'Get to the point,' said Seeker.

'As I am doing,' protested Dirk. 'Anyhow, this vagrant, soldier, whatever he might have been – he'd been in a fight at a tavern up by the Speye Poort. Fight started when another ne'er-do-well fell over, knocking over a whole table of beers, hit his head on the floor, clean out.'

'Go on,' said Seeker, resigned to having to let Dirk tell it his way.

'Well, this one that had passed clean out had got a wound in his shoulder that he'd been telling people he'd got falling onto a broken bottle. But my new soldier-vagrant friend – call him what you will – says it was a lead ball that did that, from a flintlock like as not. Badly cut out by someone that didn't know what they were doing. Says he's seen it plenty before and seen them putrid too. Now, weren't you telling me the fellow you were looking for might have been hit by a pistol shot . . .'

'Where is this soldier?' asked Seeker, looking back towards the other cells.

Dirk shrugged. 'Don't know. His woman came and got him out.'

Seeker let out a sigh of exasperation and made for the door.

'But,' continued Dirk, 'before she did, he told me where the other fellow went, the one you're looking for.'

Seeker stopped. 'Where?'

Dirk raised his eyebrows and nodded towards Seeker's pouch.

'This better be worth it, or I won't be coming back.'

'Oh, but it will be, John Carpenter. Trust me, it will be.'

Seeker drew out one last coin but held it out of Dirk's reach.

Dirk nodded. 'The man you're looking for, that arm of his was putrid, and when he came round from his fall he was raving. Something about shooting the Queen of England. They took him to Sint-Jans.'

A moment later, Seeker was headed back through the dungeon to the guardroom, with the sound of Dirk's voice calling after him, 'Tell that lazy fellow I need someone to run over to the Swaene for a jug of its finest, and there's a penny in it for him if he looks quick about it.'

The brother on duty at the entryway to Sint-Janshospitaal opened the eye grille at Seeker's banging in a state of some alarm. 'What is it? Pestilence? A fire?'

'No,' said Seeker, 'but I have urgent need to see one of your patients.'

'And who are you, that has such an urgent need?'

'My name is John Carpenter.'

'English?' Even through the grille, Seeker could see the monk's mouth pucker in distrust.

'Yes, but loyal to His Majesty King Charles's cause. I beg you will give me admittance. I have heard that an old comrade of mine was brought here yesterday, fevered, of a wound from a pistol shot.'

'Hmm,' said the monk, only partially convinced. 'Such a one was brought here yesterday, but he is not long for this world. I doubt he will even know you. Father Anthony has already administered the sacrament.'

'Well, that's a comfort, at any rate,' said Seeker. 'But it would do me good to see him one last time, even if it can do nothing for him.'

The monk relented and drew back the bolt on the smaller door that was set into the larger one. He handed Seeker a candle and led him down the stairs and behind the chapel before knocking on an inner door to the hospital proper. A small, elderly nun answered.

'A visitor, Sister, for the unfortunate who came in yesterday, with the shot wound.'

'Piet?' she asked.

The monk looked to Seeker, and Seeker nodded. 'Yes,' he said, 'Piet.'

The woman leaned towards Seeker in sympathy. 'I'm afraid your friend has little time left in this world.'

Seeker lowered his voice. 'Might I see him, Sister, all the same?'

She inclined her head. 'Of course, if you will follow me.'

Seeker went after the small, shuffling figure. He did not like hospitals. 'Hospital' to him meant something other than a place where the sick might be tended. To him, it meant somewhere that friends, comrades, were brought to die. 'Musket shot, right through the head, that's what you want,' an old army surgeon had once told him, 'or a cannon ball taking it clean off.' He hadn't needed to say what Seeker did not want: half a leg, crushed beneath a horse, half his brain blown away and the rest left, his face burned back nearly to the bone, some small wound that, ill-tended, would fester and slowly turn his living body putrid.

Never before had he had cause to visit Sint-Jans. The place was one vast space broken only by row upon row of stone columns twenty feet in height supporting the massive oak beams of the ceiling. To one side, a series of archways formed a cloister, leading to the hospital chapel. Seeker felt that he might indeed have been entering a cathedral, save that for where nave and aisles might be expected, rows of cots covered the marbled floor, and around and between these cots glided nuns, carrying trays or with strips of dressings and clean linen hanging from their arms. The smells of the sickroom were there, the groans of the sick, but nothing like what he had known in field hospitals or what he had expected to find here.

The nun came to a halt by the foot of a cot around which a screen had been placed. 'Your friend is here. May God grant him rest,' she said, before shuffling away.

Seeker drew back the screen and immediately flinched from the odours it had been holding back. All the rosemary and lavender and balms in the world could not have outdone the stink coming from the man's rotting shoulder. Many of the patients Seeker had passed were housed two to a bed, but the nuns had taken pity on this Piet's fellow sufferers, and no one had been condemned to share a cot with him.

Seeker went to the opposite side from the offending arm

and crouched down. The man's face was the colour of grey flagstones and covered in a sheen of moisture. His head twitched slightly, and he seemed to be murmuring something. Seeker leaned in, bringing his lips close to the man's ear. 'Piet.'

A jerk, a panicked 'Wha . . .?'

Again. 'Piet. You must listen to me.'

Another jerk, the eyes still not opening. More mumbling. 'Who?'

'I'm your conscience, Piet.'

The man let out a cry and, clutching at the thin linen sheet over him, tried to move away, across the small bed.

'You can't hide from me, Piet,' Seeker said, 'you know that. That priest has mumbled the last sacrament over you, and yet I'm still here.'

Another cry, muffled this time.

'Your last chance to redeem yourself, Piet, to choose between Heaven and Hell.'

Now it was a whimper.

'That's better,' said Seeker. 'Now, the old woman you shot on the road to Damme . . .'

Again there was an attempt to move further across the bed. 'That's right, Piet, you stood at that windmill window and you shot her with your musket, don't deny it!'

Another whimper.

'But it wasn't your fault, was it? It was his fault, he paid you to do it. You say his name aloud now, and you'll be freed of the blame of it.'

Seeker was aware of a desperate rallying of strength in the dying man. He managed to muster one word. 'English.'

But Seeker knew that already. 'Not enough, Piet. Remember: Heaven or Hell. Now, the name?'

There was a rustling of distress. 'Don't know.'

'Come now, Piet . . .'

'Don't know!' the man repeated more forcefully. 'Other one. Was another one there that shot me.'

'He was there, when you were shot, this man who paid you to kill the old Englishwoman?'

The man managed a slight nod.

'But it was his companion who shot you?'

A small noise of relief that his point had been made, and Piet was beyond further effort.

'All right,' said Seeker, getting up to walk out. 'All right.' It had been known all around town that Thomas Faithly had got in a shot at the man who'd killed Lady Hildred. And now Seeker knew that the man who'd hired the assassin in the first place had been Faithly's companion that day on the road to Damme: Evan Glenroe.

Seeker left by a different door to that he'd come in by, averting his eyes from paintings on the wall that depicted various stages of the crucifixion. The ghoulish idolatry turned his stomach more than the smell of Piet's gangrenous arm.

He was through the courtyard and almost out in the street when a figure he thought he recognised went rushing past him, only to collide with a young nun who'd just emerged from the dispensary carrying a tray of ointments. To the sound of the young woman's cry was added the smashing of ceramic pots and the clattering of her wooden tray on the cobbles. The racket brought others, monks, nuns and lay-workers, from doors around the courtyard.

'What in Heaven's name is the cause of such a commotion?' demanded a grizzled monk whose gown still bore the marks of a recently spilled breakfast.

'Terrible news!' panted the young man, whom Seeker now recognised as a stable lad from the Engels Klooster. 'Terrible, terrible news!'

In the Bouchoute House, Evan Glenroe was swearing. 'This damned heat, Faithly. I tell you, another night of it and I'll be hurling myself into the nearest canal.'

'I'll alert the quay porters. Anyhow, you can hardly blame the weather for your lack of sleep. It was almost light by the time I heard you come stumbling up the stairs, crashing into everything that couldn't get out of your way.'

Glenroe turned up his hands in appeal. 'Ah, Thomas, you know how those ladies at the House of Lamentations are – they wouldn't let me away. I had practically to sneak out in my stocking soles when they finally consented to sleep.'

'Indeed,' said Thomas dubiously.

'It's true,' protested Glenroe. 'And anyhow, you must shoulder some of the blame – coming home here as soon as you'd had your supper and leaving me – you and that long streak of English misery George Barton, that wouldn't set foot in the place, not even for a song. Can you believe it? So it was left to me to reassure the ladies of their charms.'

'Hmm. Well, you're lucky Dunt didn't reassure you of the accuracy of his aim, that's all I can say.'

'Oh? How so?'

'He's as bleary as they come this morning. Said he couldn't sleep, so sat up on guard half the night with his pistol pointed at the front door. If you'd come through it before he finally gave up and took to his bed, it would have been the last thing you'd have done.'

'Lucky the ladies kept me late, then,' said Glenroe, 'for I've never known him miss a target.'

Thomas waited until Glenroe had had a chance to restore himself over their breakfast of hard bread and pickled herring before saying, 'You can make your complaints to Barton in person – I've asked him to join us this morning.'

'You've what?' said Glenroe. 'I thought we'd agreed we should keep him away from the house, at least until her ladyship's money is safely out of our hands and into the King's.'

'And that very thing doesn't look well for us, Evan. I'm no more convinced than you are by his story of making his way here after the Dunes, in the hope of finding some employment in His Majesty's cause. I think he's been planted here by Hyde, to keep an eye on us.'

'By Hyde?' said Glenroe, through a mouthful of bread.

'Think about it,' said Thomas. He waited a moment to give Glenroe time to do so. George Barton, Sir Thomas knew, was just the type of influence Edward Hyde – the King's chief advisor and 'the only one of them with any sense', as he'd once heard Damian Seeker say – would wish to encourage in the circles in which Charles Stuart entertained himself. It was a thing still unspoken, but increasingly difficult to ignore, that their exiled sovereign was not conducting himself as a monarch should. Thomas himself had watched with growing disappointment the descent of the courageous soldier prince into a state of boredom and indolence, which found its outlet in card tables and taverns and the worst sort of women. He himself had heard Edward Hyde lament the way the King spent his days and the quality of people he spent them with. Thomas looked at Ellis, Daunt and Glenroe, thought of what they had lost, and of the friends they would never see again, and not for the first time wondered if it might all have been in the cause of a man who, should he ever come into his inheritance, would hardly be fit to rule.

Glenroe continued chewing then washed his bread down with a slurp of ale from his beaker. 'You might be right,' he said at last. 'Hyde's sent him here to make sure we're behaving ourselves. It seems like enough. Still no reason to let him wander about the house here alone though.'

As for Sir Thomas, he was happy enough at the prospect of George Barton's company. Marchmont Ellis was a coiled spring of tensions, uncomfortable to be around, while Glenroe's relentless heartiness and Daunt's unshakeable faith in the rightness of their cause had begun to weary him.

Barton, in contrast, seemed a man of pragmatism and good sense. Exactly what the King needed around him.

There had been a time when Thomas would never have questioned his loyalty to Charles, but over the years, what he had lost had begun to outweigh for him the value of what he was fighting for. He had had one chance, only one, to claw back some of that old life, the life he had been born to on his own manor, on the North York Moors. The price had been to live in London as Damian Seeker's spy, and in the end, for Thomas, it had been too great a price to pay. Instead, he was existing now in a house that wasn't his, with companions he'd never have chosen, waiting to fight again in the cause of a King he was not certain was worthy of his kingdom.

Thomas had yet to see George Barton in a flippant mood, but when the maid announced him and showed him in to the dining parlour, he looked even more serious than usual.

'You look almost as grim as Ellis there this morning, George. Do you bring us bad news?'

'Nothing good, at any rate, and I fear it will redound to us one way or the other.'

'Oh?' said Daunt, ready to bristle. 'What now?'

George glanced at Glenroe who appeared not to be listening. 'The old English nun at the Engels Klooster ...' He paused. 'She's dead.'

'Dead?' said Daunt. 'Old nuns die all the time. How should that redound on us?'

'Because,' said George, glancing again at Evan Glenroe

whom Thomas had noticed had gone very pale, 'the news is running about the town that she was found dead in her bed in the middle of the night, with the bolt from a crossbow through her heart.'

Anne was beginning to wonder if she'd misheard George Barton when he'd mentioned in passing that he was lodged on Kreupelnstraat, on the southern edges of town. She had spent the night hidden in an outbuilding a few streets away from the Engels Klooster before daring to venture out at first light to try to find her way to the only person in Bruges she thought might help her. She'd been standing for over an hour now in a passageway off the Blindekenskapel, in the desperate hope that George might appear without her having to expose herself by knocking on doors. She was just about to do that when she at last saw him appear at the end of the street. Checking that there was no one else in view, she moved out of the entrance to the passageway and raised her hand. Having exchanged her nun's habit for Ruth Jones's old clothes, she was dressed now like a maid or a housewife, and it took a moment before George Barton appeared to realise who she was. He surveyed the street in both directions before hurrying over to where she waited.

'Lady Anne,' he said, under his breath.

'I need your help,' she said.

He looked her up and down, took in her new clothing and nodded. 'Come with me.' He led her to a small white-painted brick cottage with a pantiled roof. Only once he had closed the door behind them did Anne feel safe at last. George Barton was moving around the small room, lighting candles against the shadows, finding a clean beaker and pouring into it a large measure of brandy which he insisted she should drink. He had not asked her anything yet. Even when she had taken down the hood and removed the cloak she had worn to disguise herself, he'd said nothing, although she could clearly see that the sight of her in such an ill-fitting, frayed green jacket and old brown woollen dress, in the place of her nun's habit, had given him something of a jolt.

She'd looked down at the garment. 'It doesn't even fit me − it was made for someone shorter and stouter, but it was all I had to hand when I fled the convent.'

The truth was, Ruth Jones had been somewhat more full about the bosom than Anne was, and the dress could not disguise this. It was little wonder it had taken him a moment to cover his evident awkwardness at the change in her appearance.

'I heard what happened there last night. I'm glad you were able to come away safely.'

'There was too much shock and upset for anyone to notice what I did. But I suspect they will have noticed my absence by now, or even have come looking for me.' She slumped, her head in her hands. 'It was hideous, barbaric. Who could even think of doing such a thing?'

'Investigations have already begun, I believe,' he said. 'Did you know that the bolt that killed Sister Janet was marked with the symbol of the Schuttersgilde of Sint-Sebastiaan?'

Anne shook her head, and then the full horror dawned on her. 'The Schuttersgilde? Then it was Marchmont Ellis, and it is my fault.'

George Barton looked astonished. 'Ellis? Your fault? But how so?'

'Because he learned from the bookseller at Sint-Donatian's that I – at least the "she-intelligencer" charged with tracking him down – was at the Engels Klooster. He must have thought it was Janet. I have brought her to this and she showed me nothing but kindness.'

George took a moment before he spoke. 'It may well have been Ellis, but you cannot blame yourself for another's evil. I've been at the Schuttersgilde with the Cavaliers most of the morning. The gilde's stores were gone through, without success, for evidence of any weapon having gone missing. But then one of the janitors, who had unearthed some tattered inventory, found a lock broken on an old, almost forgotten cupboard. It was from here, it seems, that the lethal item had recently been stolen.' He rubbed his hands over his eyes. 'If it was Ellis, he has shown remarkable cunning, for it's impossible to say who might have taken the crossbow. And of course, wild rumours, contending with each other for improbability, are swirling all around town. The general opinion though is that it might have been anyone at all.'

There was silence in the little one-roomed cottage. Anne

looked down at her lap, then at the hem of her skirt, and the specks of mud that might have been blood. 'I feared,' she said at last, 'that people might say it was me.'

The look George Barton gave her, awkward, as if taken unawares and not knowing what to say, told her everything she needed to know: some people were saying it was her. He cleared his throat. 'We'll talk more of this, but first you should refresh yourself a little,' he glanced at her worn dress with its mud-spattered hem, 'and have something to eat.' Then he left her alone a few minutes, while he went to draw fresh water from the pump at the end of the street.

When he was gone, Anne looked around the small lodging. It was modest, and even in the glow of candles that struggled to enhance the light coming through the apartment's one mean window, it seemed devoid of ornament or colour. Anne wondered what sort of home a man of George Barton's evident upbringing had come from – a better one than this, that was certain. But then, so many men of his sort had had to live hand-to-mouth for years in the King's service, with the comforts of their former life only a memory, and she herself no longer had any home at all. The place was sparse, and clean, and tidy – an empty grate, a bed, a simple table with the chair on which she sat, a stool and a small travelling chest. Nothing to tell her anything more about George Barton than she already knew – a gentleman in the King's service, well-ordered in his habits and serious of purpose.

When he returned she said, 'It must make for a pleasant sanctuary, this.'

Barton looked around him and gave a rare smile. 'I have come to conceive a sort of affection for the place. It puts me in mind of home. Not my father's manor house,' he added, seeing her surprise, 'but it's not unlike the cottages in which some of our servants resided. Some of them were very kind to me. There was a dairymaid, very pretty, when I was a young boy, who would tease me that when I was older I must marry her. I was fervently in love.'

Anne smiled at the image.

'But then of course, I could hardly marry a dairymaid, could I? No doubt she lives in a cottage such as this now, with a stout husband and a brood of children. Or perhaps,' he continued, his voice hardening, 'her husband was killed in the war and her children too, of hunger or disease, and she is a hag from overwork and poverty.'

Anne felt any warmth or comfort go from the room, but George appeared not to have noticed anything strange in what he'd said. 'Anyhow,' he said, 'to business. Tell me what happened.'

As she had done in her own head a dozen times already that day, Anne went through for him what had happened as she'd been leaving the convent the night before. It took her some time.

George listened carefully, nodding from time to time and not interrupting. 'But,' he said at last, 'why were you trying to leave the convent in such a manner and at such an hour in the first place?'

Anne moved what was left of the food and drink he had given her aside before opening her bag. As succinctly as possible, she told him of Sister Janet's secret room, and of what she had found there. 'These are the papers and ledgers,' she said, 'of Sister Janet's activities in placing Jesuits in the homes of English Royalist families. This column lists the names of the men who have compromised themselves, this the families and estates on which Jesuit priests have subsequently been foisted.'

George was astonished. He lifted a candle and bent over the table to look properly. Then something in his demeanour changed. There was a sudden alertness, an air of excitement. His lips started to move.

'What is it?' she said.

He lifted a finger and indicated an entry halfway down the page. She followed with her eyes and read out the names of the family and estate noted there, before looking up at him for some further explanation.

'They're in Leicestershire,' he said, quickly adding that he had grown up in neighbouring Warwickshire. 'I'm almost certain that that estate borders the Beaumont lands. Lady Hildred very probably knew that family well.'

Anne looked again at the entry and then ran her eye across the page to its accompanying entry. 'Father Felipe,' she almost whispered.

'Is that not the priest from Sint-Walburga's?'

Anne nodded. 'He confesses Sister Janet and others amongst the sisters. He is rarely away from the convent.'

George studied the entry. 'Father Felipe was the Jesuit placed in that house from,' he bent lower over the page with his candle, '1653 to 1656.'

He put the candle down on the table and looked at Anne. 'Do you realise what this probably means?'

She nodded. 'Lady Hildred recognised him. I should have guessed it before. She almost told me herself, that last night we were at the Engels Klooster: "I'm sure I know that fellow." It was someone she said she'd seen before, in England. Anne closed her eyes and swallowed. 'I didn't ask her. In the morning. I was too taken up with other things. If only I had asked her—'

George dismissed her thought. 'What could you have done? The man seems to have the whole convent in his thrall.'

'Some have no choice. He made it clear he had plans for me. It's why I left when I did.'

'Plans?' Then she saw the realisation in George Barton's eyes. 'Ah,' he said. 'So he is at least a man, after all.'

Anne bit back her expression of shock. This matter of the Jesuits was enough of a distraction from her true purpose in Bruges without her falling out with her one confidant over it. She said instead, 'I couldn't risk being detained by him, when I had other business of such importance on hand.'

'Which is to expose Marchmont Ellis,' he said.

'I need to meet with him.'

George paused in his pacing and stared at her. 'Meet with him? You cannot meet with him. The man has been prepared to send his former comrades to the scaffold. He as good as murdered them. If you are right in thinking it was he who killed that nun last night, what do you think he might do to you?'

Anne was unmoved. 'I am not a defenceless old woman, sleeping sound in her bed. I will be ready for him. Some of those he betrayed were my friends. I need to be certain it is him and to find out if others are involved.'

George made no further effort to dissuade her. 'How do you intend to go about it?'

'It's why I had planned to come to you anyway – even before the horrors of last night. There is a letter I need you to deliver to him in the Bouchoute House. It is written in the code I know him to have been using. It will draw him out, and any who might be acting with him.'

George nodded. 'I'll deliver it. But when do you propose to meet with him?'

'At eleven tonight,' she said.

'You'll need somewhere safe to stay in the meantime.' He glanced around his cramped quarters and at the ladder to the attic. 'They will be hunting for you high and low after last night's events at the convent.'

'I've been told of somewhere that I might find sanctuary for a few nights.'

'Where?'

'There is a place halfway across the town between here

and the Engels Klooster. Just across the bridge from the Augustinian monastery. They call it the House of Lamentations.'

George Barton's face paled and he leaned closer to her. 'Lady Anne, you cannot go there. It is a—'

'I know what it is,' she interrupted, 'but I have been assured that I can find shelter there until I have accomplished what I came for.'

His eyes searched hers. 'But who would give you such an assurance – not Evan Glenroe? Surely you will not—'

'It wasn't Glenroe,' she said. 'The young woman with whom I exchanged this dress, who took my place in Lady Hildred's carriage after the ambush on the road to Damme, had sheltered there a while. It was Sister Janet herself who had sent her there.'

George stared at her for a moment then stood up. He looked truly shaken. 'If you must,' he said at last. 'And is that where you plan to meet with Ellis?'

She nodded.

'I'll be sure to be near at hand then,' he said.

TWENTY-ONE

News of Mr Longfellow

Thomas Faithly pushed away his trencher and wiped his mouth. It had been an excellent supper, and the Vlissinghe was as pleasant a place as any to pass the hours until the time came for them to meet with Mr Longfellow. Daunt was arguing with Glenroe over the virtues of German as opposed to Italian gunsmiths when Thomas saw George Barton walk into the hostelry's courtyard. He shifted along the bench to make room for him.

'We hadn't expected to see you again this evening, Barton,' said Glenroe.

'Your housekeeper told me I would find you here. I wondered if you had any more news of the Engels Klooster?'

'What?' said Daunt. 'More news than that an old nun was shot in her bed? Surely you cannot wish for more news from that benighted place?'

'I heard that another nun had gone missing,' said George.

'What other nun?' asked Glenroe.

'The one who was with her that day we encountered them outside Sint-Walburgakerk.'

'When did she go missing?' Thomas was surprised at the degree of interest Glenroe was showing in this.

'Last night some time. She must have left just after the old woman's body was discovered.'

Glenroe stood up.

'Where are you going, Evan?' Thomas asked.

But the Irishman didn't even turn around as he made his way between the tables of the courtyard and through the back door of the tavern. 'There is someone I need to see,' was all he said.

'You will not forget our appointment?' Daunt called after him.

'Never fear, I'll be there.'

'You must not be late – he will not wait on us!'

'Ten o'clock. I'll be there.'

'A late hour for an appointment,' commented George, affecting to examine the cards Ellis had just dealt him.

Thomas Faithly shot Daunt a murderous look. 'An old friend, making a brief visit.'

Some time later, on returning from a visit to the privy, Thomas found that Ellis had got into conversation with a Welsh officer of their acquaintance and left Daunt and George Barton alone, playing cards. Barton stood up when Thomas arrived back. 'Well, I must not keep you all, for fear you will miss your appointment at ten.'

'Never fear, Barton. It's not so far to Our Lady's.'

'Of the Pottery?' asked George, casually. 'Just a short stroll along the quay there.'

'Oh, no. Not of the Pottery. Back into town. The big one – Onze-Lieve-Vrouwekerk.' He leaned closer to George and winked, oblivious to the thunderous look Thomas was sending his way. 'Much more the thing for Mr Longfellow, don't you think?'

'Oh, much,' said George, pocketing the proceeds of the trick he had just won. 'I am sure.' Then he put on his hat and gave a rueful smile. 'Well, I fear Dunt has all but cleared me out. I must retire to my lodgings and lick my wounds, gentlemen.'

No one but Daunt made any attempt to stop him leaving, but just before he reached the door to the parlour, George turned back. He reached into his doublet and produced what looked to Thomas to be a letter. 'Oh, I almost forgot. Ellis, they gave me this for you at the Bouchoute House; they said it had been delivered for you earlier.' And with that, he made a bow to all three of them, and left.

Seeker often took his supper at 't Oud Handbogenhof. The innkeeper never asked the English carpenter any questions other than what he would have for his supper, and how his work had gone that day. The other workmen of the district had learned that John Carpenter had little conversation, and so left him to his own devices. He was finishing off a dish of mussels at his usual quiet table behind the door, and studying the letter that had come for him, when George Beaumont walked into the inn.

Seeker folded the letter and slid it into his jerkin. 'So, what have you learned about the carry-on up at the Engels Klooster?'

'The death of the old nun, you mean?'

'What else would I be talking about?'

George took the seat opposite him.

'Well, the Cavaliers all appear to have been genuinely shocked by the news, but I have had it from Thomas Faithly that both Daunt and Glenroe were up and about for several hours in the middle of the night. The weapon used to kill the old woman was an old one, taken from a half-forgotten cupboard in the Schuttersgilde.'

'By Evan Glenroe,' said Seeker.

George frowned. 'You think it was Evan Glenroe?'

'I think it more than likely.'

'Why him more than another?'

Seeker finished the last mussel and washed it down with a draught of beer. 'Because he was behind the murder of your mother.'

'What?'

Seeker tore a hunk of bread from the loaf in front of him. 'The man he paid to shoot her told me so.' He gave George Beaumont a brief account of his visits that morning to the Oude Steen and the hospital of Sint-Jans. 'He told me, this Piet, that the man who paid him to kill your mother was there when the ambush took place. He said it wasn't the man who shot him that had paid him, but the other one who was with him. It was Thomas Faithly who tried to go after their attacker and shot at him. The man on escort duty with him was Evan Glenroe.'

Beaumont looked puzzled. 'I still don't understand,' he said. 'If my mother was shot because your spy feared she was the she-intelligencer sent to find him out, then surely Marchmont Ellis is the man behind it, not Glenroe.'

'For all we know, your mother was killed for some other reason entirely. The money, for instance. Glenroe has as much need of that as any of them. What's he up to tonight?'

George told Seeker of an encounter he'd had earlier in the evening with the Cavaliers at the Vlissinghe, and that Glenroe had made a hasty exit after the subject of Sister Janet's death had been introduced.

'Where was he off to?' demanded Seeker.

George shrugged. 'He wouldn't say.'

'I bet he wouldn't,' said Seeker. 'Tell me, what are they saying up at the convent about Anne Winter?'

George lifted his beer stein and took a draught. 'I heard it was only the old woman who had been targeted.'

'It was, but Lady Anne has gone missing. She hasn't been seen since last night.'

Beaumont looked surprised. 'So what are you saying? That she's been abducted by Sister Janet's assailant?'

Seeker practically snorted. 'Abducted? Her? Have you listened to a single thing I've said about that woman, Beaumont? Anne Winter isn't the kind of woman to get herself abducted.' He pushed his bowl away. 'Mind you, she's not the kind of woman to murder elderly nuns in their beds, either. Either way, we'll need to get hold of her before anyone else does.'

'It's the Jesuits,' said George, as if to himself. And then directly to Seeker, 'I think the Jesuits will have her.'

'The Jesuits?' The sight of Anne Winter being led away from the Augustinian priory came back into Seeker's mind. 'Go on,' he said. Beaumont relayed to him a story of Sister Janet and Father Felipe and the blackmailing of patrons of the Bouchoute House he said he had got from Anne Winter. 'They've been placing Jesuits all over England, amongst families that would never otherwise have sheltered them.'

Seeker shook his head in reluctant admiration. 'I knew Janet was up to something. No wonder she got herself killed. But what about Anne Winter, what was she going to do with this information?'

George frowned. 'I believe she planned to copy the materials. Father Felipe's name was on the list of those priests who'd been sent to England. Anne Winter believed my mother recognised him.'

'Did she now? Well, if Lady Hildred recognised him, it's more than likely he recognised her too, and if he did, he'll have taken steps double-quick to keep her quiet – got Glenroe to do the dirty work. If Father Felipe's got hold of Anne Winter, it's the last we'll see of her. She'll be in a cell in the Prinsenhof until she gives up what she has discovered and then – well, who knows?'

George gave Seeker an appraising look. 'You seem remarkably untroubled on her behalf.'

Seeker had heard, over a long period of time, from his friend, the Jewish apothecary John Drake, what the Spanish inquisitors did to people.

'That's only because I doubt very much that my old friend Lady Winter has allowed herself to be caught by Father Felipe or anyone else,' he said. 'I wouldn't wish the horrors of the inquisition on anyone. Glenroe's obviously mixed up in this business too. We'll need to get hold of Lady Anne, and those lists of hers, before either he or Felipe does.'

George nodded. 'Where should we begin looking?'

Seeker took a moment to think before he responded. 'I doubt she'll make for Damme – too much chance of meeting with more Jesuits there. She'll not want to hang about Bruges, that's for certain, but she'll need help to get away. She'll have to take a chance on enlisting one of the others – Faithly, Glenroe or Daunt to help her. I hope for her sake it's not Glenroe, but my money would be on Faithly. Their paths have crossed in the past.'

This was obviously news to George. 'How?'

'Never mind. But if she knows your friends are expecting Prince Rupert or the Duke of Ormonde or some other star of Charles Stuart's firmament to show up any day now in Bruges, I suspect she'd risk almost anything to get to him. Stay close to Thomas Faithly, regardless of what the rest do or say. And get a message to me the minute you know anything about the plans for this Mr Longfellow's visit.'

Beaumont leaned forward. 'That's what I've come about,'

he said. 'They're to meet Mr Longfellow in Onze-Lieve-Vrouwekerk at ten tonight. Daunt let it slip.'

'Tonight?' said Seeker, puffing out his lips. 'Well, that gives us almost two hours at any rate.'

'For what?'

'For you to start looking for that woman.'

'And what are you going to do?' asked Beaumont.

'Oh, I have business with another woman tonight.'

George Beaumont left, and as Seeker returned to his stable loft, he wondered why it was that Beaumont hadn't told him yesterday of Anne Winter's discovery of the Jesuit plot. The first answer that came to mind – that Beaumont hadn't known of it yesterday – was troubling, for if Beaumont hadn't known about it yesterday, how was it that he knew about it today?

Seeker had taken some care over washing himself at the end of his working day. He had trimmed his beard and put on a shirt newly laundered by the innkeeper's wife. Now, back in his stable loft, he took off his jerkin, carefully laying aside the letter from Lawrence warning him of the Ellingworths' imminent departure for Massachusetts, that he'd read again and again. From a hook set in the rafters of the loft he took down and brushed his best grey worsted coat, new made for him by a tailor up north on his last visit to Yorkshire and worn only on Sundays. He pulled out the loose brick behind which he kept his money and filled a small bag with coins. On his way out through the stable yard, he crossed over to the kitchen garden of the inn and plucked a stem of mint. Madame Hélène was no fool. The only way he was going to get the girl Beatte to himself for the hour he could spare before he set out for Onze-Lieve-Vrouwekerk was to play his part beyond suspicion. He pulled the leaves from the stem of mint and began to chew, as he set out on the short walk to the House of Lamentations.

TWENTY-TWO

View from a Window

He'd never been in the House of Lamentations by night before, only by day. What was shabby, jaded and faded in the light of day took on a completely different aspect, one full of unnamed promises, by candlelight. Madame Hélène, the tokens of whose profession were rendered all too visible by the harsh hues of the morning sun, was restored by night to something of what must have been the exceptional beauty of her youth. She was dressed in a low-cut gown of lush green silk, and what appeared to be emeralds sparkled at her neck. Her dark-red lips curled in amusement as she looked him up and down. 'The English carpenter. But where are your leather apron and cap tonight, Mr Carpenter?'

'I'm not here to earn tonight, but to pay,' he said.

'Indeed?' she said, and now her eyes showed genuine interest. 'And I wonder what it is you have come here to pay for?'

'A woman,' he said, 'what else?'

Her eyes widened. 'What else indeed, Carpenter? But you

will find we are above the common run of establishments. This is no dockworkers' tavern.'

'I know it,' he said. 'You need not concern yourself that I haven't the money.'

She was openly appraising him. 'Oh, I have no fears about any . . .' she paused, 'deficiency, John Carpenter. Anna,' she called, and a young girl appeared almost instantly from somewhere beyond a set of heavy velvet drapes. 'I expect to be engaged for some time. Have Nette greet any clients who arrive meantime.'

The girl bobbed a curtsy and Madame Hélène drifted towards the stairs. A mother-of-pearl encrusted, satin-slippered foot on the lowest step and an elegant hand on the banister, she turned to Seeker who had not moved from his position in the entrance hall. 'You may follow me, Carpenter.'

'I've not come for you.'

Her cat-like smile briefly faltered before re-establishing itself. 'You must not worry about the fee. It would, I agree, be prohibitive for most men of your station, but I am *from time to time* inclined to make an exception.'

'I haven't come for you,' he repeated.

The smile froze on her face and he continued. 'The girl Beatte.'

'She's busy,' Madame Hélène snapped.

'I'll pay double.'

Her laugh was derisive.

'Double your price, not hers.'

'You couldn't afford it.'

He held up the bag of coins. 'Count them, if you like.'

She did. Sweeping back from the stairs she snatched the bag from him and poured its contents out on the top of the huge dresser in the hall. Her fingers moved quicker than a fishwife's gutting herring. Scooping the coins back into the bag she tied it and kept it in her grip. 'Griet,' she called, then more angrily, 'Griet, you lazy wretch!'

The girl came running.

'Tell Beatte to hurry that fat butcher along; she has another customer.' Then she turned to Seeker. 'One hour, and don't dare to cross my threshold again.'

A short time later, Seeker was standing in a small room overlooking the bottom of Kortewinkel and the Augustinians' Bridge. The last of the evening light was gone, and the canal waters glistened with the reflection of lights from the merchant's house at Ter Brughe and the monastery opposite. Merchants, monks, harlots, all living their lives in this quiet quarter of this small town, hundreds of miles away from anything that mattered to him. One more night, and then he'd be gone.

Within little more than an hour, in a church across town, Marchmont Ellis, the man who had been his spy, would be meeting a high-ranking courtier of Charles Stuart. Whether Rupert, Ormonde or the Duke of York – it would make no difference in the end. Ellis had not told him of this meeting, therefore Ellis had turned again, was not to be trusted, was dangerous. By all the protocols he had learned or been taught, Seeker should have been effecting his own escape from Bruges right now. His source's turning meant it was he who was now compromised. Within little more than an hour, he would be betrayed – if he had not been already – and he would be hunted. And yet he was standing here, in a young whore's bedchamber, trying to uncover the truth of the murder of a young man of little account whom he had met only for an afternoon. He just couldn't shake off the memory of Bartlett Jones, who'd come all the way to try to find his sister. Tonight was Seeker's last chance to somehow lay that image to rest by finding out for himself what might have become of the girl before he himself had to leave this city, for good.

'What are you doing here?'

Beatte had come in almost soundlessly, and just as soundlessly closed the door behind her. He had seen her before only by the light of day, when she might have been taken for perhaps a lady's maid or merchant's daughter. Now, by night, there could be no doubt as to what she was. Her face was powdered like an old daub and her lips and cheeks were stained with a rouge that they did not need. Her dress, more voile then gown, was cut lower than was decent and the bodice only half-laced. The room, now that he looked at it, was hung about everywhere with drapes, and the bed covered in satin and velvet cushions. The cloying incense burning in a censer hanging from the ceiling could not fully mask the pervasive odours of human sweat and other men.

Seeker cast about for somewhere to sit. There was only the bed. He remained standing at the window. 'I'm here about Ruth Jones,' he said.

Panic flitted across her face before she mustered her lie. 'I don't know her.'

'Oh, but you do, or did. She slept on a small cot behind a wall of empty barrels in the cellars of this house. She was English, and the brother who came looking for her was murdered within sight of your window. And hers. Want to start talking?'

Beatte backed against the door. 'I told you, I don't know her.'

'All right then, Sister Janet.'

'I . . .'

'Don't even pretend you don't know who I'm talking about now. The English nun, in business with Father Felipe. Blackmailing the men who came to this brothel.'

'Not all of them . . .' she began but stopped when she realised her mistake.

'Just the English ones, eh? Like the men who come here from the Bouchoute House.'

'We had no choice. Father Felipe—'

'Oh, I know all about Father Felipe. But Father Felipe wouldn't have risked being seen here, would he? Unless, of course, he came by the tunnel. Very handy, that.'

'The tunnel is for our protection. It offers a means of escape, should we ever need it. Madame Hélène knows what happens to houses like this when enemy soldiers come.

And then . . .' She hesitated, but had clearly gone on so far she decided there was no going back. 'Sister Janet used it.'

'To spy on the men?'

Beatte smiled. 'No! The idea! She would have been greatly shocked. No, she used it when she came to collect our . . . depositions, she called them – and to bring girls here.'

Seeker had not even begun to consider this. 'You mean she procured young girls to work in a brothel?'

Beatte's face opened up in delight; she could not hide her amusement at his misunderstanding. 'No! Sister Janet a procuress? Never. She brought girls – women – here who needed to be safe, somewhere to hide.'

'Hide? Who from?'

She threw up her hands as if he were stupid. 'Cruel husbands, or fathers trying to force them into marriages with men they cannot abide. They flee to the convents, but sometimes the convents are worse than the places they have left.'

'Because of men like Father Felipe?'

Beatte nodded. 'Sister Janet knew – what he liked. If a woman or girl turned up seeking refuge at the convent, and she thought Father Felipe or others like him might prey upon her, or give her up to the men they were running from, she would bring her here, and Madame Hélène would allow her to work in the kitchens or the laundry until some other escape could be found for her.'

'She brought them in by the tunnel,' said Seeker, a hint of admiration creeping into his voice.

'Yes. And they left that way too when the time came.'

'And Ruth Jones was one such girl.'

Beatte swallowed and she looked frightened again. 'I cannot tell you anything about Ruth Jones.'

Seeker took a step towards her, but she shrank back further against the door. He held up his hands. 'All right, all right. I mean you no harm, believe it. But I must know more about Ruth Jones. Her brother came looking for her and the next day was dead – his body fished out of the canal beneath your window. Sister Janet, who, if what you say is true, is likely to have tried to help her, is also dead, murdered. Ruth herself and any other who tried to help her may be in grave danger. I cannot help her if you will not tell me what you know.'

Tears had formed in the girl's eyes and were now spilling onto her cheeks.

'Please,' he said. 'Has any man, any but me, come to the House of Lamentations here asking about Ruth Jones?'

At last she nodded.

'When?' he said, almost scared to breathe lest he put her off.

'The night . . . her brother had been found dead in the morning, and the man came that night.'

'Who saw him?'

'Anna. Only Anna,' she said, the words from her trembling lips almost inaudible. 'She usually worked in the kitchens but the upper-house girls were all – busy – that night. He came in well after dark, she said.'

'Did she know him?'

Beatte shook her head and sniffed. 'But Anna wouldn't know the patrons anyway. He scared her terribly. As soon as she said "no" to his enquiry as to whether Ruth was there, he accused her of lying. Began to threaten her. Eventually she told him that Ruth had been there, but had left that day, after her brother's body had been found, but she didn't know where she'd gone. The man threatened her again – threatened to do worse to her than he'd done to Ruth' – Beatte looked up at him – 'have you seen her face?'

'I've heard,' said Seeker.

'Anna took fright, that he would come back when he found she'd lied to him.'

'Had she lied to him?'

Beatte nodded. 'Ruth was still here, in the cellar – she didn't get away to the Engels Klooster until the early hours of the next morning. Anna had used up all her courage in the lie for Ruth's sake. She was too terrified to stay and face the Englishman should he return. She left us the next day and wouldn't tell us where she was going for fear Ruth's husband would make us tell him.'

'Ruth's husband?' said Seeker.

'You didn't know it was her husband she was running from?'

'No,' he said. 'Tell me everything you can.'

Beatte took a breath, a little calmer now. 'This man had been quartered on her father's house in their English town. He was a gentleman, an officer, and he took an increasing interest in Ruth. Ruth's parents were greatly flattered, and so, for a time, was she. When his regiment moved on from the town, he persuaded Ruth's parents to send her after him. The war had removed almost all the suitable young men of the town, and they were only too glad when they thought she had got a husband. Her brother was away from home, so had no say in the matter.'

'What happened then?' asked Seeker.

'She travelled from her home and family to join this man. The further they journeyed from her home, the crueller he became. She got away from him once, but she had no money and no connections and he soon found her. He beat her so badly she . . .' she looked up at him, biting her lower lip, 'she could never have worked above stairs here, as I do.'

'She's very badly disfigured?'

She nodded. 'When he crossed the sea, he took her with him. She got away at last, with the help of an officer's wife, and found her way to Bruges, where she sought refuge at the Engels Klooster. But Father Felipe didn't like seeing her around there – he said it *offended* him.' Beatte invested the word with almost more disgust than she had used in speaking of Ruth's husband. 'Sister Janet brought her here. When her brother was killed, Sister Janet helped her flee again. I don't know where to.'

'What was his name?' asked Seeker.

'His name? Bartlett, I think.'

'Not her brother,' said Seeker, trying to be patient, 'the man she was running from.'

Beatte shook her head. 'I don't know. She would never say. She said he would make us believe it was she who was lying and he telling the truth. She said he'd managed to do that almost everywhere they went. Do you know who he is?'

'No,' said Seeker. 'I don't, but I promise you, Beatte, I will find him, and I will see to it that he can never harm her again.'

After extracting all she knew from Beatte, Seeker had made haste on leaving the House of Lamentations, and by the time he reached the Dijver he could see the Cavaliers ahead of him, making for Onze-Lieve-Vrouwekerk. Faithly and Ellis went in at the main door of the church, whilst Daunt and Glenroe took up their positions outside. As he drew closer, Seeker saw that others – Spaniards among them – were already standing guard there and at the side doors. There was no possibility of him getting into the church undetected. He had half-suspected that that would be the case, and so turned to his remaining option: the Gruuthuse.

Lodewijk van Gruuthuse's palace had seen more than one incarnation since his descendants had sold it to the King of Spain. For now, it was all but abandoned, save for the wing housing the pawnbroker's store, the *mons pietatis*. The town kept a guard on the place all the same, for fear of idlers and vagrants.

The gatekeeper at the main door was sleeping when Seeker arrived, but a couple of knocks roused him.

'We're closed,' the man grumbled. 'Come back tomorrow.'

'Can't. I have to make my report at the Stadhuis tomorrow – there's been talk of rotting floorboards upstairs. The Burgemeester insists that it's looked at tonight.'

The man looked at Seeker, craned his neck. 'You've no tools tonight, John Carpenter.'

'Just a report and a price – that's all they need from me. I don't need any tools for that.'

The man was unimpressed. 'What need call a carpenter to say if a floorboard is rotten or not? This town goes to the dogs.' He let Seeker in nevertheless and passed him a lit lamp. 'You know where you're going?'

'Oh, yes,' said Seeker. 'I know where I'm going.'

He passed quickly through a series of empty rooms and was soon going through a side door into what had been the grand entrance of the Gruuthuse palace. He'd been here once before, as part of a squad of workers doing essential repairs to the house. He'd taken time then, to admire the quality of the carving of the staircase and balustrades, the ceiling pendants and corbels, all shut off now, wasted. Tonight there was no time for any such admiration. He made his way as quickly as possible to van Gruuthuse's oratory. The Lord of Gruuthuse had, almost two hundred years before, built a private chapel in his house and secured the permission of the church authorities to have the windows of this private chapel cut into the very walls of the neighbouring Onze-Lieve-Vrouwekerk. Lodewijk and his family would not mix with the lower sorts, the other wealthy merchants and burghers even, at their worship. Rather, they would sit in the grandeur of their own home and hear the mass through the windows of their oratory, which opened directly above the choir of the church. 'Good man, Lodewijk,' Seeker murmured to himself as he passed beneath the ribbed vault of the oratory to take up his position at the window. 'Good man.'

He'd left his own candle in the anteroom of the private chapel for fear of attracting the notice of anyone in the church below. Beneath him, the church, a confusion of ideas laid one upon the other over the centuries, was lit as if for a feast day. In the chancel below, Charles the Bold and his daughter, Mary of Burgundy, lay, as they had done for over a hundred years, beneath their golden sepulchres, glinting in the flickering light. Above the stalls of the choir were the arms of the Knights of the Golden Fleece, who had met here once, he'd been told. It wasn't the Knights of the Golden Fleece who met here tonight, though, and the man in whose name they met could only dream of wielding a tenth of the power that had been Charles the Bold's.

Faithly and Ellis were standing just beneath the altar, looking down the aisle. Armed men stood at doorways or archways leading off the side aisles to chapels or corridors of the huge church. There was no other sound or movement from anywhere in the church until suddenly the great bells in the tower began to toll the hour, and Seeker heard the oak doors at the other end of the aisle open, and a trio of brisk footsteps begin to make their way down the aisle.

Edward Daunt appeared first, but Seeker couldn't crane
his neck enough to see who came behind him. He looked
instead again at Thomas Faithly and Marchmont Ellis, just
as each sank on one knee. And then Seeker knew. This was
no Prince Rupert or Duke of Ormonde, no Duke of York
either. Not Charles the Bold but that other Charles, that
impoverished, rootless, vagabond Charles, that King that
had never had a kingdom.

A half-head taller than any other man in the place apart
from Seeker himself, hair black as the ace of spades and
the skin of a Spaniard, Charles could have been no one
other than who he was, and yet Seeker knew him to have
travelled half of England and many miles of the Low Countries too, in disguise. The pauper, beggar king, the man of
fable. Charles leaned forward and touched Thomas Faithly
on the shoulder and Thomas stood up, to be embraced.
Ellis received a gracious nod and was permitted to kiss the
King's hand, no more, as if Charles already knew who was
his Judas. Daunt and then Glenroe drew alongside them,
and Charles addressed all of them.

Charles was in buoyant mood, his words carrying to
Seeker as the acoustics of the church did their work. 'Our
hour is almost come, friends, and the good Lord has seen
to do it in the most unexpected of ways. It behoves us to
give thanks, which is why I have called you to this place.
We will see to the business I have come upon, but first let
us give thanks.'

It was clear to Seeker that the Cavaliers, no more than

he himself, knew what they were to give thanks for. Nevertheless, the next moment they were on their knees in emulation of the man they would have as their king. Charles was praying, a litany of texts from the prayer book that had brought his father's throne to destruction. Seeker settled to observing the men below him. It was impossible to hear now what was said, although he thought he recognised snatches of the Prayer Book that had heralded the Stuart dynasty's downfall. Charles then rose from his knees and drew the Cavaliers closer to him. Even less of what he now told them was audible to Seeker, but it was plain to him from the expressions that appeared on their faces that they very much liked what they heard.

The conference was short, though, and soon Charles was back on his feet and clapping his hands. 'Now, our devotions done, a toast I think, my friends. The tide turns at last and by God! It will carry us home!'

If any of the Cavaliers were shocked by their King's blasphemy in such a place, they masked it well. Daunt smiled broadly and slapped Marchmont Ellis on the back. 'You see, Ellis, did I not tell you, a little faith was all that was wanted.' From his vantage point, Seeker could see that while Ellis's jollity was half-hearted, Thomas Faithly looked unconvinced.

'We have known false dawns before now, sir. I would urge you to caution.'

Daunt stepped in before the King could speak. 'Caution, Thomas? Caution be damned! God smiles on us tonight!'

Charles reached out a hand and clapped his exuberant countryman on the shoulder. 'I begin to believe it, my faithful Dunt. I begin at last to believe it. But let us go and celebrate this news in a more suitable place.' And then they were all making their way back down the aisle of Onze-Lieve-Vrouwekerk. Seeker was instantly on his feet and sprinting back down the great stairs and through the suite of empty rooms, waking the watchman once again as he passed.

'What the devil?!' shouted the man, but Seeker didn't stop to answer him.

He was through the courtyard and out onto the street in time to see that Charles, surrounded still by the four Cavaliers, was headed off in the direction of the centre of town. He leaned back against a wall to catch his breath a moment, then, taking care to keep to the shadows, followed.

At the Grote Markt Ellis suddenly quickened his pace to stand in front of the others. He said something, gestured in a direction different to where they were headed, and on Charles making some response, made a deep bow and stepped back to allow the others to continue on their way. Seeker watched as Ellis observed the others disappear towards the burg and then himself make off in the other direction, towards Vlamingstraat. Which way should he go? Seeker decided to follow Marchmont Ellis.

TWENTY-THREE

Beneath the House of Lamentations

Anne Winter shivered. It had been cold coming through the Augustinians' tunnel and it was little better in the cellars of the House of Lamentations. She had not thought it wise to continue to wear her nun's cloak in town, and Ruth Jones's old green jacket might once have been of good quality but now it was worn and thin. Anne thought of the blue velvet jacket with marten trim that she had had made in London last year, and wished she had it with her, but lady's maids did not wear blue velvet jackets with marten trim.

Her whole body was tense with waiting. Every unexpected sound had her on the alert. The gusts of laughter and music, or the outburst of the cook at some imaginary catastrophe in the kitchen above her were a comfort, a reminder of normal life going on close by. But down here in the cellars, with their dark recesses, their creaks and their echoes, their proximity to the depths of the canal, it was different, and Anne couldn't help feeling apprehensive. It might well be that her ruse had not worked, and that Marchmont Ellis would either not come alone, or not come at all.

At least someone – George Barton – would know where she was. He'd gone to arrange for the horses and the drawing up of papers that would be necessary for their departure from Bruges. He'd been certain he would have all ready, and be waiting above, in the kitchens of the House of Lamentations, to come to her aid should she need it. After her appointment with Marchmont Ellis, he'd assured her, there would be nothing more to detain either of them in this city.

The bells of Bruges began to ring: it was eleven. Anne watched the door at the far end of the cellar. She'd learned of the tunnel and the sanctuary it led to in a letter from Ruth Jones that she'd found amongst Sister Janet's papers. She'd told Marchmont Ellis to come this way. She'd placed a candle in the sconce by the tunnel door, so that she might know for certain who came through it. As the muffled sound of the last peal of bells died away into the night, the handle started to turn.

The door opened and she saw him. 'Marchmont Ellis,' she said, stepping into the light.

Ellis's eyes met hers in shock. 'You!'

Anne felt a little rush of power at the look on the turncoat's face. 'Who had you been expecting?'

'Someone – else.' He looked about him, as if that someone else might materialise from the darkness. 'The letter – the code.'

'Yes,' she said. 'The code by which you have been communicating your information back to London, to Secretary Thurloe.'

'Through John Carpenter,' he said. 'Why didn't he fore-warn me of this?'

She looked at him quizzically. Something Sister Janet had said hovered in the shadows of her mind. 'And who is John Carpenter?'

'Surely you know, if you have come from Mr Thurloe?'

Anne smiled. 'But I have not. I have been sent here by the Great Trust to uncover the traitor who has been delivering our every plan to Cromwell's agents. If this John Carpenter is someone you are working with then I think I must deliver to him the same message I have for you. Your time is up.'

Marchmont Ellis looked genuinely amazed. 'Astonishing. Absolutely astonishing, Mistress whatever-your-name-is. This is really quite amusing. But I have been getting bored of Bruges. I had decided to leave anyway. Your happy revelation has given me a much better idea. A transaction, if you like.'

He moved towards her and Anne tried to step back another pace but found her way blocked by the stack of barrels. 'There will be no transactions between us,' she said. 'You will sign the paper I have prepared and your family will be permitted to live with honour. If you do not sign it, your treachery will be published across England.'

Ellis now let out a small explosion of laughter. 'My treachery published? By whom?'

She wanted to knife him that very minute but controlled

the impulse. 'By those you have wronged, or those who are left, at least. By the men and women of the Sealed Knot and the Great Trust, whose brothers-in-arms your betrayal sent to Cromwell's dungeons and then his scaffold.'

He looked a little chastened, but soon recovered himself. 'That's a pretty speech, but we have hardly the time for pretty speeches. If we go now, I can lay my hands on more money than you have ever seen. We can be gone from Bruges, you and I, go our separate ways into Europe and no one ever find either of us.'

'You are mad, I think,' was all she said in reply.

'Not so,' he said. 'Your old mistress's money lies in a strongbox in a safe space in the Bouchoute House. An hour from now, my good friends Edward Daunt, Thomas Faithly and Evan Glenroe will be removing it from its place of safety and carrying it to De Garre, where they are currently carousing with His Majesty the King. We can get to it first but we must go now.'

Anne was bewildered. 'You think I would risk everything I have risked for mere *money*?'

'Why else would a maidservant take the risks you have taken? Why should you care more for one cause than the other? It is surely all the same for the likes of you.' He turned as if to go back to the tunnel.

Anne unsheathed her knife and held it up. 'Sign the paper, Ellis.'

He spun round to grip the wrist of the hand that held the knife. For a man who looked slight of build, he had immense strength. He lifted her arm so that the tip of the blade came within an inch of his own throat, before twisting her arm behind her back so quickly she thought it might break. The knife clattered to the floor. 'Sign it yourself, my pretty,' he spat, before forcing her down onto the ground.

As she hit the floor, Anne managed to roll away and started to get to her feet. Ellis lunged at her but she kicked out and caught him on the side of the knee. He stumbled and swore and came after her again. She could see the light beneath the door at the top of the stone stairs leading to the kitchens and bolted for them, knocking over a pile of empty barrels as she passed. The sound reverberating around the vaults was like a battery of gunfire. George Barton would surely hear it. She heard Ellis curse again as he pushed the rolling barrels aside. She reached the stair and managed to catch hold of the guide rope secured to the wall. She was up three steps, and then four, when she felt the pull at the back of her skirts. She strained to keep going but he was pulling her back. She cursed the material that would not rip. She tried to kick out behind, but only succeeded in losing her footing and falling. Still the door to the kitchens remained closed. And now Marchmont Ellis was on her. He turned her over, had her pinned by the shoulders. Without thinking, she twisted her head and sank her teeth as hard as she could into the exposed flesh of his arm. He called out in pain and let go her shoulders to grasp his injured arm. Anne rolled again and fell the few feet off the side of the stairway to the floor. That was when she saw he had dropped the knife.

Anne lunged across the floor for the knife but before she could reach it she felt the thud of his boot below her ribs and into her stomach. She doubled up and wheezed before reaching again for the knife. A swing of the other boot caught her in the side of the jaw and she felt her upper teeth sink into her lower lip. The blood was streaming down her chin as she staggered once more to her feet, just in time to see Marchmont Ellis lift his bleeding arm, the knife in his hand, while grabbing her with his other arm. She tried to turn away but his grip was too strong for her and she felt her knees go from under her, her body give up the fight. He pulled her up by the hair, which he twisted around his fist to bring her very close to his face. 'You've had your chance, and now it's over.' He lifted his arm and she saw the point of her own knife aimed at her neck.

As the knife started to move towards her, there was an almighty crash, not from the kitchens above but from the direction of the tunnel, and Ellis's arm was momentarily frozen in mid-air before being twisted up behind him. Ellis let out a yell, dropping the knife at the same moment as he loosed his grip on her hair. Suddenly, not only his arm, but his whole body seemed to twist round before being lifted into the air and flung against the wall of the cellar. Anne watched in disbelief as Ellis slid to the floor before trying to get up again, one hand flailing for the dagger she now saw sheathed beneath his torn doublet. He never reached it, a heavy boot forcing him back to the ground before powerful arms reached out and snapped his neck. Ellis's body slumped again to the floor but this time did not move. Shaking almost uncontrollably, Lady Anne looked into the face of her deliverer and realised, at last, that she too must be dead.

Seeker flexed his fingers. It was a long time since he'd snapped a man's neck, and he hoped never to have to do it again. He turned Ellis's body over with his foot and crouched down beside the trembling form of the woman.

'You just can't stay out of trouble, can you?' he said.

Even in the slight golden light of the candles, Anne Winter's face was deathly white. She was staring at him. She moved herself back against the wall, pushed the hair away from her eyes. 'You're supposed to be dead,' she said at last.

'And you're supposed to be behaving yourself,' he answered.

'But the bear, people saw your body . . .'

'People will see what they want to see,' he said. 'Enough people that wanted me dead thought they saw me dead. It seemed a shame to disappoint them.'

'But Manon, Maria . . .' she said.

'Are my business. And I know what yours is. Or was,' he corrected, nodding over to the dead form of Marchmont Ellis.

He saw the understanding dawn. 'You're John Carpenter,' she said. 'You were his handler.'

'More or less,' he said, 'in as far as he was worth.'

'He betrayed countless good men,' she said.

'They'd set themselves up for it, traitors to the Lord Protector.'

'The Lord . . .'

He'd lifted a finger to stop her. 'Another time, I think, Lady Anne. There are other things requiring my attention for now.' He leaned towards her. 'May I . . .' He lifted away the hair that had fallen down about her face before gently examining the damage to her jaw. 'It's not broken, but you'll be black and blue for a while. What about your teeth?'

He saw her probe her mouth. 'Still there,' she said.

'Good. Right, I'll help you up those stairs to the kitchens – they'll look after you – and then I've to be elsewhere.'

She pressed her hands on the floor and began to push herself up. 'I'll manage myself,' she said. 'Just one thing?'

'What?' he said, starting to haul Marchmont Ellis's body towards a darkened recess of the vault.

'Was it only Ellis, or was one of the others involved too?'

He pondered a moment. He didn't need to answer her anything at all, but she deserved something for her courage. 'No,' he said. 'It was just him.' He didn't tell her that everywhere Charles Stuart went, wherever his threadbare court settled, Secretary Thurloe had eyes and ears at the very centre of things. Ellis's job had been to report on any conspiracies fomenting in Bruges. Europe was full of desperate Englishmen like Marchmont Ellis. If the Stuarts didn't know that, they were even greater fools than they had already shown themselves to be.

She nodded, then began to make her slow way towards the bottom of the stairs. Seeker watched her a moment but knew he really had no time to wait any longer. He had an appointment with Mr Longfellow.

TWENTY-FOUR

De Garre

Thomas Faithly laughed, but his laughter came a beat after that of the others. Daunt gave him a concerned look. 'What's up, old fellow?'

'It's nothing,' he said as quietly as he could.

The King turned his attention away from the fiddler in the corner. '"If it be nothing, I shall not need spectacles."' Thomas had noticed before that he missed very little. 'Lear,' Charles added, in response to a bemused look from Daunt. 'I always preferred a comedy. But tell me, Thomas. What do you think Will Shakespeare would have made of our present predicaments?'

Thomas measured his words as best he could. 'Perhaps he would have found the matter for his greatest hero, Your Majesty.'

'Or perhaps not?'

Thomas thought for a moment he had gone too far, but eventually the King's features relaxed and he lifted his own glass. 'A history, I would have, but no more of tragedies.'

'Then we should proceed with caution, sir,' said Faithly.

'Too many of our friends and your loyal servants have lost their lives for the lack of it.'

'And how are we to guard against the treachery of those we think our friends?' asked Charles. 'Shouldn't Ellis be back by now? What manner of errand can be keeping him this time?'

'Nothing good, I'll wager,' said Glenroe, who had been growing increasingly restless.

Daunt and Faithly glanced at one another. 'Ellis has gone to the Bouchoute House, to make ready Lady Hildred's . . . consignment . . . for transport with Your Majesty. He said he would send word when it was ready.'

'He appears to be taking an uncommon length of time over the matter.'

Glenroe clenched his fist. Daunt glanced at Thomas and cleared his throat. 'Ellis has disappeared a little too often of late – always something to see to, something he has forgotten, something he has promised to do. Always vague, never any details.'

'What are you saying, Dunt?' asked Thomas.

'What we're all thinking, Thomas,' said Glenroe before turning to the king. 'By your leave, Your Majesty, but I think one of us must go and see what's keeping him.'

'All of you go,' said Charles. 'Safer that way, and I daresay it will take at least two of you to transport the money. I can come to little harm in this tavern.'

Thomas gave a careful smile. 'Changed days, sir, if you can find no trouble in a tavern.'

Charles laughed but Thomas broke into the laughter. 'You have always been too careless of your safety, sir. Glenroe and I will go back to the Bouchoute House. Dunt will stay with you.'

'Then all will be well,' said Charles. 'Now go, both of you. Go and see to my money.'

Daunt sat more upright, the look of befuddlement gone. 'Go on,' he said to his friends, 'and keep your wits about you.'

'We'll be back as soon as possible.' Thomas nodded to the King and followed Glenroe down the stairs to the ground floor. Glenroe impatiently brushed aside a couple of porters and a carpenter attempting to come up the steps from the narrow alley. By the time they reached the Markt, his sense of foreboding was almost overwhelming.

After scanning the ground-floor taproom and finding no sign of who he was looking for, Seeker climbed the wooden steps to the upper gallery of the tavern. All might have been up a moment before, had Faithly and Glenroe not been so obviously bent on getting somewhere else in a hurry. Not once in the months since Faithly had appeared in Bruges had Seeker come anything like as close to him, and now, at a crucial moment, they had almost come face to face. The means of escape from this tavern were not the best. Till now, it was he who hid himself, found exit routes, always considering his means of escape. A turning of his head, a drawing in of his shoulders and the affecting of a stoop as Faithly had hurried past had allowed him to escape the other Yorkshireman's notice. He was not sure that this tactic would work here.

As soon as he was at the head of the stairs he saw them: Charles and Edward Daunt. Seeker could have laughed. Not another soul in the crowded tavern seemed to be paying the slightest attention to the fact that the man who called himself King of England was sitting, laughing and drinking in their midst. Here, Charles was not a fugitive, but neither could he move quite freely. The Spaniards gave him sanctuary whilst refusing openly to acknowledge him. The Dutch, over the northern border, would not allow his sister, the Princess of Orange, to have him in her house in the Hague. His mother was a princess of the blood in France, his cousin the King, but the French would not have him either. So Charles Stuart, who called himself King of England, spent his days like the third son of an impoverished English gentleman for whom a role in life was yet to be found. When he was not pleading with his Spanish hosts that they might allow him to visit them in their palaces, or rouse themselves to join him in attempting to regain his own, he went fowling, he practised at the butts, he drank with reckless Irishmen and slow-witted men of Kent in crowded, lowly taverns.

But Glenroe was not here, only Daunt. Seeker had not yet reached the empty bench he had spotted in the far corner of the upper parlour when the Englishman announced of a sudden that he must get to the jakes and the King laughingly dismissed him. Hardly three minutes after Faithly and Glenroe had left De Garre Tavern, Charles Stuart was sitting utterly unprotected and alone.

Seeker continued along to the empty table, sat down and brought a deck of cards from his pocket. He began to lay them out in a cross for Florentine. The tavern-keeper's daughter soon appeared beside him with a mug and a jug of ale, and Seeker began to play.

He was laying a seven of hearts on a six when he became aware of a figure making its way through the crowded tables towards him. He kept playing, steadily, and didn't look up as he waited. And then the tall man's shadow fell across the table and he did look up. Charles Stuart said something in heavily accented Flemish.

Seeker took a gamble. 'I'm sorry, sir, my Flemish is not so good. Do you speak English by any chance?'

The dark man's smile broadened and he swept off his hat. 'With all my heart, friend. Charles Longfellow, as far from home as you are, I daresay. Would you give a fellow Englishman a hand of cards? I have withal to make it interesting.'

'I'm just a carpenter, sir,' said Seeker. 'I doubt I can match what you stake.'

Charles Stuart sighed heavily. 'Few men could match what I have staked and lost, friend, but I'd play you for a handful of buttons for a half-hour's companionship and talk of England.' He hesitated. 'But I would not have you end your game too soon.'

'Oh, my game's nearly done,' Seeker replied, 'and I tire of it anyway.' He gathered up the cards and looked at the King. 'Piquet?'

'Learned at my mother's knee,' said Charles.

Seeker began to sort through the pack, taking out the unwanted cards. 'Are you out of England long, sir?'

'Too long,' said Charles.

'Aye,' said Seeker. 'Me too.'

'What took you here?'

'Following the King,' said Seeker.

Charles's smile broadened and he called for wine. Seeker offered Charles the remaining pack and soon they had cut for dealer and were beginning to play.

'You are from Yorkshire?'

Seeker acknowledged that he was.

'I never fared well in Yorkshire,' said Charles.

'Nor I,' said Seeker. 'But I miss it, all the same.'

'You may see it again, sooner than you think.'

Seeker was wary. 'Oh? How so?'

Charles leaned in closer across the table. Seeker was suddenly aware that he was close enough to plunge a dagger in the man's throat. 'I have been assured this very day that England will soon be back to its senses. I have brought this news to my friends, and it is what we – when they return, of course – came here to celebrate tonight. The tyrant will soon be dead.'

Seeker felt a chill creep through him. If there was a plot against the Protector, he should have known of it before now. He played his cards out carefully. 'The King's supporters are to adventure something new . . .'

'Adventure?' Charles's brow wrinkled in amusement and he shook his head. 'The time for adventuring is done, my friend, and not another drop of loyal blood to be spilled. Almighty God has at last stirred himself in the matter of England and likes not what he sees – and now by the Divine Providence of which he is wont to speak, the tyrant lies close to death at Hampton Court, in the very bed of the man he murdered.'

It was as if the sounds and life around him had suddenly stopped. It could not be true; Thurloe would have told him. 'Cromwell is dying?' said Seeker.

The King nodded, smiling to turn over an unexpected ace before declaring his hand. 'Of grief and a fever. The plagues of a new Egypt have been visited upon Oliver Cromwell. Sons-in-law, daughters, grandchildren go to their graves, beating a path for him to follow.'

Seeker suddenly realised he was gripping his cards in his hands so tightly he had begun to crush them. Ingolby had written to him of it, having had it from Andrew Marvell, how the loss of his adored youngest daughter after that of her baby son had all but broken Cromwell's heart. But he had not been ready to believe that the Protector himself could be truly ill.

Charles was so intent upon his cards that he hadn't noticed the damage Seeker had done to his. 'Yes,' he said, 'the tyrant is not long for this world and soon his followers will be clambering over one another to leave the sinking ship.'

Seeker was just considering how to respond when there came sounds of some sort of commotion downstairs. Before he could tell what they signalled, the sight of Thomas Faithly emerging at the top of the stair suddenly caught his eye. In the instant it took for Faithly's look of blank astonishment to be replaced by the drawing of his sword and a roar of, 'Glenroe!', Seeker had tipped the table and everything on it over onto Charles Stuart and begun his run across the upper parlour. Faithly was knocking people out of the way as he attempted to reach him, but as the tip of his sword came within inches of Seeker's chest, Seeker barged his arm with all his force to get past him before swinging himself over the balcony rail and dropping the ten feet or more to the floor below. The whole place was now in uproar, Glenroe bounding up the stairs to collide with Thomas Faithly coming down as an astonished Daunt emerged from his visit to the jakes. Seeker barrelled past Daunt and down the steps back into the narrow alley. He chose to turn right, towards the side streets rather than risk going back out towards the wide-open Markt. He had just reached the far end of the alley when he heard the shouts of the Cavaliers emerging at the bottom of the steps and demanding of a terrified clerk to know which way he had gone.

The sound of his boots on the cobbles seemed to reverberate through the darkness of the near-empty streets, but it was not long before the shouts of Daunt and Glenroe had faded to nothing and it was clear that the Cavaliers had separated in their search for him. They had gone towards other parts of the town: only Thomas Faithly had picked the right direction — south-westwards. Before he left the city, Seeker knew he must tell George Beaumont he was going. What Beaumont himself then chose to do was up to him. When Seeker reached the precincts of Sint-Salvatorskerk, he came to a halt for a moment and reached into his pouch. He held up a coin to the vagabond taking shelter for the night beneath the porch. 'The man coming after me,' he said, 'tell him I went towards Sint-Jans. There'll be more tomorrow if he doesn't find me.'

The vagabond nodded and eagerly took the coin, and Seeker began to run again, away from Sint-Jans and down across the canal towards the Beeste Markt and then 't Zand. Long before the spire of the Blindekenskapel came into view, the sound of Thomas Faithly coming after him had dissolved on the air. At the church, Seeker stopped at last and leaned against the door a moment to catch his breath. Then he looked across at the little house that was George Beaumont's refuge in Bruges.

Seeker was troubled by George Beaumont. It wasn't just the inconsistency in the timing of what Beaumont claimed to have learned from Anne Winter about the Jesuits, nor Seeker's suspicion that it was because Beaumont actually knew where she was. It was more that there had been something not right in Beaumont's reaction to learning the identity of his mother's killer. The man had claimed that finding his mother's killer had been his prime motivation for coming to Bruges and yet he had displayed very little emotion at hearing Seeker's revelation, or curiosity as to the whereabouts of his family's money. He was beginning to wonder if there was some other reason George Beaumont had come to Bruges. That he had seen no sign of the officer anywhere since their conversation much earlier in the evening, despite the many dramas of the night, had done nothing to reassure him. George Beaumont should have been anywhere tonight but at home, but as he looked across the street, Seeker could discern a glimmer of light where the old red shutters of Beaumont's cottage's window did not quite meet.

Seeker crossed the street and approached the house with care. He looked at the door which did not appear to have been interfered with. He put his ear to it but heard nothing. The gap between the shutters afforded him very little information to begin with, but then, just as he was about to pull away, a movement past the window temporarily obscured the light.

Seeker went back to the door and rapped softly. He caught the sound of a slight movement and then utter stillness. He rapped again: nothing at all this time. He recognised this silence: it was the silence of someone trying very hard to make no noise at all. This was a time when his carpenter's tool-belt would have been extremely useful, but as it was, in his dressing for his assignation at the House of Lamentations, he had come out without having brought his special keys or even a chisel with which to gain entrance to the place. There was nothing for it, and it would no doubt attract attention in this quiet street at this hour of the night, but he had no option. He stepped back and kicked hard. The door flew open with a minimum of resistance.

The room was empty, the candle flickering alone in the middle of a table on which sat the residue of a simple meal. Seeker crossed quickly to the back door, but it was bolted from the inside. Whoever had been moving about in here a few minutes ago must still be in the house. Seeker lifted the candle and stooped to check beneath the bed: nothing but a chamber pot and a pair of brown shoes. There was only one other place in the cottage anyone could be. Seeker raised his eyes towards the hatch in the ceiling. At the top of the ladder, evidently having had no time to go any further, were the soles of a pair of feet, almost obscured at the back by folds of brown woollen cloth hanging down around them.

'Come down, whoever you are.'

The feet disappeared up the ladder. Swearing, Seeker bounded up after them. He swore again as he reached the top and made the error of standing up, banging his head on the central beam of the roof before he was more than halfway straightened. He lifted the candle to see that a few yards away, watching him with a modicum of fear overlaid by a much greater degree of defiance, was Lady Anne Winter.

He groaned. 'You! Again? I left you at the House of Lamentations. What, in the name of all that's holy, are you doing here?'

She lifted her chin and Seeker saw that her face was still streaked with blood and dirt from the attack by Marchmont

Ellis. The bruises were already deepening too. 'I would ask you the same question.'

'Aye, I've no doubt you would. But where's George Beaumont? What have you done with him?'

'Beaumont . . . no. This is George Bart—' but even as she said the name, he could see realisation dawn on her. 'No. It can't be.'

Seeker let her disbelief fill the air a moment. Then, he said, 'Oh, but I'm afraid it is, Lady Anne. Now where is he?'

That she was genuinely shocked to learn the true identity of the man was clear.

'Come on, Lady Anne, you know how it works. I mean, it's not as if you were here under your own name either, is it? Lady Hildred's maid? And then a nun? They'll laugh at that one a good long time in Whitehall. I almost smiled myself. I'll ask again – where is he?'

'I don't know,' she said, her look distracted as she tried to untangle what he was saying to her.

'Come on. I haven't the time for this.'

She spoke slowly, as if the ideas were only coming to her through a fog. 'He's gone to get us horses – and papers.'

'He told you you'd be leaving together?'

She nodded.

'How long ago did you last see him?'

'Hours,' she said. 'He was supposed to be there – in the kitchens of the House of Lamentations – when I met with Ellis below. But he wasn't there. I thought he might have come back here.'

Seeker didn't like this news one little bit. Earlier in the evening he'd told Beaumont to look for Anne Winter, but it was plain now that Beaumont had already known where she was. Nevertheless, he hadn't been, as he'd promised her, at the House of Lamentations, and he hadn't been with the Cavaliers either, so where was he?

'And he is really Lady Hildred's son?'

'Aye, he is. And he risked a great deal to come to Bruges to find her killer. Or at least that's why he said he'd come.'

'And he has been working with you?'

'Lucky for you, or I might never have followed Marchmont Ellis to the House of Lamentations tonight.'

'But Marchmont Ellis was also working for you – you are John Carpenter.' She looked away and then back at him in disgust. 'Are you real, Damian Seeker? Is there to be no escape from you? Was even Hell not enough to hold you? You were supposed to be *dead*! I was even sorry for it.'

'I'm very touched. But as you can see, I'm not dead, Marchmont Ellis is, and neither of us know for sure about George Beaumont. You'd better tell me everything you know. Where did he say he going to get the horses?'

She shook her head. 'I don't know.'

'And the papers he spoke of? Who was he to get those from?'

Again, 'I don't know.'

Seeker was exhausted. He let out a long breath of frustration and squatted down on his haunches opposite her, setting the candle down beside him. His head touched the sloping roof. He leaned his elbows on his knees and screwed up his eyes a moment, trying to clear his thoughts. It was when he opened them again that he saw it.

'Dear God,' he said.

'What?' Lady Anne was looking at him, but he was looking past her to the end of the attic. He raised the candle the better to see.

'Dear God,' he said again. And then, slowly, he turned to Anne Winter. 'What did you tell George Beaumont, Lady Anne, of how you effected your escape from the ambush in which his mother was killed?'

She screwed up her face. 'What has that to do with anything? I told him I had exchanged places with a girl Sister Janet was helping to flee the town.'

'Ruth Jones,' he said.

'Yes, Ruth Jones.'

Seeker took a deep breath. 'And did you tell him where Ruth Jones is now?'

Anne Winter nodded. 'Yes, that as far as I knew, she was still at the house of the Grote Sterre, in Damme.' She turned to look in the direction in which he was staring: the far corner of the small attic. What Seeker was illuminating by the light of his candle was a wooden stand and hanging from the stand were a large black felt hat and a good grey woollen suit. They were the clothes he'd been searching for, the clothes worn by the man with whom Bartlett Jones had last been seen alive.

TWENTY-FIVE

De Grote Sterre

The house was very quiet now that that the Spanish governor and most of his soldiers had left. Ruth wondered how close they were now to Brussels and hoped that the French would not have got there before them. She liked the Spaniards. She liked the formality of the officers and the friendliness of the men; she liked the way their religion allowed beauty and beautiful things. The intonations of their priests, so little of which she could understand, sounded like poetry to her, and devoid of the endless haranguing of the Puritan preachers who had so enraptured George.

How was it she had not realised, at the very beginning, that it was not possible that someone like George Beaumont could truly have loved her? He had been like no man she had ever met, certainly not like her brother's friends. Bartlett's friends had been so coarse – farm boys and merchant's apprentices. Her mother's prohibition on Ruth having anything to do with them had been unnecessary – she'd had no inclination whatsoever to make their acquaintance. And then the army had come into their town and her father and the other aldermen had gone out to meet them and to assure the commanders of the town's good morals and affection to the Protector.

George had been billeted on their house and had charmed them all. It might have been different had Bartlett not been from home at the time. Bartlett might have noticed as she had not, at first, that George accommodated himself too easily to the stated interests of others, paid too much court to their mother's empty prattle. For herself, at first, George had kept a polite distance, but before long he was exhibiting a strong interest in her welfare and her comfort. She'd been flattered, for a time. An older man, handsome and an officer – no one like that had ever paid attention to Ruth before. But then, after a while, George had spoken to her mother, advising against permitting Ruth the freedom to walk around the town in the company of her friends as she was used to do, for fear of the rowdier elements in the army. When Ruth had protested that the New Model had no rowdy elements, her mother had scolded her, told her the captain knew better.

George was often with them when he was not required on army business, or to be going back and forth to London. He spoke of the immorality of London women and the immodesty with which they conducted themselves. He spoke of his admiration for the simpler, plainer dress of the Puritan woman, whose inner beauty shone through all the more clearly for that it was not obscured by vanities of ribbon and fripperies of lace. Privately, Ruth's father chided her mother, and told her to look better to her daughter's wardrobe. Ruth's pretty silk gowns – her favourite blue, and the yellow embroidered with scrolls of flowers – were removed to be replaced by deep black stuff, her pretty lace falling-bands displaced by plain linen partlets and collars.

George had been taken aback at her level of learning. Never had he come across a young woman of such intellect and promise. He had surveyed her little library and found it charming but wanting. It would be no trouble, he told her mother, for him to bring more suitable reading material for Ruth, when next he journeyed back from London. He hinted that there were certain qualities he looked for in a wife, and that Ruth certainly came *closest* of all the young women he had encountered, to what would be required from the future mistress of Beaumont Manor. Her parents had lost no time in enquiring what other qualities George looked for, and how Ruth's deficiencies might be suitably made up. George had been magnanimous. He felt sure Ruth was such a God-fearing and biddable young woman, that he could address any small difficulties himself.

No one consulted Bartlett about his sister's welfare, and no one consulted Ruth. She, at first carried away that such a man should have such an interest in her, had in time begun to question whether she was up to the task of being Lady of Beaumont Manor. A question had also whispered itself in her mind as to whether she truly wished to be the sub-missive, obedient, good Puritan wife of George Beaumont. Her mother hushed her doubts and Ruth allowed herself to be carried along with the excitement of the planned wedding. It would not be an ostentatious affair, of course, but there was still much to be done.

And then had come the news that George's company was to be called away, to ready for war in the Low Countries, against the Spaniards and the treacherous supporters of Charles Stuart. George was to travel instantly – there was no time for even the simplest wedding, but he assured Ruth's parents that if they would but send her after him to the coast, they would certainly be married there. Ruth had been despatched, two days after the departure of the troops, for Portsmouth.

And there in Portsmouth George had married her – or so he claimed, although it did not seem like any wedding or marriage ceremony that Ruth had ever known. The wedding breakfast had been without friends or family or any adornment, the deflowering without tenderness or preamble, a vicious awakening to the realities of her new situation. Ruth's attempt to flee their lodging had been thwarted by the landlady, who had been well paid in advance against such an eventuality. A package and letter sent by her mother had been returned with a note that the regiment and all in its train had already left the town. Day by day, things had grown worse, until eventually, belittled and brutalised, she had been told to tidy herself up and make herself respectable, and fit to go out in the world like other officers' wives. The walk from their lodging to the harbour had been a short one, and Ruth had boarded the ship like a woman already dead.

There had been brief moments of hope. The Spaniards might sink their ship, the French might forget that they were now friends of Cromwell's English rather than their foes; she could break free from the other women long enough to throw herself over the side and into the foam below. Brief moments of hope, and all futile, but no disappointment had been so great as when George had returned, all but unscathed, from the Battle of the Dunes. Ruth had prayed, every hour he had been gone, for his death, but God clearly had had other business on hand that day.

Dunkirk, though, had been the saving of her. George had been too busy with his new duties, in establishing English control of the town, to pay her as much attention as he would have liked, and Ruth had used her time wisely. She had made friends, used the limited French she had to learn something of where she was, of how far away the 'enemy' Spanish-held territory lay, of where their seat of power was. Little by little, Ruth had managed to transmit an idea of her plight to those inhabitants of the town who were no friends to their new masters, and in not much more than a week, she had learned of a place of sanctuary where Cromwell's officers would never be allowed to set foot: an English convent, in Bruges.

All that remained was for her to find the courage to leave. And then George had given her the courage. He had come home one night and found his supper not to his liking. As Ruth had cowered in the corner, he had slowly removed his belt. She had scrabbled like a rat for some means of escape but had found none. She had been glad that night of the thick black puritan dress and its staunch linen collar, but there had been no protection for Ruth's face, and George had seen to it that he fashioned her a face that, he told her, would cure her of her weakness for the looking glass.

'You will tell people you tripped in the stables and caught your face on the side of a shovel,' he'd said, as he'd tied on his belt once more and straightened his jacket to his satisfaction. Through torn, bleeding lips, Ruth had promised him that he would never again find fault with the supper she made for him.

She had been so cautious in her leaving the next day, and yet he had almost caught her. He had returned earlier than planned from a meeting of the governing military council, to find her gone from their lodging at a time when he had not authorised her to be so. It had taken very little effort on his part to beat the truth out of their terrified housekeeper, and George had very soon been on her trail. But somehow, by some providence of the God that she had almost stopped believing in, he came within sight of her just after she had crossed into Spanish territory. He had fired off a shot after her, but she was just out of his range and he'd missed. And the last thing she had heard as she'd run for her life, was the sound of his promise that he would come after her, and he would find her.

She had found her way, in time and through the kindness of strangers, to Bruges. The gatekeepers at the city walls had been dubious at first, about this foreign woman who looked at best to be a camp-follower, until she had said the name she had been given by her well-wishers in Dunkirk. The name had opened the gates to her, and several doors thereafter: Sister Janet. A kindly carter had taken her then – she had not even had to walk – through this strange new town of canals and spires, through streets and over bridges right to the front of the Engels Klooster. A novice at the gate had taken her through the small courtyard and into an anteroom, where she'd left Ruth waiting on a bench. When the short, portly old nun had come to the iron gate saying, 'Well, my dear, I have not the whole night to wait upon visitors, so I suppose you had better come in,' Ruth had collapsed at her feet.

And that had been Ruth's sanctuary until the day the Spanish priest, Father Felipe, had caught sight of her. Her ruined face had displeased him, had 'offended' his eyes. 'Surely,' he'd said to Sister Janet in her hearing, 'such a face could only be a mark of God's displeasure?' That night, Sister Janet had led Ruth away to the House of Lamentations where she would be safe, until a way out of the town and a new and better sanctuary could be arranged.

Only once, during her time in Bruges, had Sister Janet pressed her for the name of the man from whom she had fled, but Ruth wouldn't tell her. She knew George. She knew how he charmed people without seeming to be charming, won them over, made them believe him over anything anyone else might say. And she was George Beaumont's wife. As far as she or anyone else knew or understood, she was his wife.

Would even a Papist nun deny his rights over his own wife? So Ruth told no one the name of her tormentor, and waited for the day she could disappear even deeper into Spanish territories and even further away from him.

Sometimes, when she was not busy at her work in the convent garden, or later in the kitchen or laundry of the House of Lamentations, Ruth had let herself imagine that perhaps the one person who she knew would take her part against George Beaumont would receive the letter she had smuggled out to him from Dunkirk just before she'd left, that he'd make his way, somehow, to Bruges, and find her. Last thing before she settled to sleep each night, whether in her little cell high up in the convent or her basement hiding place in the House of Lamentations, she would look out of her window, telling herself that soon she would see Bartlett, walking down the street to find her. Even so, she had hardly been able to believe it when, one night, she had received a note from Sister Janet telling her that a man calling himself Bartlett Jones and claiming to be her brother had called that day at the Engels Klooster. Ruth had read over the note again and again, looking for some invisible sign in it that what it said was true, and not some cruel hoax of George's devising. She had scarcely been able to breathe for the next long hours as she had watched the streets leading to the house, such was her fear, such was her hope. She had determined to watch all night, if need be. But somehow, sleep had taken her, and the sight that had greeted her when next she'd looked out through the bars of the basement window had almost finished her. Bartlett, lying dead on the Spaanse Loskaai, canal water in his hair and a bloody gash at his throat. She'd known then no one would believe her, she was certain, but Ruth knew. George – who else could it be? George was in Bruges and he was coming to find her.

But now, through the miraculous intervention of Sister Janet, and the help of the maidservant who had been so eager to exchange places with her, she was here, in the house of the Spanish military governor, in Damme. There had been an irony, she realised, in her having sat at George's mother's side, like the most loving and dutiful of daughters-in-law, tending to the old woman's comfort as she'd died. She had not told Lady Hildred of the irony, for fear it might somehow add to her pain. But now Lady Hildred was dead, and terrible news had come to Damme from Bruges only that evening that Sister Janet was also dead. Ruth had taken herself away and prayed that God would be merciful to Janet, as Janet had been tender and merciful to her. She'd traced her hands over the scars that Janet had taken such care to tend to. In her mind, she saw again the tenderness in the old nun's eyes as she'd carefully applied salves and ointments and heard her curse the evil that men do. Even as she'd heard the news of Janet's death, Ruth could feel George's presence. She could feel him coming closer. Her skin prickled at the thought of it; she was almost certain she could smell him.

But one hope remained to her. The news of Sister Janet's

murder had been carried to Damme only incidentally, the main reason for the Spanish messenger's despatch being the rumour, reported in several quarters of the town, that Charles Stuart, King of Scotland, had come to Bruges for Lady Hildred's money, and would be passing through Damme next day as he journeyed once more northwards. Ruth would throw herself on the King's mercy and beg to be allowed to travel in his train. She cared nothing any more for her name, and her honour had been torn from her. She cared nothing more for hunger, or cold, or fatigue, or work with little dignity and no wage. All Ruth cared was that George Beaumont would never touch her again.

The house of De Grote Sterre was empty, save for herself. The handful of men the military governor had thought prudent to leave in the town were billeted elsewhere and the house largely shut up until the governor's return. The cook and her boy lived above the warm bakehouse across the back courtyard, and the gardener in his little house at the end of the kitchen garden. Two stable hands shared a loft above the now near-empty stalls. Ruth had been permitted to sleep in Lady Hildred's chamber, even after the old woman's death, until such time as the governor and his officers had moved out. Since then, on perceiving her reluctance to return to Bruges, the housekeeper had deemed it reasonable to allow Ruth space in the kitchens, until she might join the next party of English passing through Damme. So, each night for the past few nights, before she retired to bed, Ruth had got into the habit of going through the house,

floor by floor, checking each room. The chambers of De
Grote Sterre had echoed their emptiness as she'd climbed
the stairs and passed through rooms so recently taken up by
the governor's retinue but now sounding only to her own
footsteps. When at last she had reached and surveyed the
little attic room five storeys up, at the very top of the house,
above which was only to be found a pair of nesting storks,
Ruth would begin to make her way back down, checking
windows and shutters and doors, and closing them all fast
behind her as she did so.

Tonight she took more time in looking out over the little
town. There was the Stadhuis. What would the aldermen
of her own town have given to have such a place to meet,
so imposing and so grand? Women as well as men, sculpted
in stone, looked down on the town from their niches in
the Stadhuis walls. Even Ruth had been shocked at first to
see it. They'd have been smashed in England, she thought;
smashed, and all made ugly. An elderly Spanish soldier had
told her that Charles the Bold had married his English wife
there, Margaret of York, a long, long time ago. The soldier
had meant it for a kindness, perhaps thinking it would
make Ruth feel less far from home, but all it had done was
make her wonder what Margaret had felt as she'd walked
up those steps to a destiny she surely had little choice in.

The town around the square was sleeping. Ruth pulled
fast the shutters then the windows, then crossed to look
out over the gardens, and the rooftops of the little houses
as they extended back from the street, all the way to the

church of Our Lady. They were a picture of contentment. They reminded her of the rooftops of her own town. Ruth wondered what happiness they might contain or what horrors they might hide. She closed the shutters and went down to the next floor. Her favourites were here – a man and a woman, husband and wife, five feet apart, carved into the chimney cheeks of the huge fireplace. They did not interfere with each other and had each minded their own business a good three hundred years. The hearth had not yet been properly cleaned out and a pile of logs that had tumbled down in the packing of the governor's belongings had not been put straight. Ruth knew the stern stone housewife would not rest easy over such disarray and glancing upwards she promised the matron that she would see to it tomorrow.

Ruth was just reaching out to close the shutters of the windows facing onto the square when she froze. A horseman, a lone horseman, had been permitted through the town gates and was crossing the canal. He might have been anyone, but he was not anyone. He was not wearing his cavalry officer's garb tonight, but Ruth knew instantly who he was. She stood there, her hand on the window catch, rendered motionless by terror.

As he rode off the bridge and into the square, George Beaumont looked up. He looked up at the windows of the De Grote Sterre and he looked directly at her. Still Ruth could not move. She could not move her hand, she could not make her lips move, she could not take her eyes from the horseman in the square and she could not blow out the candle she had set down on a table behind her and that was now illuminating her, like a gift, in the window. She was making of herself a gift to George Beaumont, just as much as her mother and father had done.

George continued across the square and disappeared from her view. Ruth ran to the back of the house in time to see his horse pass complacently and unchallenged beneath the archway and into the courtyard of De Grote Sterre.

Ruth's instinct was to run, but she needed to know where next to run to, and so she forced herself to keep watching. The courtyard had been in semi-darkness, but now the moon emerged from behind a cloud and bathed everything in a startling blue light. George remained on his horse and surveyed the courtyard before looking up towards the window behind which she now stood. She had blown out the candle now though, and she could tell from his expression that he wasn't certain whether he could actually see her or not. A sudden half-smile, that she remembered very well, appeared on his face and he swung himself down off the horse and began to walk towards the back entrance of the house. Ruth thought she might be sick. She turned, looking desperately into the darkness of the room, trying to think of somewhere that she might hide. Behind settles, beneath tables – no, no, he would find her in those places. She imagined she still felt the bruising on her arm where he had grabbed it and dragged her out from under the bed she'd been forced to share with him in that Portsmouth lodging.

Now came a knocking. Two, then three raps. Louder,

harder. Ruth tried to think: upstairs? No, she would be trapped. Down then. But what if he should force his way in? How would she pass him? Desperate ideas flashed through her head, one after the other, and in her mounting panic she could grasp hold of none of them. And then came the sound that made her actually cry out – the sound of George Beaumont breaking through the back door and entering De Grote Sterre.

Ruth crept to the top of the stairway. He was two floors beneath her; she could hear him moving around, checking doors, pushing things out of the way. She did not move. And then, his voice.

'Ruth,' he called. 'Come downstairs, Ruth. I have found you now. Come downstairs and be a good wife.'

She heard his foot on the stair, and she ran across the landing, ran back to the room where the well-matched fifteenth-century merchant couple kept eternal watch from either side of the huge fireplace. Ruth hurriedly picked up as many as she could of the tumbled logs and laid them across the hearth and the front of the uncleaned firedogs to make of them a low screen, before slipping in behind it and lying as flat as she could amongst the ashes of the fireplace. Before she laid herself down she cast a desperate glance at the stone effigy of the merchant's wife, gazing implacably upon the scene unfolding beneath her. 'Please,' she whispered. 'Please.'

George was moving slowly. She could hear him now in the room below, methodically working through it, pushing back furniture, opening the lids of chests. All the time, he kept up his refrain, so measured, so reasonable, of, 'Come now, Ruth, let us be friends. We have much to talk of. What would your poor parents think, if they knew what a bad wife you were to me? Come now, Ruth, it is your husband come to fetch you.'

It carried on, the reasonable tone, the methodical searching, until she heard him sigh and then begin to climb the flight of stairs leading to the room she was in. Ruth pressed herself as flat as she could to the floor and began to pray. When George got to the top of the stairs, he halted, and he stopped talking too. There was utter silence in the room and Ruth was terrified to breathe. The ashes were finding their way into her nostrils, her throat. She could feel her eyes begin to water, her cheeks begin to burn with the effort not to cough. Just when she thought she could stand it no more and that her lungs must burst, George at last began to move again and this time, rather than talking, he did something she had never heard him do before. He began to whistle.

Ruth heard him come closer. There was less in the way of furnishing in this room, fewer items which he might pause to lift, or push aside to check behind in his search for her. He was very close to the fireplace now. She dared to open her eyes and past the firedogs and the stacked-up logs, she could see his boots. Even through the dust and the ashes, she could smell him.

'Oh where are you hiding, my pretty little wife?' he said.

He reached out a hand to lean on the mantelpiece whilst he surveyed the room. 'Where are you?' he repeated. And then he looked down, at the stone effigy of the merchant's wife. He laughed. 'Well, Mother dear, have they turned you to stone so soon? I would rather they had burned you, you evil old baggage. But where is she, baggage? Where is my wife?'

He cursed, and kicked at a log, sending it rolling across the wooden boards, threatening to expose her. Ruth's fingernails were digging into her own palms. Every limb was in agony from the effort not to move. Just as she thought she could not hold her position any longer, the whistling resumed and George began to move away, in the direction of the next flight of stairs. 'Up and up we go, my dear, but soon my little bird will have nowhere left to fly.'

As the sound of the whistling became more distant, Ruth allowed herself to breathe properly at last, and to move. She lay there a moment, enjoying the blessed relief, but she had a decision to make and she would have to move soon. She listened as George spoke while he shifted pieces of furniture in the room above. She heard him proclaim that he was beginning to tire of her game, and really, she should come to him now or he would be forced to chastise her. Ruth waited until she heard the whistling start up again, and when at last it seemed to emanate from halfway up the stepladder between the upper floor and the attics, she pulled off her slippers to creep quickly and quietly out from her hiding place and begin to run for the stairs. She did not notice, in the darkness of the room she had shuttered earlier, the log that had rolled out into the middle of the floor when George had kicked it. All her attention was on trying to discern the upper banister of the stair leading down to the floor below. She was almost there when her toe caught the log with such force that she cried out in shock and pain before she properly realised what she was doing.

She stifled the cry almost instantly, but it was too late. The sounds of movement two floors above her stopped suddenly and then were just as suddenly replaced by the clattering of George's boots coming back down the step-ladder. Ruth cried out again and hurled herself downwards, not caring for the splinters on the steps or that she slipped and missed the last two and banged the base of her spine on the edge of the step. She scrambled up and ran to the top of the next flight down. All the while she could hear George coming down from above.

She carried on, in desperation and panic, down the last flight of stairs to the ground floor. At last, here, she didn't know where to go. A few yards away, on the other side of the main door, were the steps giving on to the square, and surely to help and freedom. But the door was heavy and locked and she did not have the key. To her right was the door George had left open on his way up from the kitchen. Ruth ran through that, but instead of going to the kitchen as George would surely assume she had, she made for the vaults that gave out on to the back courtyard.

As Ruth entered the vaults and closed the door softly

behind her, she heard the sound of George jump down the last few steps from the ground floor. She hurried towards the next door and the final chamber of the vault, but as soon as she put her hand on it to open it, she heard the door behind her swing open and she heard George's grunt of satisfaction. 'Caught. Like a doe in a trap.'

'No!' she screamed and wrenched open the final door. She was almost at the hatch. She had her hand stretched out for the handle, when she heard his laughter reverberating around the cavern of the vault and felt his hand lunge at her waist. 'No!' she screamed even louder, propelling herself forwards, but it was too late. He had her.

TWENTY-SIX

Portrait

The King sank down on the stool from which Daunt had hastily removed a dust sheet. It had taken some effort even to find candle and flint, so shut up and abandoned was the house on Hoogstraat where the King had latterly held court whilst resident in the town. For a moment Charles said nothing and Daunt wondered whether he fully understood what had happened. In all justice, Daunt himself did not entirely understand what had happened, but he knew it wasn't anything good. He was still pondering the turn of events that had unleashed itself upon Glenroe's and Thomas Faithly's return to De Garre tavern, when the King suddenly cursed and shot out a foot to kick over the coal scuttle beside him. Daunt was momentarily dumbstruck and unsure as to whether etiquette demanded that he pick up the coals or leave them where they were. The King seemingly oblivious to the mess now spilled over the hearth onto the floor, Daunt elected to leave them as they were.

'Damn him to Hell!' Charles repeated. 'Damn them all to Hell!'

'Indeed, sir,' agreed Daunt, now on surer ground. 'Best place for 'em.'

'But how in God's name could this happen? Was there no guard put on the place?'

Daunt attempted to clear his throat, the appropriate response as ever eluding him. The truth was that they had not even considered that anyone would find the hiding place behind the wall in the small upper chamber of the Bouchoute House. When Faithly and Glenroe had returned to the Bouchoute House in search of Ellis, it had been to find no sign of Ellis, and Lady Hildred's money gone. Worse, the servants of the house, who had not even known of the fortune secreted away within its walls, had told them that Ellis had never returned after leaving with the rest of them earlier in the evening. He must have stolen the money at some earlier stage, and then had the gall to actually look the very sovereign he was betraying in the face and kneel before him. Such behaviour was beyond Daunt's comprehension. He could have believed it of the Roundheads, of course, but never of one of his own side. And then, as he observed his dejected and so-often betrayed monarch, Daunt reflected that Ellis had not, after all, been one of their own.

An uncomfortable thought had begun to niggle at Daunt since he had hastily escorted the King to the Zeven Torens for his own safety. When Thomas had reached the head of the stairs in De Garre as Daunt had been returning from the jakes, he had suddenly roared something about Damian Seeker. Daunt had heard of this Seeker from many an exile but never met him and never wished to. He'd had no time to enquire of Glenroe or Faithly what they were about, for he'd been near enough knocked over by a fellow who'd just jumped down from the tavern's gallery when Faithly and Glenroe had gone hurtling out of De Garre after the man. He'd had little enough time to look but Daunt had a horrible feeling that the man his friends had been pursuing was the English carpenter he had come across, in that special upper chamber, in the Bouchoute House.

The King groaned and Daunt saw how weary Charles actually was. Where was their dashing hero prince, their Cavalier king, who had escaped Parliament's clutches time and again, who had begged Spain to let him lead his own troops, and been forced to see his brother, the Duke of York, garner the glory instead – where was he now? Daunt had more than once drawn his sword to teach a lesson to fools who'd dared claim, in his hearing, that the King was becoming a gambling, womanising sot for lack of any other purpose. Did they know what he had lost? Did they truly know what he had suffered, of the privations he had faced and still faced, the humiliations? Looking at his dejected, abandoned King, Daunt had seldom felt such rage.

'They'll pay, Majesty. One day, all those who have betrayed you, they will pay, if I have to send every one of them to Hades myself.'

Charles looked up and there at last was the smile, the glint in the eye. 'And you would too, wouldn't you?' He slapped his own leg. 'Devil take them all, Dunt! As long as

I have such as you by my side, England will be ours again. Now, there should be some brandy left in that cabinet there. First pull off these blessed boots of mine, and then we'll drink to it.'

Daunt felt tears pricking his eyes and feared he would disgrace himself. 'Your Majesty,' he said, getting down in front of the King to begin the process of pulling off the boots, 'it has been the greatest honour of my life—'

But Charles merely waved a hand at him. 'Indeed. Indeed. But you'll take a drink with me, old friend, and then you can tell me about this carpenter that has Thomas Faithly jumping over banisters.'

Faithly and Glenroe mounted their horses after leaving Seeker's lodgings.

'But how is it you never saw the fellow before? He was always working about the town somewhere – the House of Lamentations, the Engels Klooster, even our own house, Dunt tells me.'

'What?' said Sir Thomas, turning to Glenroe in astonishment. 'Damian Seeker was in the Bouchoute House?'

Glenroe threw up a hand. 'Dunt mentioned it the other day. I had no notion then that this English carpenter was Damian Seeker – if indeed he is Seeker.'

'Oh, it's Seeker, all right. If anyone can come back from the dead, it's him. And he's been in the Bouchoute House?'

'Yes, Dunt found him last week, claiming to be mending window frames.'

Sir Thomas began to experience a horrible sensation of dread. 'Where, Evan? Where did Dunt find him?'

There was a pause, then Glenroe groaned. 'In the room on the upper floor where . . .'

'Where Lady Hildred's money was hidden.'

Glenroe nodded. 'God curse him. Dunt said he checked that the box was still there.'

'And it was?'

'Aye, but he didn't check inside.'

Thomas Faithly cursed. 'It wasn't Ellis that took it then, it was Damian Seeker.'

'We don't *know* that,' said Glenroe.

'Oh, I know it,' said Thomas, through gritted teeth. 'You may have avoided dealings with Damian Seeker until now – for which you should thank God – but I haven't. If he was in that room, he's got that money, and he probably knows what's become of Ellis too.'

They'd lost him in the chase through town, they'd gone back to the tavern and eventually, after much asking around, had discovered that the English carpenter lodged in the stable loft above the yard of this inn in Sint-Gillis.

The innkeeper had been able to tell them that John Carpenter had woken him from his sleep less than half an hour ago and on the spot had bought two horses at a price that would allow the innkeeper to replace them with four.

'Not much more than nags – the Spaniards took all the decent horses – but he gave me a prince's ransom for them,' he said.

'You speak the truth, friend. A prince's ransom it was,' Glenroe had remarked. 'But why two horses?'

'One for himself, and one for the woman,' the man said.

'What woman?'

The innkeeper shrugged. 'Never saw her before, and I never saw him with any woman at all before.'

'What did she look like?'

The innkeeper sighed. 'How should I know? It was dark.' He called over his shoulder to his wife who was standing a few feet behind him, wielding a broom against their second intruders of the night. 'Jennike, the woman with John Carpenter, what was she like?'

'Tall, well made. Walked like a lady.'

Now the innkeeper nodded. 'That's true, now you say it. Sat a horse like she knew what she was doing.'

'And where were they going?'

Again the man shrugged. 'They didn't say. But he paid well over the mark for those horses and cleared all his things out of my loft. I checked. Plain enough to me John Carpenter has no plans to be back.'

They were almost at the Speye Poort, having had no luck enquiring after Seeker and his companion from the guards at Kruispoort, when Glenroe suddenly pulled up. 'You don't think this "woman" he is apparently travelling with might be Ellis in disguise?'

'Seeker is back from the dead,' said Sir Thomas, 'I would believe anything of him.'

The guards at the Speye Poort were no happier to open up

to them than the innkeeper had been, and enquired whether
any other Englishmen were bent on Damme before dawn,
for they were the third such to disturb them that night.

'Third?'

'Aye, John Carpenter and his woman, but before them
there was the red-haired fellow. Tremendous hurry he was
in.'

'George Barton,' said Sir Thomas. 'He must have heard
of our search and gone after Seeker himself.'

'No,' the gatekeeper said. 'Not Barton. Beaumont. He
was very particular that I should make that point to anyone
who came looking for him. That his name was George
Beaumont.'

Ruth Jones's wrists were bound so tight behind her that she
thought the blood must soon burst out of her veins. Her
upper arms, too, burned with discomfort.

'You mustn't fidget so, my dear. It is most unbecoming.'

Ruth was in terror, but she had been in terror before
George many times, and the only defence that came to
her was to slip into the deference that had allowed her to
survive his rages up until now.

'I'm sorry, George,' she said.

He smiled. 'I'm sorry too, Ruth. I'm very disappointed.
Are these the actions of a loving wife?'

Ruth tried to answer, but could not find the words, and
then it was too late: his face was inches from hers, the
spittle from his snarling mouth hitting her chin. 'Well? Are

they? Answer me, slut!' The last words were accompanied by a heavy slap across her left cheek. Without her hands to balance her, Ruth fell over sideways, her temple hitting the hard flagstone floor.

'Sit up, slut!' he ordered.

Ruth managed at last to manoeuvre herself up.

George surveyed her, his lips curling in disgust. 'What a despicable, filthy sight you are. To think that I ever thought to make you mistress of Beaumont Manor. But tell me, you did not tell my mother you were my wife?'

'No, George,' she managed, her words barely audible.

'I can't hear you!' he shouted, bringing his left hand this time across the right side of her face, splitting her lip and sending her keeling over once again.

Gathering more strength than she thought she had left, Ruth forced herself upright again. 'No, George,' she repeated loudly.

George grunted. 'Well, that is a blessing at least. What pleasure it would have given the old harridan to think I had saddled myself with such a worthless specimen for a wife. Her satisfaction would have been insufferable.' He reached into his satchel and brought out a flask which, by the smell as he took a drink from it, was filled with brandy. He gave a sound of satisfaction and got down on his haunches against the wall, alongside Ruth. He leaned into her almost affectionately.

'And tell me, slut, did my dear mother speak of me at all, in her dying hours?'

Ruth swallowed. The blood in her own mouth almost made her gag, but she knew it would anger him if she did so. 'Yes,' she said, praying inside that this was the right answer, for it was the truth.

'You're not lying to me, slut?' he said.

'No, George,' she said desperately. 'I promise. She kept asking for you.'

'Did she now?' The thought seemed to please him.

Ruth sniffed and nodded. 'She was asking for you, and for a locket. She became very agitated when it couldn't be found. "My locket, my Guy and my George," she kept saying. I went through the jewels she had with her, but I couldn't find it.'

'No, because that old bitch nun stole it.'

Ruth's mind was scrambling to follow him. 'Sister Janet?'

'Yes. *Sister Janet.* Janet who thought my father was going to marry her. Can you imagine? A dumpling of a woman like that? The thought turns my stomach.' He set down the flask and rifled once more in his bag. The only light was that coming from the two candles she had left burning in the kitchen, before the nightmare of this evening had begun, yet Ruth saw something glisten as he pulled it from the bag. He held it up closer to her and tilted his head – she wasn't sure whether it was the better to observe her reaction or to look more closely at the thing himself. The chain was old and heavy, and the casing of the locket somewhat worn, but inside, the miniature portraits looked almost as bright and fresh as if they had been painted only yesterday. The portrait on the left was of a man of about George's age, with dark brown hair and kind eyes. His clothes were old-fashioned, and he looked nothing like George. That on the right was of a boy on the brink of manhood. It must have been painted years ago but it was indubitably of George.

George snapped the case shut and tossed the locket back into his satchel. 'People can be so dishonest. I knew some of my mother's belongings were still at the convent and the woman Winter told me she was certain Sister Janet had been through them.'

'Who?' asked Ruth before she could stop herself.

'Winter. Anne Winter. The one who swapped place with you in my mother's carriage. It was her, you know, who told me where I could find you. It was an unexpected bonus, meeting Lady Anne. I mean, it had taken me long enough in the first place to track you down to Bruges, but the right sort of *persuasion*, shall we say, amongst your acquaintances in Dunkirk got me there in the end. That Anne Winter was so ready to tell me where you were really was quite a boost. Oh – don't look so hopeful – she'll be dead by now too.'

'She too,' Ruth repeated. 'How?'

'I left her on her own to deal with a spy, a double agent. Marchmont Ellis – did you know him at all?'

Ruth shook her head.

'Oh, well. I suspect he'll have killed her. So she won't be coming looking for you now, will she? And no one else knows where you are. You won't be missed, I'm afraid.

Anyhow, where was I? Oh, yes. Sister Janet and my mother's locket. Well, I went to Sister Janet's cell and had a look around — all the nuns were busy in the garden, you see. I made sure some of them saw me leave by the back gate, and simply didn't close it properly, so that I could just slip back in before they all went to terce or sext or whatever other nonsense they get up to in their chapel. Anyway, sure enough, there in her cell, beneath her pillow was my mother's locket. So I took it.'

'It was you who killed her,' said Ruth, her voice a husk.

'Well, yes, of course.' His tone was the height of reasonableness. 'She'd had the locket, you see, and was bound to have looked in it. She would have recognised me. There would have been quite a row. So, I went back to the convent at night and paid her a visit.' He smiled. 'I'd taken the precaution of opening a window onto the street when I'd been there earlier, and do you know? No one thought to close it. The convent all shut up for the night and that one window giving out from a back stairway — left open. You would have known to close it, wouldn't you, slut?'

Ruth nodded, but said nothing. George didn't like to be interrupted when he was in the middle of a story. Satisfied, he continued.

'She woke up, of course. And she did recognise me. Her hand went under the pillow straight away, as if to check I was safely there, shut inside the locket, and not standing in her cell with a crossbow in my hand. But I shall give this to my wife, of course.'

'Your wife?'

'Of course. When I return to England I shall find myself a suitable wife.'

Ruth could barely muster more than a whisper. 'But I am your wife, George.'

He looked at her and shook his head. 'Oh, dear, slut, it is too late now to make protestations of love, of duty. After your shameful behaviour? Your ingratitude? Oh, no. I'm afraid it's much too late for you to mend your ways. Then there's the misfortune of your face, those scars from when you fell on that shovel. Can you imagine *that* looking down from a frame in the Great Hall on generations of Beaumonts yet to come? *And* yet,' he sighed and put his hand up to touch her cheek – she tried not to flinch, 'you are still rather pretty, after all.'

He leaned closer to her and forced his mouth onto hers. Without thinking, she turned her face away in disgust. And then she knew, suddenly, but too late, that it was over. George roared and pushed her to the ground.

'Whore!' he shouted, kicking her in the stomach whilst struggling with the leather belt of his coat, the belt whose burning lash she knew all too well. He had already opened up her face again, and she thought of the weals on her back recently healed under the tender administrations of Sister Janet and the apothecary of the Engels Klooster. Even after her flight to the House of Lamentations, Janet had made sure pots of soothing balm had reached her. Beatte had helped her apply it, with the greatest of care and gentleness. Ruth missed Beatte. She would never see her again. She would never see anyone again. At last George had managed to remove his belt. She buried her bloodied face in the floor, and waited for the first blow, which came soon enough, almost slashing the backs of her wrists where they were tied at the small of her back. The one mercy was that it would not take a great deal of time. Such was his fury, she would surely be dead soon.

Thinking she would see her brother's face again before too long, Ruth steeled herself for the second blow, silently praying that she might be taken quickly. But the second blow didn't come. Instead, there was an almighty roar, someone shouting George's name, a clash of metal on stone, and the belt landing, limp, on the floor beside her. There were the sounds of a tremendous struggle behind her, and then next to her there was the face of the maid, the kind woman who had exchanged clothing with her in Lady Hildred's coach, telling her that all would be well.

TWENTY-SEVEN

Reckoning

Thomas Faithly felt as if his stomach had been filled with lead. He almost wished it had been – stomach, heart, head. So many battles he'd fought, fights he'd been in, and almost negligible scars apart, he had come away unscathed, and for what? For this, for a beggar's life in the service of a stateless prince whose best years now began to slip unnoticed behind him, whose family had all but abandoned him, and who had begun to fear that his own brother, James, already a better soldier, might make a better King. Thomas had come to realise, moreover, that amongst his companions in this destitute existence were men who would betray their friends and their families for the sake of a few coins or to save their own necks. Marchmont Ellis: a traitor and a spy; George Barton: a spy; and now Evan Glenroe – what? What was Evan Glenroe? As they had left Bruges in pursuit of Seeker, Glenroe had finally unburdened himself of the secret he was sure Damian Seeker had discovered he carried with him. Glenroe was an agent of the Jesuits, who had spent his time in the city arranging for his friends to be caught in such compromise that they would put their families at home in jeopardy in order to save their own face and name. But Glenroe, at least, believed in the justice of his cause.

'You didn't see it, Thomas, what I saw, when Cromwell came to Ireland. Drogheda. Wexford. You didn't see the slaughter – men, women, children, priests – it didn't matter. And for what? Do you know what he said when he came to Ireland with his white flag of peace to bring us "the Protection of the Parliament of England"?'

Thomas knew, because he'd heard it from Glenroe, in his cups, many times before. But he'd heard it from others too, who'd been there.

Glenroe answered his own question. '"For the propagation of the Gospel of Christ, the establishing of truth and peace and restoring that bleeding nation to its former happiness and tranquillity." For the Gospel of Christ, he slaughtered my father, my brother, my nephew, the priest who first taught me my letters as a boy.'

Thomas would not defend it. 'I know it, Evan. But that was Cromwell. It is our own and not Cromwell's people that you target in this scheme of the Jesuits. Our own, the King's own, whom you entrap in their web, force to endanger their families.'

'To a greater end,' insisted Glenroe. 'Do you think if I could get some of Cromwell's men into a brothel in Bruges I wouldn't serve them the same? But that is hardly to be done, is it? I was just a foot soldier, Thomas. Felipe and Sister Janet had their campaign going a good long time before I ever got here. Janet never forgot the persecution of our faith that her own family suffered. And why should she? I was just helping her out. Anyway, they'll have their reward, the families we persuaded to take in the priests, when our time comes.'

'England will never accept the Jesuits, Evan.'

'We'll see,' said Glenroe. 'I'd warrant the ends will justify the means.'

'The means? Blackmailing your friends? Killing Lady Hildred?' asked Thomas. 'She put her faith in us.'

Glenroe had at least had the grace to look shamefaced. 'She'd recognised Felipe. She all but told Janet about it. The whole thing would have blown up in our faces, and there would have been no way of keeping the priests or the families they were with in England safe then. And no one will miss her. Her own son made that plain enough.'

'No one would miss me either, Evan. Is that why you never tried to entrap me with your scheme, because I have no family left to shame?'

Glenroe attempted a smile. 'That and the fact that the girls said you did little but drink and talk of home. But yes, with your family being gone and your estate in republican hands, it would hardly have been worth our while trying to get you.'

They were clattering over the bridge into Damme. Since the departure of the Spaniards from the town, the gate-keepers had all but given up their vigilance over new arrivals and had let them through with only the same grumble about

Englishmen as they had had from the guard on the Speye Poort in Bruges.

'Seeker and the woman have definitely come through here then,' said Glenroe as they approached the Stadhuis. 'Beaumont too.'

'But where?' said Thomas, looking around him at the hushed buildings surrounding the market square. All appeared utterly still in the Stadhuis. Around the square, shops and booths were shut up, and the business of the taverns was long done for the night. There was something, though, about De Grote Sterre. One or two shutters not closed, a suggestion of light leaking out into the street from the stable yard. 'The governor's house.'

'Surely Seeker would never risk it,' said Glenroe.

'He'd risk anything,' returned Thomas, spurring on his horse. 'Besides, the Spaniards are gone. Come on.'

The carriage gates into the rear courtyard of De Grote Sterre were indeed open, which was a warning already that all was not right. Thomas and Glenroe advanced through them with caution. They had not got very far when they heard the sounds of some commotion and, somewhere, a clashing of swords. A torch burned in a brazier on the outer wall of the stable, the only other light coming from a window above the bakehouse. At first Thomas had trouble making out anything at all, then a noise to his left took his attention and he could hardly believe his eyes. Two women, dirtied and bloodied, were emerging from a small, splintered door at the back of the house, one clearly supporting the other. Glenroe leapt from his horse and took hold of the more injured of the two just as she was about to collapse.

'Who did this?' he demanded of the other woman. 'Seeker?'

She was shaking her head as Thomas drew his sword. 'Damian Seeker never did that,' he said.

The less badly injured of the two women looked up at him. Through the blood and the dirt, without the wimple or the maid's cap, he saw her at last. 'Anne Winter!' he said.

'You must get in there, Sir Thomas. They are killing each other.'

Thomas called over his shoulder as he charged through the shattered door. 'Come on, Evan.'

'Wait, Thomas!' Glenroe grabbed an unlit torch from a bracket by the smashed door and ran with it to the bakehouse, whose inhabitants had clearly been woken by the commotion. 'Light!' he demanded of the terrified woman who came to the door. She quickly brought a candle and the torch was aflame. 'See to these women,' he told her, and then ran to join Thomas. 'Right, Faithly, me first.'

But Thomas grabbed the torch and pushed ahead of him, through the destroyed doorway and into the house. 'No, Evan, you can have Beaumont. I've been waiting a lot longer for my reckoning with Damian Seeker.'

As they entered the vault at first Thomas could discern nothing but chaos. They were in some sort of cellar or storeroom that had a strange, damp, sweet reek from bottles and jars of preserves knocked from their shelves and smashed on the floor. Thomas almost slipped in some sticky, wet substance that oozed over the dirt floor. A door at the far end of the cellar was open, and it was clear from the sounds coming through it that the antagonists had taken their fight into the body of the house. He ran in the direction of the noise, putting the torch to candles in their sconces as he passed. Glenroe was close behind him. Each arc of light revealed the same thing: devastation. Everywhere, furniture was toppled over or pushed askew, jugs, bowls, vases knocked over and smashed to pieces, drapes pulled from tables or torn from walls. The sounds of clashing steel, of human beings colliding with walls or furnishings, sending objects hurtling across wooden floors, did not abate but each moment seemed to come from just a little further away.

It was on the second floor that they at last came upon them. In the time it took Glenroe to shove his burning torch into an empty bracket, the two men who had been struggling near the window had approached the central stairs. Thomas readied himself for an assault on Seeker, but Glenroe pulled him back. 'Wait, Thomas.'

'What?' yelled Thomas.

As he did so, Damian Seeker glanced around for the briefest of moments and George Beaumont managed to swipe the point of his sword across his cheek. With a roar, Seeker lunged at him, but Beaumont parried and managed to scuttle backwards up the next set of stairs. Seeker charged after him. Thomas began to follow but didn't know how to get amongst them and again Glenroe's hand was on his bandolier, pulling him back.

'The odds, Thomas. We'll wait till they've shortened the odds.'

'What are you talking about?' Thomas snapped.

'Just now it's evens. Us and them. Let them fight it out and it's two to one in our favour.'

Thomas shook him off and continued up the stairs but didn't make it to the next landing as Seeker's elbow swung back and connected, hard, with his jaw, sending him stumbling backwards into Glenroe.

'Trust me, Thomas,' Glenroe gasped, steadying them both. 'I know my odds.'

The fighting went on, the adversaries well matched. Seeker's bulk and strength were balanced by Beaumont's agility and greater battle-readiness: the man who had fought the Spaniards only a summer's season ago was more practised than the man who had played the part of a carpenter for the last eighteen months. But even as he watched, Thomas could see George Beaumont begin to lose his discipline as the momentum of the fight brought Seeker back to the height of his skill. To avoid one of Seeker's thrusts, Beaumont jumped onto a dresser and launched himself to take hold of the brass candelabra hanging from the ceiling. Swinging forwards as the candelabra pulled loose of its fixing, he managed to connect his booted feet with Seeker's shoulder, knocking the big Yorkshireman sideways, but Seeker quickly regained his footing and landed a blow on Beaumont's arm, sending Beaumont's sword scuttling across the floor.

It should have been over then. Thomas thought it would be and prepared himself to face Seeker when George Beaumont had been dealt with. This was their reckoning, at last. The final act in the drama playing out between them for the last three years, since Thomas had first given himself up to Seeker, in Yorkshire. What a mistake that had been, to think he could get back his old life in return for becoming Cromwell's spy! It had been a disaster that had reached its climax in a disused bear pit in Southwark and almost cost the life of Maria, the woman both himself and Seeker loved. And up until tonight, Thomas had believed it had ended in the death of Seeker himself. But here the man was in front of him, flesh and blood and fighting for his life. Thomas made ready but suddenly, Evan Glenroe had dived across the floor in front of him and picked up the sword that Seeker had kicked further out of the way. As Seeker's head whipped round to see what was happening, Glenroe threw the sword back to Beaumont. 'Here, George, entertain us a little longer!'

Thomas turned in disbelief to Evan Glenroe.

'For the fun of it,' said Glenroe. 'Let's see what the big fella can really do.'

But Seeker had dropped his arm a moment on his approach to what he thought was an unarmed man. The sliver of time before he understood what was happening might as well have been an eternity, and now it was too late. George had him off balance and managed to slash Seeker across the shoulder in such a way that it was now Seeker's sword that fell, not to the floor, but clattering down past a gap in the stairway to the storey below.

Instantly, Seeker had his knife out, but there was no chance that he could get close enough to George Beaumont to bring it to bear. Thomas's heart was racing. His eyes swept between Seeker and Beaumont as if he was watching a bout between a favoured fighting cock and a new-arrived, unwanted interloper. They had reached the top floor proper of the house, the wooden steps which Seeker had begun to back up leading only to a loft beneath the rafters. The trapdoor above Seeker's head was closed, but one forceful thrust of his arm had it springing up and open. As he disappeared through it, he kicked out at the advancing George Beaumont, but Beaumont ducked his head in time and then lashed out with his blade, ripping the leather of Seeker's boot. Then George continued up into the darkness.

And that, Thomas realised, was George Beaumont's mistake, because it would be the advancing predator and not the hidden prey that needed light in the last act of this struggle.

'Come on,' said Glenroe, putting his foot on the bottom rung of the stepladder.

'No,' said Thomas, 'wait.'

'What for?'

'To even things up, Evan.'

Glenroe gave a snort of derision and started up the steps anyway.

★

Seeker had studied the building as he and Anne Winter had approached it less than an hour earlier, run his eye over it, front and then back, for points of likely entry and exit. He had not intended to find himself at the very top of De Grote Sterre, directly beneath the roof, with three men coming up behind him, intent on killing him. As he'd finally heaved himself backwards through the hatch at the top of the stepladder, still trying to kick out at George Beaumont, Seeker had swiftly recalled how the top of the house had looked from the back. Beaumont's sword proved almost as great an encumbrance to the man himself in progressing up the stepladder and through the hatch as it had done to the toe of Seeker's boot, and it afforded Seeker a vital opportunity to get to the back of the room, and the wall. He stood about a foot and a half out from it. He would like to have been further back, but this loft room was not deep enough for him to go any further. He didn't have long to wait before Beaumont began to emerge through the hatch. The time of the wait was a matter of a few breaths, but it was enough for Seeker's eyes to start to make something of the gloom. The blade of the sword came into his sightline first and then the man holding it. Seeker was ready. The pain in his right shoulder from where George had slashed it was intense, but his aim with his left was not so certain. It would have to be the right arm.

Beaumont came slowly through the hatch, looking about him in the darkness, trying to sense Seeker's presence, expecting him to be close. Seeker began to raise his arm.

Something in the movement took Beaumont's attention, and he turned his head in the direction of the sound. Seeker let fly. He could only see shapes, forms in the darkness. He couldn't see the look on the man's face, in his eyes, as the dagger flew through the air with all the force he could muster to embed itself in George Beaumont's forehead.

And then there was only a short, strange pair of sounds before George's body started to crumple and fall back down through the hatch – the contact of blade with flesh, through bone, and the astonished gasp of the dying man. Then, as the body collided with Glenroe, coming up just behind it, and the Irishman called out in alarm and confusion, Seeker bounded across the floor to take the sword that had fallen from George Beaumont's grasp. He paused only to slam shut the trapdoor, before making straight for his only escape route – the wide window hatch that looked out onto De Grote Sterre's courtyard, over thirty feet below. As Seeker fumbled in the darkness with the catch on the shutters, it seemed that Evan Glenroe had at last managed to wrestle George Beaumont's body out of the way and was pushing up the trapdoor.

'Evan, wait!' Seeker heard Thomas Faithly cry.

'What for? I'd swear even that Devil hasn't another knife on him.'

And then Glenroe was in the loft and Faithly close after him. Seeker braced his left forearm and finally smashed the shutters open. And there, as he'd seen when he and Anne Winter had entered the *hof* not an hour ago, was the rope.

Seeker silently blessed the Flemings that built their houses thus: broad windows with hooks above by which to haul goods up to any floor of their house. Glenroe and Faithly were coming for him as he launched himself through the window to grab hold of the rope. He travelled downwards with tremendous speed, the shouts of the other two men still in his ears as he hit the ground. He quickly ran to the coil of rope wound round the winch at the foot of the wall and sliced through it with George Beaumont's sword so that Faithly and Glenroe could not replicate his exit, then he started to run towards the stable. And then he stopped.

The torch on the wall was still lit and illuminated a woman, Anne Winter, standing there with one hand on the bridle of a horse, the other outstretched, holding a pistol. Seeker's heart was thumping, his lungs almost bursting in his chest. Now. This was it. After all he had been through, all he had done, this was it. A stable yard in a small town in a country very far from home. And for what? What was any of it worth? The cause he had so long fought for was in its death throes, its values betrayed, and he would never see Manon or Maria again.

Anne Winter appeared to be very calm. 'Where is George Beaumont?' she said.

He gave a short flick of his head back towards the loft.

'Dead?'

He nodded.

She looked at the pistol in her hand. 'I doubt he'll be mourned.'

'No.' Seeker nodded to the pistol. 'Best be done with it then, Lady Anne.'

She looked at him in confusion and laughed. 'Done with it? No, not like this. You saved my life tonight, twice. You saved Ruth Jones's too. This is not the reckoning I want, and I will not live in your debt.' She took another step towards him and put the pistol into his hand. 'There's powder and some of the King's money – enough to get you away – in Glenroe's saddlebag. His is the best horse. I've loosed the others. They'll not have wandered far, but it will give you a start. I've kept the rest of Lady Hildred's money for the King, of course.'

'Of course,' he said.

The shouts of Faithly and Glenroe coming down through the house were getting closer.

'For God's sake, get away,' she said, exasperated.

For once, Seeker had no idea what to say to this woman, and so said nothing. She shook her head as she hurriedly passed him the rein of Glenroe's horse, and there was just the glimmer of the old spark he knew in her eyes. 'A gentleman to the end. A "thank you" would have done, you know.' Then she began to walk away. 'Be gone now. For the love of God, Damian Seeker, be gone.'

EPILOGUE

England was there. A beacon glowed from the hill fort, lights twinkled out of the darkness, the moon was silver on the water as the prow of the ship advanced up the estuary. Seeker felt something surge inside him: England was there, still, and all that England held, all that mattered to him.

The storm of their first night at sea was now so abated there was hardly sufficient breeze to take them into harbour, and yet inch by inch, it seemed to him, the lights of Harwich came closer. Inch by inch, what had passed in Flanders was further behind him. All round him, the crew made ready for docking and Seeker stood out of their way, watching. The journey from Damme to the coast had been short, but there had been times when he had thought he would not see England again. Faithly and Glenroe had been after him in no time, Glenroe at one point coming so close that Seeker could have reached out his hand and gripped the Irishman's ankle. But the heifer behind which Seeker had been lying in that Flemish barn had not encouraged further human intrusion, and after a brief inspection of the place,

Glenroe had left. Worse had been the moment Thomas Faithly had rapped on the door of the fisherman's cottage only moments after Seeker had stepped into it. As Faithly made his enquiries of the fisherman's wife, to whom Seeker had just shown a handful of coins from Lady Hildred's fortune, he himself had stood a mere few inches away, obscured only by cottage's opened door. But the promise of money, as it had a tendency to do, had done the trick. The fisherman had assisted Seeker to Ostend, where he'd finally made contact with Thurloe's agent and obtained a pass to travel back over the sea, home.

Such a storm had raged on that very first night that Seeker had wondered whether he would see another morning. The superstitions and omen-reading of the seamen were such that Seeker himself had begun to wonder if God was indeed expressing his wrath, but when dawn had brought some respite and he found he was still alive he knew they had survived the worst.

Or so he'd thought, but the worst was waiting for him in Harwich, on the boat slipping out to meet them and guide them into dock. The town they were drawing closer to had a quiet to it, a stillness, that did not fit a naval port. Seeker felt as if they were coming upon a vigil. Debris from the late storm floated on near-still waters and gathered around piers and boats at anchor in the harbour. The sky, grey clouds giving way to darkness, lowered over all with a heaviness that the lamps being lit in windows could do nothing to alleviate.

A rope was thrown out to the boat that had come along-side them, and a ladder put down for the naval lieutenant about to board. The man was young, must have been little more than twenty, but his bearing very sombre. Seeker looked at the stillness of town, at the flags flying a flag's depth lower than they should be, then he looked back at the young lieutenant's face and he knew before the words were spoken. Cromwell was dead.

It took him a day and a night to get to London. He went through a country not in uproar, but in shock, and calm. Richard Cromwell had been named successor by his father, on his deathbed, to rule as Protector in his stead. This Seeker had learned in a tavern in Colchester. Dick, the country squire, not his brother Henry, the soldier. There was no consternation amongst the people. There should have been. Dick Cromwell would never control the army or Parliament. Dick would not make the people love him, as his father had. He had not the style nor the guile to stand against Charles Stuart and those who intrigued for him. Dick Cromwell would never bestride the world and make the ambassadors of Europe bend the knee. It was over.

The country was not in turmoil and yet all was not quite right: the authorities were alert, the foreign posts suspended. Seeker travelled in his carpenter's guise and with his carpenter's papers. He arrived at Aldgate a little before dawn. The pull of London had been growing stronger in him, more insistent, with every mile that passed. He smelled the city, its smoke, its humanity, the beast of the river, before his eyes began to discern the first spires rising heavenwards as if nothing had changed. Everything had changed. Everything.

As he passed through the gates, Seeker kept his head low and avoided catching anyone's eye. Images from the past flooded his vision, crept up, had their moment, then slipped away again. There, down to his left, beyond Poor Jewry was Crutched Friars, where Anne Winter had thought to make a traitor of Andrew Marvell and had plotted to hide the King. Further down were the almshouses of Gethsemane, where a wicked, deluded preacher woman had believed she was preparing for the coming of Christ. Seeker did not turn down Poor Jewry for Crutched Friars, but kept straight ahead, making for Leadenhall and then Cornhill. London was stirring, and amongst the smoke beginning to rise from its chimneys, Seeker imagined he caught the drift of that from the chimney of Kent's coffee house. Perhaps Samuel was already starting to warm the embers beneath the stove, as Grace checked her stores and the boy Gabriel scrubbed benches and swept floors. There, ahead, was the Royal Exchange, where no doubt the merchant George Tavener would be, in two or three hours, seeing what profit might be made from the Protector's death, for there was nothing George Tavener could not make a profit on. At the bottom of Threadneedle Street, Seeker glanced up to his right, towards Broad Street, and felt that familiar ache of the knowledge that his daughter slept there safe, under a roof that was not his. But it was not time, yet, for him to make his way to Broad Street, and the sanctuary of the Black Fox.

He carried on, his heart beginning to beat faster, along Poultry till it met with the bottom of Old Jewry. Seeker stopped. There, as ever, was the Angel, and there, just opposite, the old, crumbling arch of the passageway into Dove Court. Twenty yards way, three flights of stairs, a door that stuck in the winter with the damp. There, behind the door, was Maria. He remembered again the time as he'd sat at the table in that barren room, with its little jug of winter green and berries, watching as she struggled to put together a meal that a man could eat, when all he'd wanted was to reach out and touch her, pull her to him. Maria. Twenty yards and three flights of stairs away. He straightened his stance, pulled back his shoulders, took his courage in his hands and walked towards Dove Court.

At first he thought he was hearing wrong, a child's cry as he rapped gently at that swollen wooden door. A woman's voice, hushing the child. Grace, perhaps. Grace here with her newborn child. He rapped again, but then came a man's curse and another as the door was yanked open.

'Who in Hell's name . . .?' An angry man in a dirty nightshift, red hair dishevelled, stopped in his speech suddenly, and Seeker saw ire change to recognition, shock. The door was shoved shut and Seeker could hear the sound of furniture being dragged across the floor towards it. He put a shoulder to the door and forced it open.

Inside the old familiar attic he was confronted with the

same few sticks of furniture as he had always known there, but a different smell and different people. The red-haired man was standing by the window, brandishing a Bible in one hand and a broom in the other. A woman Seeker had never seen before cowered against the wall at what had once been Maria's bed, a squirming bundle of swaddling pressed to her chest.

'Get back, in God's name, whatever you are, get back!'

Then Seeker understood, at least some of it. This man that he had no recollection of having set eyes on, had recognised him as Captain Damian Seeker, of Cromwell's guard, that was supposed to be dead.

'What I am,' he said, 'is your worst nightmare, if you don't tell me where the woman has gone who used to live in this attic.'

The man began to shake his head, eyes wide. 'Don't know anything about any woman. It was a lawyer had this place before us. Ellingworth his name.' He looked desperately to his wife, who also shook her head before burying it in the bundle of swaddling. 'Don't know any woman.'

Ellingworth. Surely Elias could not have gone already? They were not yet in the second week of September. Surely George Tavener's last ship of the year was not ready to cross the Atlantic yet?

Seeker left the attic without saying anything more and stormed down the stairs of Dove Court and back out into the street. Where to go first – Kent's coffee house or Elias's chambers at Clifford's Inn? At the bottom of the street he turned right and began to stride westwards, careless now of who might recognise him, in the direction of the Fleet and Clifford's Inn. How many times had he gone to this same place, armed and with all the authority of the Protectorate behind him, in search of the recalcitrant lawyer? How many times had it mattered more to him than it did now?

The porter on the gate at Clifford's looked almost as shocked as had done the stranger in the attic of Dove Court. Almost, but not quite, and with a twinkle in his eye the man quickly recovered himself. 'I knew it wasn't true, Captain. I knew they'd never have got you, bear or no bear.'

Seeker clapped the man on the shoulder. 'Thank you, Bennet. I'm back on the trail of that rogue, Ellingworth though. Still in the same rooms, is he?'

Bennet opened his mouth and Seeker could see he was about to impart some information he'd rather not. But then the porter's expression lightened with relief and stretched into a smile as he looked out past Seeker's bandaged shoulder to the approach down Clifford's Inn passage from Fleet Street. 'Ah, now, here's a gentleman'll be able to tell you better, Captain.'

'Captain?' The voice behind Seeker was incredulous. Seeker turned and found himself face to face with a disbelieving Lawrence Ingolby.

'Where is she, Lawrence?' said Seeker.

Ingolby looked about him. The gardens of Clifford's were still empty at this hour, but already lawyers and servants were starting to make their way along Chancery Lane. He ushered Seeker towards a bench set in an alcove by some apple trees. 'Are you mad? Does Thurloe know you're back?'

'It doesn't matter any more. Oliver's dead.'

Ingolby raised his eyebrows and lowered his voice. 'Aye, well, I know that, don't I? But surely Thurloe can't have called you back for that already. Even you couldn't have got here from Flanders in that time. I thought there were agreed messages you'd send, according to the protocol, when you were coming back?'

'Thurloe doesn't know I'm here,' said Seeker.

Ingolby's eyebrows went even higher. 'Are you mad?' he repeated. 'They're as jumpy as fleas since Cromwell died.' He shook his head in disbelief. 'Well, if he doesn't know now that you're back, he will by dinnertime.'

'Then I'll have to be gone by dinnertime,' said Seeker.

'*What?* They've never turned you, have they? The Stuarts?'

'Don't be daft. But there's plenty they will manage to turn, now that Oliver's gone. It's over, Lawrence. The Stuarts will be back on a sea of blood, and there's precious few of ours left worth fighting for to stop them. I need to find Maria and then we need to leave.'

'Leave? We? Where? Who?' Lawrence leaned towards him, his brow furrowed. 'You're too late, Damian. She's gone.'

Four days ago. The morning after Cromwell's death it had been. It was Andrew Marvell that had got word to them, before almost anyone else had found out. Dick Cromwell. A recipe for disaster. The army would chew him up and spit him out for the dogs. Freedom, the merest notion of freedom, would become a thing of the past, if it had ever been. And if Charles Stuart's supporters should rise, as surely they must, what new horrors would visit themselves upon England? Elias would not keep his family here to see it. Almost everything had been readied for their departure anyway. George Tavener, fearing riots on the news of the Protector's death, had swiftly made arrangements for his ship to sail early, and was night and day planning the security of his other stocks.

'She's gone, Damian. Four days since. She kicked up quite a stink, I can tell you, but Elias persuaded her finally that she might end her days here, waiting for you, and never see you again, but if you wanted to find her again, you would.'

Seeker nodded. 'The first sense the man ever spoke.' He stood up. 'Come on then, lad, there's no time to be wasted.'

Bur Lawrence remained seated. 'Time for what?'

Seeker looked down at him and wondered what it was that Lawrence wasn't seeing. 'The England that's coming isn't one for me, or you, or Manon or Dorcas either.'

Lawrence gave a short laugh, more blowing air through his nose in amusement than anything else. 'Dorcas? Dorcas'll never leave England, Seeker, come what may. And you don't really want her anyway, do you?'

'She knows.' Seeker searched about for the right words. 'She knows what she is to me.'

Ingolby's gaze was steady. 'Aye, and she knows what she isn't too. One or the other, Seeker. You can't have both.'

'I can't leave her here, in the middle of it all.'

'Well, you'll never take her with you, I'm telling you that now. Dorcas'll come through whatever she has to face, and she doesn't need you or me to do it.'

Seeker knew this. 'Right,' he said, 'well we'd better get up there anyway.'

'I've only just come down,' protested Ingolby. 'I've clients to see. Cromwell or no, the law's the law.'

It was now Seeker's turn to be disbelieving. 'Do you understand what I've been saying? There's another war coming.'

'I think you're wrong,' said Lawrence. 'The people know what war means. Besides, I never noticed much difference for myself, between Protector or King.'

'You'd stay in London?'

Lawrence shook his head. 'London? No. I've had what I need from London. I think I'll head back north, to York. There's merchants there with money falling out of their pockets, just waiting for a good lawyer to help them sue each other.'

'You mean it too, don't you?'

'Oh, I mean it, all right. Ten years from now I'll have my own house on the Castlegate and a brood of children running around their mother's skirts.' He gave Seeker a particularly piercing look as he said this.

'"Mother"?' said Seeker.

Lawrence seemed to gather his courage and persuade himself that having gone thus far, he should just carry on. 'That's what I said. I intend to marry your daughter, Captain. Whether you like it or not. I love Manon, and I'd be prepared to wager everything I have that she loves me. And I reckon, her and me together, well, there's no one'll stop us – not Protector, nor King, nor wealthy merchants of York nor anyone else. I intend to make your daughter the finest lady in the north of England, and if the price I have to pay for that is that one of my sons, or God forbid, one of my daughters, looks at me with that look you're giving me now, well so be it.' Lawrence then sat up straight, as if somehow stunned himself by what he'd just said.

'No one to stop you, eh?' said Seeker, not sure if it was rage or pride he felt rising through him.

'No,' said Lawrence, attempting to be resolute but now avoiding Seeker's eye. 'No one. Leastways, no one but you.' He looked back at Seeker now. 'If you ask her to, she'll go with you, wherever it is you're going. I know her, and I know fine well I can't compete with you as far as she's concerned.' He shrugged with a resigned half-smile. 'God alone knows why.'

'But if I tell her she can't come, if I tell her to go with you . . .'

Lawrence stood up and looked resolutely at Seeker. 'She will. And I swear on my life and hers and the souls of everyone I ever cared about that no one, no one will ever harm a hair of her head and I'll make her the happiest woman there's ever been.'

Seeker felt his lips move as if a smile threatened to prepare itself. There was moisture prickling somewhere in his eyes. This man, this infuriating, clever, determined length of Yorkshire grit, polished but not impressed by all London had to offer. He'd buy and sell them all in a few years. Seeker knew now, that almost since the day he'd met him, he'd never have considered entrusting his daughter's future to anyone else. He leaned in closer, and fixed Lawrence Ingolby with a look he'd last used on a Whitehall bootboy who'd burned his best boots by leaving them to dry too close to the fire. 'You see you do, or I promise you this: every one of those grandchildren of mine will look *exactly* like me, and they'll make you wish you'd never been born.'

The streets of London were growing dark again by the time Seeker walked out of the door of the Black Fox for the last time. Dorcas hadn't wept. He'd held her a long, long time. He knew Lawrence was right – Dorcas would never leave England. He'd tried, all the same, to persuade her. She'd have none of it, refused even to leave London. With Manon it had been the other way round. She'd wept, and clung onto him, and threatened to come with him wherever he went so that he'd had to tell her she couldn't. 'I don't know what's ahead of me, Manon,' he'd said. 'But I know what's ahead of him.' He'd nodded towards Ingolby. 'Luckiest beggar that ever walked the face of this earth. Always lands on his feet. And he doesn't look much, I know, but he'll look after you, give you a life I never could. And if he doesn't, he knows that not a hundred oceans would be enough to keep me away.' He'd left Lawrence with most of the money he had on him. 'Get her up north as soon as you can. The Stuarts'll be back one day, and they'll be out for revenge. Never tell anyone she's mine.'

He'd left the Black Fox then. There were many people and places he had not the time to bid farewell to, but before he headed out of the city for Liverpool, and the agent he'd been sending a good bit of his wages to for years, in case of just such a time as this, there was one more thing he did have to do, one person he did have to see.

The lamps were lit in the chambers of Lincoln's Inn, but not in John Thurloe's rooms, which were dark. The Chief Secretary would be in Whitehall now, burning other lamps, preparing for Cromwell's funeral, writing endlessly to every outpost of the Protectorate, shoring up an authority that Richard Cromwell would never otherwise have. He might even by now be reading Seeker's last report, sent from Ostend as he himself prepared to board ship, detailing the treachery and death of Marchmont Ellis, the madness and death of George Beaumont, the whereabouts of Thomas Faithly and the clandestine presence in England of Jesuits. Lady Anne Winter, he wrote, had eluded his grasp. He'd said nothing of his own impending return to England. Perhaps Thurloe was reading of that too, now, from some other source, or listening to London's latest rumour. Seeker had not come to Lincoln's Inn tonight to see John Thurloe.

A friendly wisp of smoke still curled from the small chimney of the gardener's hut, a glow of candlelight from the window near the door. The low growl of a dog inside was soon accompanied by the squealing of a pup. Seeker walked almost the length of the path and then waited, silent, a few feet from the door. And then it began in earnest, the barking, the thump and scrabbling of huge paws against the door, the boy's voice attempting to calm it before the door opened and the hound flew out and was upon him, almost knocking him over for joy. Seeker laughed and wrestled happily with the dog as he tried to catch his breath, before a squealing and nipping at his boots made him look down, to where three small bundles of fur were clambering over each other to lay hold of his boots. And there, calling to them all, was Nathaniel, the one person Seeker had gone to see before he'd left for Flanders, the one last person he knew he must tell he was returned.

Nathaniel's open face was filled with delight. 'You've come back, Captain. You said you would. And I never told a soul.'

'I know you didn't, Nathaniel. I knew you never would. But I am leaving again.'

The delight went out of Nathaniel's face. 'Are you going after Maria?'

'Well, that brother of hers will never keep her out of trouble, will he?'

Nathaniel shook his head in agreement. 'Massachusetts is a long way away.'

'It is, but it's where I must go.'

Nathaniel shrugged at the truth of it. 'You'll have come for the dog, then?'

'If the old fellow doesn't mind keeping me company?'

'Oh, he won't. He's been watching for you all this time. When he hasn't been with Lawrence, or up at the Black Fox for titbits from Dorcas, or . . .' and a shy smile came on Nathaniel's face as he indicated the puppies.

'Oh!' said Seeker. 'Got himself a lady friend then?'

'Stablemaster's bitch, from the mews.'

'They'll be fine pups then.'

'I'm keeping one of them, and one of the gentleman here has offered me a good bit of money for the other two.'

'Well, you see and charge him double what he offers.' Seeker knew Nathaniel wouldn't, but it made him feel better to say it all the same. 'I suppose I'd better be getting on then.'

'I suppose you'd better, Captain. It's a long way to Massachusetts,' he repeated.

Seeker bent down to tousle the head of each puppy. 'You mind your master now.' Then he started to walk. 'Come on, boy,' he said to his own dog, who turned once to look at Nathaniel before trotting after him.

He was almost at the gate when Nathaniel's voice stopped him.

'Captain? Will you ever be back?'

Seeker took a moment to look around him, to breathe in the air of the city, take in the sounds of its night. 'I don't know, lad,' he said at last. 'I don't know.'

AUTHOR'S NOTE

At the foot of Spanjaardstraat in the city of Bruges, just across the Augustinians' Bridge from the site of the former Augustinian priory, is a building known as Huis Den Noodt Gods. Alternative names have been the Phantom House (Spookhuis) or the House of Lamentations. Once a convent, this house is said to be the most haunted building in the city. Legend tells of a monk of the priory who used a secret tunnel going under the canal to visit one of the nuns of the religious house. When she fled from his declaration of love, he murdered her. The spirit of this young woman is said to haunt the House of Lamentations, giving the place its name. This is what gave me the idea for the entirely fictional events I portray as taking place there in the year 1658. The House of Lamentations should not be confused with the Engels Klooster, or English convent, which still exists on Carmersstraat and is still dedicated to the religious life. The events I portray as taking place in the Engels Klooster are also entirely fictional.

While Sint-Donatian's cathedral and the Augustinian

priory are both gone, the vast majority of the locations mentioned in *The House of Lamentations* are still to be found in Bruges. At the end of Carmersstraat, not far from the Engels Klooster, the Schuttersgilde Sint-Sebastiaan survives to the present day. Sint-Walburgakerk is still a living place of worship. The activities ascribed to the fictional Father Felipe are entirely of my invention. The Bouchoute house remains on the corner of the Markt, a restaurant now taking up its ground floor. The Huis van de Zeven Torens has been incorporated into an hotel. The Gruuthuse is a magnificent museum, open to the public, and incorporating the oratory from which I have Seeker spy upon the Cavaliers and Charles II as they meet in Onze-Lieve-Vrouwekerk. Also open to the public is the Hospital of Sint-Jans, one of Bruges's most iconic buildings and now a hospital museum. The basement of the Oude Steen, one of Europe's oldest prisons, with its grim displays of implements of torture, can also be visited. The exceptional Jeruzalemkapel founded six centuries ago by the Adornes family on the Adornesdomein – their private estate within the city – remains in the family's ownership, and is open to the public. You can still have a beer at De Garre, or, like Seeker and the Cavaliers, take your supper at 't Oud Handbogenhof or De Vlissinghe. A short canal-side cycle from Bruges is the small town of Damme, known today as Belgium's Book Town. On one side of the square is De Grote Sterre, home to the Spanish military governor in the seventeenth century, now housing the information centre and a folklore museum. I would like to thank the custodians, past and present, of all these places for their dedication in preserving their heritage.

But why send Damian Seeker to Bruges? Because of Charles II. Aside from his disastrous adventure with the Scottish Covenanters (June 1650–September 1651) the young king spent the years between his father's death in 1649 and his own Restoration in 1660 in exile in Europe. Initial sympathy for his plight was eroded over time, partly because of the behaviour of some of his followers, but in the main due to political expediency, as the increasing power and international profile of Oliver Cromwell forced foreign powers to recognise the Protectorate. Charles's mother, Henrietta-Maria, had found sanctuary in her native France and his sister, the Princess of Orange, was resident in the United Provinces, yet both the United Provinces (1654) and France (1655) would come to terms with Cromwell's government, and Charles found himself unwelcome in both. Having left Paris in 1654, he spent much of his time in Germany, particularly Cologne, but the outbreak of hostilities between England and Spain encouraged him to sign a treaty with Spain in 1656. He moved his small court from Cologne to Bruges, with a view to being near to hand should the Spaniards launch an invasion across the Channel. Such an invasion never happened, the King's plans perpetually caught in the irreconcilable difficulty that a sufficient number of supporters in England could only be persuaded to rise on his behalf if they were assured of Spanish military support, while Spain would only agree to embark on an invasion attempt if there was sufficient evidence of support in England.

Added to this was the problem of money. Charles and his followers in exile were in desperate financial straits and he himself almost irretrievably caught up in labyrinthine Spanish bureaucratic protocols in attempts to extract from them his promised pension. The Spanish crown itself was at the time experiencing great financial difficulty and used their inability to host Charles appropriately as an excuse to keep him in relative obscurity, away from the centres of royal power in Madrid and Brussels. From around the summer of 1656 the exiled King was mainly resident in Bruges, long a popular place of Royalist resort and intrigue. It had been in Flanders that the plot to assassinate Oliver Cromwell (treated in Seeker book 4, *The Bear Pit*) had originated, hence my decision to send Damian Seeker to the city in early 1657 to keep an eye on potential plotters.

By the summer of 1658, Royalist hopes of Spanish help were utterly in tatters. With an eye to acquiring Dunkirk from the French and better controlling the Channel, Cromwell in 1657 had agreed to send six thousand troops to aid the French campaign against Spain in Flanders. This alliance heavily defeated Spanish and Stuart forces at the Battle of the Dunes in June 1658. Charles, desperate to lead his forces, which included Irish and Scots as well as English regiments, had not been allowed to fight. His brother, James, Duke of York, who had learned his craft in the armies of France and was hugely popular with soldiers on both sides, was forced to serve with the Spaniards, who lost twice the number of men as their opponents. Spanish forces then had to muster themselves for the march to protect Brussels from the advancing French forces. I would like to thank Doug Kemp of the Historical Novels Society for alerting me to Eva Scott's *The Travels of the King: Charles II in Germany and Flanders, 1654–1660* (1907), which was particularly useful in outlining the difficulties faced by Charles Stuart in Flanders in this period.

To military dejection on the continent was added the crushing of Royalists at home. Thurloe's intelligence operatives were now so far embedded in Charles's circle abroad and amongst supporters at home that their every plan reached the ears of Whitehall before it could be put into action. The discovery of plots by 'The Great Trust' – which had replaced 'The Sealed Knot' as the main clandestine Royalist network – was met on the Protectorate side by the re-establishment of the High Court of Justice, previously used to try Charles I. Public revulsion at the brutality of resultant executions of relatively minor figures, as well as the Protectorate's understanding that its point had been made, eventually led to the High Court of Justice falling into disuse.

Having faced down Royalist plots and republican dissidence, and finally refused the Crown (May 1658) the Protector's personal power was at its height, his position seemingly unassailable. But as the year 1658 progressed, shadows lengthened over Oliver Cromwell: the recurring illness, thought to have been malaria, which had dogged him since his first expedition to Ireland, laid him low. The deaths of a son-in-law, a favoured niece, his baby grandson and finally his favourite daughter, Bettie, seem to have been too much for him and he spent much of the summer at Hampton Court, bedridden and despondent. Charles Stuart, meanwhile, having grown bored of Bruges and with little else to do, spent that hot summer at Hoogstraten, just north of Antwerp, hunting and playing tennis, which is what he was doing when the astonishing news was brought to him that Oliver Cromwell was dead.

Cromwell had died on the afternoon of 3 September 1658, the anniversary of his victories at Dunbar and Worcester, as a tremendous storm raged over England. On his deathbed, he named his son Richard as his successor. Or so at least his advisers thought – they couldn't really hear him properly. Despite the fears expressed by Damian Seeker in this book, England did not descend into a bloodbath. Rather, yet more ill-conceived Royalist plots came and went, and there ensued a mainly peaceful struggle between Army, Parliament, and the ineffectual new Lord Protector, Richard, who was induced to demit office in June 1659. The struggle came to an end when General Monck marched down from Edinburgh in early 1660 to restore the Long Parliament for long enough to vote for its own dissolution. There now seemed to be only one solution to England's political impasse: on 8 May 1660, it was declared that Charles II had been King since 30 January 1649. The Stuarts were coming home.

Under the Stuarts, the fates of those who had held sway during the Republic varied widely. Some, like George Downing, who deserted the sinking ship of the Protectorate just in time, or cryptographer Samuel Morland, slipped smoothly into the new administration. Both would betray former comrades and intelligence agents. Others, such as John Thurloe and John Milton, suffered brief periods of imprisonment, Thurloe on his release working quietly for a time for the restored government. Those whom Charles held to be irredeemably responsible for the death of his father, however, were hunted down without mercy, some in England, some on the continent of Europe, and some, as detailed in Charles Spencer's *Killers of the King*, and Don Jordan and Michael Walsh's *The King's Revenge*, even to the Americas. But that's another story.

Shona MacLean, Conon Bridge, March 2020